About Donna Maree Hanson

Donna Maree Hanson is a traditionally and independently published author of fantasy, science fiction and horror. She also writes paranormal romance under the pseudonym of Dani Kristoff. Her dark fantasy series (which some reviewers have called "grim dark"), Dragon Wine, was published by Momentum Books (Pan Macmillan digital imprint) in 2014. *Shatterwing*: Part One, and *Skywatcher*: Part Two, are now re-published independently in digital and print-on-demand formats. *Deathwings* and *Bloodstorm* were published in 2017. The final installments in the Dragon Wine series, *Skyfire* and *Moonfall,* were published in 2018.

In April 2015, Donna was awarded the A. Bertram Chandler Award for "Outstanding Achievement in Australian Science Fiction" for her work in running science fiction conventions, publishing and broader SF community contribution. Donna also writes science fiction romance, with *Rayessa and the Space Pirates* and *Rae and Essa's Space Adventures* out with Escape Publishing. *Opi Battles the Space Pirates* was published independently in 2017. In 2016, Donna commenced her PhD candidature at the University of Canberra researching feminism in popular romance. Also available is her epic fantasy series the Silverlands: *Argenterra*, *Oathbound* and *Ungiven Land.* Donna lives in Canberra with her partner and fellow writer Matthew Farrer.

In 2018, Donna's SF short story collection, *Beneath the Floating City* was short listed for best collection in the Australian Aurealis Awards. Donna also won the ACT Publishing Award for her book, *Australian Speculative Fiction: A genre overview* in 2006.

You can contact Donna at her blog http://donnamareehanson.com

Or sign up to her newsletter, *Wing Dust.* https://landing.mailerlite.com/webforms/landing/u6u1f6

Or on Twitter @DonnaMHanson and www.facebook.com/donnamareehanson

Also by Donna Maree Hanson

The Silverlands (Epic Fantasy)
Argenterra, The Silverlands: Book One

Oathbound, The Silverlands: Book Two

Ungiven Land, The Silverlands: Book Three

Dragon Wine Series (Dark Fantasy)
Shatterwing, Dragon Wine: Part One

Skywatcher, Dragon Wine: Part Two

Deathwings, Dragon Wine: Part Three

Bloodstorm, Dragon Wine: Part Four

Skyfire, Dragon Wine: Part Five

Moonfall, Dragon Wine: Part Six

Love and Space Pirates (Science Fiction Romance)
Rayessa and the Space Pirates

Rae and Essa's Space Adventures

Opi Battles the Space Pirates

Short Story Collections
Beneath the Floating City: Short Science Fiction Stories

Through These Eyes: Tales of Magic Realism and Fantasy

Skyfire

Dragon Wine: Part Five

By

Donna Maree Hanson

Copyright information

Skyfire was first published by Donna Maree Hanson 2018

Copyright © Donna Maree Hanson 2018

National Library of Australia Cataloguing-in-Publication Entry

ISBN   978-0-6482795-1-8 (ebook)

ISBN   978-0-6482795-2-5 (print on demand)

Cover design by www.crocodesigns.com

Edited by Stephanie Smith

Proofread by Jason Nahrung

Dedication

To all those lovely readers who get it. Thank you from the heart of me.

Prologue

A seething cauldron of fire and rock brewed above Margra. Soon the boiling, churning mass would be ready, and skyfire would pour on the world below...

Part 1

Drop by drop the dragon wine leaks away, drop by drop your life fades away…

Chapter One
MORE THAN A TRACE

Karol hated the compound where his kind were imprisoned. This morning, his mother had said that Nakel, his father, was never coming back, and then she cried. Ilania was so sad and Karol hated that she was like that, without hope. She spoke with so much conviction that he had to believe, and to grieve. He remembered before, before they'd been brought to this compound where their poor circle of tents barely kept out the wind and the dust. Surrounded by rock on three sides, there wasn't any place to go in this prison. Not one that the guards knew about, at least. Their village had been neat and tidy and happy, and hidden from the outer world. Now, Karol understood why they hid away from the awful humans, who knew nothing grand, who had no culture and were just miserable, evil creatures, preying on everyone.

Karol was small for his age. But he didn't mind that so much for it meant he could explore where the adults could not and, even better, he could go where the guards could not. His favorite place was a fissure in the cliff face behind his family's tent. There he had found a small spring. Water gurgled pure and clear from the ground then it slipped over a small rock to disappear into the nooks and crannies of the cliff, never to appear again. It was his secret place. The camp had a dam half-full of murky water that had to be boiled before drinking.

He dipped his hand in the sweet-smelling water and sipped his fill.

His loincloth had seen better days. His mother wanted him to wear his tunic, but it lay abandoned in their tent. He didn't mind that his ribs stuck out or that his knees were bony knobs on thin legs. He would grow big and tall like his father one day.

And one day there would be enough food. Food for them all. And he'd lie around with his belly protruding and sleep for an age without being prodded awake by hunger pains.

His long hair was tied back, which made climbing and drinking from the spring easier. He peered down to the camp below, careful to keep his body in shadow. The guards didn't know he climbed up here and he wanted to keep it that way.

Like his mother, his hair was white. He didn't mind that it wasn't like Nakel's, for his father praised him for his looks. Praised him for being true kin.

The water helped ease his hunger. There was never enough to eat. Once a day they were given dried bread and a few beans. The cliff held no edible plants, nothing to supplement their diet. The spring was the only treasure. His mother said his growth was stunted forever now because of the poor diet. Thinking of his mother, he watched the water trickle. He had forgotten to bring a cup to take some back to her.

The sun moved while he sat there staring at the interior of the fissure. What he thought was a shadow disguising nothing suddenly seemed more. With thin arms and legs, Karol slid into the dark cleft. The slit in the stone was long and gloomy, and as he peered in he saw that there was an opening. Not a big space, but if he could squeeze through it might make a good hiding place.

"Karol? Karol!" His mother's words reached him, echoing around the rocks as if her voice came from everywhere. No time now to explore. His mother needed him.

Back in their tent, he saw nothing had changed. His mother was still stooped with grief.

"I'm glad you're back," she said in a low voice and hugged him to her.

Yelling in the compound jerked them apart. They shared a terrified look and then let their breaths roll out of them. "Roll call?" his mother ventured.

"Could be early food delivery?"

His mother bit her lip. "You wait here and let me see."

She slipped out of the tent with its ragged flap that kept nothing out. Karol went to his sleeping space. Rolled up and placed at the rear of the tent was his sleeping blanket. It was where he could be the most unobtrusive. Where he could be unnoticed. He folded himself among the bedding, hidden.

It was so quiet and the sound of his breathing annoyed him. His mother hadn't returned so Karol crept to the tent flap and peered through the strips of torn fabric into the compound. Bent old men, ragged women and a bunch of thin, white-haired children stood in a group, surrounded by guards. There were not many of them left. Some had died of disease and hunger. Karol's stomach clenched painfully. He could see no signs of food.

A scream rang out. Karol started. His heart raced as he squinted against the setting sun. A child ran across the clear area and then fell down. Karol stared. A spear stuck out of the child's back. Karol gasped, not quite believing his eyes. With sweaty hands, he moved strips of fabric out of the way to run forward.

More screams. Splashes of red. Then his mother's voice: "Run, Karol. Hide!"

Karol bolted from the cover of the tent. Feet pounded the hardened ground behind him, but he didn't look back. He closed his eyes and thought of his mother. Was that her scream?

Their captors were killing them all. Karol ran harder, so hard he thought his heart would fly out of his chest. He was ten years old. He could do this. He was the man of the family now.

With a quick leap, he landed on a protruding rock and then scrambled up. A spear hit the boulder near him and it clanged and then clinked when it dropped. A deep voice yelled, "Stop where you are!"

Karol didn't look and scrambled faster, higher and sideways.

A dispassionate order rang out: "Follow him."

"Hey, kid, is this your mother?"

A whimper echoed around Karol's ears.

"Hide," his mother screamed.

Karol didn't look, couldn't look. If he did, he'd go back to her, he would die with her. He knew they were baiting him.

"I'll kill her," a deep, angry voice raged.

Karol scrambled up the rock face. He was heading for his little stream. There he could survive for a while without food. Karol's legs shook; his muscles were starting to feel the exertion, the lack of food, the fear. This was a dash to safety, not the fun climb he did for a lark.

"I will kill her. Stop!"

But Karol knew his mother was already dead. She didn't want him to come back. She didn't want him to die too.

An odd sound reached him, amplified by the rocks. It was followed by a dull thump. He had to look, had to see. The man had cut his mother's throat.

There she was, blood pooling around her head, legs twitching. Standing over her was a man, a brutal-looking man, thick muscled, bearded. A beast.

Something snagged his foot. He'd been still too long. A hand tugged at his ankle. Karol kicked, kicked like one crazed, but still he was dragged down. He was caught. As if a demon possessed him, he screamed and kicked.

The man held him around the hips, and then changed his grip. Karol took his chance. He kicked out hard, blindly, and connected with something soft, something that left a wet smear on his foot. A crunch, a pain-filled *whoof*, a hail of curses. The man let go. Karol flung out a hand and a foot to stop his plummet to the compound below. He slid and then caught a nub of rock, clawing for a hold. Dirt and stones hissed as they moved beneath him, but Karol was driven by fear to climb like a spider up and away from pursuit.

I am a leaf, I am a feather, I am light and I can scuttle like a beetle so fast no one can catch me. Soon he was out of sight of the compound. The tell-tale trickle of his little spring beckoned. He took a different path, behind a boulder, and squeezed between it and the cliff face. A small cave captured the spring and made a stream.

Panting, he slid down at last to a tiny cobbled bank, a space just large enough to crouch in and no more. He drank and he wept but only for a minute. They were coming. More of the men were climbing to where he was. Pulling himself up to where the water emerged, he stared into the fissure. He was small. He could fit. He had to try. Climbing up and over the canyon wall to escape by the plains was beyond him. He'd tried and there was no easy way out. Not without ropes and supplies.

He could hide. He had to hide. He had to hide or die.

As Karol inserted himself into the fissure, the cold water ran over him, startling his sun-warmed skin. The rock surrounded him, and beyond, where the light did not reach, loomed dark. The sounds of pursuit were wiped out by the crash of the water, his own frightened breaths and beating heart. The fissure grew very tight and even smaller after a few sideways shuffles. Karol flattened himself and squeezed farther in. If he was far enough in they wouldn't see him—they wouldn't know he was there.

Karol squeezed and squeezed…first a leg, an arm, and then managed to wiggle his pelvis and chest into the narrow gap between the rocks. He ought to have been scared, but Karol wasn't. The rock was safe, welcoming. While he had not been underground before, he knew that his forefathers had lived in the ground. Nakel had told him. Told him of the great cities. Regaled him with tales of their people.

As the darkness embraced him, Karol didn't fear anymore. The water provided cover at the entrance and he was now hidden in darkness.

The pursuer's large face jutted through the water. Karol drew back, jammed between the rocks of the fissure, water pushing around his body. He had to keep pushing through or they would notice the current wasn't as strong, that the flow was less.

Karol slid and squeezed, used the palms of his hands as they pressed against the rock face, pushed with the soles of his feet, keeping the pressure on himself so that he could get through. Karol held his breath and then let it out slowly and pushed harder.

His lungs were desperate for air. Water smothered his face, ran into his nostrils, his mouth, his ears. There was no sound except for water in his ears. Karol knew he was going to die. Here. He was going to drown here. He should have died with his mother. He shouldn't have let her die alone.

Then, as his strength was draining away, something shifted. His body passed through and he landed in a heap on the other side of the fissure. Choking and crying, he looked around him. It was a cave. Here the water was but a rivulet and passed through a channel in the floor. He saw where it fell from above to the right of him. He'd lost his loincloth and his pale skin had dark smears where he'd torn flesh from his torso.

Shaking his head, he sucked in breaths and checked his body for further injury. Scrape marks ranged over his chest, hips and knees. He rubbed at his chin and his hand came away with blood on it. He cried more, releasing his pent-up fear and grief. His mother was dead. His people were dead and he was alone.

He calmed himself. His mother wouldn't have wanted him to cry or be sad. She wanted him to live and live free. His father would have wanted him to be true to his people. Nakel had said there was a place for him in the world. He only had to look.

After wiping his eyes and clearing his nose, he looked around the space, serenaded by the fall of water hitting the floor. It was surprisingly light inside, with the sun filtering through the fissure and reflecting off the rivulet. He realized the floor was tiled. He ran his fingertips through the spaces between the mosaic patterns. This was no natural cave. He quickly scanned his surroundings and in a dim recess he saw something strange. He crawled forward, rubbing tears from his cheeks. In front of him was an archway, embellished with strange writing. He staggered to his feet and went up to it. It was a door.

ॐॐॐॐ

Karol slept, turning fitfully due to his various aches. It was a sound that woke him. There were men outside the fissure. He crept forward to hear what they were saying. His heart hammered so loud he missed a few of the words.

"...the debris will cover the dead..."

"...explosives...here..."

Karol blinked, trying to understand. They couldn't come and get him, but they could kill him by blowing up the cliff he was hiding in. He backed up and detected a waft of smoke. He didn't have any time left. He turned and faced the door.

He knew what it was. He knew what lay beyond. It was a secret that his father had died for, that his mother had died for. It was what was going to save him.

He knew the chant off by heart. It had been a lullaby when he was young, something that made little sense to others.

"High for the sun, down for the ground, once for the right and twice for the left. There you can enter into the Travel Ways of your forefathers…"

The door slid open. The smell of smoke was stronger, the rumble under his feet making him sway. He dashed inside the darkened Way and groped around in the dark when the door shut. As he moved away, praying that the Way Gate would hold, Karol tapped his feet in front of him and put his hand out to the wall. A faint glow grew outward from where his hand touched. The longer he was inside, the more he adapted to the low lighting. Soon he saw stairs and the various directions they took. He had no idea which way to go. He had no food or water. He wasn't going to go far or last very long, but at least he was free.

The ground lurched suddenly, throwing him off his feet. He fell into the wall, which glowed light gray, and the substance of it smothered him. Karol fought and fought, and then relaxed: he was either going to die or be all right. He moved his legs as if walking and found he could move. Not back out into the Way, but within, or through, the tunnel wall.

Donna Maree Hanson

Chapter Two
THE LAST DAYS OF
TRELL OF BARR

In Nils's office, deep in the tunnels beneath the city of Barrahiem, it took Salinda many days to decipher Trell's writings. If Nils had been out of the healing tray this work would have been a few hours, but not for Salinda. She knew the code but it was laborious translating it. Trell's word use was different than the present day and that made the task of translation even harder. In many places she had to write "undecipherable" where she could not make out the words. Some of the sentences didn't make sense to her.

She read over what she had written down, shaking her head, certain that Nils would be able to correct her work and fill in the spaces. Salinda went over the translation of a particular section, tidying up the words so they made sense. This particular section sounded like she had it right, but she wondered if it was useful at all:

The last days of Trell of Barr and the tale of the Falt of Ruel moon.

> *I do not know if any of my kin will read my final words. I find I do not care. They will perish as surely as the Sundwellers if nothing is done. But here in the Sundweller city of Unethea I found others who saw the danger and planned to make a stand. Bright minds and brave hearts so like my kin in their better days. Not like the [undecipherable undecipherable] my kin have become.*

In the end there were seven of us, seven of us who dared the [undecipherable]. Two great minds instigated this. It was not I, I was a willing contributor. [Undecipherable and undecipherable] Benenge and his sister Annabeau were a scientific team of astrophysicists who had been studying the bands of power that bound Ruel moon. They were not interested in the mystery of the Moon Binders for they felt that the mystical aliens who had placed them there were not likely to return to save Margra. [Undecipherable] maggots! Ruel [undecipherable] moon. No, they were more interested in what was happening to Ruel, what kind of elements and rock it was made up of and how this knowledge could be used to save Margra.

My knowledge was scant as well. Curse my [undecipherable] soul. I had only the writings of our great astrophysicists and historians who theorized that Ruel was once a mine, that the Moon Binders took something so essential from the moon that it became destabilized. We have their artifacts but not [undecipherable] written account of who they were and what they did. We do not even know how long ago they left this planet or if indeed they died out. [Undecipherable]

It was Annabeau who developed a telescope that identified the elements on the moon. It worked on the stars too, but much better so close to home. Annabeau was a dark beauty, along with an amazing mind. My kin would renounce me for such an act as loving her. [Undecipherable] dotards. I was an old Hiem, but she didn't care about that. I had a family, although my mate had [undecipherable]. Annabeau loved me in return. While Annabeau calculated, Benenge worked on his matter converter. Annabeau explained it to me thus: Benenge's ray would target the heavy elements in the moon fragments, transmuting them to gas or other types of matter so that the mass was less. It sounded damn near [undecipherable].

In these last weeks, we know we cannot deflect the moon. My heart is [undecipherable] heavy. My spirit is low and [undecipherable]. Merkon and Taha have been developing scenarios of how the moon will break apart. We cannot avert the impact totally but we can lessen it. It could be all for naught. All could perish. But our efforts may leave a few alive to carry on. When I think of the lives I cannot save, that we cannot save, I cry and I cannot sleep and it is Annabeau who soothes me. Dark eyes light the black of night [undecipherable] warm and smiling just for me. We are not just these bodies, she said, pinching me. We are more than that. We live on. We come back. I [undecipherable undecipherable].

My faith was not as strong as hers. I was jealous of my life, my identity, my personality and I was not sure I would ever be the same. My attachment to my life and who I am was too strong and [undecipherable]. If I wasn't going to remember myself, remember who I was, then that was death for me.

Rinul built the machines that would target the moon with Benenge's invention. The Sundwellers had surpassed the Hiem with their ingenuity and their desire to save. Not so my [undecipherable] Hiem brethren who ignored my warnings. My first observations were but conservative estimates of what a broken Ruel moon could do. Now that I have joined with my learned colleagues I know it is going to be far [undecipherable] worse than I could have [undecipherable] imagined.

So I am faced with the [undecipherable] knowledge that I will die whatever decisions I make. I am faced with the choice to make my [undecipherable] death matter. There is the rub. I know what is coming and I will spend my life to give life to others that come after me.

My grandson, Nils, lies in a prison of sleep. Maybe he will [undecipherable] survive and read these words from me. Maybe he will perish along with my kin. I cannot tell, I do not have such foresight. The [undecipherable] Hiem cities are well protected. The observatory may survive. It was they who led me to the city of Unethea. My learned friends. How I mourn for thee. [Undecipherable, undecipherable, undecipherable…]

Salinda's heart rate thumped as she translated each word then read each sentence. Her excitement was immeasurable. The names were familiar to her. She cast her mind back to the time she broke through the layers of the cadre to learn how to transfer it. She had seen a vision— seven people who went into a machine. Could this be the same people? The names given in this tale—were they the seven that the cadre spoke of? The vision of a machine...there had to be a connection. Trell mentioned machines, so there was more than one. Where were they? Did they still exist? If only Salinda had paid attention in her history lessons, studied the maps of the world, she would understand more. If only Nils was awake, he could do this so much faster with greater precision.

A noise in the corridor alerted her to Garan's approach.

"Salinda," Garan said as he entered the study. He held a platter and Salinda smelled food. "You have been down here for so long I thought you might like something to eat." Garan's smile didn't quite reach his violet eyes. He could not hide that he had some worries.

"Thank you, Garan. I am hungry." Salinda sat up and realized her back and neck muscles were stiff and sore. How long had she been at this?

Garan supplied the answer to her thought before she could ask. "You have been down here for ten hours straight."

Salinda smiled and gestured for Garan to put down the tray of food. She lifted the lid on the bowl of steaming vegetable stew and noted with interest the freshly cooked cacti bread. The people of Vanden dried the cacti and ground it into flour. It made the most delicious bread. Because the observatory traded with the Vanden, they had been making it for years, and Garan had had the foresight to learn how to bake it. "I thought it was longer. Oh, that's so good," Salinda said, inhaling deeply. She took a nibble on the edge of the bread, closing her eyes and savoring it. "I didn't realize I was so hungry." Salinda opened her eyes and noticed the little tells that Garan's food delivery was for another purpose. "Sit down and talk to me."

Garan leaned his back against the wall and slid to the ground. He ran his fingers through his dark curly hair. His tanned skin had paled after being underground for so long but it was still a creamy olive, not so much lighter than her own. His straight nose and full, vulnerable-looking mouth made him an attractive lad. Not that he had had any joy in the love department. "'Tis Laidan," he began. Salinda took a sip of the liquid from the casserole and bit into the bread. Closing her eyes briefly, she enjoyed the taste. "This is so good." Then she realized what Garan had said and apologized. "I'm sorry. I'm listening. Does she still think you hurt her?"

Garan grimaced. "I think she is beginning to understand that I didn't. She misses Nils. She has come to depend on him and I thought it was going well between us…"

"Until Brill arrived."

Garan let out a long sigh and leaned his head back against the wall to stare at the ceiling. "Yes, maybe…I don't know. 'Tis not that he has done anything or she…I find I am reacting to ghosts…to what went on before."

"You know her brain was damaged. She may never be the girl you fell in love with. You have to temper your expectations, you know that."

"I know!" he said, rather too fervently. "I am sorry. 'Tis just so hard…so hard…so much harder than I thought it would be."

Salinda took a spoonful of fungi and swallowed before answering. "I understand that. If we live through this moonfall then we will have time to see to our own relationships. Our hearts will do what they will. So how is everyone else upstairs?"

"Danton has come down with a fever. Brill suspects another infection."

Salinda's lips compressed at this news. It had been her decision to put Nils in the healing tray while leaving Danton to recover from his horrific injuries the natural way. It had been touch and go already and the damage done to him by the baron was too awful to contemplate.

Yet Salinda had contemplated it—she had cleaned and dressed every wound, every cut, every burn, every bruise. She had nursed him until she could barely stand. Every minute of his suffering was a cut to her soul and every look of blame from Brill burned a hole in her mind.

The call had had to be made. There was but one healing tray. Nils was important for the future of Margra. She had to be right about that because one doubt about that decision was likely to cause her to lose her grip on sanity. Danton suffered so much. Suffered because of her choice. Salinda didn't think she could cope if it had been the wrong one.

Salinda thought she had been through the worst this life could give. She had survived torture at Gercomo's hands, rape by Ange, brutalization by the people of Gunner, and still she had persevered. She had found Nils, or rather, he had found her and saved her. It had to be fate. It had to have meaning. But letting Danton suffer? Letting another soul continue in agony. It had been the worst. Absolutely the worst. Salinda doubted she would ever come to terms with the outcome of her decision. But she didn't let on, didn't let Brill's pained looks and Danton's fevers get under her armor. She couldn't show weakness. Not now.

And Laidan. Oh Laidan! Her suffering was on Salinda's conscience, more and more each day. The constant "if only I had done this" or "if only I had done that" plagued her endlessly. But looking at Garan and how well he had settled the cadre within his mind, she knew she had that part right.

She finished the meal he had brought and piled the bowls on the tray again. Garan stood to take it from her. "Are you coming back up tonight?" he ventured to ask.

Salinda frowned as she looked at the book. "In a few hours. I will come to check on Danton, too."

Garan lifted his chin, indicating the book open on the desk. "What is that?"

Salinda realized that she had kept the most exciting news from Garan. "Source preserve me! You don't know. Garan, you did it. You found the book. The book Nils was searching for." She tapped the book with her hand. "This contains the last writings of Trell of Barr."

"I did? From the old observatory?"

Salinda nodded eagerly.

"Trell of Barr. Nils's grandsire." Garan shook his head. "I found the book. It's been sitting here?"

Again she nodded.

Garan's eyes flashed, his skin reddened and a smile bloomed on his face. "That is wonderful." He leaned over to examine the script. "You can read it?"

Garan studied her. Salinda squirmed under his scrutiny, conscious that she wasn't quite up to the task, then shrugged. "Yes, but not well. Nils did teach me the Hiem code language when I came here. It's a bit of a slog for me, and the language Trell uses is archaic."

"And?"

Salinda knew what he was asking. Did it provide the answers they sought? Salinda thought it would, but didn't know for sure, not yet. "There is so much in here. I think this is the clue we've been looking for. I'll let you know when I've translated a bit more."

Garan backed away, a lopsided grin on his face. "That is really good news." He took the tray and headed out.

"Garan..." She stopped him before he reached the corridor.

"Yes," he responded, the smile still there but damped down.

"You recall how I went inside my cadre?"

Garan nodded. "Yes, you needed to find out how to transfer Laidan's to me." His brow furrowed. "Why?"

"I think you might learn more by doing something similar. The key name for you would be Trell of Barr."

Garan's head jerked up. "You think Trell of Barr is inside my cadre? Inside my head?"

"If what I read in here is true, then yes."

Garan gulped, his neck bump moving up and down. "I will see what I can do... in my spare time," he said reluctantly. "I'll tell the others you will return to check on Danton soon, then."

"Yes, thank you." She bit her lip as she continued to stare after Garan long after he was lost from view. Salinda moved her tongue around her dry mouth, and then leaned over to take a drink of water.

There was a sense of disappointment. Why wasn't the lad as excited as she was? Yes, he said it was wonderful, but it didn't set him on fire. Didn't he understand the importance of what he'd found, of what she had discovered? She smiled to herself, thinking his head was just too close to his heart. But no time to think about that. It was back to translating Trell's words. She took another sip of water, picked up the pen she'd been using and tackled the next paragraph.

It would have been easier to read sections of the text and only translate the relevant parts, except she still had to translate each word and writing them down was the best way to do it so she could then read each sentence aloud to ensure it made sense. Too many words were labeled "undecipherable", but she suspected they were mostly curse words because she could make sense of most of Trell's writings: a lot of technical details about their plans, about his growing love for Annabeau, and bitter recriminations about his kin.

A few hours later she needed a break. Stiff shoulders and her head ached. She'd been working on the same word for over ten minutes. It was time to call it quits. She pushed herself off the chair and turned to the door. Before she could take a step, Brill bounded into the room. "Come quickly. It's Danton!"

Brill turned and fled back up the corridor. Salinda shuddered once, forgot about her aches and pains and ran after Brill.

Chapter Three
A WOMAN TAKES
A STAND

Toola had a very personal attachment to Linel. So much so that she couldn't bear to live without him. He stood in the corner, looking as he always did, except his eyes were made of glass and his complexion had a waxy sheen of preservative. She ran a hand down his stiff chin and rested her head against his silent chest. She would never forgive Mandin for striking that killing blow.

That Toola had had her revenge was not enough, not enough to fill the storm of anger that raged inside her. She had stabbed Mandin, stabbed and stabbed, but still the rage would not die. The woman couldn't die enough times for Toola. But Mandin's death did not bring her obedient dog Linel back. Her sometime fuck. He was her creature and now she had him no more.

Mandin had been cut into tiny pieces. Some had been flung in the dung heap, some thrown into the river, some fed to the burden beasts in the corral.

Now Toola was empty. It was all for nothing. Business went on as usual. Toola sat down and poured her tea, but she couldn't remain seated. There was a blade waiting to fall. She just didn't know when. Surely the baron's spies would have told him that Eneit was gone. The young virgin that would have been her star attraction, who would have earned her price back in short time, thus allowing Toola to repay the debt. Toola had no means to pay the baron what she owed him.

Restless, Toola went to the mirror and smoothed an imaginary strand of hair and turned her head left, then right, admiring the high pile of dark hair held together by long pins. The small curls curving on her cheeks. She was made up in her best style. Wafting, sheer robes gave more than a hint of the body beneath, perfume light and spicy lingered in the air around her, and her body was massaged and moisturized, smooth and subtle to the touch.

It was too much. The sounds of the brothel went on around her, but she felt two degrees removed. The brothel she had built up through hard work and cunning strategy. To think she could lose it. She could be homeless when the baron came to throw her out. He had taken Danton—the only person she cared about. He had outmaneuvered her and that stung. How many regimes had she survived? How many near misses had she survived? How many times had she pimped herself to gain what she wanted?

And still she had no idea what the baron was up to.

A knock at the door disturbed her train of thought. "Yes, what is it?" she grumped, unable to disguise her mood.

Lexia poked her head around the door. "Oh, there you are. My lady, the bartender asks if there are any special orders."

"None."

Lexia bowed her head. "Madam Tyree said there have been five cancellations in the bathhouse this morning. She asks whether she should use this opportunity for cleaning."

"Of course she should. Is she stupid?"

Lexia bowed her head. "Is there anything I can do for you?" Her gaze slid to Linel in the corner. Toola saw the lines of Lexia's face, the hint of revulsion.

"No. Get out or I shall beat you for your impertinence."

Lexia's eyes widened and she retreated into the corridor, shutting the door quietly behind her. Toola lifted her chin and turned her gaze to the ceiling, trying for patience. It wasn't their fault she was ruined. What was going to happen to them? Just the thought of the baron claiming what was hers was too much to bear, but she knew there was nothing she could do. The best step she could take was to send everyone away and close the business, even burn it down and hope it took her competitors as well. But her people had nowhere to go. She owed them a livelihood and, except for the debt for the purchase of Eneit, her business was profitable. Could she bargain with the old lecher? Could she? Would she dare?

She shook her head. What choice did she have? The best face was a brave face. Her people stood a better chance if they were gainfully employed. So what if there had been cancellations. Rumors traveled fast, but she could show they were unfounded.

Hiding in her room drinking tea wasn't going to bolster morale. She stalked up to her table and drank off the cooling liquid. She would do a walk-through, inspect everything, get everyone motivated. Then she would come up with a plan to deal with the baron and his inevitable takeover.

The kitchen was not expecting her impromptu inspection and they received a tongue-lashing. The young apprentice cook she sacked on the spot. Better he was out of there. She scribbled down a note and gave him directions to another establishment where he would be safe. She gave him some coin, then mussed his hair and pushed him out the door.

The cook stood, nonplussed. "Who will scrub the pots?"

"The girls aren't busy. Get one of them. Just keep your lecherous hands off them or I'll be feeding you your own cock in white sauce. Got it?"

He bowed his head and wiped his hands on his aprons. "Yes, ma'am."

Tyree was in the middle of having some bath attendants scrub out the main bath. Toola nodded in approval. Others, she saw, were cleaning the urns and scrubbing towels. They were hard at work. Tyree appreciated the need to keep everyone busy. While Tyree didn't know it all, she'd been with Toola long enough to know that the situation was bad.

The brothel proper was in the middle of being spring-cleaned. Mattresses were being carried out to the rear courtyard to be put in the sun. Girls bent over small brooms and cloths, cleaning diligently. In the bar, customers were few. Here, the sluts were cleaning too. The barkeep was polishing his tools of trade and his serving bench shone darkly in the light. Toola said nothing, just looked it over.

The means to pay back her debt were few. The only thing she owned was the brothel and even then she didn't think it was enough. She had overextended herself. It was Mandin's fault, with her talk of stolen virgins and confiding in Toola. She wouldn't have known anything about it if Mandin had shut her big, fat mouth.

A smile twisted Toola's lips at the memory of seducing that country wife. The woman had never had an orgasm in her life until Toola gave her one. Not that Mandin was grateful. All her life she'd been poked at by men who knew nothing except their own pleasure and need to reproduce. Mandin could have been something more than she was. Now she was just dead. Stupidly dead, and her darling daughter, the next star whore, had escaped her fate.

Well, if you can hear me, Mandin—fuck you!

Toola reentered her room and put her kettle on to boil and it was doing so when she heard them. Booted feet stomping through her halls. Her heart leaped at the sound, but she kept herself calm. She'd known this was coming. Continuing to make her tea, she put some aromatic leaves in the pot and inhaled them as if doom was not coming in the door. She poured in the water and put her face over the rising steam. Then she put the lid on and grabbed her favorite cup.

Dark liquid streamed into the mug. It caught the light and glittered. She smiled. How silly to notice such a mundane thing at this moment.

A thumping on the door failed to shift her calm. "Enter!"

It was Jent, the pompous, hated servant of the baron's. "The baron requests your attendance. He is in your upstairs parlor."

Toola lifted the cup to her lips and sipped, then lowered it and lifted her eyes to Jent. "I will be there shortly."

"You will come now or you will be dragged naked up the stairs." Two burly men in uniform stood behind him, dark shadows in the hall.

Carefully, Toola put her cup down and stood, stopping to adjust her clothing and run a hand over her hair, ensuring her pins were in place. "After you," she said sweetly.

Jent lifted a dark eyebrow. "No, after you." There was no trace of sweetness in his words. The brothel was unnaturally quiet, as if its inhabitants were holding their collective breaths. With as much dignity as she could muster, Toola ascended the stairs. Her stomach was a bit riotous, but she admitted to herself the baron was one scary customer.

Toola glided up the stairs, head held high. Eyes were on her. The guards that the baron had brought were arranged around the corridors and key points. It brought to mind Danton's capture, how snared he had been. But Toola wasn't going to run. There was no point in that. Other eyes were peeping out through the cracks in the doors and the spyholes. These were her people and she would show no fear. She would do her best for them.

The door was shut so she stood there until a guard knocked on the door and opened it. Here was where Danton had fought his last fight. Toola sniffed and tried to forget her betrayal. She tried not to think about how she had played the game and lost. What a fool she had been to think she could weasel her way into the baron's inner circle. If it hadn't been for Mandin, she might have succeeded. *Mandin, you fucked me utterly.*

The baron sat on a chair, arranged so that it was the only one against the wall. All the others were stacked in a corner. His servant stood out ahead of him like a pompous herald. Guards were arranged beside him on both sides and from the loud shuffling some had moved to block her escape. The baron really didn't know her. To her dismay, the kitchen boy she'd fired was standing by the baron's knee, his face a bland mask. Toola sighed. She had tried to save the boy. Now he would be consumed by the baron.

Hate for the baron burned like liquid fire in her gut. She didn't care if he saw it. The baron would not care either way. Love or hate would make no difference to him.

"So, Toola, where is the girl?" the baron asked, rat eyes squinting.

"Gone," Toola replied in a bored voice. She couldn't help getting a dig in.

"Gone where?" the baron asked. It had to be a kind of game. His spies would have already told him.

"Ran off with Brill, Danton's rebel friend."

"And where did they run to?"

"I have no idea."

The baron lowered his chin. A guard strode up and slapped her across the face. The blow was hard and Toola staggered back, but then righted herself, not even bothering to touch the sore part of her face. Her eyes watered, though, and there was nothing she could do about that.

"I don't know where they went. I had them chased, of course, but I had other problems at the time."

The baron grinned at her and it chilled her to the core. "Your little fuck toy. I heard you cried and screamed like a child. You're too emotional by half. That is why you don't succeed, Toola. Too much heart, not enough balls."

Toola didn't deign to reply. Toola had plenty of balls. She just wasn't a sick fuck like the baron. Even she had limits.

"You have defaulted on your loan. Do you have the means to pay me?"

"I have and, no, I do not. My wealth is in this brothel."

"Then the brothel is now mine. Agreed."

"Yes, that is reasonable," Toola replied, knowing there was more. It wasn't enough, not nearly enough.

"You are mine."

Toola stiffened, not quite able to repress her reaction. His? That was a shock. Unexpected.

He lifted an eyebrow in query. "Agreed?"

The words stuck like ice in her throat. She managed to squeak out, "Yes." *Owned by this man? Never.*

"You will sign the contract Jent has prepared." Toola hated Jent beyond reason. He was a mere servant and thought himself superior to her.

"I will. What will you have me do, baron? As your slave, I mean?"

The baron sat forward on his seat, elbow on his knee. He gave his hand a casual flick. "Anything and everything. Your slave price will not even dent the debt of honor to me and the penalty for failing me."

Toola's hand went nervously to her coif and relaxed when every hair was in place. "What is your first order, baron?"

Her eyes flicked to the boy, and then she looked to the ceiling. His face was fresh and young. Too innocent of the world to know what was to come. The baron placed his hand on the boy's shoulder and the lad trembled. Perhaps the boy was already regretting his decision. Toola had to control her stomach in case she vomited. Most of the girls were safe provided they brought in a good return. The baron didn't like girls. At least she hoped so. For herself, she had a pretty good idea what was in store. It was an open secret what he had done to his wives.

"After you sign over the deeds to this place and sign your slave contract, you will be stripped naked and placed in the bar. You will be our new lowliest whore, doing tricks for spit and small change."

Toola shuddered. *No, not that.*

Everything came crashing down on her. Manage the place for the baron and send him the profits, take a beating and fuck some official for information she could do willingly. But not that. Not that lowly whoring. The full meaning of what the baron intended hit her full force.

She took a step toward him, just as the servant took a step toward her. The guards had taken a step too. She held out her hands showing she had no weapons. They did not relax. The rustle of the documents drew her attention. She took another step closer, but not close enough.

The servant smirked at her and took another step closer holding out a pen. Toola's lips were drawn into a straight, hard line. Her gaze slid to the papers. The servant took a step closer.

Toola reached up to her hair. The servant's eyes widened in puzzlement at her action. She should have been cowed, she supposed. Shaking in fear. Crying up a storm. No. Not Toola.

In a blur of motion, she drew out two long hairpins. Her hair fell long and lush down her back. She grinned and then lunged, stabbing the servant in the neck. There was a yell from the baron and the clink of weapons. Toola turned the other hairpin on herself. It had poison on the tip. She didn't need to stab it far.

Bodies fell on her and tried to stay her hand, but she was unstoppable. A guard gritted his teeth as he held her hand. Toola grinned and bent her arm up to meet the tip of the pin. The guard did nothing. He didn't know it was poison.

The pin fell from her numb hand. Four burly men held her and the baron stepped up now that she was held tight. The baron leered at her. "You thought you could trick me."

Toola spat at him. "No man tells me what to do with my body. None."

Her body shuddered and then she writhed, a scream ripping from her lips as the poison burned. Her throat closed, her breath was hard to draw in.

"Damn you," the baron seethed. "You stupid fools. She's used poison."

The baron punched her in the gut then sideswiped her across the head. Toola could not feel it over the fire in her nerves. She tried to smile. Her mind was full of gloating.

Toola looked to where Jent, the stuck-up servant, lay stiff and dead on the floor. If only that had been the baron.

Another shudder as her muscles contracted. Her diaphragm would not move. The baron didn't know she had won. It was a pity that his was the last face she saw. Then, everything went dark.

๛๛๛๛๛

Gercomo's damaged left wing hung down on one side and, no matter how he placed himself either in the dirt or the sun, it just would not heal any faster. He was in so much pain that he couldn't transform. A very annoying thing, that. Bertha licked him, licked his wounds, and he was too put out to even growl at her. She'd proved her worth, her loyalty.

Gercomo couldn't believe how well Bertha had fought. Ruthless, cunning and wholly vicious. If he had trained her himself, he couldn't have taught her any better. Her skill came naturally. In the battle over Eternity, they'd lost the alpha male. Lost four bulls. Their numbers were sorely depleted. Gercomo wasn't going to give up, though. He'd come so close. Salinda had been so close and her power was like an itch behind the eye. If only he could scoop it out and take it.

The baron had got away. Gercomo could sense him too, smell him. As he lay there feeling his body ache, he wondered why? Why did he serve the baron? What sort of twisted desire existed in him? He should have ripped the man to pieces. Should have, but didn't.

There was a link there, some kind of inexplicable joining. The baron had shaped him, had molded him as if he was a clay model. That's why there was the need to serve, the need for recognition. He thought he'd outgrown that, had shrugged off that cloak while he rotted away at the prison vineyard, but it had come back like a thirst. He needed and wanted the baron.

Bertha sighed listlessly beside him. He really needed her to get food. He projected thoughts of hunger and food at her. And threw in a few curse words and insults for good measure. *Get me food, you lazy cow. Now!*

Bertha nipped at him. *You get it.*

Gercomo nearly fainted in shock. *Did you just speak to me?*

Yes. Did you think I couldn't learn your mindspeak?

Gercomo stared at Bertha and then laughed. Bertha hadn't said anything. No. He was going crazy. She understood emotions and strong thoughts. She didn't talk back. Bertha eyed him inscrutably and said nothing more.

She lumbered to her feet and called to some of the other dragons— young males, a few females. Together they took off in search of food. Gercomo lowered his snout and nosed it into the sand. If only he could get comfortable. If only...

☾☾☾☾☾

Later, after he'd finished off a delicious meal of old burden beast, Bertha nursed his wounds again. He stretched out his injured wing and found it moved freer than before. Once again, he had hopes that he could fly and that he could change. He needed to seek out the baron. They had plans they needed to make. Salinda couldn't be allowed to get away from them. That power could not be allowed to slip through their fingers. He licked his claws. Slip through his claws, he corrected.

The baron was useful, and Gercomo was bound to him, but if he was objective about it, he could break that hold. He was more powerful than the baron and smarter, and he had less dangerous proclivities.

Perhaps it would even be possible to regain his old self. That was something to work toward. Being Gercomo again.

Donna Maree Hanson

Chapter Four

SUFFER UNTO ME

Salinda had to cut into the infected tissue and drain it. Danton was going to find it hard to walk for a while. Keeping him lying down was not going to be easy. As she sliced into the puckered red skin, she realized that the infection went deep. This meant digging farther into the wound to drain the infection.

"You're going to have to sit on him, I think," she said to Brill.

"What?" Brill asked her, brows knotted together, fists balled up and resting on his thighs.

"Just do it. Sit on him," she said as she flamed the blade again. No point in introducing infection on top of the one he had.

Brill grumbled, but he swung his leg over and sat astride Danton, effectively blocking Danton's view of the proceedings. Danton lapsed in and out of consciousness, babbling insensible words half the time.

As she dug deeper into the wound, Danton's body stiffened and he screamed. It unnerved her, that sound. That pitiful, scared and pained sound. And she was causing it. Salinda's hand shook, but she fought for steadiness. The tip of the blade touched the source of the infection and pus shot out, hot and green. Within the wound, she spotted a small sliver of metal that had not been removed when she first tended him. In the tray of equipment she found a pair of tweezers with which to grip the metal and draw it out. Then she flushed out the wound until no more pus exuded.

While she washed her hands, she nodded at Brill and he climbed off Danton. He'd passed out, which was a mercy for him and them. Sick and vulnerable, Danton lay there, and Salinda's heartstrings grew taut. *Please live. Please, Danton.*

Danton, covered only in a scrap of sheet, had lost weight and his skin was pink with fever. She took a cloth and wiped his face. She pursed her lips in concentration, trying to keep the emotion in check, the despair. If Danton died it would be on her conscience as well as her heart.

Blood ran freely from the wound. Ideally, she'd stitch the flaps of flesh together, but perhaps if it didn't bleed too much she would leave it open to drain, and when it was clear of infection in a day or two she could attempt to stitch it up. Or, she could use dragon wine. They were running low, but it was worth using it on Danton's wounds. She just had to wait this time, wait for the gore to drain before using the power of dragon wine to heal the wound.

"Can you do anything else?" Brill asked anxiously at her side. His hair stood up from running his hands through it. Danton and Brill shared a house in the node next to hers. The place was sparsely furnished. All they had done in there was care for Danton. Not much time for making it seem like home.

She met Brill's gaze and shook her head. "I've done all that I know how to do. Give it a day, maybe two, and then I'll use the wine. He's strong. He will fight."

"Strong? Look at him, Salinda. He's wasting away because…" Brill stood and turned his back to her, tension radiating off him. He could not forgive her decision. Danton was a beloved friend. Nils, to Brill, was a strange and barely understood creature. No amount of reasoning would get Brill to understand, even though every dig, every needling complaint about her decision, cut her to the quick. Brill was young, impetuous, still bound by ideals. He didn't understand that leadership took more than that. Leadership required hard decisions.

"I will stay with him tonight," she said. "You go and take some rest. Use my abode."

Brill's eyes glittered in the reflected light when he faced her. "No…I mean, I appreciate you staying up with him, but Garan told me you've been working on some text for ten hours or more. Perhaps we can take turns in case he has another crisis."

Salinda gazed at Danton and pulled the thin blanket over his pale and sweaty torso. She didn't think he'd survive another crisis. "You go first then. I'll wake you in a few hours."

Brill nodded and went into the living area. She heard him rustling blankets as he made a bed on the sofa. He wasn't going to take up the offer of her own abode. Salinda washed out a cloth in cold water and placed it on Danton's forehead.

"Danton?" she said as she took another cloth and wiped over the slight smattering of chest hair. It was sad that the only time she had touched him like this he was sick, perhaps dying. She leaned over and spoke directly into his right ear. "Fight for me, Danton. Fight this. I need you. I really need you right now."

Salinda knew it was wrong to burden him in his condition but it was the only thing she thought he'd respond to. He may be angry with her because of Nils, but she knew he still loved her, loved her as she loved him.

Her eyelids were heavy, and it was hard to stay awake after so long in Nils's study, translating the text, but she fought the weariness as best she could. If she was smarter she could skip ahead in that book, find information about the location of the machines, but she wasn't and couldn't. She had to read Trell's words one by one and not all of them were relevant to their current need. Doubtless, Nils would rejoice in every one of those words. Salinda wanted to know about the machines. There was more than one. There were hints that it was so. Where were they? Did they still exist? Had they survived Moonfall?

The rift where the largest piece of Ruel moon struck Margra was likely to have been near one of the machines. Likely, she thought, but she had no real idea. She was no scientist. And if it was there, would it help them? She needed the observatory for that. She needed someone from the observatory to help them. Garan was useful, but he was not a Farsighter. He couldn't do the calculations.

Salinda lay down next to Danton as weariness closed in on her. She tried to keep her eyes open, but couldn't.

She awoke with a start when Danton shuddered violently. She sat up and wiped her eyes, as Danton's arm flew out. His leg jerked and his body twitched. Tentatively, she rested her hand on his forehead. So hot.

She sloshed the water around with the cloth and wiped him down. It wasn't enough. "Brill. Brill," she called out.

She picked up the bowl of water and tossed it on Danton's chest. Brill stumbled in, wiping sleep from his eyes.

"More cold water. Hurry," she said without preamble.

"What?" He shook his head and focused.

"Hurry, it's a crisis. We need to bring his temperature down."

Brill lurched from the bedroom. He came back with a bucket of water. "Good. Wet the sheets and drape them over him."

Together, they dampened Danton down. He shivered, jaws clenched tight, neck arching back. Salinda chewed her nails as she watched. If the source was something that she could appeal to for mercy she would have, but life and death did not work that way. She lifted the sheet to check the wound. The blood flow had lessened. No pus was in evidence.

"I think I should use the dragon wine now." Salinda met Brill's worried frown.

"Are you sure? The shock might kill him." Brill ran a hand over Danton's face.

Salinda looked to the ceiling as she tried to sort through her jumbled emotions. "Wing dust! I will wait a little longer."

Brill squeezed her shoulder and Salinda's head shot up at the touch. It was the first tender thing he'd done since she made the decision to put Nils in the healing tray instead of Danton. It was too much, too unexpected. She burst into tears, great sobs of tears.

Brill drew closer and rested her head on his shoulder. "I know," he said. "I know."

Danton continued to shake and shiver and jerk. Then, just as suddenly as they'd begun, the convulsions stopped. Salinda gasped and Brill fell to his knees. "Danton!" he blurted, loud enough for his voice to fill the room.

Salinda sat down next to Danton and put her hand on his chest. He breathed. She shook her head and smiled. "He's through the worst."

"The wine?"

Salinda inclined her head. "Yes, I think now is the time."

There could be worse things than having pure dragon wine poured onto an open wound on your groin where a maniac had cut away your testicle, but Salinda didn't think so. She winced as Danton screamed. Brill's face screwed up in sympathy and he had to look away.

Danton jerked and fitted as the wine soaked into his wound. After about ten minutes, he collapsed, totally inert. When Salinda checked him, he was sleeping like a limp rag, no strength left even to whimper as she and Brill changed his wet sheets for clean and dry ones.

Salinda stood and ran her hands through her long hair. Her fingers caught in the tangles and she winced. She hadn't brushed her hair in ages. "Now, Brill. I'm going to sleep. I'm exhausted. When he wakes feed him broth. Bread, if he can manage it. Keep him quiet. I'll check on him in the morning."

Brill flashed her a grin. "You deserve some sleep. Thank you."

Tears slid down her cheeks. "Why do you thank me?" She was close to losing control. "It is because of me he is like this."

Brill looked up, his head tilted to the right as he regarded her. "I was wrong to blame you. Forgive me."

Salinda found it hard to speak. "There's nothing...nothing to forgive. Your anger...was...warranted. I..."

"No, not warranted. Danton wouldn't have wanted it any other way." Brill changed his expression and Salinda realized he was impersonating Danton: "What? An alien contraption for me? No. Of course not."

Salinda's eyes narrowed and her chest relaxed. "Did he say that?"

Brill grinned. "Yes. Stupid fellow. For the record, I'll take the healing tray and what it offers without argument. Provided someone worthier than me doesn't need it first."

Salinda wiped at her tears and nodded. She moved to the door and bent down to exit. She was heading for her own bed this time. Her bones were so weary she thought they'd break. "Good night...and thank you, Brill. I will sleep better now."

When Salinda had washed and eaten she lay down on her bed, her body so heavy and tired that she didn't think she could rise again. At that moment she didn't care. Closing her eyes, she was at peace for the first time in weeks. Danton would be okay. She was sure of it. Brill forgave her.

Now there was just the world to save.

Donna Maree Hanson

Chapter Five
NEW BEGINNINGS

Nils's eyes snapped open and he drew in a shuddering breath. The healing tray lid was down and the healing webs were still attached to his naked flesh. Something had called to him, something had awoken him before the tray had finished the healing process.

He pushed up the lid and slid his legs down the side. He did not have any memory of major injuries. Whatever had happened to him must have been bad for him to be in the tray, without his memory. A robe lay folded on the edge of the tray. He picked it up, unfurled it and put it on. He cocked his head, but he could hear no one nearby.

Closing his eyes he sent his senses out into the world around him. There had been something. A sharp prick of awareness. A warming of recognition. A dark corridor lay to one side. It drew him. Not to his abode or even his study. The Ways called to him.

Nils shook his head. That hadn't happened before. Yes, he had shared his essence with the Ways and the Ways had been hungry for his life force. Surely that did not mean they called to him now. His heart *thunked* uncomfortably in his chest. Fear! He was afraid of what he had awoken in the Ways.

A smile lingered on his face. *How fickle you are, Nils of Barr. First, you long for death and then you quake at the first sign of it.* Yet there was much to consider. Being reckless with his life could damage Salinda's cause. When he thought about her, he thought of their unborn child. He had not wanted it to be brought into being. He did not want it to be alone on this world. Now, though, he had softened his attitude. Much had happened, he realized. They had found good people on the surface of Margra, people who, while not eclipsing the Sundwellers, were certainly worthy descendants.

In his early days of being awake, he had seen what existed above. That any good existed on the surface had to be some great cosmic chance or miracle. Or maybe the goodness and wisdom of the Sundwellers had passed successfully to a few.

No one came to investigate whether Nils was awake. If he was going to slip away, then now was a good time. He could be back before they even noticed he had gone. Not that he wanted to cause his companions any distress...but something...something niggled, something itched in his mind, in his soul, in that part of him that was essentially Hiem and linked to the Travel Ways.

Without shoes, his feet trod softly across the tiled floor. While in the city his passage would be easy, but once into the stairs to the Travel Ways he would be sorry for the lack of foot protection. He did not falter. He would travel carefully.

He climbed the stairs where the Way Gate loomed above him like some hungry mouth. He had never considered it thus before, but now there was something there, something waiting. An awareness.

Small chips of rock dug into his bare feet. Nils winced and tried to be more careful and to take the passage slowly, but the Way called to him at a level he did not understand, increasing his excitement, quickening his breath, his pace, his anticipation.

At last, he was through the worst of it and stepped through the gate. It was as if the Way exhaled when his foot touched the path. The gray substance of the Ways glowed slightly. He was sure of it. How could that be? It had seemed so dead before, but something lived.

Closing his eyes, he sought his inner compass to lead him where he must go. He started walking, faster and faster, until he was jogging at a quick pace. Soon he was running full pelt down the dark corridors, taking steps two at a time and then climbing them the same way. The Way grew perceptibly lighter the farther on he ran. He was getting closer to whatever it was.

Then, just ahead, light spilled onto the dark Way. Nils almost stopped, staring in awe as the walls of the Travel Way glowed pale blue. He stepped more carefully along the path to see what was causing this manifestation.

By the source! Trapped within the substance of the Way was a boy. Not any boy, but a Hiem child, thin, pale, naked. Nils fell to his knees and bowed his head. A Hiem child had been caught all this time in the Ways. To be preserved in the very substance of Margra. Tears leaked from his eyes and then his breath caught. There was a flicker in the light. Puzzled, he glanced around and then studied the boy trapped in the Way. He was moving. He was alive?

Nils sprung to his feet and thrust his hand into the substance of the Ways. It gave easily under pressure and closed around him like thick gel. He pushed hard to reach that small flailing hand. He was in up to his shoulder and he grasped blindly as he tried to find that pale, flailing limb.

"Reach for me," he said, and thought, *Reach for me.*

As if the child had heard, the Way gave a little and the small hand grabbed onto his forefinger. Nils pushed just a little more, not willing to surrender himself to the Way completely. He crawled along the child's fingers and found the wrist, circling it with his own hand. He latched on and then gradually drew back, bringing the arm and the boy with him. Once the movement began the Way did not stop him, but appeared to loosen, to make it easier for the child to get free. Then, with a loud sucking sound, the child was freed. They both fell to the ground.

Nils lay there gasping, holding the child's cool body. It took a moment to realize that the child was near to death. It was thin and frail and naked. Nils bundled up the child and started back to Barrahiem. The Way back was not as fast as the journey to this place. Once, Nils would have been tempted to use the in-between, but he was without a shroud and without the strength for such a feat. He could not face Salinda, either. He glanced down at the child. The child had no more life force to give to the hungry Ways.

The small boy began to weigh heavily in his arms. Long blond hair draped over his arm from the small head. The head lolled back, giving the impression of lifelessness. Nils, though, still sensed a thread in him, something he thought the Way had given the child. How? Why?

The child had the Hiem forehead, the slight build, the hair and even the skin color. This child was Hiem. Up ahead was the Way Gate entrance. Nils near cried with relief.

Stepping over the broken masonry and stones, Nils felt the cuts but didn't care. He had to get this child to the healing tray. Wetness smeared the ground as he walked. Blood. His strength was ebbing, but here was the threshold of the Hall of Elders. Not far to the healing tray now. He glanced back and saw his bloody footprints. Later, he would clean it and tend himself. There was no time for such niceties…

The tray was open as he'd left it. No one was near. Nils lifted the lid and placed the child on it and shut the lid. Then he went to the wall where the machine was and programmed it to heal.

Soon the child was covered in mist. Nils sank to the ground. It was only then he could make an accounting of his shredded feet: cuts, bruises, blisters. They were painful, but he could not truly feel the wounds. He had saved the child, a Hiem child. That was amazing.

"Nils?" Salinda's distant voice cut through his thoughts. "Nils," she shouted when she saw him. Loping awkwardly, Salinda held her rounded belly as she hastened over.

"Salinda," Nils said quietly with a slight bow. "You are well, I see."

"Where have you been?" Her gaze ran from the top of his head to his toes, where she saw his feet. "By the source, what have you done to yourself? When Garan came at a run to say you were missing we went into a panic. I went down to your office, but you weren't there." She met his gaze, her dark eyes glittering. "Where did you go?"

Nils cocked his head. "I am sorry you were concerned. I did not think. Something called to me, something woke me."

Salinda drew her head back. "Woke you? While you were still in the healing sleep?"

Nils glanced at the tray. "Yes."

"Can you tell me?"

Nils folded his hands in front of himself. "I believe the Travel Ways called to me. I cannot explain it. Perhaps because of my excursion to the in-between I have developed some intimate connection."

Salinda swallowed once and Nils thought he detected skepticism in her expression. "And what did the Travel Ways want?"

Nils shifted, the pain in his feet making itself known. Salinda's gaze dropped and she bit her lip. Just then the sounds of running feet reached them. Garan came in, panting heavily, wiping his curls from his forehead. "Oh, good. You found him."

Salinda turned to him. "Garan, Nils is hurt. Can you fetch hot water and some towels to clean his wounds and then bring his slippers? They are in our bedroom."

Garan looked at her and blew out a breath. "Right. I will be back." Garan ran back down the corridor.

"Perhaps you should sit down," Salinda said to Nils. "Do you need to go back into the healing tray?"

Nils smiled slightly, not quite sure how to reveal what he had done. "Perhaps if I sat on one of the benches in the Hall of Elders."

She moved forward to offer her arm, but Nils held back.

Her surprise was evident in her wide eyes and growing confusion. "What is it, Nils? Tell me," Salinda said, reaching up to slide a finger down the outside of his hand.

Nils smiled wider and moved toward her as Salinda glanced at the healing tray.

"If you are here," Salinda said, regarding him earnestly, "who is in the healing tray?"

Nils turned toward the tray. Fine webs obscured the boy. "I was about to explain about that. You see, when I went into the Travel Ways, I found a Hiem boy."

Salinda's eyes shifted between the tray and Nils. "A Hiem boy," she enunciated carefully. "You're sure about that?"

"I am fairly confident. I am not saying he is a pure breed or from my time, you understand."

"Oh," Salinda replied as if she was contemplating Nils's degree of sanity. "Then where did he come from?"

"That remains to be seen."

"Nils, are you telling me you brought a stranger into Barrahiem?"

Nils blinked. "To own the truth, I did not consider him a stranger. But, yes, you are right. I know nothing of the child, but it seemed to me that his life was hanging in the balance and that the only thing that sustained him was the in-between. You do not know how strange that is. If you recall, it drew from me."

"Drew from you, but gave it to this boy?"

"So it would seem."

"Come along then, let's look at the damage you have done to your feet. Then I should go to bed." Salinda frowned. "But…I have so much to tell you."

Garan could be heard approaching again. She narrowed her eyes at Nils. "You know what? I think we'll get your feet sorted and then I'm going to sleep. Tomorrow I will tell you the news."

Nils let Salinda lead him to one of the stone benches in the Hall of Elders. They were not obviously benches since they were built into the walls of the hall and somewhat disguised by being in the same design style as the walls. He recalled the first time Salinda had discovered their existence when she'd found him sitting there while he contemplated the eternal flame.

By the time they had taken a seat, Garan had arrived. "Wing dust," Garan exclaimed when Salinda took up Nils's left foot. "What did you do? Run across the plains in bare feet?"

Nils glanced up and winced as Salinda probed his injuries. "Nothing so careless. I just entered the Travel Ways through the north-west stair and, as you know, there is a lot of debris there."

Garan nodded as he busily tore cloth into strips.

"Thank you, Garan." Salinda took the strips in a businesslike fashion and focused on Nils's injuries. Nils saw, then, the black rings around her eyes and the skin sagging around her hollow cheeks. Salinda had been using herself ill.

As Salinda bathed his feet, Nils tried to keep his reaction under control. He knew he had recklessly damaged himself. Although not severe, the wounds were painful. Garan's gaze roamed about and Nils saw that he was very soon inspecting lamps and giving the eternal flame a good checking over. If it hadn't been for Garan relighting the city's lamps, there would be no eternal flame. The boy was gifted in many ways. Nils forgot about Garan when Salinda started bandaging up his left foot. It was a secure bandage and his wounds were clean, but his foot throbbed. Salinda started on his right foot.

A loud exclamation alerted them that Garan had discovered the boy in the tray. He came back at a run. Arms gesticulating, eyes wide with surprise, Garan asked, "Who? What? How?"

Salinda *tsked*. "Really, Garan. It is obvious. Nils went into the Travel Ways and brought that child here and put him there."

"Oh," Garan said as a small vee creased his brow. He made eye contact with Nils, an eyebrow raised.

"It is essentially what happened," Nils said, deadpan.

Garan opened and closed his mouth, eyebrows pumping up and down as he thought it through.

"Right then," Salinda said, dusting off her hands as she climbed to her feet with the assistance of the bench for leverage. "I'm done. Garan, I'll need your help getting Nils back to the abode."

Garan grinned. "Of course," he replied. "Leave those things. I'll come back afterward. You look done in."

Nils studied Salinda as she drew his arm over her shoulders. "What ails you?" Nils asked.

"I'm just very tired. I've been busy. But I'm not going to talk about it until tomorrow. I would have been asleep by now if you hadn't gone missing."

Nils nodded. "I see. I look forward to hearing about it in the morning." Nils was not used to Salinda speaking like this to him, so he took at face value that she was tired and upset with his disappearance and, he supposed also, that carrying around the child inside was taking its toll. He accepted Garan's support and together they made their hesitant way back to the Barr family node. On the way, Garan told him that Danton was recovering from his injuries and that Eneit and Laidan were getting on well together. Of Brill he said nothing, but Nils was sure he would eventually.

Donna Maree Hanson

Chapter Six
A GOOD BOOK

Garan made his way back home. He could hear laughter coming from Laidan's abode, the one that she shared with Eneit. Brill's voice could be heard speaking and then more laughter. Garan tried not to be bitter. Laidan was so much better now. Not the same as before the attack, but more able to do and to think. Eneit helped her a lot. Then Brill. For some reason the young rebel was able to reach her and teach her in a way that Garan couldn't.

In order not to appear surly, Garan paused at Laidan's door. He should wish them good night.

"Hello," he called.

The sound of steps reached him and then Brill peered out. "Garan! Come in! You should see. Laidan has beaten me at a game of match and grab."

Garan smiled and followed Brill inside, bending and moving carefully so he could glide his body inside. Eneit waved to him from where she sat cross-legged on the sofa. Laidan's face was alight with delight. In her hands were all the playing cards. Brill had drawn the whole pack for her. They were really quite beautiful. Garan couldn't match such a gift as that.

"I won," Laidan cried and then laughed like one drunk on too much wine. For an instant he paused, because the light in her eyes was like the old Laidan and then it was gone, the spark lost as the ever-present stupor came over her.

"We are playing a game, Garan. Want to play with us?" Eneit asked.

Garan grinned and ran his hands through his hair. He really needed to wash and get some rest. He'd been running all over the city looking for the missing Nils and then half-carrying him back to the Barr family node. He shrugged. "Not really. I should go to bed."

Brill slapped him on the shoulder. "Come on, there's some watered wine there. Just sleep in in the morning. You can miss out on some beauty sleep."

Garan shook his head. "I do not think so. Nils is awake. We might be making plans when Salinda gets up and tells Nils about the book."

Brill sobered, glanced at Laidan, then stepped closer to Garan to whisper in his ear. "You mean she hasn't already?"

Garan shook his head. "By the time we located Nils, she was dead on her feet. She went to bed and said she would tell him in the morning."

Brill acknowledged this news with a slow nod of his head. "Makes sense to wait, I guess. Salinda was exhausted."

Garan turned to go. "Have fun." He paused at the door. "I take it Danton is doing better?"

Brill's smile dimmed. "Yes, much better. He's suffered though. Really suffered."

"Yes, I know." Garan squeezed outside then walked to his abode and repeated the process of squeezing through the door. He really wished it wasn't bad manners to make the door larger. He had suggested it to Salinda and she had ranted at him for half a day. So Garan had sucked his belly in and pushed himself inside the Hiem abode. Once inside, he put some water on to warm. After sniffing himself, he realized he really did need to wash. Hair and all. Who knew, it might be the last time he experienced such luxury.

After pouring the water into the bowl and soaping up his torso, he paused. Why had he thought that? Was it some kind of premonition?

Rinsing off, he started on his hair. No foresight required, he thought, as his nails scraped at his scalp, now slick and smooth with suds. The moon was falling and the world was ending. It could end tomorrow for all he knew. He was doing nothing to stop it. He was powerless to stop it.

Dried off and dressed in clean sleeping pants, Garan stretched out on his bed. His mood was somewhat improved. Coming after his wash, the mattress against the tired muscles of his back lulled him to sleep. Still, his mind was engaged with the state of the world and their role in it. To be fair on himself, they *were* doing something, just not yet, not this minute. They had saved the wine for the people, but who was going to save the people?

He rolled on his side, punched the pillow. *Tomorrow*, he thought. *Tomorrow, things will happen.* They would know more. Make plans. Do something. They had to.

Nils was awake. He could study the book and find out what they needed to do. *Tomorrow*, he repeated to himself. *Tomorrow*…then his eyelids lowered. They fluttered open again when he registered the sound Brill made as he left the girls' abode. The rebel sang to himself, hummed a tune. Why couldn't Garan be carefree like that? Garan hardly ever felt like humming.

He rolled to the other side, squeezing his eyes shut against the ever-present light pouring in through the window. Garan didn't hum or sing to himself, because he was not Brill. He neither thought like him nor loved like him. Garan was different. He had to accept who he was and what he had to do. He had the cadre now. Things were different.

Just then his cadre stirred and Garan groaned. Why now? Why did he have to think of it and rouse it? He was trying to sleep. He didn't need any visions right now, or displays of power. He wanted to sleep. He was so tired.

The book, the cadre said, *the book. THE BOOK.*

Garan clutched his bed covers. *I know*, he thought at the cadre. *I know. Tomorrow. Sleep now.* And before Garan could blink, the cadre went quiet and Garan's body relaxed so quickly and so completely, he did not even recall the transition to sleep.

It was with some annoyance that Garan found himself awake again later. He had no idea what woke him, but then he sat up in bed and cried out in startlement. Nils was outside the window, peering in with his eerie silvery eyes.

"Garan," Nils said.

"Nils," Garan replied on automatic, sure that Nils peering and talking through windows was a major breach of etiquette. Putting that first stupid thought aside, he bounded over to the window. "Is everything all right? The baby?"

Nils frowned and lifted a finger to his lips to signal quiet. "The baby is fine. I need your help." Nils limped toward the front door.

"What?" Garan said a tad crankily as he pulled on his tunic and shoes. Nils had not entered, but waited outside the door

"There you are," Nils said. "You slept so soundly I was not sure I could wake you."

Garan groaned and stretched, wishing he hadn't. "Why did you wake me? How did you wake me?" Garan grouched a little, recalling how hard it had been to go to sleep, and finally he had slept so deeply it was a disappointment to be awakened.

"I had to throw some stones at you since you did not wake when called."

Garan screwed up his face. "Stones? What in Magol's name made you wake me in the first place?"

"I really need your help."

"Obviously." Garan sucked in a breath and shucked the bad mood. He had no call to be angry at Nils. They had been waiting for him to leave the healing tray with a great degree of anxiety, so being ungracious now would be, well…ungracious. "How can I help?"

"Salinda finally told me about the book you found. Good work, Garan. I need to get to my study."

"Now, not in the morning?"

"I have no need of sleep right now. I have been resting in the healing tray for weeks, but it's my feet. I am afraid I cannot make it there without assistance." They spoke in soft whispers and even then the sound seemed overly loud.

Garan nodded, rubbing his eyes, which felt full of grit, and then ruffled his hair with the palm of his hand. "You need me to carry you down to your study?"

"Yes, that is my desire. If you would be so kind."

"Could I not go fetch the book for you?"

"No," Nils said, folding his hands in front of his abdomen. "I prefer to work in my study, surrounded by my things."

"Am I to carry you on my back?"

Nils considered Garan. "Yes, I think that would be easiest. You are tall and strong."

"Let me get dressed."

Garan put on his trousers and a belt. He threw some food into a sack and tied it to his waist. Garan didn't trust Nils not to keep him waiting so it was better to be prepared. Already Garan's stomach grumbled. He squeezed out his door and went to Nils. "I am ready." He presented his back and Nils limped over to him. Bending his knees, Garan stood still while Nils arranged himself. Garan had thoughts of playing games of carry the baby and smiled. He almost laughed at the picture they made, but did not dare to. Nils's sense of humor was...different.

Once he secured Nils, he set off out of the node and down the stairs. As he descended the stairs carrying his burden, he began to wonder about the design of the city and Nils's current predicament. Nils was surprisingly light for one so tall. "Are you safe back there?" Garan asked.

"Very secure, thank you. More speed would be good."

Garan grimaced. "Faster. On the stairs? You are in an awful hurry." The bag of food hit his knee when he increased his pace.

"That I am. Much time has been wasted. Time grows short, Salinda tells me."

Garan was travelling well. Up ahead he could see the entry to the lower levels where Nils's study was. Down there was that machine and the presence that was in his mind. He did not exactly hate going down there, but it made him feel uncomfortable.

"Tell me, Nils. The city is full of stairs. How did people get around if they could not walk or they had health issues and could never walk."

Nils was quiet for a moment. Garan was about to prompt him by repeating the question when Nils answered, "They had glides."

"Glides," Garan replied, a bit shocked. He pictured sleds rocketing down the staircases, but then came up short on imagining how they went upstairs. "What are they?"

"They came in several sizes. Personal ones were shaped like a disc, larger than a chair, and they floated and moved of their own accord."

Garan nearly slipped when the mind picture came to him courtesy of the cadre. "Oh. I had not...You did not...Are there any left?"

Nils changed his grip on Garan's shoulder. "I had not thought to look. Why?"

The present situation was in Garan's mind rather prominently. "I just thought they would come in useful. If we could get them to work. We could float supplies around rather than carry them on our backs, for example."

"Yes, you could. I am not sure, even if we found one, whether we could get it to work."

"Why is that? Are they not like the technology for the lights?"

Nils stayed silent and they continued on.

"Nils?"

"To own the truth, Garan. I do not know. Ah...here we are."

Garan's shoulders burned from carrying Nils, so it was with great relief he lowered the Hiem to the ground. Nils limped over to his desk. Garan wanted to go back to his bed, but Nils had not dismissed him yet. Nils's long fingers trailed over Salinda's translation and it was with awed reverence that Nils picked up the plain black book containing Trell's writings.

Nils's shoulders hunched and his body shuddered. Garan stared at the floor when he realized Nils was weeping. "This is it! Oh, Garan, wonderful Garan. You found it."

Garan's cheeks heated. He was glad he had done good. Salinda hadn't reacted so emotionally or as gratefully. Yet Nils was a sensitive creature. These were the words of his lost kin, his grandfather. Other than Thurdon, who was once his adoptive father, Garan knew none of his family. The observatory was all he had. He had lost the Master Elder, too, and Laidan...well, Laidan was not the same and they were not together in any case. He cared for her but expected no romantic attachment. He barely expected civility these days.

Nils wiped his eyes with a cloth he pulled from his robe. Garan's eyes widened at that. Carefully, Nils sat in the chair and began to read. He compared Salinda's words and nodded. "Her translation is awkward but mostly accurate." He laughed suddenly. Garan straightened in surprise. He had not heard Nils laugh before. Nils glanced up. "There are words that Salinda could not translate. They are mostly curse words, hence my amusement. They are very Hiem."

Garan nodded and waited. Nils was absorbed in reading. Garan winced as he spoke, hating to interrupt. "Do you need me anymore, Nils?"

Nils turned to him. "Does this not excite you?" He placed the book down and patted it. "These are the words of Trell of Barr."

Garan's unease grew. He did not know why, but he had to leave. "To tell the truth, it does not. I want to go back to bed." Garan was far from sleepy now so that was a lie. Garan had lied. He floundered. "I, er…I cannot tell you why, but being near the book makes me feel on edge. That is the only way to describe it."

Nils stood up and limped over with the book in his hand. His eyes narrowed as he studied Garan. "Odd indeed. Hold the book, Garan."

"What?"

"Hold the book. Just a few moments."

Garan swallowed and took the book. His hand shook and he looked at the book. It was innocuous yet something stirred within him. *Strange.* Then he wondered: the cadre? It squirmed inside his mind. Not revulsion. Not abhorrence. Just unease. He handed the book back. "I think the cadre does not like the book."

"The cadre?" Nils said, eyes suddenly bright. "How interesting." Nils limped back to the desk, wincing as his feet hit the ground. He wore slippers on his bandaged feet but still they pained him. "You may go now. Let Salinda know where I am when she wakes. Come back for me to see if I wish to return."

"Here is some food. I thought you might need some." He untied the bag from his waist and handed it over. Garan had packed the food for himself but thought the supplies better served Nils's situation than his own.

Nils glanced at it. "How thoughtful you are. I tend not to get hungry when I work." He opened the first page. Garan still stood there stupidly, then Nils asked, "Did you put in some of that bread you make?"

Garan let out a relieved sigh. "Yes." He turned to go, catching Nils's movement as he opened the bag. The one thing Garan did that pleased everyone was making the flat cacti bread.

෧෧෧෧෧

Danton's body was like a heavy stone. Illness and privation had exhausted his reserves. Yet, he was alive. Something he didn't think he would ever be when he was in that prison. Something that he had not wanted to be when the torture was at its worst. He didn't want to see himself in the mirror. He didn't want to see how Salinda looked at him. Ugly. Destroyed. Brutalized. Less than a man. These thoughts hit him like arrows from the dark. *How vain you are, Danton. Salinda has no more need for handsome than she does for dust.* She wanted to save the world.

Brill entered. "Oh, you're awake. Food?"

Danton nodded. "Yes, and then I need to get up."

"Up. But…"

"Yes, up. I have to get my strength back. Something tells me I'm going to need it."

Brill tilted his head from left to right and back again, as if weighing something up, then shrugged and passed Danton a plate. Danton didn't care what it was—some kind of cold porridge—as long as it did the job. At first it was hard to eat. Nausea overwhelmed him, but he shut it down. Eat and live, he told himself. When his meal was down and he decided it was going to stay down, he rolled over on his stomach and pushed up onto all fours. He was naked and Brill, seeing that he was looking around, handed Danton some clothes. They were too big for him so he figured they had been borrowed from Garan.

"I think you should take it slowly," Brill suggested, passing him some watered wine.

"I intend to. A swim, I think. Care for a dip? Garan said there was a big lake here."

"I believe there is a part of the lake that Nils doesn't mind us using. As long as we stick to that." He paused and watched as Danton finished dressing.

Danton sat to put on the boots. These fit him reasonably well. This was odd, because he didn't remember his clothes surviving. When he examined them he realized they had been recently repaired, perhaps cut down. He nodded to himself as he put them on and wondered who he owed a favor. He really didn't like being beholden to people. However, if he was going to repay debts and contribute meaningfully to Salinda's cause, he needed his brain and his body in fine order.

"Ready then?" Danton asked.

Brill agreed. "I'm pretty unfit myself. Can you manage the stairs?"

Danton grimaced and said, "Don't patronize me, kid. If I can't get down there I'm not likely to be able to swim."

Brill followed along behind as Danton lurched to the small opening in the abode and tried to climb out. *Damn door*, Danton fumed. It took quite a lot of his energy to just leave home. Once out, he swayed, blinking at the bright lights of the city. Although he had heard about it, he didn't have much recollection of seeing the ancient wonder. Salinda and Garan had not exaggerated it. Yet, such a waste. Houses and shelter for thousands and it was only inhabited by a few.

"Give me a hand, Brill," Danton said softly, almost apologetically. Danton was determined to swim. It was the one thing that he thought would help him build strength, or at least fool his body into thinking it had some.

Danton put his arm around Brill's shoulder and clasped him. "Thank you for everything. For tending me and being my friend."

Brill's cheeks grew pink. "You're very welcome. Never hesitate to ask me for anything."

"Good, because I have another favor to ask."

"Oh," Brill replied, his blue eyes widening. "Will it hurt?"

Danton laughed. "Maybe later. I need your support to get down these steps. Do you mind?"

Brill grinned and grabbed the hand that was dangling over his shoulder. "The trick is to synchronize."

Together they took each step slow and steady. Danton was tempted to quit, to crawl back up the stairs to his bed, but Brill kept a steady pace, not commenting on the panting, sweating man he was assisting. To Danton the stairs were endless. His calf muscles cramped and he had a stitch in his side. His wound throbbed.

"I need a break," Brill said. "Bloody stairs are a killer. Do you mind if we stop here and sit?"

Grateful, but with no energy for barter, Danton just nodded and let Brill assist him to the ground. The lake was nearby. He could hear it and he could detect the dampness in the air. It was a dark mass to his left. How big was the thing, anyhow?

There weren't many lakes on the surface, or not that Danton had seen.

Brill passed him some dried fruit. It was sweet in his mouth when he bit into it. "What's this?" he asked Brill.

"Lairn apple, I think. It's something that grows in the gardens. You will never believe how big the gardens are. It's like a closed-in jungle. I have been in there many times now and I have not walked the length of it."

Danton's eyes brightened. "Then we could live here a long time. I mean, people could."

"Yes, I think so. Nils said he wasn't sure why his people died off. Many survived Moonfall, but later fell ill. He said the records were not well kept at that time. He said it could have been a disease or the dust in the air that made its way into the Hiem cities."

Danton met Brill's gaze. "Interesting, isn't it?"

Brill nodded, his expression losing its humor. "It is very interesting, Danton."

Danton was pretty sure Brill knew the direction of his thoughts. Feeling a bit more refreshed, Danton asked Brill for a hand up and they arranged themselves once again to descend to the lake. They had come a long way already and it was less than a half hour later when they made their way to the spot where they were permitted to bathe.

"Have you been in there yet?" Danton asked.

Brill shook his head. "No time. Garan has, I think. Also Laidan and Eneit."

At the mention of Eneit's name, Danton's head shot up. "Mandin's daughter. I remember now…you said you saved her."

"Yes, I'm sorry about Mandin. She died to save her daughter. You have to respect that."

"I do. I just wish…I wish I had handled the situation with Toola better."

Brill kept his gaze on his for a moment and then directed it out to the lake. "Last one in is a shitty dragon's ass."

Danton laughed and struggled to rid himself of his garments. Brill was in the water before Danton had taken off his trousers. These were saturated when Brill heaved a big splash of water at him.

"Right then, like that, is it?" Danton said and then slid carefully into the water. At first he couldn't breathe. It was like his diaphragm was frozen. Then the needles of cold punched into his skin. Danton was in danger of sinking. And then it was over. He adjusted and lunged forward, drawing his arm over his head as he began a slow crawl, cutting across the water and sending ripples out over the surface. Brill said nothing, but he closely shadowed his friend.

The water buoyed up his heavy body and something in the water, maybe, made Danton feel more alert, more alive. He took it easy and when he really did think his energy would give out, he flipped over onto his back and floated.

The dark water surrounded him. Brill's hair was wet and dark and he trod water close by. "Do you want me to tow you back to the edge?"

"Not yet. The water feels good, you know."

"Apparently this lake has a lot of meaning for the Hiem," Brill said quietly. "There's another city across the lake. I haven't been there. I haven't asked Nils about it, but it was like a small sister city or something. They traded across this lake."

Danton looked up to the roof of the cavern. It was so high—not like the sky—but the cavern which held the underground city and this lake was larger than anything he'd ever seen. It was like some buried hidden valley. And Nils had it to himself. Yes, he shared it with them, but only with promises of secrecy. It was such a waste. This place could live again. Admittedly not with Hiem, but with people. Danton let out a sigh. Which people? Who were worthy? Was there anyone left to judge such a thing? Danton wasn't worthy.

"Penny for them?" Brill said.

Danton's body bent and he went under after suddenly losing his buoyancy. He pushed up again and trod water. "Nothing…"

"Do you need a tow?" Brill asked. His eyes were hooded and Danton thought Brill wasn't fooled. He knew Danton had something on his mind.

"I think I do. Now, tell me how Laidan is while we make our way back." Brill caught Danton's outstretched hand and began to make his way toward the shore.

Danton panted and spat water. "Do you think we could have a rest before we go up all those steps?"

Brill laughed. "Of course."

Brill continued towing and grimaced as he looked back to Danton. "About Laidan…you…hmm, okay…you probably haven't caught up on what happened to her."

Danton listened to the tale. His heart thumped. How could she still be alive after suffering at the Inspector's hands? He hadn't been aware that Gercomo could transform at will between dragon and human. That was…not quite…real…but if Brill was relating the story to him then it had to be. Brill did not tell tall tales. Brill's tale was long and they were halfway up the stairs to their shared abode when Brill stopped.

"Source preserve me," Danton exclaimed, shaking his head. He reached for the next stair and lowered himself to the ground. "So Nils has a healing machine?"

"Yes, he used it to cure Salinda, remember?" Danton nodded. He couldn't remember if he had heard it. He and Salinda had not had that much time to talk about everything. He seemed to remember Salinda crying and begging forgiveness. Then it made sense. She had not put him in the healing tray to save his life. She had chosen Nils.

Brill shook his shoulder. "Danton? What is it?"

"Nothing," he said, and picked at the fine layer of dust on the stair. "Just remembering and fitting things together."

Brill lowered his head and stared at his knee. "You understand then, what Salinda did?"

Danton nodded slowly, not able to form words.

"She spent long hours tending you. Don't think she doesn't care, because I know she does."

Both he and Brill sat quietly, staring at nothing in particular. Danton thought it behooved him to speak, to break the awkward silence. "Don't sweat it, Brill. I understand. I've always understood what comes first with Salinda. She thinks Nils is the key to saving the world and nothing is going to change her mind until the end is nigh."

Brill let out a sigh and lifted his bright gaze to Danton. "You forgive her? Just like that?" His fists were balled as they rested on his knees.

"There is nothing to forgive. I'm alive, aren't I?"

Brill reacted, gesturing with his hand at Danton. "But your injuries…"

Danton flashed him a grin. "Some would consider them a just punishment for my evil ways."

The flippant reply was regretted when Danton saw the look of horror that crossed Brill's face. "I don't think that. I'm sorry I ever tried to preach to you. It was wrong of me."

Danton nodded, remembering Toola's brothel and Brill's righteous indignation when they first arrived there. It didn't make him think less of the lad. "No, Brill. Not wrong. Just wasted on me. Do something for me—don't change. Don't change who you are." And then the memory came back of an old man, starved and barely alive. Should he tell Brill about his father? No, he couldn't do it. Brill already grieved for his father. Why open that wound up again? Why put salt in it? No, he would keep that to himself. Better to pretend that the old shell of a man he had seen was nothing but the ghost of Hubert of Duval. Brill had already mourned him and there was no point in bringing back that particular pain.

Danton was desperate to be horizontal in his bed. He would rest, but he knew he would get up again after a while to walk around their sleeping level. He had to keep moving.

"How about a hand up?" he said to Brill.

Brill grinned, stood and reached down to haul Danton up.

"Thanks, lad," Danton said, giving the young rebel a smack on the back. "You're a good man. Your father would be proud of you."

Brill looked askance at him. "Thank you. Any particular reason you speak of my father?"

"No, only thinking about the past and about how good you turned out. He did a good job with you."

Brill stayed silent for the rest of the trip up the stairs. Danton was too busy concentrating on putting one foot after another to think of opening his mouth again. He buried the ghost of Hubert in his mind, taking comfort in the knowledge that he had passed on and was no longer subject to the baron's whims.

By the time they arrived at the abode, Brill was virtually carrying him. Danton couldn't even complain, but sank down gratefully on the bed. He took the offer of watered wine and gulped it down. He was asleep before his head hit the pillow. He was wrecked. Totally and utterly wrecked.

A couple of hours later, he climbed out of bed again and shuffled to the door. He would walk around their node and then come back. He had to keep moving. Tomorrow, he would swim again.

Chapter Seven

GAMES OF STRATEGY
AND GAMES OF RISK

The next morning, Salinda yawned and rolled to her other side. The pregnancy made sleeping difficult. While she wished the child to be born for personal comfort reasons, she also had reasons to wish for it to be delayed. There was so much to do and so little time. She could feel it ticking away in her mind, the inevitable end of the planet, of their lives, her life, her child's life.

After having a bite to eat, she wandered over to Laidan's abode. When Brill spotted her, he helped her through the door.

Laidan was studying a puzzle game. Salinda knew that Laidan had taken to the games that Brill devised for her.

Eneit brought Salinda some tea after she'd sat down on the sofa with a slight groan. She was annoyed at herself for acting like some old person with a multitude of aches and pains. Mez, her old mentor, had never complained, even when he lay dying in the prison vineyard. He was too concerned for others, for the fate of the planet, and here was Salinda groaning about being heavy with child. She shook her head, thanked Eneit for the tea and watched Laidan.

"It's a strategy game," Brill said from the sidelines. "She has come along in leaps and bounds."

Salinda watched silently and sipped her tea. Her eyes narrowed when she saw how Laidan solved the puzzle and won the game. Salinda did not have time for games, but she saw how useful they could be. Laidan was more focused, more aware. Not the old Laidan, though, and Salinda was ashamed to own she was not sorry. The old Laidan was self-absorbed, whiny and difficult. She reproached herself. That was uncharitable, to say the least. *What did Laidan suffer? Remember that. You would likely not have survived.*

"You are doing very well, Laidan."

Laidan looked up, her cheeks pink with pleasure. "Thank you, Salinda."

"So what do you want to do now?"

"Now?" Laidan asked, frowning as her gaze leaped to Brill.

"She means now that you are feeling better."

Laidan lowered her head and pulled at her lower lip. "I'm not sure. What choices do I have?"

Salinda didn't really know what Laidan knew of the larger situation. Ideally, Laidan should be sent to the observatory out of harm's way. But there was no such thing as out of harm's way anymore. Not that there ever had been, really. "What about learning to defend yourself? Learning to lead others?"

Laidan's head shot up, her pale eyes flashed. "You'd trust me to do that?"

Salinda shrank back a little. There was so much of the old Laidan in that statement and so much truth. Indeed, Salinda had not trusted Laidan.

"Yes, I would. We need all the help we can get."

Brill raised a hand. "Salinda, I don't think—"

Salinda quelled him with a look and engaged the girls in conversation. She spoke to them from the heart about what they could do to help.

Eneit hugged her impulsively and Laidan reached out and squeezed her forearm and nodded, tears in her eyes.

As the conversation had come to its natural end, Salinda tried to get up from the sofa, but stalled. "Help me up, will you? I have to get some work done."

Brill came over and assisted her to stand. "Thank you, Brill. Train both of them. I have an idea."

Brill helped her through the door and followed her out. "Are you mad? Laidan isn't ready or fit for something like that. And Eneit? How could you think of it? She's a child."

Salinda turned round, impatience running through her veins. That ticking clock wasn't going to spare anyone. "Look, Brill, we don't have time to be precious about anything. People. Places. The end is nigh."

Brill bit back a response. After a minute's thought, he nodded. "I will train them. Have you spoken to Danton?"

"Not since the crisis."

"Maybe you could talk to him. He's trying to get himself fit again." Brill gestured to the lake below. "He's in the lake right now."

"I will, but right now I have to go see Nils. If Danton is up for it, get him to help you train those two. Actually, add Garan as well. He could do with some training."

"Garan?"

"Yes. He has power, but sometimes he might need something else. I see that your training develops strategy. Strategy is good. Don't be surprised if I sit in on some of your sessions. I can use all the strategy I can get."

Brill backed up, eyes wide. "I see. You think it will be that soon."

Salinda's eyes watered and she wiped a tear. "Sorry. Emotions are a bit wild. Baby issues. Yes, I do. I am waiting on Nils finishing with that book. It has to have some coordinates in it. Some hints of where we go next."

☞☞☞☞☞

Salinda took her time descending the stairway. Looking out at the lake, she saw tell-tale ripples and realized that Danton was swimming just as Brill had said. It was good to see him trying to get fit. If it had been her with his injuries, maybe she couldn't have brought herself to do it. Then again, maybe she hadn't expected him to fight back because she had denied him true healing. Danton exceeded her expectations. It warmed her knowing how hard he tried to be of use.

Taking the left-hand path, she walked to the lake's edge near where Danton was swimming. His stroke was strong and he had energy. Uninvited, a smile landed on her face. Then Danton did a slow crawl stroke in her direction.

"Have you come to join me?" he asked, and there was a cheeky twinkle in his eye, a touch of flirtation.

Salinda laughed, really laughed, picturing herself trying to get out of the lake after swimming. Danton laughed, too, so she understood he knew exactly what he was playing at. He, she thought, was trying to put her at her ease, letting her know that he held no grudges for the choice she had made.

"It's good to see you looking so well." Her gaze assessed him. Only his shoulders and head were visible above the water. The scarred tissue that was one of his eyes didn't shock her. He'd been without his patch since they rescued him. There were more shocking signs of violence on his body, which she was intimately acquainted with, having stitched, bathed and salved the injuries.

"It's good to be feeling well. I'll be ready when you need me, Salinda. I won't let you down."

Ah, he thinks he let me down. She couldn't kneel to talk to him so she decided to sit. Her movement was inelegant but soon she sat comfortably with her feet dangling in the water.

"You didn't let me down. You didn't let any of us down." Salinda spoke plainly. No preamble. She knew him too well. Knew what was on his mind.

"Oh, but I did. It was my stupidity that got me snared and I don't even know what I told him…"

She reached out a hand. "Don't, Danton. I understand…"

Danton didn't try to come close to touch her hand. He looked at it and then met her gaze directly. "That's the worst thing about this. He terrorized and tortured you as well and he still lives…"

"I…"

The water rippled of its own accord and beneath her the ground vibrated.

"What the hell is that?" Danton exclaimed. "A quake?"

Her head shot up to the cavern roof. "Yes," she replied, finding it hard to swallow with a suddenly dry mouth. *Pray, don't let it collapse.* It didn't. The tremor eased off.

"I'd better go," she said.

Danton dived for the edge and pulled himself out. "Wait. What was it?" he asked, standing in wet sleeping trousers that clung to his body, revealing much. His chest was concave with loss of weight, though his arms were strong.

"The beginning of the end, I fear." Salinda kept her voice low, afraid of speaking it.

Danton grabbed her arm. "Tell me."

Salinda patted his hand and he let her go. He rubbed water out of his eyes and smoothed his hair, sending trickles down his neck and back. "It's the moonfall. It's starting. That had to have been a sizable chunk hitting the surface."

"No," Danton replied, "we are still here."

"It's not a quick process until the end. I have to go to the observatory."

"I'll come with you."

Salinda shook her head. "No, Danton. There is nothing you can do there. You need to stay here, train the others. Brill will fill you in."

"But—"

"I understand, Danton. More than you know. But for now I must go. I have to—"

Danton cocked his head. "We need to talk. All of us. There are some things I want to say...to ask..."

"Yes, I agree. Can you arrange it? This evening. There're too many for one house so we will convene in the common area of the Barr family node." She looked up to the ceiling. "There's no chance of rain."

Danton flashed her a grin and turned away to pick up his dry clothes. Salinda backtracked and continued her way to Nils's office. While she didn't expect miracles, she had high expectations that Nils had translated a lot more of the book than she had managed to. The Hiem code was a second language to him.

Her legs ached as she took the stairs. *Not long now*, she told herself. *Not long now either way. Please hold on, child. Don't come yet.* In the gloomy passageways, she walked along trying to keep her thoughts light. It was hard. So very hard. What was it about pregnancy that made one more emotional than normal?

Salinda snorted and said to no one in particular, "What is it about the end of the world that makes one more emotional than normal?"

Clenching her hands, she fought this morose thinking. She wasn't giving up. She wasn't giving in. They were going to win this. They had to.

Nils was poring over the book when she made her way into the office. He didn't even hear her approach. She didn't want to stand there awkwardly, so she looked about the room. There was a spare chair. It had been there from when she was with Garan in this room. Garan…someone else she needed to talk to urgently. She was seriously considering leaving the city to get to Trithorn Peak and see what the impact was and where, and what had happened. Garan would want to come. He had a great desire to see what was happening on the surface, just as Salinda did. Sometimes one was too insulated here in the depths of Margra.

"Nils," she said, when he hadn't acknowledged her for some time.

She had to repeat herself louder.

"Oh," he said, lifting his head, "it is you." He looked at the book. "I'm not finished yet."

Salinda squeezed her fingers together. There was no point in complaining about that. It was obvious Nils was working very hard. "Did you feel the tremor?"

Nils rubbed his forehead and then scrubbed his face with his fingers. He must be tired. She'd never seen him do that. "Tremor?"

That answered Salinda's question. "Something has happened on the surface. We need to investigate. Can you join us for a meeting? Probably in a couple of hours?"

"Do you need me there?" Nils asked, his eyes trailing to the text in front of him instead of staying on her.

"Yes, Nils. We need to talk about a lot of things. Important things and we need you."

He nodded and then turned back to the text. Salinda eased herself to her feet and rubbed her lower back. *Don't make me come get you*, she thought. Nils was already oblivious to her presence. Salinda waddled along the corridor and made her way slowly back to the Barr family node. She took her time. She had a lot to think about.

☾☾☾☾☾

Gercomo was desperate. He hated being isolated. When he had changed back to a man he had been caught up in the worries of the world, and now he wanted back in, except he hadn't been able to transform to a man again. Not since he was injured. Things with the dragons hadn't been too good since the battle over the buried city.

Bertha was standoffish. With many of the bulls being killed outright, or later dying of their wounds, the herd was in disarray. His mate was probably the strongest among the remaining dragons and she was growing more aware of that fact. Soon, she would turn on him.

Gercomo had to act fast. Act before the situation took a turn for the worse.

With one wing dragging behind him, he shuffled up to Bertha. She barely lifted her head at his approach and didn't bother to open her eyes. Gercomo was wise to her game. He struck out and bit her on the flank, sucking down the hot, rich blood. Erupting from her pose, she shoved him off and struck back, but not before he got a taste of her blood. It burned through him, swelling his flesh with power. He stood his ground and dove back to get more, aiming for the small wound he had made. He attacked under her guard and latched on with his jaws and held as she writhed and clawed at him. The low moan she gave out spoke of pleasure. Bertha liked it rough. He supposed he was up to rutting with her. She still had a use. She had influence with the others.

The transformative effects of the blood tore at tendons and flesh. The pain was excruciating but pleasurable too. His erection throbbed and Bertha flattened herself to the ground, wanting him, craving him.

He thrust into her and then struck at her, gnawing at her flesh, drinking and eating from her. Her groans of pleasure became screeches of pain and she shoved back and forth to throw him off. *Power!* He burned with it. His stomach filled with a chunk of her living flesh was like a sun in his gut.

Replete, he fell off his perch and staggered back. Dissatisfied because he had not completed the mating, Bertha came after him like a shot. Gercomo darted and sped hither and thither until he found shelter within some boulders, squeezing himself down so she could not get at him. Soft sand sheltered him, letting him burrow deeper. After trying to claw him out, Bertha roared and spat flame. Whatever reached him was harmless against his flesh. The next outburst was a pathetic wail. Gercomo grinned. *Teach her a lesson.* Bertha blurted a wild mental torrent of rage at him. Gercomo ignored it.

Then a scream and a roar filled the air. Stupefied, Gercomo shook his head, trying to clear it. But then he realized it wasn't within his head. It was external. The dragons around him screamed too. Long agonized cries of terror. Throaty roars that made his skin tingle and vibrate. Gercomo peeped through the gap in the boulders above his head and gasped in horror. A large ball of fire streaked across the sky. Immediately, he knew the danger. Grateful that he was mostly protected, Gercomo worked at burying himself deeper in the sand.

A concussive wave bowled him over. Small particles of grit rammed against his hide. He whimpered. He cried. He struggled to breathe. The world was ending. It had to be. Fear fueled his blood, his mind. The ground shook and shook. A flash of bright light burned across his vision and mind. Hot fire rolled over the land. He felt the sand solidify and the roaring hot wind blew a gale. Great chunks of earth and rock rained down. Fire pounded the soil like hail. It went on and on and on.

Gercomo could hardly breathe and dared not try to claw his way out. He could feel it, sense the power raging overhead. Even as a dragon he could not survive that. Only the odd happenstance that had put him in this place at this time had saved him. What of the others?

The searing destruction of a fallen piece of Shatterwing had ripped the planet. Yet Margra was still here, solid and sure. He was still here, so the planet hadn't been totally destroyed. This was not the forecast end. Relief swept over him. There was time still.

Just the beginning of the dance of death.

In the aftermath, dirt and debris fell like thick rain. Gercomo didn't know if he was the only one of the dragons alive. If he was alone, he had to make plans. He needed to be with people who thought logically, who had knowledge of the greater world. One person immediately came to mind. The baron. The baron knew where they could be safe. The baron knew many things.

Soon. Soon. I will find the baron again.

There was no sense of the other dragons being in his vicinity. Gercomo stayed nestled within his sand and boulders, full of power and a will to survive.

If it hadn't been for Salinda, he would have been safe in Eternity and not out here living like a beast, in the open, exposed to such heavenly horrors. He was going to rip her limb from limb and suck her bones dry. It was all her fault.

Days later, the rain of earth had lessened to a mist of dust falling lightly across the land. Each speck registered on Gercomo's consciousness as if the tiny atoms were enlivened with energy. Using his snout, he pushed his way through the crust of glass that lay above his resting place.

The hatchery had been a desolate place of grays and browns and dirt and dry. Now it was pulverized. He made out a dragon corpse nearby. He clawed his way free to investigate. The air was thick, smudging smells, but he could breathe at least. The luxury of dragon lungs, he supposed.

The dragon flesh was cooked. Gercomo wasn't fussy. He bit into a leg and tore it loose and sat down to eat. It was a younger dragon, a male. Gercomo didn't care. There was enough to feed him for a few days. He looked around. He saw no other dragons though dust-covered mounds might be hiding more bodies. Others might yet be alive.

He used his dragon sense and there, just there, he detected some. Not all dead then. After a few hours, the sense of the others grew. Bertha had survived. How he did not know. Then the query came and the images from her mind. Bertha had fallen into the hatchery pit, which had collapsed upon her.

Later, she had dug her way out and had gone to investigate the crater. An image of a hot fire pit was small in his mind's eye, but he knew it must be large by human terms. There was no anger in her thoughts. It was if they had never fought, as if he had never taken a piece out of her. As he moved around to investigate further, he noticed something else. His wing was healed. He noticed the absence of pain first and then stopped to examine it and test it.

He grinned, broken teeth catching on his bottom lip. He growled in pleasure. Time to see if he could fly. He looked around for a place that had enough room for him to run. He would have to clear a space. He nudged and pushed at the layers of dirt, shifting fallen rocks and the occasional dragon corpse.

When he was satisfied, he started the run, opened his wings and took flight.

Chapter Eight

A LITTLE BIT
OF SWEAT

Laidan was excited. Straight after Salinda's visit, Brill had started training them, taking them for a short run to warm up. She liked learning things and she liked being with Eneit, too. Eneit was a quiet girl, but she was attentive and helped Laidan to learn. Laidan had a lot to learn.

Apparently, she had forgotten almost everything she had known before Gercomo's attack. She could talk and she could remember some things about herself. She remembered Thurdon, but only from when she was a little child. Long, dusty roads, and his voice, featured in fragments. Thurdon had told her stories but in her mind they were jumbled up, just bits and pieces that she couldn't put together. The pieces of memory didn't match. That made her sad. Something essential was gone and those story fragments were a constant reminder of what she'd lost.

Nils said he didn't know if she'd get those memories back. She had been severely wounded and she was lucky to be alive. That's what she had been told. Nothing but a ball of black pain hovered in her mind when she tried to focus on the attack. Nils said it was best not to. Somehow, the memories would return, those that were still there.

Laidan had to focus when she nearly lost her footing as she reminisced while running. "Keep up, Laidan," Brill said as he led them to the next node where he and Danton shared an abode. There was a clear area there, like a town square, but much smaller. Danton and Brill had constructed benches to sit on, at times, particularly in the evening. At present, the benches were shoved against the walls of the abodes so that they had room for practice.

"First of all, we need to increase your level of fitness," Brill said with a grin.

Laidan smiled back. Brill was always nice to her. He always smiled and that made Laidan feel safe. Well, as safe as one could be when the world was going to end soon. She remembered asking Nils why he had saved her when they were all going to die. Laidan smiled to herself because before Nils could open his mouth, Salinda had butted in, saying, "We may yet save the world." To which Nils nodded and said, "We still have hope and saving you gave us hope in our hearts."

Laidan's smile widened. That was a lovely thing to hear. She liked putting hope in people's hearts.

That morning, Salinda had sat down with her and Eneit and said that she wanted them to help save people. Laidan's heart had soared. If she saved people she could give some hope back, like when Nils saved her and she gave her friends hope. "But first of all, you have to be able to take care of yourselves," Salinda had said. "Protect your person and others and think strategically in case there are problems. You, Laidan, are showing great promise in strategic thinking. Would you like to help?"

Laidan and Eneit had given a resounding "Yes". Laidan had changed out of the robe she always wore into some trousers and a tunic top. They didn't fit very well, but they were easy to run in. She was ready to learn and to train.

"Right, follow me," Brill had said. "We're going for a proper run. Upstairs and downstairs and over obstacles and then we will come back here. If you need us to halt, call out to me, but only if you really, really can't go on."

Brill had scanned them and started jogging away, out to the main stairs. When Eneit and Laidan had nearly caught up, he increased his pace. They went up and away from the Barr family node, through pathways to other nodes, one where the houses weren't in such good condition. No one lived there now, but when Nils was young it was full of people like him. Like her, too. Nils said she was part Hiem and that the city was part of her heritage.

Laidan couldn't help liking being special. Being special was good. It helped one focus and gave life purpose.

Laidan breathed heavily as she ran and noticed that Eneit had moved in front of her as the path became narrow. Eneit could run and run, it seemed, without getting tired. Brill turned and shouted, "Down", and then he disappeared from view. Eneit checked her step and turned down the stairs, Laidan followed. Here, she had to concentrate lest she fall. She didn't want to ruin her first day of training by falling down. Her feet felt light as they took each riser. Brill turned and now he made them leap over the low walls that separated a group of abodes. Shuwai hung down and she had to brush it out of her way. She didn't mind touching the light-emitting fungi as long as there wasn't too much. Some, she ducked. Eneit, being shorter, passed clear under the glowing strands.

"We are heading back now," Brill said, and the fire in Laidan's calf muscles told her it was none too soon. Up the stairs they ran at a fast pace. Now her lungs burned and sweat gathered in her lower back and between her shoulder blades. Her upper lip was itchy and she swiped the perspiration away. Laidan didn't think she had ever worked so hard before. But she must have done. She had walked and walked all her life. That was the truth.

Once back in Brill's node, they took a short rest, caught their breath and drank some water. Laidan was very tired and her leg muscles ached and throbbed. Although tired, Laidan didn't mention it. She didn't want to be the one to put a stop to their training. Eneit was tired and sweaty too. She just grinned at Laidan and squared her shoulders.

"Now, we will do some exercises and then we will move onto this." Brill held up a pole, shorter than he was. "I made these for you. I made them shorter than normal because I want them to pass for walking canes, but they are actually staves. I figure this is the best defense I can teach you."

Brill showed them some exercises to stretch their muscles, and also to quickly move on their feet, sort of like a fast dance. Then he gave them both a stave and Eneit grinned, and Laidan just looked at hers. She remembered Thurdon had had a cane once when she was little. He used it to walk, but once someone had attacked them. She couldn't remember the details but she did remember Thurdon attacking back with his cane and taking those three attackers down. They hadn't so much as touched him. He'd managed to fool people into thinking he was a doddery old man, but his mind was sharp and he was remarkably nimble.

At the time, Laidan had been afraid. She just stood there and gaped as it all happened very quickly. Her job had been to hold the reins of the burden beast that carried their gear. The burden beast hadn't even lifted its head from cropping on the desert grass it had been munching on.

"You are strong," Laidan remembered saying to Thurdon. The memory held her. There were lots of emotions there, feelings that were somehow strange but not. He'd hugged her and she had felt safe. Thurdon had smiled at her and she experienced such burning love in her chest she wanted to burst.

"Laidan," Brill said, touching her arm gently, "are you all right?"

Laidan shook her head, making her hair shimmer and shift down her back. "I am. It was just a memory. I'm ready now."

Brill's eyes glittered. "A good memory, I hope."

She smiled. "Oh yes, one from my childhood with Thurdon."

Brill showed them how to hold the stave and then he had them move forward and bring the stave down. Then they shuffled, holding the stave in a protective stance. They did this so many times that Laidan got blisters on her hands and her feet were as numb as rocks. Before they could finish the training session, she and Eneit hit their staves together in a blocking action, learning how to avoid getting their fingers smashed.

Afterward, Eneit and Laidan heated water for baths. There was only one small tub so they were going to take it in turns. It didn't help that Brill said that their aches and pains would get worse before they got better. Laidan couldn't imagine hurting more than she did at that moment. She could also sleep for a week.

"You go first, Eneit. I'll get some soap to wash your hair."

Eneit had stripped off and was in the tub before Laidan had even turned away. The girl's long sigh made Laidan grin. If she didn't get in the hot water soon, herself, she might be too stiff to ever be soothed, yet it was Eneit's turn, after all.

Eneit's dark hair fascinated Laidan. Always had. Laidan being very fair, which was unusual, made her wonder at other people, particularly when they were darker. Skin color was so many different shades. Eneit's was creamy, with a flush of tan on her legs and arms. Her eyes were brown with flecks of yellow and that was pretty too.

Eneit stood up and stepped out of the tub. "Your turn. I'll heat more water to top it up. I think I made it cool down."

Laidan laughed and stripped off. Her toes touched the water and it was warm to her, but she didn't stop the other girl bringing more hot water. The water would cool and Laidan was in no hurry to get out again, not until every aching muscle and every creaking bone was soothed and she was ready to sleep.

The next morning Brill banged on their door. "Come on, up you get. Time for training to begin."

Laidan put the blanket over her head. Was he joking? She had been exhausted the night before even with a hot bath and Eneit rubbing her leg muscles.

"Come on. I have some hot bread here straight from Garan's excellent kitchen."

Laidan lowered her blanket. Eneit stuck her head in. "First one there gets all the bread."

"No!" Laidan exclaimed as she bolted from the bed and scrambled to put on her clothes.

Brill was laughing at the sounds they made as they hurried to get ready. "Oh, by the source, this bread is good," he said, teasing them, theatrically inhaling the aroma of the fresh-cooked bread.

Eneit and Laidan screamed in horror and laughed as they charged out the door to be handed two pieces of hot flat bread. "Good morning, ladies. Ready to begin again?"

"Yes," Laidan replied after swallowing a mouthful of bread.

Eneit found a pot of tea sitting by Brill's feet and poured each of them a cup. "Right then, now that you have finished we will do some gentle stretching exercises to ease those tired muscles before we go on our run." Brill demonstrated and they copied him.

Laidan eased the kinks out of her whole body. Brill apologized that he had forgotten to get them to stretch before they started the run yesterday.

"Danton was none too pleased with me when I told him our routine. If you are up for it, we can finish the day with a swim."

Eneit's mouth dropped open. "What is it?" Laidan asked.

"I don't know how to swim." Eneit turned to her. "Do you?"

Laidan couldn't remember. "I don't know."

"Well, then, we will have a swimming lesson," Brill said. And then he was off, leading them in a jog first, and then speeding up before he followed the previous day's route.

༄༄༄༄༄

That night everyone, except Nils, was gathered in the common area that the three abodes faced. After the tremor, they should have had a formal meeting to discuss the situation. Nils, though, wasn't ready and they needed his translation before making firm plans. Yet that didn't stop them from wanting to talk and eat together.

Ledges that had been carved on the outside of abodes were used as benches and allowed them to sit facing each other. In his own abode, Garan had cooked up a meal, with Eneit helping him serve it out. Root vegetables simmered with mushrooms and spice, with a side of lairn apples and some dark leaf that combined the sweet with the peppery. Nursing her plate on her lap, Salinda thought about sending Brill to fetch him when Nils arrived. He looked around in surprise. "I thought we were just eating. This looks like a meeting."

"We are eating, but it may be the last time we can join together for a while," Salinda said. Then she sat up straighter. "Unless you have found something?"

Nils wasn't always up with the social niceties. "No, nothing to share just yet."

Salinda kept her expression bland. There was no point in advertising her disappointment.

"I will join you for a meal before going back to the translation." Nils sat, taking the bowl of vegetable stew Eneit handed him and giving her a nod of appreciation. After he inhaled the aroma, a genuine smile lit his face. He was probably famished after working for nearly two whole days on the translation. Salinda studied him from under her lashes, trying to gauge if he had found something useful.

70

Danton groaned suddenly and her attention was diverted to the rebel. Danton seemed okay so perhaps it was a minor discomfort as he changed position and then took a spoonful of stew. The expression of delight on his face made her realize it was just Danton expressing his appreciation for the food. After swallowing another mouthful, he sent a stream of compliments in Garan's direction, making him blush.

Salinda found she couldn't resist the smell of the steaming bread. As Eneit passed around a plateful, Salinda snagged two. Taking a bite, she let out a sigh. Truly, Garan was a wonder.

Once all were served and Eneit and Garan sat with their bowls in front of them, Salinda started the conversation. While this wasn't "a meeting" or "the meeting", there was no point in wasting the opportunity to share information. "Thank you all for coming. We have a lot to consider. We also have a lot to be grateful for. We have Danton healing nicely." Danton inclined his head and swallowed another mouthful, his dark eye glittering. He was wearing an eye patch again. Brill had said he would fashion an eye patch and Brill had been true to his word. "And Laidan is doing really well," Salina continued.

Laidan smiled shyly as she looked around the group and then studied her food. Eneit reached over and squeezed her forearm.

"As you no doubt felt, there was a tremor in the city. Its origins lie outside and, given the pending moonfall, we can safely assume that it was an impact of some kind."

Brill caught her eye. "What if it's just a natural phenomenon? I mean, there are tremors and earthquakes some of the time."

Salinda smiled. "That is true. If it wasn't an impact, then investigating the situation at Trithorn Peak would be beneficial."

Garan swallowed a mouthful of stew. "So who will you send?"

Salinda read that as "send me", and, since that was her intention, she smiled. "I will be going and you, Garan, will accompany me."

"You!" blurted Danton. "You are in no condition to go anywhere." His voice was sharp and he blushed profusely when everyone looked at him. He lowered his gaze. Eneit popped up to get him more stew, which he took without meeting anyone's eyes.

Nils looked up from eating and frowned at her. "Are you suffering from some ailment that I do not know about?"

Salinda chuckled. "I think Danton means because I am so far gone in my pregnancy. He assumes I am not fit for travel."

Salinda looked around the group and realized that most would not meet her gaze. "What?"

Brill glanced up. "You have to consider what will happen if you give birth while we are away."

Salinda sat up straighter. "I prefer to be positive and consider that I will do what I have to do before then. Besides, the observatory have people who know how to assist in giving birth." She tapped the side of her head and Brill looked back down at his place.

"It's not safe," Danton blurted.

Salinda schooled her features. She knew his comments came from concern about her well-being. But none of them were safe. Not in the grander scale of things. "Danton, please let me finish. Then we can discuss what is to be done. I am perfectly able to get to the observatory. Women have been having babies for a very long time."

He glared at her and when the anger in his eyes died, he nodded and resumed his meal. She turned in her seat so that she was facing Nils.

"Nils," she said gently.

Nils looked up, his eyes flashing silver with the reflected light. "Yes?"

"I have something important I want to discuss with you."

Nils gestured with his hand for her to continue.

"You know how we agreed to keep the existence of Barrahiem secret and that we shouldn't bring anyone here?"

"Yes," he replied. He didn't frown, but his gaze travelled around the group. "Necessary, I assure you."

"Well, I've been thinking about—"

"Me too," interrupted Danton.

He was echoed by Brill and then Garan. Salinda paused as she looked around at their faces. "Oh?" Then she smiled, pleased that they had been thinking along the same lines.

Nils sat back quietly. After a beat, he asked, "What have you been thinking?"

Voices talked over one another. Nils raised his hands, but to no avail. What Salinda heard were the same thoughts that had been on her mind.

"There's so much room here," Brill said.

"We could keep people safe, give them a chance," Danton added.

"The people of the observatory and Vanden could shelter here," Garan said.

Nils turned to her. "Is that what you think?" he asked.

"Nils, oh Nils." She took a breath, gathered her thoughts. "This place is a wonder. A blessing. It kept you safe. It kept us safe for now. Maybe we will perish here in the end. I can't say. I can only try to make a safe place for people now. Give them time, a chance to live on if we succeed. Elder Titina said there would be much debris falling to the surface before final moonfall. Think of the terror and the death above from that. They have doomsday caves, but they aren't as secure as here, not as deep inside Margra. Here they could live a better life, if there is a life to be had."

"Yes," Danton interrupted, "there are gardens and food and water."

"But this place is sacred to my people, to me," Nils protested. "You gave your word."

Brill stood up and then knelt in front of Nils. Nils sat back, aghast at this gesture. "Nils, I ask you. I beg you to release me from my promise."

"For what purpose?" Nils asked, panic written in his voice.

"So that I can bring people here to save them, to give them a chance."

"No!"

Salinda rolled her eyes. She had not meant for Nils to be overwhelmed. She had hoped to bring him to this logically and carefully. Yet, she sympathized with the others.

"What about the lesser city?" Danton asked.

"N'Barek?"

"Could you not share that place with the humans above? Those that are worth saving?"

He looked to Salinda, a helpless expression in his eyes.

"Nils," she said and smiled at him gently, "I think what is in people's minds is that if we are to die, what difference does it make that people know the secrets of Barrahiem. How can we stay here in safety, if there are people up there that we can help, that we can give comfort to? If we don't succeed, then everything, including this city, will be destroyed. But in those last hours, we could give balm to troubled souls. We could give them a chance to survive if we find a way to stop final moonfall. So why not share our safety with others? Spare them the terror raining down from above? If by some chance we survive or they do, they will be better able to live here and then go above if there is anything left to return to."

Danton added, "When it is safe to return to their homes." Her eyes met his and he inclined his head with a grin.

Nils shifted his gaze, checking each face in turn. "You all want this?"

The chorus of yeses was overwhelming. Nils put his empty bowl down by his foot. "I did not feel this tremor that you experienced. Until recently, I was in the healing tray and I did not have time for thinking on the situation as you do. These people you seek to bring here are your kin." He paused. "Maybe they are my kin, too. There is a boy in the healing tray right now. Somehow, he found his way into the Travel Ways. This tells me that my people went to live with yours in the past. I don't know why and I don't know how, but the evidence is there. I can see that you believe this is the end, or close to it. You seek to give hope where there is none.

"I have lived without hope. I have lived with despair and loneliness. I do not wish that on others. Therefore, I release you from your promises of secrecy and you can bring your kin to N'Barek."

Salinda ungainly climbed to her feet and waddled over to Nils. He stood to receive her embrace. "Thank you, Nils." She turned to the others. "Now, we have to plan."

And so it began. Salinda and Garan were to depart for the observatory. Nils was to continue to decipher Trell's book. Brill was to continue to train Eneit and Laidan, while Danton developed a plan for evacuating people from Vanden, and even Sartell. First, he had to go to N'Barek to assess the city and whether it was habitable. Salinda and Garan were to bring people from the observatory there, those who were willing and who could be saved. They would enlist the elders' help in evacuating Vanden and securing as much food as could be gathered. It was a big undertaking.

When the observatory folk were settled, Brill, Eneit and Laidan would then venture to Sartell to help evacuate others. By then, Nils should be able to help them navigate the Ways. It was a daunting task. Salinda looked around her, at the enthusiasm—at the light in Danton's eyes, the smile on Brill's face—and knew they had done right.

The plans were to run in unison if possible. They didn't have time to wait for one expedition to be completed before the other was commenced. They spent the next two hours nutting that out.

Nils didn't look happy about the arrangements, but Salinda was sure he would get used to the idea of having more people in the Hiem cities. If they did not find a way to avert moonfall, then what they did now was for naught. Somehow, that didn't matter. What mattered was that they try to do what they could, try to share the relative safety of Barrahiem and N'Barek, and give other people hope. That was what mattered more. Hope.

♋♋♋♋♋

After the meeting and Nils's decision, there was a buoyant mood. Garan came up to her as the group was dispersing. "You know, Salinda, this had been on my mind for a while now. Brill says that he and Danton had also started thinking about using the Hiem cities as a safe haven."

"That is good to know. Now, can you pack for us for our trip to the observatory?" She rubbed her back. "I'm afraid that I can't be of much help carrying supplies."

"I'll be ready in the morning. I take it that's when you want to go, rather than straight away."

She nodded. "Yes, I'm afraid pregnancy does take its toll on me. I must sleep. It's been an exhausting week."

"I may have an answer to the haulage problem." Garan scratched his chin, the stubble of his beard showing this late in the day. "But maybe I don't have time to organize it for this trip."

"Now you are being mysterious."

"Not really, but if I am being coy, 'tis because I am not sure it can be done. Just trust me."

Salinda smiled. "And the cadre? How has it been?"

"Quiet most of the time, but now that I have started thinking it has perked up."

"Keep doing the exercises as I taught you."

Garan stood with one leg bent and smiled at her. "Nils is very thoughtful. He's been to the healing tray already to check on the boy and to

75

read his reports. He's making some clothes for the boy he found in the in-between."

"That isn't surprising. Did he say anything about the boy?"

"Only that he didn't need the report to tell him the boy was almost pure Hiem. Apparently, he looks Hiem and that's enough for Nils."

"Well, the child is certainly a mystery." Salinda couldn't help reading something into the boy's appearance. She didn't know if it boded good or ill, or whether she was just being superstitious. Nils had been rattled by the Hiem he had found helping the baron and he said there were more Hiem somewhere. More than he had suspected. If the baron had them, Salinda didn't think they'd survive long. A huge yawn escaped her and she couldn't repress it or even hide it with her hand. "I'm so sorry. I had better go to bed. I'll see you in the morning."

"Good night, Salinda."

Garan turned away as Salinda headed to her door. Nils was there to assist her, something that she found comforting. Nils wasn't normally so considerate. Yet, by the time she washed and stripped off her outer clothes, Nils was fast asleep in their bed. He really had been working hard. "Wing dust! I wanted to talk to him about the book." She rolled her eyes and climbed into bed. She'd just have to tell him in the morning to focus on where the machine was, what was required and anything else that was pertinent. She didn't want Nils rhapsodizing about his grandfather and reading a lot of personal recounting. He had to focus on what was important. As much as she knew it meant a lot to him to have Trell's writings at last and to add them to the archives, she really only wanted some simple bits of information. And quickly.

Unfortunately, she wasn't going to get it before the morning. Nils's sleeping face was peaceful in repose, the skin paler than she remembered. He was just out of the healing tray and had been straight into translating. Of course he was pale. Yet, they all had to work. Each had a role to play, even if it cost them more energy than was desirable.

She thought of Danton swimming in order to build up his strength. She appreciated that about him. That he was willing to give everything to help save Margra.

☾☾☾☾

Next morning, Salinda was ready to leave but Garan was being difficult. "What do you mean, we can't go yet?" Salinda asked testily as Garan stood before her, perfectly relaxed.

"Look, you are finding it hard to walk about as it is. Do you know why?" Garan had an excited edge to his voice.

"Besides from being very pregnant?" she blustered. "However, if you must know, I think the baby is pressing on something. My leg hurts."

"Nils mentioned to me that the Hiem used glides. He has given me permission to look for some in the storage areas and attempt to repair them."

"A glide? You mean like a cart but without wheels?" Salinda had a growing sick feeling in her gut that had nothing to do with being pregnant.

"Yes. Just think if we need to move a lot of things. If we find a large one, it will help."

Salinda pursed her lips and then let out a sigh. He was quite right. "That is a brilliant idea, Garan. Thank you. Do you need help?"

He gave her an up-and-down look. "It's pretty dirty and cramped down there. Maybe you should do something else while I work."

Salinda wanted to argue against this, but decided that she should stop organizing everyone else and let herself be guided instead. She could rest. She could make some swaddling for the baby. She could help Nils finish sewing the slippers he had started making for the boy in the healing tray. Yes, she could take a few hours to just *be*.

"Don't get carried away down there. Don't take forever or I will come looking for you."

Garan chuckled and gave her a mock salute. "If I cannot find one, I will be back before you know it and we will have to travel the old-fashioned way."

Salinda turned and headed to her abode. She was tempted to crawl back into bed with Nils, but thought better of it. She really did need to make some preparations for the baby's arrival and she liked working on the slippers. In some way, the boy was like a son to them. She considered that was how Nils thought about it. Some kind of bond had formed between the boy and Nils and that made Salinda happy. Nils forming bonds was a good thing. It made him care. So different to the early days, when he cared for nothing.

෨෨෨෨෨

Garan huffed out a breath as he surveyed the storage area. His first look had uncovered nothing that resembled a glide, so this time he explored farther back. He swelled with pride that Nils now trusted him to search the warehouse for a glide without supervision. A relaxed Nils was actually a joy to be around. It occurred to him that he should have prevailed upon Nils to draw a diagram of what a glide looked like. Then again, Garan knew he would enjoy sorting through a wonderful array of equipment. Who knew what other wonders existed here?

Except for a few hard-to-reach malfunctioning lights, the area was well lit. It was messy. It had not been left in good order. It was a state of affairs Nils lamented over, so he had previously forbade exploration. As a result, not much was known about the contents of this vast warehouse. Piles of equipment lay on shelves and hidden underneath them.

Walking along the first row of shelving, Garan drew out the pencil and paper he had scrounged from Brill. It turned out that Brill carried writing utensils in his gear and Garan had agreed to cook extra bread in exchange. He had heard the squeals of delight from Laidan and Eneit and thought it was well worth the trade.

Drawing up a list, Garan wrote what he saw and then wrote *not shelf one, not shelf two*, and so on as he visually scoured the shelves, looking for anything that resembled a disc. The big issue for Garan was time. Salinda was not likely to wait for days. If only he could just casually put his hand on the thing and repair it. Walking down the aisles, getting ever deeper into the warehouse, Garan perused the shelves, looking for items that were large, rather than smaller components. As he walked, he heard a few *whirring* sounds and noticed some gadgets lighting up. The power residing in him still had the tendency to excite Hiem technology into life. It was rather disconcerting, but at the same time he couldn't afford to be distracted or alarmed by it.

As he passed by, he wrote down the aisle number and shelf number of items that, on first glance, appeared big enough to be a glide. He knew there was another locked storage bay that they had never looked into, but Nils

78

might be persuaded if no glides could be found. The locked storage bay was at the back of this area. It had only been discovered by accident when Garan had gotten too curious when he was repairing the city lights. He blushed when he remembered how he had kept quiet about that.

Near the back was an object that looked like a large shallow bowl. It did not respond to Garan's touch like some of the other equipment had. As this was the first promising item he had come across, he lifted it down. It was lighter than he had expected. It was made of a dull metal, not quite black, not quite gray. Garan moved it around in the light and saw that the surface changed color, almost seeming to disappear from view. Garan wanted to take it to Nils straight away and ask, "Is this it?" But Nils was sleeping and Salinda would not allow him to be disturbed. The translation of the book was the most important thing, more important than finding a way for Salinda to travel a long distance with ease.

He put it on the ground and went searching for more. He found another in pieces and left it on the shelf. Then he searched farther, sometimes moving components out of the way so he could see to the back of the shelf and then lying flat on the ground to be sure he had missed nothing underneath. It was during one of these ground searches that he found a similar contraption. This one was a long oval shape. It was light, too, considering it was made of metal and was of some size. This he placed next to the smaller one.

Buoyed by his success, he rummaged farther and found another small one. Just as he was giving up, he noticed something propped up against the back wall, right next to the doors of the locked storage area. This one was twice as tall as Garan and it was narrow. Garan pondered this and then thought more about the Hiem city. If this was one of the glides, where would it have gone? His mind's eye travelled through the city and then in the Ways. Then he backtracked. The Way Gates were narrow. So, while inside the Ways the size didn't matter, it did matter when entering and leaving. That led him to think about the Travel Ways. Could some of the larger glides be inside the Ways? They would have been left there, surely—abandoned.

Perhaps. It was hard to know unless they went looking. When travelling through the Ways, they had not explored the actual space inside. There were probably storage areas at the bottom of stairwells, or near exits.

As he stood there, he looked down at his collection, convinced that these were the glides. Now all he had to do was figure out how they worked and how to repair them. If he was lucky just charging them would be enough, but they were in the storage bay, where things were often placed for repair. He sat on the ground and lifted the first one onto his lap. Its surface was smooth and there did not appear to be any obvious switches or mechanisms. Having worked with Hiem technology before, he figured that was probably the norm. He lifted the shallow bowl to the light, angled it this way and that, flipped it over, and then did the same with another one. He ran his fingers slowly across the surface of the top and bottom, and, finally, around the rim, and it was there that he detected a slight join. He went back to the spot and stared. There was an almost imperceptible line that outlined the hatch. It was very ingenious. Tricky, too.

Now to open it. He tried a few things. Yelling at it. Pressing. Shoving. Using his fingernails to pry the hatch open. None of them worked. Then he studied it for a bit longer. If it was a glide, how would it have worked? He placed the glide on the ground, assessing which was the forward section, and then he sat on it, as he supposed a Hiem would have done. They did have arms and legs like he did so it was a fair assumption. So how would they have operated it?

Sitting there, meditating, he thought about functionality. If it was him, he would have put the on/off switch there. Just where his right hand dangled if he took it off his knee. He felt around, pressed, probed and got nothing. Then he tried the left-hand side. Still nothing. What if you were transporting something or someone? It would involve someone walking alongside or behind the glide. He got off, lay flat on the floor and studied the back and then turned the glide to the front. *Hmm*, he thought. It certainly wasn't obvious. He would have to ask Nils how the glides were operated. He went back to sitting on the floor and trying to open the little hatch. He checked the glides he had gathered and all had the little hatch. So they were a similar type of mechanism.

His shoulders ached from working a long time without a break, so deep in study he had been. He placed the glide on the floor and stood up. Where would Nils be now? Still asleep or back in his study? He bent down and picked up the small glide. His stomach rumbled. He was on kitchen duty so he'd better get back to the Barr family node and get to work. Luckily he had set the dried fungi to soak, so actually cooking it should not take too long. Then he could tax Nils with his glide and how to use it.

That niggling feeling came at him again, that feeling of a presence. The sense of someone looking at him was so strong that he nearly staggered. What was it? This time he touched the cadre, hoping that it could shed light on the matter, but all he detected was curiosity. There was no alarm. The presence he had detected had not moved, but somehow while he was absorbed in examining the glide, the presence had found him. Garan walked around, wondering whether he could get a better direction on it. He stopped in front of the locked storage bay doors. Moving his head from left to right, he studied them. Was it in there? But they had explored the bowels of this place and all they had found was a blank wall and a machine that switched on when he touched it.

Letting out a sigh, he turned and went on his way, past the shelves laden with alien machine parts, past the doors that were always ajar these days, and then headed to the garden to gather some root vegetables for their supper. Garan was mightily hungry so he was going to pick some lairn apples too. Something sweet for afters.

As he passed into the corridor, he paused and looked back. He could almost feel the touch of the mind, or presence. And then it shrank away, leaving him there with his brow furrowed in puzzlement.

Donna Maree Hanson

Chapter Nine
SEEING EYE TO EYE

Salinda put aside the sewing she was doing when Nils came into the living area of their abode. He shuffled around in the kitchen area, making Pardu tea. There was a small pile of cacti bread that he put on a plate for himself and then joined her on the sofa.

"Did you sleep well?" Salinda asked. What she really wanted to say was: *Nils, have you found the location of the machine yet, and what else of importance did Trell say?* But alas, that tactic wasn't going to work on a tired Hiem, a reluctant archivist with breakfast on his mind.

"I do not recall," Nils replied, turning his bowl of tea in the four directions, which was his custom. He took a tentative sip of the hot liquid before placing it back on the low table. He picked up the bread and tore a piece off, mumbled something under his breath and then put it in his mouth. Salinda folded her arms over her distended abdomen and waited. Nils gave her a side-eye and then went to fetch her a cup with slow, shuffling steps.

He poured her some tea and handed it to her. "So you are still tired?" she asked.

Nils eased his shoulders and broke off more of the bread, contemplating it before answering. "I think I will improve once I wake up a bit more. My mind was full of Trell and his words and deeds, so my sleep was not restful."

Salinda sat up straighter and blew on her tea. Probably not what she should do with it. "And have you found anything?" she asked mildly, after taking a swallow of the hot liquid.

Nils took another sip of tea. "Salinda, the value of this book is incalculable. It gives such an accurate picture of the last days of the Sundwellers and Trell's sojourn with them. He had actually broken off contact with his kin, my kin." He shook his head. "I can hardly believe it. And," he added, "he mated with a Sundweller."

"Wasn't he mated with your grandmother?" she asked tentatively, not fully aware of the disposition of Nils's extended family.

Nils frowned as if bigamy was nothing in comparison to cross-species breeding. "Well, yes, he was, but my grandmother had passed away before I was imprisoned."

Salinda nodded and made encouraging noises in the hope that Nils would continue. "And does he speak of how they worked to prevent Moonfall? Did he mention a machine?"

Nils shook his head. "Not yet. I'm not that far in."

Salinda frowned. Hadn't Trell started on the machine when she had translated part of the book? "Nils? What do you mean? I thought you picked up where my translation tapered off."

Nils's eyes grew large. "Why would you think that? Of course, I have to read all the words myself. He was my grandsire."

Salinda lowered her eyelids and begged the source for patience. "I know and I appreciate that, but we are in rather a hurry. Remember moonfall?"

Nils reared back. "Do you dare mock me? Of course I remember moonfall. But I have to make sure I have all the information. Why do you seek to reproach me?"

Salinda screwed her hands into fists, doing her best to keep her tone neutral and her voice calm. "I am not reproaching you. I just seek to expedite the process."

"*Expedite.* You are reproaching me."

"Look, Nils. Maybe it is being pregnant and uncomfortable that is making me less than polite. I want you to prioritize your work. Once we have," she said and then threw her arms wide, "saved the world, you can read every single word of Trell's book. But right now we need to know everything about the machine they built. Where is it? Is there more than one? How do we operate it? All of that."

Nils studied his tea and finished off his bread. "You do not understand what this means to me. You would not speak to me like this if you understood. I thought you knew me."

"It is because I know you that we are having this conversation. I do understand, I really do, but we need that information. If I thought I could do it faster and better than you, I would be down there working on it right now. But you are far superior to me. You taught me well, but I cannot match you. I'm depending on you, Nils. We leave for the observatory as soon as Garan can find me a glide or whatever it is and get it working. He thinks it won't take long, but already we are delayed. I need that information when I get back. Do you understand?"

Nils's nostrils flared. Instead of getting red with anger, he grew so pale that even his lips turned white. "You ask much of me. You ask too much. You want me to open the Hiem's secrets to the world. You want me to let humans inhabit our cities and now you are angry with me for being who I am."

Salinda let out a breath. "No, I am not angry at you. I love who you are. I'm only asking—no, begging—that you give priority to the information I need. That is all I'm asking. I'm not saying don't read Trell's book. Once I have that information you can read it to your heart's content."

Nils drank his tea and sat in silence. For a long drawn-out moment, Salinda thought he would not speak. Then he turned to her. "I will do as you ask. But I have a small favor to ask in return."

"What is that?" she asked, her heart beating a steady beat. What could he possibly ask of her?

Nils let out a breath slowly. "Come with me to see the boy. I think he should be coming out of the healing tray today."

Her eyelids lowered to hide her surprise. "Of course I will. See, I have finished the slippers you started."

She held up the small slippers and Nils took them. "You have done splendid work. I really do not know what to say. We are different. You have a lot of patience with me. You understand that it is not easy for me to fit in with your ways. I appreciate that. I did not mean to be so reactive. I am very tired and I must go back to the translation."

She reached over and squeezed his hand. "I know, Nils. It isn't easy for any of us. You most of all. I am aware of that."

Just then, Garan appeared in the doorway, a strange metal object in his hand.

"Oh, look, Garan has come."

Nils stood and took the object from Garan while Garan bent and slid through the door.

"I hope I am not interrupting anything important. I wanted to ask Nils whether this is one of the glides he mentioned and whether he could tell me how to operate it."

Salinda smiled at both of them. Nils didn't notice as he was too busy studying the metal thing and Garan was eyeing him closely. "Nothing too important, Garan. Is that the glide then?" She seriously doubted she could sit on that and float through the air. Not in her condition, and what if she fell off? Perhaps they should have walked. It would be slow, but they would be nearly there if they had left already.

"Mmm," Nils commented as he twisted the object this way and that. "This is a personal glide."

Garan chuckled. "I thought so."

Salinda reserved judgment, resuming her seat so that she could watch these two enthuse over Hiem technology.

"Can you turn it on?" Garan asked, practically panting with enthusiasm.

Nils drew his fingers along the rim. "Ah, here is the switch—"

"But I could not find it. Show me?"

Nils lifted the glide and showed the rim to Garan. "But that is so small."

"It will not engage unless you are sitting on it. A safety device. "

"So what about the larger ones for carrying goods?" Garan asked.

"Oh…" Nils closed his eyes as if he was remembering some long-forgotten detail. "They had a tether, something to guide them."

Garan grinned. "That makes perfect sense."

Nils pointed to the glide. "We should go outside to test it."

Garan looked around the small room and nodded. "Yes, perfect idea." Salinda was relieved. With three people and furniture, there wasn't much room for flying seats.

With a nod to Salinda, Nils headed for the door, with Garan pressed up close behind so that he could squeeze out straight after him. *Those two!* she thought. *If only we didn't have better things to do.*

The test proved to be in vain. It didn't start. Salinda counted herself secretly pleased as the more she thought about it, the more she decided she wouldn't like to ride on one. She was about to voice this as a firm objection when Garan picked up the contraption and headed out of the node.

"What? Wait?" Salinda called after him.

Nils gathered his robes. "He has gone to fetch another."

"But…" Salinda ground her teeth. "Shall we check on our boy then?" she countered. Perhaps after that they could get going. Garan would be back by then and she would put her foot down firmly. No more waiting for alien contraptions.

In consideration of Salinda's slow gait, Nils deliberately slowed his pace as they took the stairway down into the city. Salinda heard noises, strange noises like grunts and moans, and realized it was Laidan and Eneit training. Brill's voice was interspersed with the clicks and clacks of wooden staves. Salinda thought hard about Laidan. The girl had worked hard to come back from that place where her memories were jumbled and her past was erased. Brain injury, Nils told her, could be fickle and Laidan was lucky to have language, motor skills and some memory. With time, she could recover more and also make new memories, learn new things. Laidan was a hundred times better than she had been in the early days and there didn't seem to be a limit to what she could achieve. Laidan no longer spent her time thinking about herself, but thinking about others. Placing Eneit with her had obviously been a helpful move. Eneit was a good, steady girl. Salinda hadn't had the heart to send her away. Where was there to go that was safer than here? And she was willing to fight, to help, and that counted for much. Salinda had an idle wish, a fervent hope that there was a future for them both.

By the time they reached the bottom of the stairs, Salinda had developed a stitch in her side. Nils guided her to sit on the bottom steps until she recovered. He gazed at her in a whimsical way. "What?" Salinda asked.

"Mmm?" Nils replied absently.

"What are you thinking about or looking at?"

Nils's silver eyes glowed and then he grinned in that way he had. "I was thinking of the child within you. It is uncomfortable for you. An impediment, yet you do not complain about it."

Salinda's eyelids flickered. She thought she was always complaining. *I can't walk that fast. I get pains when I walk. I'm so fat.* Obviously these hadn't registered as complaints to Nils. Salinda put out her hand so he could help her to stand. "Believe me, when the baby comes I will complain a lot."

"There is much pain then?" Nils asked. "I do not have much experience in these matters."

"I also do not have experience giving birth, but I believe it can be painful and dangerous."

Nils shuddered and stood still. "Dangerous?"

"Yes, of course. A lot of women die in childbirth."

Nils's eyes widened. "I did not realize that the child puts your life in danger."

Salinda squeezed his hand. "We did not plan this and it can't be helped now." She did not add that they would probably all die before the baby was born. She didn't think that was the type of mood she wished to project. These days her optimism was hard to summon and, sometimes, she wanted to wail and pull her hair, but always she fought against such despair.

The corridors were cleaner than they used to be. With better lighting in the place now that Garan had restored the city's lamps, she supposed there was more reason to sweep, the main corridors at least.

The sacred lamp dominated the Hall of Elders and she stood back while Nils bowed to it and chanted a prayer before bowing herself. Salinda then followed him to the room where the healing tray stood. The fine webs over the boy's body were fading fast. He was very pale, like Nils. Salinda could understand now why Nils felt he didn't need to read the reports. This boy was so like Nils that they could be father and son. She could see, too, why Nils put so much store in the likeness. He had told her of the part-Hiem he had encountered in Gateshead and the deadly outcome. It had rocked Nils, then, thinking he had killed the only other person who was as close to being a full Hiem as Nils himself. Nakel had mentioned that there were others being held. They had no idea where. Finding this boy was further proof that his people did live on after Barrahiem was abandoned. He didn't know what exactly had happened to his people and, being a Hiem, such lack of knowledge was a burden to him. But this boy was something. Proof. Irrefutable proof. There were more Hiem out there.

"Will you wake him now?" she asked reverently.

"Soon," Nils replied as he placed the slippers they had both worked on next to the tunic he had laid out.

It hit her then how thoughtful Nils was. Yes, he was strange and sometimes difficult, but that was no doubt partially due to her imperfect understanding of him. The boy, she thought, was most likely the reason Nils had let them bring humans into the city and the reason he had lifted their vows of silence. He was now in this with them. No holding back. No taking refuge in being alone or a Hiem. His blood was mixed with theirs. His people, what was left of them, were in danger, too. Nils finally cared.

Salinda smiled at that realization. There was a hiss and the lid on the healing tray rose. The boy's chest rose and fell as he breathed. Salinda thought they should stand back, but it was too late. The boy's eyes snapped open and they were as pale as Nils's. For a moment, he just stared, registering them slowly. Then his eyes widened and he sat up.

"Papa?" he said, tears in his voice. He stopped, looked at Nils and then cried, "Not papa. He's dead. They are all dead." The way he spoke was very familiar to Salinda: *a child of these times*, she thought.

Nils cast her a look of such tragedy that tears burst from her. He scooped the child into his arms, patting his back and saying soothingly, "You are safe now. Safe."

"What is your name, child?" Salinda asked.

"Karol."

The child quietened and Salinda stroked his head gently. "And what was your father's name?"

The child sniffed and turned pale eyes on her, his bony fingers clutching tight to Nils's tunic. "Nakel."

Nils hissed in a breath. Salinda felt her skin chill. It couldn't be. This was the child of the Hiem Nils had killed at Gateshead.

The boy drew back and gazed up into Nils's face. "You knew my father?"

Tears trailed down Nils's cheek. He nodded and he opened his mouth to speak and gave up. He buried his head in the boy's shoulder.

"It's all right," the boy said, patting Nils's hair. "I'm glad you met him. The bad men took him away and mother said he was dead."

Salinda grew concerned at Nils's grief. He had told her what happened in the bowels of Gateshead. His thoughts, his deeds, his observations. It was a difficult thing for him to do, but to now be faced with Nakel's orphan? That wasn't fair.

"And what was your mother's name?" Salinda asked gently as Nils couldn't control his emotions enough to get a word out.

"My mother was Ilania." His eyes grew large and bright and distant as if he was recalling a scene from the past. "I saw them cut her down. They killed them. All my people in the compound. Dead."

"That is a very sad thing," Salinda said, still trying to comprehend the violence and the bloodshed. "Were you prisoners?"

"Yes, we had been there for half a year, maybe more. They took away some of us and they never came back. Then the killing started. Just after mother said that my father was dead. I am small and I could hide where they couldn't get at me."

The boy's voice lacked emotion, as if he was recalling a story he had read or had heard. A protection mechanism, Salinda supposed. Trauma. So much trauma and death.

"They came after me...but I ran and I could squeeze through the rocks and I hid in a long, narrow fissure. I found a Way Gate. I had never seen one before because they are forbidden, but they were going to blow up the fissure I was hiding in. I had no choice but to go in."

"You knew about the Travel Ways?" Nils asked gently, rocking the boy.

"Yes, my father taught me and his father taught him, but we never spoke of them to anyone. We never told those who kept us prisoner, no matter what they did to us."

Nils nodded at the child and pulled out a cloth for the boy to wipe his face. "And then what happened?" he asked softly.

"I was able to open the Way Gate just in time. They blew up the rock behind me. I ran and then something strange happened."

"What was that?" Nils prompted gently.

"The wall glowed. Not much, but it was so dark in there and then there was some light. It called to me. I went up to it and then it reached for me. I was scared and...I don't remember, until I woke up here."

"The in-between called to you?" Nils questioned further.

Salinda had to give herself a shake to bring her back to the moment. This was unbelievable. The in-between called to the child? That destroyed her preconceptions. Nils had said that the in-between was hungry for life force. But it could actually call out? It seemed the boy was not seriously harmed. Or was he? Had his life force been drained, or preserved? How long had he hung there, suspended in the wall where Nils had found him? Nils, too, had been jerked to consciousness while in the healing tray by something calling to him. Either it was this child, or the in-between. Salinda couldn't help standing and gaping at the child. She caught Nils's eye, but he shrugged and concentrated on the boy.

Talking had taken the boy's mind off weeping. He put his head on Nils's shoulder, hands and feet tightening on Nils's torso. "Will you look after me now?" he asked in a small voice.

"Yes," was all Nils could manage.

Salinda stepped into the breach. "Yes, we will look after you. Now, you must come and meet the others."

"Where am I?" the boy asked as his gaze shifted to the door leading into the Hall of Elders and its magnificently decorated walls. Carrying the boy, Nils led Salinda out. "This is Barrahiem, city of the Hiem, and this is the Hall of Elders and the sacred flame. I am the only one of my kin alive here."

Salinda touched the boy's shoulder to get his attention. "I am human and there are some others with us. Don't be afraid. They will not harm you. They will be your new family, if that is what you want."

The boy sniffed and brought his wide-eyed gaze to Salinda. "You have a baby inside you."

Salinda smiled. "Yes."

"I will have a little brother or sister."

Salinda patted her stomach. "Yes, I hope so."

"I'm glad." The Hiem child's face screwed up and he cried all over again. "I'm so alone."

At her urging, Nils did not linger. He provided a walking narrative of what the child was seeing. He talked about the lights and how Garan had repaired them and, while they made their way to the Barr family node, Nils described their friends and companions to Karol. This appeared to distract the child from his distress. Thankfully, Nils didn't say that the world was nearing its end. They could afford to give Karol some time before he learned they were working to save the planet. Salinda agreed with keeping silent on this issue. The child was traumatized and about to be introduced to strangers. Eventually, he should be told, because he would find out anyway. It was inevitable. She was a bit wary now of leaving Barrahiem, but duty called.

Karol gazed around in obvious wonder. "This is just like the stories my father told me. He said our people used to live in underground cities and that they were very wise and great."

Nils nodded. "He spoke true. This is what remains."

The boy studied Nils's face and then cast his gaze farther. "Is that a lake?"

"Yes, and there is a city on the other side."

The boy nodded, his brows lowering as he took it in. "I never thought I would see a Hiem city. We were warned to stay away and not to look for them."

Salinda frowned and asked, "Do you know why?"

"We were told they were dangerous."

Nils looked about him, at the lonely quiet of the place.

"I see," Salinda said. "Barrahiem has been good to us. But there are things here than could be dangerous."

"The old machines..." the boy said, suddenly weary. He buried his head in Nils's shoulder and closed his eyes, seeming to fall asleep.

Salinda and Nils shared a look over the boy's head. The look spoke of future conversations. That the child was a missing link to whatever happened to Nils's kin. That he may know other things of use, not the least being able to hear the in-between call to him. Despite the puzzle of Karol, Salinda was pleased to have him join their little family. Once he got over his guilt about his role in Nakel's death, Nils would see it that way too. Watching Nils talk and pet the child as they headed up the stairs—at a slow pace due to her pregnancy—she glimpsed what kind of father Nils would be. If only moonfall was not so close. Moonfall filled her with foreboding. Salinda often felt that she would not get to give birth to her child. Would not get to see it, or it her. The cadre admonished her pessimistic attitude. That was no way to approach the tasks ahead. See the child as a good omen, it urged. And despite her misgivings, she did.

ᏬᏬᏬᏬᏬ

Garan was pacing up and down as Salinda approached. "Where did you go?" Garan blurted out and then stepped back, aghast, on seeing the child. "Oh? I see you went to get the boy."

Initially, Karol did not lift his head from Nils's shoulder and kept his eyes closed. As they joined Garan outside their door, the boy opened his eyes and then they widened. "You!"

Garan stilled and Salinda and Nils exchanged puzzled glances. "Why do you say that?" Nils asked. "Have you met Garan before?"

"No," Karol said turning to Nils, "not in person. Only in dreams. You glow in my dreams."

Garan's complexion paled. Then, swallowing, he replied, "I hope they were good dreams." Garan's gaze flickered between Salinda and Nils, silently begging for assurance. With a slight nod from Salinda, Garan continued: "My name is Garan. What is yours?"

"Karol, son of Nakel."

Salinda's heartbeat was excited, afraid. Who was this child? What was this child? Nils had never spoken of telepathic abilities before. Yet, now was not the time to drag Nils off for an explanation. She had to be patient.

Signaling that he was ready to be let down with a tap of his small hand, Karl was eased off Nils's shoulder so that he could stand on his own two feet. He glanced around the node, at the abodes and then back at Garan. "Pleased to meet you. What is that you are holding?"

Garan held out the circular glide for Karol's inspection. "'Tis called a glide. The Hiem used them to travel, floating above the ground."

Karol moved forward and touched it. "So it is true. My grandfather told me of these. When he was old he wished for one. His grandfather had told him about them and his grandfather before that."

"Well, now we are going to see if we can get this one to work. Would you like that?" Garan asked, a sweet, tender smile on his face. Salinda sighed softly, grateful to have met Garan.

Karol hopped once, an energetic spring of glee. "I would."

Garan placed the glide on the ground and then sat on it. He reached to the front and depressed the button. The glide lifted off the ground slowly and smoothly. It hovered there.

Karol whooped with laughter and danced around Garan sitting on the glide.

Nils exclaimed, "How did you do that?"

Garan grinned sheepishly. "I caressed it for a while and when I thought it had enough power I tested it. But I can't seem to get it to work. How do I make it go forward?"

"You lean," Karol piped up. "You lean in the direction you wish to go and lean back when you want to stop. You have to do it slowly so you don't fall."

"I am not sure we should use these things," Salinda commented and then closed her mouth.

Garan did as instructed and he moved forward then stopped. "Oh, interesting. There is a cushion of some kind that holds the body in place."

Garan turned, slowly, experimentally, and the glide turned and then he turned back. Then did it faster so he was doing a glide jig. "Salinda, you should try it."

The speed at which Garan was moving made Salinda feel giddy. She rested her hands on her protruding belly and shook her head. "Me? I don't think so."

Karol turned to her. "Don't be afraid," he said. "It will be good for you."

Salinda rolled her eyes. She was outnumbered. Garan depressed the switch again and the glide lowered to the ground.

With Garan's assistance, Salinda arranged her bulk on the glide. Karol came along behind and tucked the folds of her tunic and outer robe so that they were out of the way. As there was no room for Nils to offer assistance, he stood back and watched. Salinda thought she saw him smile, but as that was so unusual she also thought it might have been the play of light on the Hiem's face.

Salinda reached down to the edge of the metal bowl she sat in. It was warm to the touch.

Garan, squatting, guided her hand. "Now," Garan instructed, "press the button here."

Salinda sucked in a breath, tried to keep calm and did as she was told. The glide lifted ever so smoothly and slowly. Salinda did her best to keep her body still. It was disconcerting to be off the ground. But she had ridden a dragon and this was a piece of technology, hence, a bit more predictable. If she could ride Plu, she could do this. However, Plu would have never let her fall. When she realized that, another disquieting thought came to mind: that this machine had no mind or heart to care about her.

"But the makers did," Karol said, looking directly into her face.

"What?" Salinda asked, nonplussed. Could the child read her mind?

"The makers wanted to make sure you didn't fall. That's what my grandfather said. And no, I can't read all your thoughts. Just the ones you project. Like questions. When I'm nearby."

Nils started and then shook his head in warning. Salinda's questions could wait.

Garan scooped Karol out of the way and gave instructions. "Now, lean forward just a bit." Garan hovered close by, hands outstretched as if that would help if she fell.

Salinda leaned forward carefully, just a tad. The glide moved. She cried out and then calmed as the movement stopped when she instinctively sat back. She tried it again and it moved forward. She leaned to the side and the glide moved that way. She moved to the left and it moved left. "Oh!" she said with a smile. "I could get the hang of this. Although, I might be slower than you like."

Garan laughed. "Good. Then I am ready to leave when you are."

Salinda didn't want to leave Karol right away. She needed to make sure he met everyone and that he and Nils would be all right together. She also needed time to practice on the glide. As she sat there she became conscious of something holding her in place. It was like an invisible hand that helped to stabilize her. She practiced for a few minutes more, enough to ensure that she wouldn't be afraid to try again, and then switched it off. It lowered itself slowly to the ground.

"Garan, can you round up the others? I want them to meet Karol. Then I think we should go."

Garan agreed and with a carefree wave he ran off, firstly to the other abodes, and then leaving their node to go to Danton's and Brill's.

Meanwhile, Salinda put out a hand to Karol. "Tell me about reading thoughts, Karol. Were you always able to read them?"

Karol blinked at her, silver eyes winking on and off. Karol frowned. "Sometimes. Maybe. I wasn't sure. Now, though, it is very clear that I can."

Nils stood behind the boy, squeezing his shoulders gently, and shot Salinda a meaningful look. "How lucky we are that you are so special, Karol," Salinda said softly and in what she thought was a motherly manner. Karol was an endearing child. He brought out protective feelings in her. Feelings she hadn't known she had.

Before they could discuss things further, Garan came back, shaking his head. "I will have to check the lake. They are not there."

As he ran off again, Nils and Salinda took Karol inside, where he inspected the abode, touching the sofa with idle fingers while Nils made Pardu tea. Salinda was feeling heavy in the legs, so she sat down and patted the seat beside her. "This is our home," she said.

Karol turned to her, a smile on his face. "It is lovely." It was then she noticed that his eyes were dark gray and speckled with silver. They resembled Nils's eyes, but were different. She wondered whether they had always been that color or whether the Ways had changed him. There was something awfully strange about the boy. Not in a bad way, just in an unknown way. Could the Ways have given him the ability to read thoughts? To know things, like knowing Garan on sight? Salinda really wanted to ask Nils about it, but feared she would not get the chance before she had to leave.

Garan had amazing powers and it shouldn't be surprising that another gifted child should come their way. Hadn't she thought that fate guided her at times?

How powerful were the Ways? The way the boy made her feel, she thought they might be sentient. Was Nils hiding some of the properties of the Ways, or did he genuinely not know? From what she suspected, Nils was as surprised by the boy as she was, and while he had travelled in the in-between he had never mentioned that it could grab people and keep them there. That it could glow of its own accord, or that it could act independently.

Nils brought the teapot over to the table and laid out the small, square drinking bowls. Karol sat up straight and watched avidly. His body relaxed when Nils finished his ritual and poured the tea. Karol bowed his head when he accepted his and it was such a natural movement that Salinda realized that this was familiar to him. His family had obviously carried on the tradition.

A smile lit her face. Nils appeared so serene and happy. It dawned on her that Nils was no longer alone.

A knock at the door and the first of their visitors arrived. Nils introduced Karol to Danton.

Chapter Ten

BLACK DAY AND RED NIGHT

Garan had done a marvelous job on the slides. Salinda had time for more practice before bed after they finally introduced Karol to everyone. The next morning Salinda found she managed the glide well. Floating through the Ways with Garan, her confidence grew. It was odd to be travelling so low to the ground, but she didn't want to be any higher. If she fell off not much would be damaged, except her dignity.

Garan tugged her along with one of the tethers he had made for the purpose. His strides were long and his brow furrowed as he single-mindedly headed for the observatory. No small talk from him. He was very preoccupied. She couldn't blame him. Trithorn Peak was his home and he had a strong attachment to the place and its people. Salinda had a soft spot for them, too, but she could not lay claim to kinship. She could only surmise what Garan's feelings might be.

She did not want to be away from the others for any length of time. She wanted to get to know Karol better and wanted to keep an eye on Danton's healing. Although he said he was fine, and exercised to the point of exhaustion every day, she was still concerned. The memory of his near death still plagued her and she couldn't help worrying that he'd have a relapse.

Danton had now joined Brill in training the girls. Salinda recalled watching them the previous day. Laidan had been ferocious and single-minded, her lithe . body having grown stronger and fitter and her movements fast and hard. Eneit stood up well to Laidan's onslaught with the stave. At that session, Danton had taken over training with Laidan while Brill trained Eneit. Laidan didn't seem fazed at fighting the rebel leader instead of the smaller girl. Eneit, on the other hand, laughed at Brill and cut him jokes while they sparred.

Salinda felt a kernel of pride. She remembered her own training and how well it had set her up to survive and to lead. That was so long ago now.

Bringing her mind back to the Ways, she saw they were coming up on the exit. The recollection of ledges and darkness and danger hit home. "Garan? How will we manage the next part? I didn't think—"

Garan flashed her grin. "I have thought about it and I spoke to Nils. We will be fine. Just hold onto the sides of the glide." He studied her. "Maybe close your eyes."

"What?"

"A jest," he said and then moved in to shorten the tether. "To be on the safe side, do not make any sudden movements."

Salinda shivered. Why was she being such a coward? Behavior she did not easily tolerate in others. This pregnancy and hormones were teaching her a lot about herself and some of it was not easy to face. Every day, more and more she had to fight to keep her brain focused on saving Margra and not on what was going on in her body, not on what her baby might be like, not on how it would feel to hold it. No, she mustn't think that way, mustn't get distracted. If she faltered now, if she relaxed for one minute too long, there would be no baby and no future.

Garan opened the door. "Right then," he said as he turned to her, "are you ready?"

"Yes," she answered a mite snappishly. She was more than ready. Then, when she saw the cavernous maw of dark on the other side, she did shut her eyes. It was better that way. She needed her wits for later on. There was no point in being scared out of them before her time.

The glide dipped to one side. It was only a slight movement, but she yelped. Garan whispered to her that all was well. He gave a blow-by-blow account of their progress. Garan climbed. She could hear the scrape of his boots and the rasp of cloth against stone. She was still sitting upright. She supposed the glide was going straight up as she was pulled along by Garan. "Not long now, I can see some light."

Salinda kept her eyes shut. She had to trust that Garan would tell her when they were clear. "There we are," he said at last. Salinda thought she was going to lose her mind for all she could hear were Garan's soft steps and the drip of water.

Salinda opened her eyes, realized she had a death grip on the side of the glide and tried to loosen it. They were near the cave mouth. "What time of day is it?" she asked Garan.

Garan had been trying to keep time with the outside while they were in their underground world. Salinda wasn't sure how successful it had been. She had tended to not worry about it.

"It should be early afternoon," he replied in a low, thoughtful voice that hinted at uncertainty.

As it happened, it was dark outside. Not middle-of-the-night black, but gray, dark-gray.

They stepped out into the darkness. The sky had patches of black and swirling masses of smoke color, ash-gray lighter tinges. The mountain peaks were shrouded in what looked like heavy smoke. The sun was all but blotted out. There was dust in the air, too. Just enough to tickle the back of her throat.

"The asteroid?" she asked Garan.

Garan pulled at his bottom lip as he turned full circle, eyes brimming with tears. He covered his mouth and nodded, coughing to clear his throat. "It was either very big or very close."

Together, they looked up to the stony outcrops of the observatory. The complex looked intact. A single light was visible from a window high up. There was someone there. Salinda didn't know why she thought they might have abandoned the place. Obviously, Garan thought the same. "They are there. Come, we must hurry!"

This was a black day, a day portending the end of the world. Salinda shivered in spite of herself. While she glided along, towed by Garan, she shored up her strength and screwed down her resolve. She could not communicate this dark mood. It would be fatal.

She noted the paths were not as well kept as previously. Small spills of dirt and pebbles had not been swept clear. Weeds grew out of cracks in the rocks on the sides of the path. It had a disheveled air. This told her a lot about the state of the observatory's inhabitants. The gate was unattended. "Wait a moment, please," she asked Garan. "I need to stretch."

While it was easier to be riding on a glide than walking, sitting cross-legged on the glide had its own issues. Her feet had gone numb and her back ached.

Garan lowered the glide to the ground and then helped her to her feet by letting her hold both his hands. She rolled her eyes, hating how helpless she appeared. Casually, as she rubbed her aching back, she looked around at the observatory, the gardens, the series of courtyards, where she had met Brill again, and Garan, back in what seemed bright days compared to the gloom that was like a soup around them.

Her back cracked and she let out a sigh. That felt better. "More glide?" Garan asked.

Salinda frowned as she considered. She could either waddle through the corridors or glide on alien technology. She knew which would have more impact on the inhabitants and would be better for her ankles. "The glide, I think. It is time to impress some people, given we have come to ask them to flee into Barrahiem with us, rather than risk their own doomsday cave."

"I agree," Garan said and then helped her take her seat. She engaged the glide, Garan gave the tether a gentle tug and once again they were on their way.

"Garan, why are we headed to the refectory?" Salinda asked, trying to mask her smile. Garan was always eating and not getting fat. She glanced down at her belly. That didn't count, she was all baby.

"'Tis the best place to find people. If we go to the Master Elder's office, there is no guarantee that anyone would be there. In the refectory," he explained, with a twinkle in his eye, "there is always someone around and they know someone who knows someone…"

"I get it. Okay then." She waved him on imperiously. Their inner joy at odds with the dire circumstances. You had to keep on going, even if it was with false joy.

While not as strong as in the past, there were gentle tantalizing aromas wafting around the corridors the closer Garan drew to the refectory. Even Salinda's mouth watered when she smelled the bread.

Garan pushed open the doors. People turned and frowned, until one by one the inhabitants recognized Garan, and some recognized Salinda. Garan lowered the glide and helped Salinda to stand. "I think sitting at a table might be more comfortable," he said to her, leading her forward. The curious onlookers parted to let Salinda through to the center table. People picked up plates and cups and vacated. A server ran over with a wet rag and cleaned the table top.

Someone ran out the door. Salinda cast her gaze around. Titina and Wylie were not there. She eased her sore and cramped back with her hands, and took the proffered seat. Someone brought her some watered wine. "Thank you," she replied and waved the cup under her nose. Their own supply of dragon wine was quite low and watered down, so tasting a fresh, different batch was good. So good. They had used a lot of pure dragon wine on Danton. She took a tentative sip and the power of it filled her very cells. She sat up straighter, her muscles were stronger and her mind sharper. A few minutes later, the baby kicked. Salinda took that as a good sign and took another hearty swallow.

Garan had gone to the servery. Salinda nodded to those she knew and exchanged pleasantries. To those she didn't know by sight, she smiled.

A woman came up to her. She was familiar. One of the Vanden women, Salinda thought. "How'd be," the woman said. "Tell me, do you have word of Mandin. She who left to find her daughter?"

Salinda studied the woman. "Mandin did find her daughter. Eneit is with us now and doing very well."

"And Mandy?" Her eyes were blue and watery. Not so old, but worn, Salinda thought.

Salinda shook her head. "She did not make it, I'm sorry. But she achieved what she had set out to do. She was brave and strong and triumphant in very hard circumstances. I wish I had got to know her better."

"She was a strong woman, aye." The woman reached over and squeezed Salinda's shoulder. "Sorely missed. You are strong, too, but you will need your strength in days to come. That child isn't sitting right. It will give you trouble, mark my words."

The woman turned away, her straggly white hair like a crown around her head where it escaped its bun. Salinda's gaze followed the woman as she left the refectory. There was something inherently sad in that exchange. Salinda shivered at the words about her coming labor. If only there was some kind of Hiem magic that would hold it off until she was ready. They did not need complications of any kind.

Garan placed a platter in front of her that held two, small round flat breads and a small dish of stew. The aroma was amazing. She was just about to tuck in when the doors flew open and Elder Titina and Elder Wylie rushed in. "Salinda!" Titina blurted.

Salinda was going to get up to greet them, but Titina enveloped her in a hug from behind and Salinda didn't get a chance. Titina shuddered like she was suppressing a sob. Salinda's gaze met Wylie's and she knew that something was wrong. Well, more wrong and immediate than the world ending.

Salinda reached up and patted the woman's forearm. "Come, sit down. Tell me," Salinda said in a soothing tone. She was amazed at her capacity for calm. Perhaps she had lost touch with reality. Finally, Margra had driven her mad. She smiled at the thought. It was the damn hormones making it impossible to think.

As she sat across from Titina after the elder took her seat, her humor fled. Wylie took a seat on the opposite side of the table. Salinda flashed a look his way and his expression was no better.

"We have failed," Titina said. "Utterly failed."

"No, we haven't," Elder Wylie contradicted. "We did not fail, we just did not completely succeed."

"I take it you mean the asteroid impact? We felt it where we were deep in the heart of Margra."

Titina burst out a sob, then controlled herself. "Yes," she said, wiping her eyes with the edge of her robe. "We had a plan to deflect it or, at worst, reduce it, but it fell anyway with devastating effects."

Salinda decided there was a lot of information to process here. "This asteroid is not final moonfall."

"Oh, no," Titina said, lifting her head. "It's just a precursor, but the method is one we were hoping would assist us when the time came."

Elder Wylie interrupted again. "It does not mean our method was wrong. Each asteroid is made up of different materials and so the blasts have to be calibrated, as does the angle. This one had a steeper angle and was not so easy to deflect. While the Farsighters had the trajectory calculated correctly, they did not have as much luck with the content of the asteroid."

"I see..." Salinda commented, her body tense. This was sounding familiar and her mind started shuffling through recent events to recall where it had been discussed before. If only her brain was not so sluggish. Then it came to her. Trell's book. It had talked about research into the substance of Ruel moon. Wouldn't this apply to the fragments of that same moon? "They aren't all rock, I take it."

"No," Elder Titina said, jumping in before Wylie or Garan, who had both opened their mouths to speak. "They can have ice, iron, and granite. A mixture of hard and soft substances."

Digesting this, Salinda asked, "You mentioned the Farsighters?" She didn't understand enough about Trell's book to confirm her thinking so she kept quiet about it.

"Yes," Wylie interjected. "Epen has been theorizing for years that he could discern the makeup of the meteors and the other matter that together make up Shatterwing. Some he can judge by light and color, which he observed as they fell. Others, he says, he judges by some kind of inner sight that he possesses." Titina's eyebrows shot up, indicating she wasn't entirely convinced. But Salinda, after what she had seen, particularly recently, wasn't surprised someone could divine the substance of space rock.

"And Epen..." Salinda prompted.

"He tried to teach others, but alas it was not perfect. And we needed perfect."

"But you haven't abandoned the idea?" Salinda asked, turning to include Wylie in her question.

"No!" Elder Wylie responded. "The opposite."

"We thought you would be angry at our failure."

Salinda sat back. "Angry?" Was she that hard a taskmaster?

"Why else did you come?" Titina asked.

Garan slipped into the conversation smoothly. "Never angry. We are amazed you had thought of this. Epen was only new to Farsighting when I was a Skywatcher. Perhaps I could talk to him and study his method."

Titina gave him a grateful look. "Would you? Your insight will be most useful for none have anything approaching your talent." Garan blushed and bowed his head. Salinda smiled. If they only knew the true extent of his value. If only Garan believed more in himself and his abilities.

While grateful for Garan for intervening, she had to explain herself and explore what was going on with Titina. "We came because...because we felt the asteroid's impact and we wanted to see what the damage was and the progress you might have made."

Titina was nodding her head and then shared a look with Wylie. "We have made some progress despite this failure."

Salinda shook her head. "Don't call it a failure. We are trying to mitigate a disaster. You may have already done that with what you've achieved. I'd really like to hear about your progress, because it seems to me that you have made inroads where I have made none and—"

"None," Garan quipped. "We found the book."

Salinda nodded her head slowly. "Yes, the book." Garan had cut her off before she could mention their plan to take people to N'Barek. Now the conversation sped away from her.

"The book?" Titina asked, brow furrowed and hands kneading the skirt of her robe. "I do seem to remember you were looking for some artifact."

Salinda nodded and placed her spoon in her bowl. "Ah...long story," Salinda said. "As he lay dying, the Master Elder mentioned to Nils that he had seen a book by Trell of Barr. Since then Nils has been searching for it because Trell of Barr was his grandsire and knew a lot about Ruel moon and predicted its explosive end. Since then, we have come to understand that Trell of Barr was involved in the mission to avert Moonfall. What should have been total annihilation was averted. Yes, there was massive devastation, but there were survivors. We are evidence of that."

"Oh, and has the book proved useful?" Titina asked.

"Not yet. Nils is working on the translation. I do know that Trell worked on a project with a team of people to avert Moonfall. So we are closer than we ever were before. I only hope that there is enough information in the book when it is translated to help us." Because she wasn't certain about Trell's research, she kept quiet about the asteroids and what they were made out of.

Titina now relaxed somewhat. "We may as well join you in a meal. What we have to show you may take a while." She turned to Garan. "Epen is getting ready for his shift. Perhaps you could talk to him now. Then join us."

Garan glanced down at his brimming bowl of stew, sad-eyed.

Titina waved a hand, understanding. "Oh, eat first, of course. Then join us for the discussion."

"I'll be quick," Garan replied, casting his glance at them. He finished his stew in a few short bites, gathered up his bread and, with a bow, left the refectory.

Two trays were brought over to the elders. They removed the plates and arranged them on the table, then stowed the trays.

"Where did the asteroid hit?" Salinda asked.

Again Titina looked to Wylie before answering. "We estimate it was west of here. There was a great storm of wind and dust after the impact. From our calculations it hit beyond the Fire Ranges."

Salinda immediately thought of dragons and Gercomo.

"You have maps?" she asked.

"Of course. We can show you and discuss how our plans will work."

"Then let's enjoy this food and then retire to your office and you can tell me your plans and I can share mine with you."

So they ate while Titina provided small talk about the running of the observatory, the success in training the Vanden folk, and the successful harvest. Wylie added comments here and there and the smile on his face betrayed the deep affection he felt for Titina. It amazed Salinda how people could find love at times like these. Her own heart was not immune either.

Perhaps in times of great desperation all feelings were heightened. Maybe especially love and hate.

Again her mind went to Gercomo. He had survived the exploding roof of Gateshead city. That much she had detected. He was a thing she hated. There was no pity in her heart for him. How she wished that the asteroid impact had taken him out. Him and his corrupted dragons, but that would be too easy and she didn't think fate was that generous. The baron had also escaped. She was sure of that. He was that canny.

Chapter Eleven

TRIAL BY FIRE

Later that evening, ensconced in Titina and Wylie's shared office, Salinda sat in a comfy chair nursing a cup of watered dragon wine. It was lightly spiced and she savored the flavor. Titina stood over the neatly drawn map of the heavens. Margra was depicted below and larger pieces of Shatterwing were shown with intersecting lines and numbers and angles and other things that Salinda didn't quite grasp.

"This," Titina said, pointing to a little circle, "is the asteroid that fell. As you can see 'tis on the edge of the debris field here." She moved her finger to a dark circle on Margra. "This is the observatory. As you can see the angle is oblique in relation to the asteroid. We thought if we struck with power from here, we could achieve two things: reduce its size and push it off course."

Salinda was amazed. "You can do that?"

Titina deflated with a sigh that made her seem half her size. She cocked her head and studied Salinda. "That is the point I'm trying to make. We tried, but we don't think it worked. Well, not completely."

She brought out another map and laid it on top of the other one. "This is the original position and size of the asteroid that recently impacted Margra."

Salinda examined it, but she was not trained as a Skywatcher. "You will have to explain it to me. I can't see the difference."

Titina pursed her lips, then made a smacking sound as she turned her attention to the map. "This says the asteroid was bigger based on our

Farsighters's estimate of the size." She trailed her finger down a dotted line. "This is where it was estimated the asteroid would impact." She tugged that map aside and showed Salinda the actual position of impact as calculated. A difference of about a fingerbreadth was evident between the two maps.

"So you did change its trajectory," Salinda said.

"That's the debate. We can't be sure. We have to allow for a margin of error. We think we made it smaller and were able to shift the trajectory. What we were aiming for was reducing its size and actually deflecting it enough so it would not land at all. In that we failed."

Salinda looked up from the map, her gaze narrowed as she spoke to Wylie. "You could try again, couldn't you?" Then the conversation about the substance of the rock fragments came to mind. "Oh, you think the makeup of the fragments of Shatterwing has a bearing on your efforts."

Wylie nodded enthusiastically. "Yes, yes. If we have enough time we could test the theory."

"Time," Salinda repeated thoughtfully. She looked at the newer map again and saw all the other objects identified. They seemed awfully close. "How long? Days? Weeks?"

Titina frowned and bit her bottom lip. Her breath hitched as if she was about to cry, but she let it out again steadily, her study of the map intense. "This is the precursor to moonfall. See here," she said, pointing. "Ruelette and Rueline are drawing closer, pushing this debris ahead of them. If we can destroy or dissipate these smaller fragments," she pointed at the depiction of the debris field on the map, "then we can survive it." She thumped her hand down on the map on the larger fragments. "These we cannot survive or shift."

"Hmm," Salinda said. "If you can lessen the impact of this you give us time…"

"Time for what?" Titina exploded hotly. "Even those we have chosen to save will not survive this." She hit the map again with a forefinger. "Nothing can survive this. I've been over the calculations again and again."

Tears welled in Salinda's eyes. Titina the pragmatic had given into despair and Salinda had little hope to offer, little true advice. "I have a plan," she nevertheless offered hesitantly.

Titina rocked back, her expression skeptical. "A plan? Have you found the means to magic us off this source-forsaken rock?"

"What? No, but hear me out. You know Nils is one of the fabled Hiem and while you do not know the location of his city, Barrahiem, you know it exists. We were sworn to secrecy before but Nils has given permission for us to speak. We felt the tremor, Titina, but it was a small thing. Barrahiem is deep within Margra. Some might survive there with us. We have come to take you and your doomsday cave people to Barrahiem. If fact, we came to take any who would come."

Wylie took a step toward Titina, who seemed close to breaking down. "Take us?" Her brow furrowed. "Abandon the observatory? Our work?"

"Yes, eventually." Salinda lowered her gaze to the table. Their grief and disappointment were too real, too raw to watch. "But given this is so close," Salinda tapped the map in front of them, "we should make preparations now. We can take the people from Vanden too. We must send word to them before it is too late."

"That's your plan?" Titina yelled. "To hide from this?"

Salinda blinked as Titina's rage washed over her. "No, not all my plan!" Salinda snapped, responding in kind. "I'm trying to save people so that my plan will have some benefit, some reason. What's the point of averting moonfall if everyone bar a handful is dead?" Salinda took a breath, noting the tears in Titina's eyes and Wylie holding her close, and moderated her voice. "This is a long shot and I will tell you all that I know. But first, I want people safe. I want to save those I can rather than chance them to fate." She gestured out the window to the red sky. "If that asteroid could do this, then skyfire that will rain down on us when the debris falls will take more lives. There may be no one left to witness moonfall. We need to take action now. The more we can save, the more chance there is for life after this catastrophe."

Titina was silently crying. Salinda was deeply wounded to see such despair and to know that she had somehow disappointed the elder. "The other plan we have is to find the machine that was used at Moonfall. A machine was built to prevent—"

"But it didn't prevent it. Even if you find this machine, it will be for naught," Titina said, pouring out her grief.

Salinda felt the tug of Titina's emotion and resisted the urge to sob along with her friend. "No, not for naught. They didn't stop it, but they lessened the impact. Somehow they changed, or converted, the rock of Ruel moon." She furrowed her brow as she fought to make them understand. "Like what you are doing. Making the fragments smaller and pushing them off course. Except more powerfully. More precisely."

Titina pushed away her tears with the back of her hands. "You believe this?" Her hands were shaking still, as if her grief had undone her self-control, her life.

"Yes, I do," Salinda said. "The cadre tells me it was done. And the book that we found has the information in it. I'm sure it does. Trell of Barr was working with the team who built those machines. It has to be in that book."

Titina shook her head. "There is a lot of has-to-be's in your statement."

Wylie spoke up. "It's as good a plan as any."

Salinda wiped at her cheek where tears had spilled without her noticing. "I know. It's the best that I can do."

And then Titina came to her, burying her face in Salinda's shoulder and sobbing. Mumbled words came out. Salinda heard how Titina had tried and had hoped and how she couldn't bear to see the end. How she didn't think she was strong enough. Wylie stood there silently weeping and moved his gaze from the map to the window and shook his head. Salinda looked out there too. The red sky was burnished with orange and black. It was like the very air was on fire. It reminded Salinda of when the vineyard had been torched. She remembered how she had felt then as if the world was ending.

Now it really was.

☾☾☾☾☾

Garan followed Epen around the observation balcony, listening to his theories. Epen was tall and thin, with a bald head and dark skin and eyes. His eyes protruded like he was in a perpetual state of surprise, which Garan found disconcerting.

The scope that Epen used for Farsighting showed signs of alteration: Epen had made some glass, different kinds of glass. "See," Epen said as he slotted in a glass disc and then gestured for Garan to look.

Garan closed one eye and peeked into the scope with the other. It was hard to see anything because the sky was not black, as it ought to be, but was filled with the gases and dust that Margra's sun enlivened with color. Then, the shape of the rock he was looking for came into focus. "It has a greenish tinge."

"Yes." Epen went to the front of the scope and inserted a different glass lens. "Now what color do you see?"

Garan studied the rock. "I think it is bluish?"

"Yes, yes," Epen said enthusiastically. "You have the ability to perceive these color variations. Excellent. Some cannot, you know."

Garan stepped back from the scope. "And you believe these tell you what the rock is made of?"

Epen bit his lip and then nodded once. "Well, yes, but it is matching the colors to the substance that is hard. We do not have enough time to test my theories."

"Ah, I see," Garan replied. "What do you think that one is?"

"Hard stuff. Iron and maybe gold."

Garan frowned. "So if I were to blast it apart, would that tell you anything?"

Epen considered this, resting his weight on one of his legs and stroking his chin. "You can reach that far?"

"Yes, with the scope to target my power." Garan again studied the rock through the scope. "Yes, I think I can."

"Let us try it, then."

The other Skywatchers and Farsighters were at their tasks and their soft murmurs spilled over them. Since Garan was going to target a stationary object, he was not going to interfere with their work.

Garan studied Epen's scope and then went to get a spare Skywatcher scope and crystal. Salinda had said he didn't need to use the crystal, but Garan wanted to enhance his blast and focus the beam. He felt more comfortable using the scope and the crystal together. Also, if the others wanted to copy him they would need the same tools as they always used.

Garan took his time setting up the scope, and then he sighted along it until he had found the coordinates and the object that he was going to target. It would be interesting to test Epen's theories. Garan only hoped it would be worthwhile. If this object was heavy and mostly metal, then they would also need to compare it with one made of different materials, say, rock and water.

Garan did not use a large crystal, just one that fit in his hand. He dropped it into the chute and let his body remember its Skywatcher ways. He cleared his mind. He sighted along the scope. He hummed and felt his power respond to the summons. He let it build and build and then he focused on the substance of the crystal and how its shape would bend and shape his beam of light. It was perfect. It would channel and focus his beam. He built up more power. He wished he could see close enough to see fissures in the rock, like they could observe on Ruelette and Rueline. But alas all that he could see was a pockmarked surface.

The power had built up and almost burned his mind. It was time to release. He let the power go and fed it steadily into the crystal. The beam shot out. The scope shuddered and nearly collapsed. Garan held it steady while he focused on what he could see of the heavens with the naked eye.

"You have reached it," Epen yelled, bent over his scope nearby.

Garan was focused on the object, which glowed mauve with his power. Yet, it did not yet break apart or move. He kept the power funneling through the crystal and the scope and felt when the rock detonated.

His scope fell silent and dull.

Epen was watching rapturously, gesticulating even as he peered through the scope. "I think...I see...oh..."

Garan checked his scope, too. The asteroid was still there, although its shape was different. It was smaller, but not destroyed. "Wing dust!" Garan said. "I'll try again."

"One moment," Epen said, lifting a hand to stay him. "Let me examine it again. I think you removed the rock. What remains may be the mineral. Let's be certain."

Garan stood back from the scope, heart torn between hope and disappointment. If only they could work it out. If only his power would do what he wanted it to do.

Chapter Twelve

DRAGONS UNDONE

Gercomo was hungry. There were no more young to eat.

Decimated, the herd had lost many breeding partners. It should not have ended like this. It was her again. Salinda. Why couldn't he kill her? Curse it, why hadn't he made sure? Why hadn't he killed her with his own hands? He'd been too sure of himself. He'd wanted to watch and gloat and see the hope leak from her eyes. He'd seen all that and still she had escaped.

Can't blame her. It's your fault. Same as being a dragon. Shut up!

Gercomo was losing it. Something, anything, had to happen. The red sky portended ill and food was just not there anymore. A few animal corpses filled his belly, but they had no purple glow, no life force to sustain him.

A large hatchling ambled slowly past his nesting place. The beast was bigger than Gercomo, but slow, befuddled by hunger. He lifted his head and looked at Bertha who lay in the sand nearby. *Eat hatchling*, he thought at her.

Her snout lifted and she blew out the dirt from her nostrils. She considered him and then her gaze moved to the hatchling, her head angling to one side, sizing it up. Gercomo got nothing back from her. No protest or surprise. She couldn't be bothered defending her herd mate.

Gercomo climbed to his feet and took a few steps. The hatchling was nosing in the ground, seeking something. Food, perhaps. The hatchling was obviously deranged and a danger to the herd. The bull gone, Gercomo didn't have to guard his thoughts.

The hatchling turned and Gercomo struck. Teeth straight into the neck. Rich blood gushed into Gercomo's mouth, filling him with power, with life. The hatchling threw its head around, trying to break free when, with a great crunch, something hit the little beast. Gercomo lost his hold and the hatchling dropped to the ground. Angry, Gercomo was ready to strike out, but there was Bertha looming over him. He saw in her eyes that she would fight him, to the death if she had to. He moved over and let Bertha tear a chunk of meat from the hatchling's shoulder. Gercomo resumed his slurping and bit a piece of ragged flesh for himself. Other dragons stumbled over. Gercomo growled at them and then continued to eat. They could have the scraps.

Belly full and reenergized, Gercomo strode back to his nesting place. Bertha eyed him. Her hunger and rage were less. She was no longer about to kill him, though she still blamed him. Blamed him for their defeat and the loss of over half the herd.

A streak of light pierced the red sky. That was not his fault. Definitely not his fault.

Gercomo slept, but his mind wasn't idle. He couldn't remain here. He had to use this energy to transform and once again join the human world. He knew where he had to go. Only with help would he survive what was coming. The baron's little haven was a wasteland. The fees the baron charged the elite lined his coffers, but what use was money when there was nowhere to spend it, nothing to buy and no life to live?

Gercomo jerked awake. The baron knew that the Eternity project was doomed. He had to. He wasn't a stupid man. That meant he had another plan. One for himself only.

Gercomo gagged with rage. He wouldn't put it past the baron to save the world just for himself. Bitter, twisted…deranged.

☙☙☙☙☙

Gercomo still had energy. A fact that surprised him. Bertha trudged on behind him, bellowing her frustration in cries that would have parted his hair in his human days. Gercomo ignored her. She chose to come because he was leaving. He didn't want her, except maybe her power and her blood. Both of those were useful, or had been.

A sound echoed across the tortured plain. The pockmarked surface swallowed shadows. It had rained rocks here recently. The roar grew louder and Gercomo tried to block it out. He was going to kill Bertha if she didn't shut up. She breathed fire at him, barely missing his hindquarters.

There was no letup of the sound and it was then he realized that the roar wasn't coming from her. His head jerked up and he saw what fell from the sky: a red-yellow ball of flame and rock and dirt went flying past. The ground shook with murderous intent, rattling Gercomo's remaining teeth.

Gercomo turned and loped away with an ungainly gait, letting out a scream as he did so.

He couldn't stop himself from turning back, from peering over his shoulder. Bertha turned slowly too. The air burned. Her wings flapped. Her panicked cry was loud and long. Gercomo almost felt sorry for her. In a desperate leap, she launched herself into the sky as flame melted the ground from under her. Gercomo dived for cover behind an array of boulders, slapping sand over his exposed flesh. The heat singed his skin and dried the saliva in his mouth. He caught a glimpse of Bertha struggling with the flame. The tips of her wings glowed dark purple, then lightened to lilac.

Gercomo shook, forepaws covering his head. Bit by bit, Bertha's wings dissolved. Plumes of violet light and shimmering silver streamed upward from her body. Her screams were swallowed by the roar of destruction around them. Air moving so fast, Gercomo could barely see. Even then he fought against the storm, lowered himself so that his underbelly scraped the rough stones beneath him.

Bertha was disintegrating as if the meteorite was gradually undoing her existence. Gercomo's heart thudded. It was beyond his comprehension that something so big and powerful as Bertha could be taken apart piece by piece, but it was happening as he watched. Her tail was a mere shadow now and her hindquarters writhed as she tried to shake whatever it was off. *Energy? Elemental fire? Magic?* The dark purple blotches covered her torso and her head, eating away at her substance. The spots left emptiness where Bertha's flesh had been.

Gercomo could bear no more. What if that came after him? Whatever that was. He shuffled around and slithered along on his belly as fast as he could go. The sand was hot and penetrating, no longer the warm protection he had enjoyed in previous times.

He scrambled faster, whimpers leaking out of his snout. The tips of his wings burned and with a glance at them, he shrieked. The dark purple blotches were on them, too. He bolted, leaped into the air and fought like his life depended on it. The burning didn't get worse. His wings worked. The air rocked him, threw him up, threw him sideways, and he kept his membranes extended. His thumping heart belied his steady flight. But he was not dissolving, not disappearing as Bertha had done.

As he gained height he saw the dust kicked up from the meteorite impact, saw it rolling along, billowing over crannies and valleys and up the sides of the mountains. Would any dragon be safe from that?

He was safe. He was clear. But not for long. He needed another way to survive.

Chapter Thirteen
INNER STRENGTH

Laidan knew her body was changing. It was firmer and stronger and she could run fast, faster than Danton, faster than Eneit, and not quite as fast as Brill. She laughed as she threw herself to the ground after making it back to their starting point in the node that held the little house that Brill and Danton shared.

Danton wheezed as he joined her on the ground where she reclined against the low wall. Eneit bent over double, catching her breath, and even Brill was breathing heavily. Maybe she had tested him after all, made him run hard to beat her. Laughter bubbled up again. For some strange reason she felt good. Happy. Happy to be doing something physical, something worthwhile.

"When do we leave for Sartell?" she asked Danton.

"Maybe tomorrow. Nils is working on a map for us. Actually, I think he said it was a series of markers so we could find our way back by ourselves. This afternoon we are crossing the lake to inspect N'Barek. Nils said he hasn't been over there to check it out, and I guess we need to work on a few logistics."

"Will Salinda be back before we leave?" Brill asked as he reached down into a bucket and scooped water over his head and took a long drink.

Danton shook his head. "I don't think so. She has to organize for an evacuation. I think that may take a few days. We can't afford to wait."

Brill shook his head. "You ready, E?" he said to Eneit, ruffling her hair, which had been cut short. It now stood up in spikes.

She pushed his hand away. "I'm always ready," she quipped. "Not like you, old man."

Brill grinned and Danton laughed at Eneit's cheek. Laidan saw the sadness in the other girl's eyes. Eneit had seen a lot. Laidan couldn't remember what she'd seen. Even Salinda said that it was best she didn't remember. It had been that bad. Salinda just gained a haunted look in her eyes when it came up in conversation.

Laidan shrugged and accepted the cup of water Brill handed her. She liked Brill. He was polite and fun, but Laidan found her mind more on what she could do. How well she could run and fight with the staves. How she had a purpose. How she could help.

Danton was going to give them unarmed combat lessons when they recovered from their run and before they ate. Laidan was hungry, but the water helped with that.

She had been curious to talk to the boy, Karol, but Nils kept him close. But she could wave and send him a smile. He did look an awful lot like Nils. She was pleased about that. Nils always seemed so lonely even though he had Salinda.

She tried to think what it would be like to be alone among strange creatures. For example, if she was the only human among Hiem. She guessed it would feel odd in lots of ways. As she surveyed her companions, she realized that they helped her feel at home and, to some extent, they understood her. Maybe not everything. How was that possible? Who really understood someone else? Take Garan, for example. He had power inside him and that must make him feel different and strange compared to others. Salinda was definitely strange, but Laidan found she did not dislike her or fear her, and something told her that in her previous life she had disliked Salinda a lot. It was there. An echo of a feeling.

"Right, then," Danton said, climbing to his feet with a small groan as if something didn't quite work properly. He had been badly wounded and Laidan shivered when she remembered his injuries when she had taken a turn nursing him after his latest bout of illness. She recalled how they all had thought he might die. She smiled at him before letting him pull her to her feet.

Eneit came up next to her and faced off against Brill. There followed lessons in trickery. Using the weight of the other person to throw them off balance. Well-placed feet, and places on hands to grip that hurt a lot and made the opponent cry out and unable to move. Laidan did all right with the lessons. She did not like being thrown or being choked, but provided she actually remembered these moves when and if she was attacked, she would be all right.

After an hour of this, they broke for a meal. "Later," Danton said, "we will get you to use those moves against us. But we won't give you warning. Then we will do more drills in the morning"

Laidan waved them off, keen to get some food. She and Eneit headed for their abode. After a quick wash, they set about putting the meal together. Eneit put food on their little table while Laidan took her turn to wash off the sweat.

"Do you think those moves would actually work?" Eneit asked as Laidan sat down opposite her.

"I hope so. Why?" Laidan asked.

Eneit cast her dark gaze down to her lap and picked her bread to pieces, dropping the crumbs onto her plate. "I know what it is like to be helpless. To fight and struggle and have it do nothing. I don't think those moves will work. Not in a real fight."

"Oh," Laidan said, with a frown. "Why don't you say something to Danton and Brill? Surely they can either teach us more or tell us we should just run."

Eneit put a piece of bread to her lips. "Running doesn't always work either."

"Are you worried? About going to Sartell?" Laidan asked.

Eneit's head rocked back. "No! No..." Her eyes narrowed. "It is just that I worry that you will get overconfident and take on someone without your weapon."

"Me? You're worried about me?" All kinds of emotions rocked through Laidan. Pleasure. Censure. Fear. Hurt. Love. "I don't know what to say...I mean, that is very good of you to think about me. Do you think I am not capable?"

Eneit shook her head. "No. I think you can fight. I just worry. I love you like a sister. Like a friend. I've lost too many people already. I don't want to lose you." Tears gathered in Eneit's eyes and she wiped at them. "I'm sorry. I shouldn't say that."

Laidan put her plate down and moved to sit next to Eneit, bringing the girl's head to her shoulder. "I love you too, Eneit. You have helped me so much and I will try very hard to be capable and not get hurt. We are going to help people remember? They won't want to hurt us."

"You don't know Sartell. Not everyone will want to be helped."

Laidan nodded. "I understand. We'll stick together and be careful."

Calls from Danton and Brill made them both scurry about and shove their food in their mouths. "They didn't give us very long."

Laidan exited first and soon had Danton's forearm around her throat. Lifting her foot, she back-kicked him in the knee. He let go. She turned and followed up with a punch, which he barely backed away from. "Sorry," she said, as she rubbed at her throat where he'd put pressure on her.

Danton was still recovering from an injury; she figured a kick to the knee might not dislodge a real attacker. Eneit's words were getting to her after all. Or maybe she was a realist. Turning the corner, Brill came at her with a weapon raised, some kind of club. She put up a defensive hand and punched him in the face with the other. Brill reeled back and fell to the ground.

Immediately, she felt remorse. "I'm so sorry," she said as she squatted by him. "I should have pulled my punch."

Brill shook his head. "No, I should have been ready for that. I thought you would trip me, not punch me." Blood trickled from his nostrils and he wiped at it with the back of his hand and sniffed. "Not bad, really," he said, examining the blood on his fingertips.

Laidan frowned. "Oh, yes, that is what you taught. I'm sorry I acted on instinct. Shall we try that again?"

Brill shook his head. "Maybe when we drill again. You two girls are pretty tough. I have a huge bruise on my shin from Eneit."

"Well," Laidan said as she helped Brill to stand, "she has been attacked, remember. I think this training has upset her."

Brill's eyes widened, the blue in them suddenly bright. He smacked his forehead. "I didn't think. *Wing dust!* I'd better talk to Danton. Maybe she should stay behind."

Laidan put a hand on his shoulder to stop him. "I don't think that's the way to do it. I think maybe...I don't know...acknowledging that these moves don't always work and it is best to stay safe, keep your stick or other weapon by your side..." She shrugged. "I don't know really...just thinking out loud."

Brill's gaze narrowed and he studied her before nodding his head. "No, you're right. They are good ideas."

"She wants to fight. Don't get me wrong...it was something she said and then I remembered what happened to her, what you said happened, I mean. She doesn't talk about it. But I think today it's come back to her."

Brill flashed her a grin. "I'll talk to Danton and then we'll start the drill again. You need to do them instinctively, and maybe other precautions too."

Then he was gone. Laidan went back to her abode and stretched out on the bed. Time to rest and to think. Had she done the right thing by Eneit? She didn't want Eneit to be scared or frightened or for her to worry unnecessarily. Laidan had to take Eneit's warnings to heart, too. Hadn't she forgotten a move and hit Brill? It had seemed effective to her, but Brill might think otherwise. She hoped he didn't get a black eye. Eneit came in later and crawled into her bed.

☙☙☙☙☙

When they assembled for the next drill session, Danton asked them to sit and Eneit and Brill and Laidan positioned themselves with crossed feet and back straight. Danton paced in front of them, hand on his chin. He'd lost the beard and Laidan wished he'd grow it back. He had a scar along his chin. It marred his beauty, more than the missing eye—the eye patch, in fact, gave him a kind of raffish air. Without the facial hair to cover the scar, he looked vulnerable or something. Not that Laidan would say such a thing to him. The scar made him look like he had lost something of himself, that was it.

"You're learning these moves to help you in case you get into trouble. However, they aren't foolproof. They are designed to give you a fighting chance. They don't make you invincible. Understand?"

They all said yes. "And you have to take precautions. That means following orders without question. I say *run*. You run. I say *duck*, you duck. If I can't give an order, you listen to Brill. We will do our best to safeguard you, but these moves that you're learning are there to help if something doesn't go to plan or we are surprised in some way. Or maybe in the future you have someone trying to touch you in a way you don't like. Get it? Then you can let them know in a flash you won't let them touch you."

Eneit and Laidan shared a look and then said, "Yes, Danton."

"All right. Assume your positions. This time Eneit versus Laidan. Brill and I will comment and make suggestions."

Brill touched his cheek where there was a red swelling. Laidan tried not to grin. She was sorry for hurting him, after all.

It turned out that Eneit was very fierce, and Laidan's rear end became covered in bruises as she was tossed, thrown, tripped and otherwise wrestled to the ground, over and over again. She had sore spots on her knees, ribs and elbows. Eneit, on the other hand, did not seem to be any the worse for wear. Laidan had managed to toss her once, but the girl was compact and wiry and seemed to morph into a wildcat when cornered. Brill and Danton tried to give her instructions and in the end just shook their heads. "She's a scrapper," Danton said.

Brill grinned. "You're not wrong. I would not like to meet her in a dark alley."

Eneit grinned. It was as if they had given her the highest praise. Laidan rubbed her sore back and then her elbow. It was all right for them. Eneit hadn't beaten them to a pulp. Yet, in her heart, she was happy for Eneit. That sense of gloom that hung around her had dissipated. Brill and Danton were really quite clever, after all.

ﾟ◯ﾟ◯ﾟ◯ﾟ◯ﾟ

Danton enjoyed the trip across the lake. It was better than he'd thought it would be. The far city was very dark from this viewpoint, but his surroundings weren't pitch black, like a night without stars would be. Shuwai cast its wan light so he was able to see. Not so well that he could pick out his fingernails, but he could make out the outline of the others on the raft.

Nils sat at the front. Danton and Brill had been building this raft as a side project as any other boats were long since gone. Some of the trees in the gardens had proved to be useful for making things, such as furniture, this raft. The trees were a cross between a palm and a fruit tree and the wood was soft and easily cut. Nils had informed them the leaves were used for making cloth, and the tall, narrow trunks were naturally buoyant. It didn't take long for Danton and Brill to consider the material useful for making a raft. Danton had drawn a picture and carefully explained how it would work to Nils before they assembled it.

They could have taken the Travel Way to N'Barek but, traditionally, the Hiem went by boat and Nils liked the idea of doing it the old-fashioned way. They were going to return to Barrahiem using the Ways to make sure that that route was functioning as it should. It was obvious that Nils, while willing to have humans take refuge in deserted Hiem cities, was uncomfortable with them coming directly to Barrahiem. N'Barek, the lesser city, was a good compromise for resettlement of refugees. They would be safe, and negotiating later transfer to Barrahiem could be tackled when Nils was more comfortable sharing with others, beside their immediate group. Nils had not walked the streets of N'Barek since before Ruel fell and thus appeared to be contemplating the visit with subdued reverence.

Danton had heard a hint or two that there was a story around Nils's survival. Salinda had mentioned a sarcophagus of some kind that had held Nils in sleep, but she hadn't elaborated. Maybe she didn't know why Nils had been in that thing. Maybe he didn't want to talk about it. Either way, Danton couldn't help being curious. Nils was so straitlaced that if he broke a rule or something it would itch at his mind, and he definitely wouldn't want to talk about it.

The lake waters were dark and still as they crossed. It gave Danton the creeps as he plunged the oar in. Brill worked at the paddle on his side, changing positions now and again to keep them on track. Eneit sat in the middle of the raft and Laidan draped her hand over the side, watching the water as it passed through her fingers. Her expression was thoughtful.

Danton liked this new Laidan. Not that he had disliked the old one, but she had been transparently a creature of her own desires, out of control and a recipe for disaster. He knew what had happened to her and no one deserved such a fate. But now, she was different, more focused and more settled. Had that Laidan always been inside, waiting for the right moment, or had it required the destruction of the young, superficial Laidan? She was still as beautiful as before, but Danton also noticed something missing, some spark behind her eyes. They no longer danced with delight when she looked at Brill. Danton let out a sigh. None of them had escaped harm. None of them were the same as they once had been. All had been shaped by events.

He did not care to look too closely at himself—what was left of himself. It was daunting. He thought that if he did, he would cut his own throat and the only thing preventing such an act was that he still had some use, that maybe he could serve Salinda and the cause one more time and, perhaps, make up for his betrayal. He had told all under torture and it unnerved him. He no longer trusted himself and that was one scary proposition.

"In my day," Nils said, "there were lights on the lake to illuminate the waters and show travelers the way. I have looked out over N'Barek and wondered about the city. About what I would find there."

"Sounds lovely," Eneit said as she watched Nils. "Why was it called the lesser city?"

Nils looked up and met Eneit's earnest stare. "It was built after Barrahiem and it was smaller, so I think that is why. Our population grew at some stage and a couple of clans moved to N'Barek. There they made new homes and made trade with Barrahiem."

"Did you have friends at N'Barek?" Eneit asked.

Nils did a good impression of a frown as he formed his answer. "No. Actually, I did not. I knew people who were from there or who had family there, but not so close as to call them friends."

"And were they the same as you?"

"What do you mean, child?" he asked.

"I mean, did you think of them as equal and the same? Sometimes, if someone is from another town people look down on them and call them names and say they are dirty or smelly or stupid. I wondered if that was what it was like if you were from N'Barek."

Nils shook his head. "Perhaps there was some rivalry, some lighthearted pranking, but no. They were Hiem, and every Hiem is Hiem no matter where they came from. Sundwellers—humans—" he corrected, "did not perfectly understand us even though they used our services. Being different and being a minority meant that we had to be careful and watchful, particularly when alone with the humans."

Eneit nodded and sent her gaze out over the lake and to the city that was growing more distinct as they neared. "Did you have a girlfriend when you were younger?"

Nils stiffened his spine and then smiled. "I did." At this he lowered his head.

"What was her name?" Eneit asked with the persistence of the young.

"Luca," Nils replied. "We liked each other very well."

"Why didn't you marry her?" Eneit asked. Danton gritted his teeth. If he had been closer he would have poked the girl to quiet her, but he could do nothing except watch and listen with interest.

"Mmm…" Nils began. "It was complicated. You see, I was betrothed to another, Acendrian, and to try to marry Luca was a big insult."

Eneit lifted her head, startled, and stared at him. "You had two girlfriends?"

Nils looked up to the ceiling. "Yes, I suppose that is a way of putting it. I was a bit of a rebel."

"A rebel?" Eneit said, turning to meet Danton's eye.

"A different kind of rebel," Danton supplied in response to the unanswered question.

Eneit sent Nils a grin. "How were you a rebel?"

Nils studied his fingers. "I wanted to have a career looking at the stars, but the elders chose the career of a historian for me. I would not agree. We were at a standoff. Then one day I tried to run away with Luca. We were caught."

"Oh, and then what happened?"

Brill cautioned Eneit. "Eneit…maybe…"

But Nils held up a hand. "The tale is begun and I have a need to finish it." Acendrian's family were very angry. Even though I agreed after pressure to marry Acendrian, she would not have me. I had given her great insult by not only loving another, but by running away from my duty. Not only my duty to her but to my people. It had been explained to me why I could not follow my chosen career. For a long time I told myself it was because there was already another in that profession—Trell, my grandsire. But it was also because I did not meet the requirements. I refused to listen to them and asked to resit the exams. Even when I failed to pass the second time, I took my anger out on them. I rebelled against the authority of my clan and my people. I would not listen to anyone…"

There was a catch in Nils's voice. Danton's eyebrows lifted when he detected it. There was more, and Eneit's straightforward questioning was going to solve a mystery.

"There was a fight. I injured someone." Nils looked up. "One of the guards who was sent to bring me to the Hall of Elders for judgment. He had to go into the healing tray as a result of his injuries. I had not meant to hurt him but…he fell badly.

"My mother, Isagar, witnessed this because she had come to beg me to see reason. I was young and unwilling to bend. But, when I saw the result of my actions, it was like a cloak had been lifted from my eyes. I saw my actions laid out in front of me. I saw them for what they were. Vanity. Pride. Overweening ambition, without any substance to aspire to such things. I will never forget my mother's weeping when the sentence was passed on me. They did not kill me—such is not the Hiem way—but they did put me to sleep, and for a long time. I went to sleep knowing I would see none of my immediate kin ever again. My mother was lost to me. My father, too, although we had not spoken for years. Sometimes I like to amuse myself by blaming others, but I see clearly now how it was my own fault."

Eneit scooted over and put her hand on Nils's. "That is a sad story, Nils. But if you hadn't been put to sleep you wouldn't be here to help us now. We would all be dead. No one would know about the Travel Ways. No one would have helped Salinda." She smiled at him, tears in her eyes. "We owe you everything. So maybe, just maybe, it was meant to be."

Nils looked at the girl, his eyes glowing silver. "You are too wise for one so young. Thank you." Eneit lifted her hand and then scooted back to her position in the middle of the raft. Out of the gloom loomed the first signs of N'Barek, white balconies appearing as if out of thin air.

"Look," Brill shouted, "there it is."

Danton turned away from watching Nils and Eneit and faced the city. Laidan, too, lifted her hand from the water and focused on what was ahead.

"There should be a shore…somewhere to put up the raft," Nils said, but the balconies grew closer and there was still no sign of a shoreline. The raft kept moving, propelled along with their momentum. Then it was clear that the water was higher than it once had been. Lower houses were half-submerged and some buildings had collapsed. N'Barek had not survived as well as Barrahiem.

"There has been some subsidence," Nils commented as his eerie gaze swept the cityscape. "There, you can tie up there." He pointed along the western edge where the roof of a submerged house would serve as a pier. Brill saluted and he and Danton paddled the raft in that direction. Laidan was kneeling and staring at the city.

"Your people lived there too?" she asked Nils.

"Our people did."

Danton did a double take and then remembered what Salinda had told him. Nils believed that Salinda and Laidan had Hiem blood. Laidan had the coloring but Salinda was as ordinary as any of them: all part something, mixed race. They had had to interbreed to survive. Danton looked down at his tanned arms, pale now that he had been out of the sun, but obviously he was not white, like the Hiem had been. Salinda was near his own coloring, her shapely dark eyes speaking of her mixed heritage. Brill, with his blue eyes and blond hair, was more of a rarity, but even then his skin had that yellow tone and he tanned easily. Garan had olive tones to his skin, but his eye color was violet, a hint of something else. Danton shook his head. Nothing about Garan was ordinary. The world was a strange place.

He picked up their rope and leaped onto the roof, pulled the raft close, and helped Nils, then Laidan and Eneit, to cross over. Brill lifted up his pole and took a leap and together they tugged the raft onto the roof so it wouldn't float away. The city smelled of water, new and old. Near where the water met the buildings there was debris, and a kind of dusty film. The inundation could be recent, then, sweeping debris from the city into the lake's waters.

Nils handed out lights, as the city was not lit as Barrahiem was. There was plenty of shuwai, but that light was muted. "Come!" Nils said as he leaped to a stair that was not far from the edge of the roof. "We must explore quickly. We must see if it is fit for habitation."

Danton couldn't argue with that so he watched as the others joined Nils, and then followed, although not without a quick look around at the lake and to make sure the raft was really secure.

Nils then led them upward. Remembering what they had discussed about Gateshead, Danton knew that Hiem cities had a similar layout. Water trickled down the stairway and here and there were piles of soil. A few houses were cracked with one slumped down and dark emptiness spilling out

"This way," Nils said, leaning over the balustrade of the balcony above. Danton saw Eneit climbing and went to follow. He had to stay focused as he did not want to get lost here. Something was clearly wrong, and it was eerie, too.

Danton joined the group. From N'Barek, Barrahiem was a bright beacon of light on the distant shore of the lake. Nils's gaze ranged over the N'Barek. "We must be careful. I think it is stable now, but this subsidence could be recent."

"The tremor from the other day?" Brill ventured.

Nils's head turned in Brill's direction. "Perhaps. But there may be other issues."

"But the water did not rise on the other side." Danton had thought of this straight up.

"No. Not noticeably. But there is some obvious local subsidence here."

They climbed up into the city and to the remains of the Hall of Elders. Here, the decline was evident. Nils's light shone on decaying walls, the murals blemished with mold and crumbling plaster. The sacred lamp had been smashed at some point. What remained was a pile of rubble. The room where a healing tray should have been was empty. The wall that should have housed a machine was a gaping hole. Danton narrowed his gaze. This place had been ransacked. Maybe long ago but ransacked just the same. Not so Barrahiem. It was a city of the dead and as untouched as the day people had died or left.

Nils's sent him a look of thunder. "Everything has been taken. Even the lights."

Danton cast his gaze around. He was right. Where Barrahiem had lights, there was nothing but empty spaces.

"Would the Hiem have done this when they left?" he asked Nils.

He shook his head. "It is hard to credit, but it's possible they took the equipment with them. But someone did this."

"A long time ago, Nils. There hasn't been anyone here recently. There is so much dust settled on what remains. Let's search elsewhere. Can we reach the Travel Ways?"

Nils backed up. His expression was lost as his gaze travelled around him. His hand covered his mouth and he shook his head. The beauty of the place had been erased.

"Nils?" Danton repeated.

Nils turned, shook himself. "You are right, of course. Let us see if we can access the Ways."

It did not take long to find the stair and the Way Gate. While there was debris lining the path, the Way was clear and unblocked. Nils keyed the gate and it opened smoothly.

"Perhaps this is how they left," Eneit ventured.

"Yes, I think so, too," Danton said and ruffled the girl's hair. She slapped his hand away.

Nils disappeared from view. Danton was not worried as Nils had agreed to check whether the Ways were clear for them to travel to N'Barek unimpeded. He studied the city. Was this going to be the right place to put these people? If there had been subsidence, would there be more? Would Barrahiem succumb?

N'Barek did not have archive tunnels beneath it, like Barrahiem did. As a newer structure, it was not built over the remains of the Moon Binder artifacts and machines. There were no archives to be lost if the city flooded. But still, could people live here?

The sounds of Nils returning warned them of his approach. Danton placed his attention on the Way Gate. Nils emerged in a flow of white robes. "The way is clear."

"What about the city?" Danton asked. "Will it be safe?"

"For the moment, as safe as anywhere," Nils replied.

"Do you want us to bring the refugees here?"

"Yes, for now. If there are problems, we can discuss bringing them to Barrahiem later."

Danton did not push the issue. Nils needed time to trust. They did not know what kind of people they were bringing in, so Nils's approach was best. It would give them all time to adjust and deal with any major issues, or curtail disruptive elements. In the mad rush to save people they had no means to recognize or separate the worthy from the unworthy.

Obviously, if Danton saw the baron or any of his cronies, he'd cull them out good and proper straight away.

For just a second, Danton had doubts that they were doing the right thing. Then he shook it off. Who was he to judge who lived and died? They weren't guaranteeing anything. They were offering a chance to survive, to make it to the next step if moonfall was averted. If they could save the planet then these people would be able to inhabit it. That was all. No promises. Just a slim chance.

Nils led them down to the foundations of the city. Laidan and Eneit preferred to explore so it was Brill and Danton who accompanied him. "What do you hope to find?" Danton asked, looking around him nervously.

There was something eerie about this place. Danton had to admit that Barrahiem was eerie, too, but it at least had some inhabitants now.

"Evidence of when the subsidence occurred. If it is recent then this place would not be any use to your refugees. We would be giving them false hope. If a lot older, then it was from another cause."

"What other cause would that be?" Danton asked, even though he could think of only one: warfare. But that seemed unlikely given who the Hiem were. Danton considered that thought. What he knew of the Hiem came from Nils and, by his own account, he had been already in his prison of sleep when the end came. What did he really know about the true nature of his people at the end? Danton only had to look to his own kind to see what desperation and fear could do. Brill had said often that given the right circumstances humans could shine again, that they could once more care for and nurture each other. It was the vision of Brill's father, Hubert. Brill still clung to it and Danton had let it creep into his heart like a faint hope.

They followed along behind Nils, his blue outer robe billowing as he took the steps down into the dark depths quickly. His light would sometimes momentarily disappear and Danton would feel a moment of panic, although he had his own light and so did Brill. They kept them unlit, though, while they were in such a narrow corridor and Nils was leading them.

"Here we are," Nils said as his voice was muffled, then echoed up to them.

"About time," Danton said, with Brill close behind. "That stairwell was giving me the creeps."

Brill chuckled. "You? Afraid of the dark? Never."

Danton laughed but stopped abruptly as Nils swung round, his eyes glowing silver. "Is there something funny?"

Danton shook his head. "No. Never mind…"

"Danton is afraid of the dark."

Nils's eyes rested on Danton. "Is this true?" He lifted his hand. "I have light."

"Look, the kid was just teasing me. I can cope with the dark. It's a joke."

Nils nodded, his expression glazing over. "I confess I do not like this place. I feel the ghosts here quite strongly."

Brill and Danton exchanged a glance. Brill made a face of mock horror and Danton covered his mouth to stop from chuckling.

Nils walked along the wall of the long room they were standing in. "See here?"

Brill stood, hands on hips. "What?"

"This was where some of the supports to the lower city were."

There was nothing there. "I don't follow." Brill made way for Danton to take a look. Danton knelt down and ran his fingers along where the wall and floor joined. "It's rather smooth."

Nils squatted next to him. "That was my thought. There were a series of pillars. They are gone. I believe they were taken out."

"How is that even possible?" Brill commented, looking up.

Danton lifted his head to inspect the site. There was nothing but gloom up there.

"I cannot say why it was done, but it would account for the subsidence."

Danton turned to Nils and looked up at Brill. "You say they did it deliberately?"

Nils stood up and dusted off his fingers by rubbing his hands together. "It makes no sense, but then, what makes sense in this world anymore? It could be that people would not evacuate so someone or a faction did this to force the issue." Nils glared at the place around him.

"It bothers you, not knowing, doesn't it?" Danton asked as he too stood and wiped his hands on his trousers.

"You begin to understand me. It haunts me. The destruction upstairs, for instance. Was the equipment just destroyed or taken elsewhere, and if so, where?"

Danton let out a long sigh. He understood. Was there something out there in the wrong hands? But Danton had heard no rumors of strange beings, or unknown equipment being in use, and he had been around a while. "You heard anything, Brill?"

The lad had had a good education, fancy tutors and the like. Brill bit his lip and shook his head.

Nils raised his light. "I think we have seen enough. Let us head back."

With long strides, Nils ascended the stairs in quick time. Danton was close behind and Brill brought up the rear. "So we bring the refugees here?" Brill asked.

Nils's answer floated down. "Yes."

Danton grinned. They were ready to go.

Chapter Fourteen
A RENDEZVOUS
AND A LOST SOUL

Gercomo sweated underneath the hooded cloak he had stolen from an unwary traveler. Coming to Sartell to find the baron was a big risk, but he was desperate. He could only pass for human if he kept himself covered and didn't speak, or at least spoke little.

After transforming back to human shape, he found he was even less human than before. It had taken a while for his mind to kick in, for thoughts to move away from dragon concerns. He had no mirror. However, the scream of utter terror when he had showed himself to the unwary traveler demonstrated that he did not look pretty, or even human, except that he now had two legs. The man hadn't had to be afraid for long, as Gercomo had clawed his throat out.

The cloak was long at the back and that helped to disguise his tail. Yet he kept his head down. There was an awful lot of guards in the streets. Gercomo sniffed the air and his mouth watered. There was dead meat close by. Lots of it. Come of think of it, normal people were scarce, and traffic, too. Just a few carts and big wagons with guards on them.

So far, he had been unhindered in his passage through Sartell. He had entered from the wharf area because that was closer to where the baron lived. While Sartell was fairly safe generally, he doubted that, grotesque as he was, anyone would have any second thoughts about mobbing and killing him where he stood. Yet, there was something in the air here. Something not quite right that he couldn't pick.

He turned the corner and looked up quickly before lowering his head again. Guards stood around at the entrance to the street.

A spear was lowered in front of him. "You there. What's yer business?"

Gercomo halted, heart thumping. He wasn't anywhere near close enough to the baron and as yet he had said nothing more than *yessth* or *nosthh* when required, which had got him by. This required more.

Obviously, Gercomo wasn't fast enough. The guard shoved him hard on the shoulder. Gercomo stepped back. Not that the man's shove was too strong, but he didn't want to seem abnormal.

"Hhhhooomeesth," Gercomo said and cringed at the sound of his own voice.

"Fuck me," said one of the guards, coming up to join them. "He sounds like a Lesseren."

The guard who had shoved him nodded slowly. "Yeah, sure does. Lift yer hood."

There was a spread of snickering as other guards took notice and then formed a ring around Gercomo.

"I'm hungry," called one. "Lesserens are food."

Gercomo stood stock-still while he processed this. The sky above was black and streaked with dark-gray clouds, a gift of dust from the meteor that had hit recently. He had survived, but what of the humans? The atmospheric conditions would have had an effect and the towns that supplied grains and other foodstuffs may not have fared as well as the residents of Sartell. If the man was telling the truth and Lesserens were food, then they were desperate. Gercomo's gaze travelled past the guards and up the tree-lined street to the neighborhood where the baron lived.

The weapon was brought up toward his face. Gercomo kept motionless. There was nothing to do but let the situation play out. There was no point in denying he was a Lesseren. Not with his present mouth and the way he shaped or didn't shape words.

The spear tip lifted the cowl on his cloak. The man jumped back in fright. "Fuck!"

The other guards recoiled. "What is it?" said the bravest of them.

They recovered their courage and moved forward, bringing their lances up as if they were going to prod him like some dead creature washed up on the beach.

Their grins widened and he saw the glee in their eyes, until Gercomo grinned. Then they recoiled again and some screamed. The guard in front of him was too late to duck the swipe Gercomo unleashed. His claws slashed the flesh of the man's face to ribbons. His hands dropped the lance and went to his face. He continued to scream until Gercomo relieved him of his guts.

Throwing off his cloak, he lunged for the next guard and brought his tail up to topple the one next to him. The spear shaft shattered with Gercomo's blow and then he bit into the man's throat, his jagged tooth catching on the soft flesh and making a large gash. Blood fountained up, landing on the dirt of the road like the patter of heavy rain. The other man Gercomo gripped by the throat, lifted him bodily and threw him at the others.

The screams were a melody. Some of the remaining guards tried to run, others whimpered, crumpling to the ground in puddles of piss and shit. Gercomo scraped up a fallen guard by the legs and bit and ripped. The man's blood spurted into his mouth and it ran down Gercomo's naked scaly body.

The taste of the man's flesh was wonderful. Gercomo's dragon aspect throbbed with bloodlust. It wanted to eat them all, but Gercomo realized the remainder of his quarry had fled as he stood alone in the street, surrounded by corpses. He scooped up his pilfered cloak and draped it back over himself. Easing a crick out of his neck, he stepped down the avenue, hoping that the baron was at home. It would be really annoying if Gercomo had to go looking for him.

Jittery voices followed Gercomo's path to the baron's residence. He glanced around him, but could see no one. As there was no threat, he didn't bother rooting them out of their hiding place, whoever they were. His tale swished against the dirt on the road. Looking down, Gercomo saw that it was ash and dust. Sartell had not escaped the asteroid's impact. No wonder there was chaos and fear. Thinking on the feeling he had had on entering the city, along with the guards' behavior, the last piece of the puzzle fit into place. Sartell was imploding. It was in its death throes.

Gercomo quickened his step, realizing that he might be too late. The baron may have already fled. He took note of the houses as he walked. Some were damn fine constructions, now with broken windows and furniture strewn on the remains of well-kept lawns. Trees that had once been magnificent were layered in dust and sagged. Some showed signs of dying. None of these were the baron's house. He moved along the street and then it appeared before him. The unkempt, disheveled exterior looked even worse, if that was possible, than Gercomo remembered from his visit so many years ago.

Memories he thought were long hidden came surging forth. The baron fucking and then discarding him. The baron urging him on to destroy one of his toys, the boy's black eyes already dead. The remaining life in them extinguished by Gercomo.

And Salinda dressed in her finery. Her frozen expression of muted joy, the mask where she hid her pain, locked in place. The cruel sound of her bitter laugh. Oh, so much had happened in this house. Why did he cling to the baron? What did the baron do to him? What made him so loyal? Gercomo didn't know the exact moment, or what it was that occurred in particular. Was it one thing? No, it was many things, piled up high like a stack of mattresses in a barracks. This was where Gercomo had been born.

Gercomo strode up the path, noting that there was no furniture spread on the lawn, no signs that the place had been ransacked and the inhabitants fled. No one opened the door when he rang the bell. The house was silent.

Gercomo inhaled and picked up the scent. The question was, did he want to break the door down? Would the baron appreciate that? Maybe not.

He pounded on the door. "Letsssth mee innnn," he said. He didn't need to shout because his voice was hard and rough and it would reach right down into the earth. No doubt the baron was down in a bunker, hiding away from the chaos let loose in the city. He thumped the door again and the wood made a ripping sound as if he had broken something.

"If you do that again, I will have you killed you where you stand," the baron said from behind him.

Gercomo lowered his clawed hand and turned. The baron stood there with his retinue. Gercomo hadn't been wrong. He had smelled them. They just weren't inside the house.

The baron cast a significant look at the end of the street. "Your handiwork, I take it?"

Gercomo gave a superficial bow of his head in acknowledgment. The baron's retinue included six burly guards holding various sharp weapons in plain sight and who knew what else hidden in their raiments. "You are proving to be interesting, Gercomo, I'll give you that. And as it happens," he said, as he casually walked forward to his front door, "I have a use for you."

Gercomo stepped back and let the baron unlock his door. A few small boys trailed him, plus two body servants. The baron did not appear to be suffering from any significant loss of status in Sartell, though the occasional agonized scream piercing the air indicated that the city was going through some traumatic final convulsions. Gercomo wasn't surprised that the baron seemed untouched, removed from the chaos.

Gercomo stepped back so that the retinue could pass inside. The guards eyed him carefully. A big bull of a man—bald, and with shoulders that rivaled Gercomo's own dragonized physical form—grunted and spat before entering the building. Gercomo just inclined his head and studied the fellow. The man's days were numbered.

The baron called out. "Come in, Gercomo. I want to look at you."

Gercomo grinned. The baron hadn't been so interested before. He'd only been interested in Gercomo's ability to summon dragons and detect Salinda. It appeared that the baron had some leisure time on his hands. Gercomo sniffed the surroundings. A layer of dust and death settled on his tongue. He was made curious by this play of the baron's. He would cooperate for old time's sake.

His clawed feet scraped against the ceramic-tiled corridor as he made his way to the main reception room. Gercomo inhaled deeply and detected hints of old blood and, if he was fanciful, old suffering.

Easing the tension from his back, Gercomo tried to get more comfortable. He had not been in a house for a very long time. Looking up, he could see that he was quite close to the ceiling and his tail swished behind him, not quite sure what it was meant to do. Gercomo only found the thing useful when flying, and occasionally as a weapon. Not that he could manipulate the appendage easily—it was more a hit and flick mechanism. More often than not with a mind of its own.

As he entered the reception room, he saw the baron sitting down in a large, ornate chair. It was the biggest in the room. The baron had lost weight since last they met and there were lines of strain around his mouth and eyes. At his feet sat the boys and his servants flanked him. The guards stood arrayed against the wall.

"Take off that cloak, Gercomo. I want to see what you look like," the baron said in a silky voice.

Gercomo considered saying no. He considered launching himself at this assemblage and biting their heads off. Yet there was something in the baron's eye, something that appealed to Gercomo. A glint of lust in those dark, beady eyes. Gercomo had not thought of himself as desirable in this state before. Given the baron's taste for young boys, he wondered that a half-man/half-beast was in his style. On the other hand, perhaps the baron wanted Gercomo to prove his loyalty and obedience. Gercomo wondered about that, wondered again why he was here now. It was that damn asteroid. It changed everything for him. That and the fact that the dragon was taking over. He had transformed back into human form, but this time he was less human, more dragon. It was affecting his mind as well.

Gercomo stepped forward and noticed the guards tense. He grinned his feral grin and flicked off his hood. The guards who hadn't guessed what lay beneath the hood recoiled. The burly guard who had spat at him didn't react like the others. His face screwed up and his eyes narrowed and a growl of pure hatred issued from his throat. The baron hissed for him to shut up before gesturing to Gercomo to continue.

The boys at the baron's knees put trembling hands out to grasp each other. Obviously, the baron hadn't worked on them yet, if they were still capable of giving support to each other, still able to fear. The baron was getting soft in his old age.

Gercomo clawed the cloak from his shoulders and stepped out of it as it fell in a heap behind him. The baron's eyes widened and he licked his lips. "Magnificent," he said, breathing hard as if the very sight of Gercomo had given him an erection. The little boys crawled away behind the seat, peeking out from the trailing end of the baron's cloak. The baron paid them no mind.

Gercomo straightened his shoulders, baring his chest for all to see. His long thick legs supported his enlarged penis. Scales and skin were meshed together like patchwork over his body. His large hands, with broken, bloodstained claws, hung limp at his side and his tail swished against the tiles. It was longer than his legs and tapered to a fine point.

"Are you aware of how breathtaking you are?" the baron asked. He lifted a hand and a servant kneeled. "Bring the large mirror. I want him to see."

Wary, Gercomo stood still and watched. The guards were nervous. A bearded one was tugging at his facial hair. One had a scar across his cheek and it had grown redder. The burly guard tensed as if getting ready to strike. Gercomo had the measure of the man.

The two servants carried out a round mirror. Gercomo hid his surprise. He was ugly, so ugly that his stomach churned. Such a grotesque excuse for a human, he didn't deserve to live. That is what he would have thought if he had seen someone like this when he was human. His eyes were like a dragon's: slitted irises, glowing with power. Gercomo could see the violet light in them. His mouth was a snout, which explained why speech was so difficult this time.

His cock was the only impressive thing. It was not limp, but nor was it erect. His was in a state of potential arousal. Gercomo turned to see behind the rest of him. His tail was pure dragon, sleek scales of mauve and green. Where his wings usually extended, sat mounds of flesh and muscle like a dual humpback. Gercomo sneered at the sight. He was repulsive. He should leave before the baron made a mockery of him.

The baron's approach caught him unawares and Gercomo hissed as a hand touched his shoulder. The baron didn't flinch. He wasn't afraid, just curious and turned on. Gercomo could smell it on him. What now? A performance of some kind? A show of fealty?

The baron stood in front of him. "Kneel, my friend."

Gercomo did as he was bid, wondering what was going to happen next. The movement was awkward, difficult with limbs that protested the bending of knee. The baron caressed his scalp, his fingers tracing the indents where flesh and scale merged. He whispered in Gercomo's ear. "I want to see you fuck."

Gercomo said nothing. The guards had moved as one and each held a projectile weapon. Perhaps Gercomo would kill some of them before they killed him. It was a show of loyalty, then. Gercomo considered just killing the baron, but where would that leave him? Gercomo didn't know what came next. He needed the baron for that.

Who was to be his meat? The baron loved pain and suffering. Gercomo's gaze raked the guards and rested on the one who had spat at him. He lifted a clawed finger and pointed. "Himsth."

The man's eyes widened and his gaze flicked to the baron, a protest on his mouth, mute appeal in his expression.

The baron grinned. "Good choice. Vult, drop your weapons. Disrobe, and come here."

To Vult's credit, he didn't argue or beg. He just methodically took out his weapons and laid them neatly on the floor as if he would be coming right back for them. With hate in his eyes, he stripped off his clothes and placed them neatly next to his gear.

"You know the rules," the baron said, retaking his seat. "Follow my instructions. You first, Vult."

Gercomo grinned, and then hissed. He was to kneel on all fours and lift his tail. Vult grinned and rubbed his cock in readiness. His massive shoulders bunched and his thighs were like trunks. His cock was impressive, although nothing compared to Gercomo's. Vult flexed his stomach muscles and his cock rose up hard and ready.

"Don't worry, Gercomo," the baron said. "I'm sure it won't hurt a bit and I'm curious about that tail of yours. I'm going to watch."

Vult shoved Gercomo's tail up and Gercomo bit back the urge to slash and slay. Gercomo gouged the floor tiles as Vult had at him. The baron had drawn near, his breathing heavy as he watched Vult fuck. Gercomo felt nothing, other than the humiliation of being an object of curiosity. He should be admired for his mind, his power.

Seeing he was being watched, Vult upped the aggression, thumping into Gercomo's hole. Gercomo was going to kill that bastard. Not that it hurt. It was the glee Vult exuded. As if fucking Gercomo made him stronger, better...more.

When it was his turn, Gercomo would try to make it slow and excoriating, but these days he had little finesse and little patience.

"It really is a tail. Fascinating," the baron said.

Vult came with a yell and withdrew quickly, spilling cum over Gercomo's hide. "Lesseren," he hissed as he stood back, shoving Gercomo's tail negligently aside.

The baron took his seat with a grin. "Now, Gercomo. I want to see you fuck Vult with that huge cock of yours. You can do what you want to him...be as soft or as hard as you like. He lacks discipline and good sense."

Vult made to protest, but Gercomo surged upright and grabbed Vult by the throat, throwing him back against the wall. Vult screamed in terror. Gercomo knelt before the guard and the man's legs shook as he licked the man's cock. Surprised, Vult's breath hitched and after a few more licks, he had relaxed. He probably thought he was going to get to come in Gercomo's mouth.

At the moment of relaxation, Gercomo bit and tore at the flesh of the man's groin. Blood curtained the man's legs. Vult screamed and tried to push Gercomo away. The sound of his panic was music to Gercomo's ears. Then he stood and shoved Vult down on all fours. The man was powerless in Gercomo's grip. Then he really screamed as Gercomo shoved his huge cock into his ass. The man gurgled and groaned, body tensing, then growing floppy. Gercomo gripped both sides of his buttocks, and rent him in half with the strength of his clawed hands and the thrust of his engorged penis.

When the remains of Vult stopped twitching, Gercomo withdrew and looked at his blood-soaked body, a grin on his face. He turned at the sound of the baron clapping. A few of the guards were openly weeping. The small boys were nowhere to be seen and one of the servants had vomited and lay on the floor in a swoon.

Gercomo bowed. He could not voice the things he wanted to say. *Is your curiosity satisfied? Have I proved myself?* He would only mangle them.

The baron seemed to understand. "Excellent. My curiosity is well satisfied. Will you serve me, Gercomo? I must leave the city and I could use you on the journey."

"Yessth," Gercomo replied.

One of the guards moved, hand on a throwing knife. Gercomo hissed and shifted out of the way as the blade clanged on the floor, deflected by Gercomo's scaled arm.

The baron lifted a hand and shook his head, as if disgusted by his man's stupidity. "He's yours, Gercomo. Help yourself to him. The others will clear up the mess."

Gercomo found he liked the taste of human flesh and blood even in this form. He no longer hungered for human-type food. He was even more dragon than he thought. The walls, splattered and sprayed with blood and gore, stood as a testament to his fervor. The baron stayed to watch the show. He didn't flinch, just licked his lips and walked off at the end as if the disobedient guard had been whipped, rather than ripped to bloody shreds. Gercomo would never understand the baron. Luckily, there was no need to. If anyone was going to survive on this planet, it was him.

Later, a servant offered Gercomo a cup of dragon wine. The man's hands shook as he held it out. Gercomo didn't blame him. Guards wept as they cleaned the walls and floor. Gercomo took the wine and drank it down. The cup clattered to the floor as cramps hit Gercomo. The power of the wine was inside him. Gercomo fell to the floor as the ceiling span above him. Heat flared in his skin and he growled low as he fought the wine.

His stomach churning, Gercomo lost consciousness.

Chapter Fifteen
A REBEL DAME

Squab hated hiding out. She was good at it, but it irked her. She'd rather be active, strike a blow.

The wine they'd retrieved from Eternity had been distributed: some into the poorer parts of town, and a goodly portion divvied up among the members of the rebel band to be taken out into the towns. Things were bad and Squab hadn't been able to bring herself to say otherwise. Those who were from outlying areas had been entitled to go back to their families and their homes to try to make the best of it. The wine would help them. As a group they were pretty smart. They had figured out what Eternity was doing and knew the end was near. They wanted a chance to find their families, find shelter and survive. Squab had no family—no family she was interested in saving.

The basement she was hidden in held a goodly portion of wine, some dried meat and about a month's supply of dried cacti bread. Even though she had eaten that morning, her stomach groaned and demanded to be filled. She shook her head, angry at her body's inability to deny itself. She was stocky. Always had been. During her time with Danton and the rebels, she'd turned her excess fat into muscle. As she sat there alone, anticipating the end, she regretted nothing. Danton had shown her that a man could be good. That they all weren't depraved, violent rapists and pedophiles. That there was good in the hearts of men and women. He'd taught her how to survive. How to help others and how to turn her anger to good.

She lay back against the wooden fake wall where she was hiding out. The looters had long gone. Squab had tried to sleep through most of it. Screams and cries. It hadn't sounded good, but she was loath to investigate. Yet, as she stared at the opposite wall, with little to ease her mind, she wondered what it had all been for. Why was she sitting here waiting for the world to end, waiting to die? Is that what she wanted?

Squab didn't want to die. She had no say over that. So maybe she had control over how she died, or what she did do while dying. She scoffed, laughing at herself. She was only three days into the serious hiding and already she was climbing the walls. It was the quiet, she told herself.

Squab had intended to kill Toola. Kill her for betraying Danton. She didn't even know if he lived. Brill had gone and her job had been to get the wine away. When the cliff had come down on the hidden city, chaos erupted. She didn't know if Brill had survived. Doing her duty with the wine had been her focus. She couldn't think of Danton laying broken somewhere and fresh-faced Brill buried in the city.

A tear broke free and its passage was a hot trail down her cheek. She shook her head in bewilderment. She hadn't cried in a long time. Not since she was a kid.

Unfortunately, her plan to kill the brothel madam had died a quick death. She'd found Toola's corpse rotting in the back alley behind her establishment. Many of the servants and working women were fleeing and Squab had quickly pieced together the tale of how Toola died and why.

After sending word via the cook for anyone who remained behind to leave immediately, Squab burned the place to the ground. The baron was also on her kill list. Pity he was impossible to get to.

After that, Sartell went to hell and hadn't come back from that place.

A roar out in the street startled her, made her hand twitch. She frowned as she listened.

"That is unusual," she said to herself, and eyed the door, which she had barricaded. Then she scooted around on her butt to study her escape hatch. She had to have an alternative exit given that someone might do to this building what she had done to the brothel.

The sound came again, and closer. "No time like the present," she said as she got on all fours and undid the panels to the little side tunnel leading out to the street. The exit was between two buildings that were so close together one could barely squeeze between them. She had a little scooped-out portion of earth under the neighbor's house. The backup to the backup plan involved going in a different direction, but since the sound was coming from the main street, she chose this way.

Outside she could hear the sound of feet marching and the roar became a growl that was more like a voice, albeit a voice cut from gravel. It was too late to make a dash for a better viewing position as the feet were too close. The first man marched into the intersection. He was followed by three others in a line and then behind them, a motley collection of people roped together. They were prodded along by another four armed men, and then in strode a nightmare. Squab thought her heart actually stopped for a moment. It was hideous. It was not human, but somehow it was. Part-man, part-dragon.

She blew out a breath between her lips. Had Brill mentioned this? No. Surely she would have remembered.

The beast punched a clawed hand in the air, directing the group down the street on the right. "I sense more humans there," he growled out.

A detachment of men came up behind him and then splintered around him as they jogged down the street in formation. Squab's heartbeat fluttered again as screams sounded. Could that beast smell her? She couldn't stop herself from inhaling to see how bad she stank. A lack of bathing facilities for nearly a week meant she reeked badly.

They dragged a few men and women up the street. These were dressed in rags and had open sores and looked half-starved. Squab's heart twisted in pity. Should she help them? She summed up the opposition and figured it would be a cheap and nasty death for her. She'd be taken or killed and win nothing. There were too many of them. If she'd had a bomb on her, possibly. She nodded to herself at the thought and grinned.

The beast's head jerked in her direction. "There. Something there."

Squab back-shuffled along her groove of earth. It was time to beat a hasty retreat or she was in danger of being rounded up with this lot.

She made it into her tunnel and put up the camouflage just in time. She could hear them. "Nothing here," one called out.

"Nothing!" replied the other.

Squab fled back into her fake room and hoped the beast didn't enter the building and sniff her out. As low as it sounded, she wished he sniffed up some other poor sod and not her. She put up the barrier and laid her head against it. Her heart wasn't up to this much excitement.

The beast gave a muffled growl. "I smelled it, damnsth yous. Keep lookingsth!"

The sides of the house were banged on. Footsteps sounded overhead. A crash and a crunch echoed through the empty house. Footsteps ran up the stairs and some feet thudded a slow beat as they entered the basement. Squab held her breath and closed her eyes. *By the source! I should not have ventured out.*

A shout from outside and the footsteps joined together, stamping their way out of the building.

"Downs theresth…" The harsh voice reached into her small, enclosed space. Goose flesh rose on her skin. Then there was silence. They had moved on.

Squab panted her relief. Some other poor sod was up for it. Squab reached out and snaffled the flagon of dragon wine. She was meant to drink it watered but she needed something stronger after that little escapade. The wine made her blood sing and her skin warm. It was an extravagance she should not repeat. Maybe save the rest for the end. She laughed at the thought, realizing that she was possibly intoxicated or verging on crazy.

The light slipping through the cracks in her small space dimmed. The sound of the beast and his horde of armed men, rounding up poor unfortunates, did not echo again. With the darkness came fatigue and the lull of dragon wine. She was tempted to drink more, to obliterate her consciousness with it, except a lifetime of frugality stayed her hand. She'd already drunk more pure dragon wine in one go than ever before.

To pass the time she tried to conjure up happy memories, but they were stained with loss and grief. She pushed away those dead-end thoughts and tried to replace them with better ones. What she had done with her life had made a difference. It had. She had saved women from being mangled.

She had loved some of them and they had loved her. Danton was a good man. Brill was, too. Some of her rebel mates weren't all that bad. They had tried to do good.

"But it was for nothing!" It flew out of her mouth and into the dark like an arrow from a bow. "No! No." She had to fight regret. It was terrible to think that one's whole life was for nothing. That the pain and suffering didn't matter. That the sacrifices meant nothing.

It was a hard battle. Wrestling with regret, Squab won. It didn't matter how it ended, or that it was ending. She had done her best. Had fought her best. The fate of Margra was out of her hands. Was never in her hands.

A sense of relief settled over her and her eyes closed as sleep claimed her. "It mattered," she mumbled to herself. "It still does."

༄༅༄༅༄

After staying holed up in her hiding place for a couple of more days, Squab found she couldn't stand it any longer. She made up a backpack of supplies and shouldered it. Weapons were in short supply, so she decided a bit of exploring was essential. If she was going to make a difference to someone, she needed to be well armed. There was some nasty stuff going on in this town. Even in her bolt-hole, she could smell the stench of rotting meat, of death. With a shiver she thought back to those people she'd seen. Now, they were no doubt just so much dragon fodder.

There was too much dragon wine to carry, so she drank a long draft of it straight. Her head spun and her blood sang so hot she thought she was on fire. Muscles were pumped, joints moved freely. She was ready for anything.

Squab was going to leave her hideout unsecured, but thought better of it. She replaced the panel carefully as she left, thinking it would be good to have that at her back. It was nice to know there was somewhere safe. Nice to know there was a stash of wine. She burped loudly. Maybe she shouldn't have drunk so much wine. She grinned and felt the scar on her face pull. She was at her ugliest when she smiled.

The street was eerily quiet when she stood on it, swaying slightly. Looking left, looking right, nothing moved except a few bits of rubbish rolling about in the light breeze. The sky was less black than it had been. It was now dark-gray with some lighter patches, and a ripe, pink glow shaded the edges of broken clouds. *This is what the end of the world looks like—a picturesque splash of color.* Squab laughed and then shook her head. She never laughed. Damn that dragon wine. The effect was increasing.

Putting her head down, Squab pictured the layout of the city. The sector she was in was close to the poor quarter, just up from the docks. The next sector over was where the merchants were. Not far from the brothel she had burned to the ground. Arms merchants had shops there. Perhaps there was abandoned stock. It was a more targeted approach than running around ransacking people's houses looking for the odd weapon. Most wouldn't have left even their knives behind.

When she thought about how little help those knives had been to most of those people, her mood fell into despair. She shook it off, bracing herself against the outer wall of a building as that movement sent her intoxicated mind into a spiral. Why was she doing this? She should have stayed in her hideout and drunk herself to death. Yeah…nah!

Taking action was the cure to wallowing in lost hope. Squab was going to end her miserable life doing something worthwhile. Her scar tugged again. She was damn well smiling. *Well, curse my dragon-infested ass!*

Although the streets were empty, Squab was cautious. There were patrols, she knew. And that dragon beast thing that could smell humans. That reminded her: she was pretty ripe. Down an alley, she passed under overhanging second floors. This sector of town had plumbing and gravity-fed water so even though the place was a ruin she might find a way to bathe. After checking that the place was truly deserted, she forced open the door of a dilapidated two-story inn. It wasn't a place she had frequented, too upmarket.

The place had been ransacked. There wasn't a bottle or a morsel of food to be had. There weren't even any scraps on the floor near the upturned tables. At the back of the place, in a room with a low, sloping ceiling, sat a large round tub, big enough for four to bathe in to the waist. The tub was full of cold, clean water as if someone had been intending to take a bath. A pile of clothes lay on a stool. A change of clothes for someone who hadn't ended up clean before they died. She pictured the man being dragged naked and screaming into the street, the imagined sound joining the very real chaotic sound rampant in the city just days before. A sound she never wanted to hear again, even though it blew through the empty alleys of her mind. She shook her head. Bloody wine was making her morose.

Upstairs, Squab found some clothes that looked like they would fit her, as the tidy garments below were too small for her thickset frame. These were surprisingly neatly stacked in the innkeeper's room. People had been hungry and not in need of clothes, even though a few weeks ago they had been worth money in trade.

Before taking a bath, Squab checked the street by peering through a broken shutter. She burped again and hiccupped, wiped her mouth with a grin. She had a stash of wine in her backpack and the thought did occur to her again that she could go out that way, mindlessly drunk. "Nah!" she told herself.

Nothing up and nothing down. She held her breath and listened. Nothing. That gave her five minutes, tops, to bathe because everything could change in that time. But having the coast clear meant she could relax enough for a body scrub. Being full of wine had her pretty much relaxed already.

The water was cool, not cold. The expensive soap smelled of flowers. Normally, Squab would hate such a feminine thing, but beggars could not choose their scent. She scrubbed vigorously and dunked herself into the water, using her palms to wipe off the grime. Ducking under, she also washed her hair. Her short crop had grown out a bit. If she had had time she would have shaved it off, but why bother? She had things to do. Besides, all that wine made her hands a tad unsteady.

Sounds began in the city again, not one minute after she exited the inn. Time had run out. She ran in the direction of the merchant houses, locating a weapons merchant pretty quickly. The door had already been kicked in and the display cases smashed. With a groan, she looked around at the room. Holes in the wall. Cabinet doors hanging loose. She walked behind the counter. Nothing there. She turned away and paused. The floorboard under her foot gave a little. She stepped back and knelt down. Wiping the dust and splinters of wood away, her fingers encountered a concealed trapdoor. With a feral grin she opened it, but she cut off her cry of delight.

Slowly, she reached into the stash and started to place weapons in pockets and belt and boot. There were throwing daggers, hurling blades, and two short swords with double edges and sharp points. They were good for slashing and stabbing. And something else caught her eye. It was finely made and she took it into her hand gently. A little bitty bomb. It was much better made than anything she could have fashioned.

Chapter Sixteen
FINDERS KEEPERS

A couple of days after having inspected N'Barek, Danton lit the beacon that Nils had supplied and nodded to the Hiem that they were ready to move on. Nils would guide them to the gate to Sartell, then return to Barrahiem, leaving beacons to guide their return. Brill had to admit to feeling nervous. It would be Danton's first time among other people since his capture and torture at the hands of the baron.

In their long talks when neither of them could sleep, Danton had admitted the mere thought of the baron made his hands shake and his breath hitch. And looking on, Brill had witnessed a sweat break out on Danton's forehead and his complexion turn gray, his lips almost white.

Brill had tried to get Danton to stay behind, but the rebel leader would have none of it. "I can't conquer my ghosts if I don't confront them. I can't redeem myself in my own eyes if I don't face my enemy."

Brill had nodded, agreeing with Danton. Yet, he could not help wishing that Danton had stayed safe, as he had suffered so much for them all.

Brill tried to remember the path he had walked when he escaped Sartell. He had wandered, lost, until he was found by Nils. He didn't want to get lost again. Danton bent and lit another beacon at the junction. They took the stair and lit another at the bottom, on the platform. Brill was pleased with the result. The gray nothing that was the substance of the Ways seemed to swallow the light, yet their path forward was obvious. "We will need to set up a watch over the lights in case they are damaged or moved," Danton whispered in Brill's ear.

"I was just thinking that. Having been lost, I would not like to see a lot of people panic in here. It could get ugly."

"No way around it. We can't take them through one at a time."

"Eneit and Laidan?" Brill suggested.

"Yes, but even with their help I don't think it will be enough."

Danton walked forward to catch up with Nils, who was leading them. "Nils, if something happened to the beacons, would you be able to detect that people are lost in here?"

Nils's eyes widened. "I had not thought about it. I have been able to detect a single intruder, but I do not know how the Ways will react to many, or how I will."

"Will you be in N'Barek when we bring some people through?"

"No. I do not think that is wise. They will be afraid of the strange surroundings in the first place. Seeing me may send them over the edge." Nils cocked his head to the side. "I can undertake to monitor your progress. If you are delayed, I will investigate."

Laidan piped up. "I think I can find my way. I've been watching and remembering." She then recited the list of stairs, and directions right down to the number of paces.

Brill grinned. "We will need your help if the beacon lights go out or are moved." Not that anybody was likely to move them.

Laidan smiled and Brill's breath stopped. It was the old Laidan. Eyes bright and intelligent, and then the look faded. She was still smiling, but it was the new Laidan.

"We are getting close," Nils said. "There is the gate. I will leave you now. Karol is waiting for me. He is fragile yet, and I do not like to leave him alone for too long a period."

"Thank you for your help," Brill said. "We will be as fast as we can."

Nils bowed. "Now, if you will excuse me. I will monitor your progress best I can, rest assured. I must return to Trell's book and to Karol's care."

Within a few minutes, Nils had passed out of sight. Beacon lamps illuminated the Way so it was a pale, dull gray, the walls seeming to eat the light. Ahead was the Way Gate that led into the sewers of Sartell.

"Let's get going. Two at a time, sticking close to each other." Eneit nodded and stood behind him and Laidan ranged up behind Danton, stave at the ready.

"Look less fierce, Laidan. You are meant to carry it like it is a walking stick," Brill commented.

Laidan smiled and relaxed her stance. He didn't blame her for being nervous. He was, for sure.

They had debated whether to wear Hiem shrouds, but Nils had argued successfully that the less Hiem technology was exposed, the safer they would be. They had agreed that if the situation was dangerous they would abandon the mission to rescue people from Sartell. They would go to their next destination, one of the satellite towns, in the hopes of finding people there.

"Open up," Danton said and Brill bent to the task. Muted light spilled in on them. Noise and smell assaulted them as they stepped out.

"What is that stench?" Brill said, as the reek of rot washed over him.

"Oh, no," Danton said. "Can you hear that?"

Brill straightened his shoulders and then shook his head in dismay. "The sounds of dying."

Screams and moans filled the air as if a lot of people were gathered together. Then, as they listened, the cries grew less frequent and finally stopped, leaving an ominous silence and a sick smell in the air.

Danton came to the front to look around the area. There was nothing, no one to be seen. Vacant houses. Signs of hasty departure.

"I'm beginning to think this wasn't a good idea," Danton commented to Brill in a quiet voice. He glanced behind at Laidan and Eneit. Brill's skin flushed, and he nodded once sharply. The eerie deserted streets were disconcerting, as was the smell and the stark sky now burnished red as the sun neared the horizon.

"Maybe we should confine our search to the schools," Brill suggested. "You know, save the children."

Danton shook himself. Were children even in school these days? And the stink. What had happened here?

They walked down the street, eyes peeled for any sign of life. Once, there would have been a market here in the square, bustling with produce and people. They rounded the corner and Danton stopped dead. It was empty of people, but it was like a wind had rushed through. Tables overturned, goods spilled, but not food, he noticed. Not a scrap of food. Dark stains on the ground gave Danton pause. Bloodstains?

"Go back around the corner and stay out of sight," Danton said to Brill.

The boy lifted his eyebrows and opened his mouth as if he was going to object, then catching Danton's look, he turned on his heel and urged the girls backward.

Danton took tentative steps forward. The square had five streets that ran into it. Danton could now hear something. He followed the main street, following that sound. A coarse guttural scrape against tortured vocal cords. He heard moans and cries of fear cut short. Something was up.

Each dark doorway held a potential threat so Danton was cautious. Empty windows. Empty houses. A doll on the street, its head crushed. It gave Danton the shivers.

He turned the corner into the side street and the noise was suddenly louder. It was the city hall, he thought, a large building with a tower and a quadrangle beyond. The noise and the stench had become more intense. Drawn onward, heart thumping hard, Danton had to see, had to know if what he suspected was true. Surely the people had not turned on each other. No food to be seen, not even scraps at the market area, told him there was virtually no food left in Sartell and that none was making its way down the river. The lack of sunlight and the dust had probably killed off crops and livestock. But he hadn't thought it could come to this so quickly.

Harsh voices shouting commands made his step falter. Memories assailed him. He tried to block it out, but fell back instead, some instinct for survival making him take cover in the shadow of a doorway. The door had been kicked in and splintered.

It was then that he saw them. Guards marched along the street, followed by a cart. Danton's stomach clenched at the sight. Arms and legs were stacked in neat piles. This was the new meat. People.

Then a sight he hadn't thought he'd ever see, though he knew it by description. A beast of a man strode into view, tail swishing as it gave out orders in a strange voice, words misshapen. "Catchssh themns." Gercomo flicked out his arm in a sharp gesture.

Gercomo was here? *Defiler of Laidan. Oh, source preserve me. She can't see him. He can't see her.* Danton panted, waiting for the opportunity to retreat, so that he could warn the others. They had to leave. Sartell was even more dangerous than they had suspected.

Then the unbelievable happened. The baron strode into view. He cast his dark gaze around as he shared a few words with Gercomo. Danton pissed himself and fought for consciousness. The memories crowded around him, fighting for precedence in his mind. Visions of what had been done to him, visions of what he himself may or may not have done, because he couldn't remember, wouldn't remember, but deep in his gut he knew and he hated it, hated himself. He backed up into the house so that he was hidden in the darkness. The smell of piss was strong and he knew then it was one of the smells that overlaid the city. The other was shit. Another was blood. Oh, and the guts and the stench of meat. Human meat.

ᔕᔕᔕᔕᔕ

Danton must have passed out, because he woke up on his back. It was quiet outside so he crawled to the door. Activity was less. He ransacked the house looking for some clean clothes and found some. He quickly wiped himself down and donned the fresh trousers. It wasn't that he was ashamed of soiling himself. It was the fear that his emotional state would instill in the others. They needed to have confidence.

The red night drew around him and he snuck from shadow to shadow to make his way back to Brill, Laidan and Eneit. Then the thought occurred to him that they'd been taken while he'd been passed out from sheer terror. Brill wasn't where he'd left him and Danton choked back a sob. Then there was a slight whistle and Danton relaxed and turned down the lane. There, coming out of the shadows, was Brill.

"Where were you? You were gone so long. I thought..." Brill creased his forehead. "What is it?"

"We need to leave right now. Gercomo is here and so is the baron."

Brill rocked back on his heels and shot a glance over his shoulder. "I agree. What else did you see? Where are the people?"

Danton couldn't hold it back even though he wanted to spare Brill. It was something that would shake the lad's optimism for humankind. "They are being rounded up and slaughtered for food."

Brill's eyes widened. "No!" He shook his head and wiped at tears that rolled down his cheeks. "No!"

Danton nodded. "I hate to leave Gercomo and the baron to their cruel deeds, but we need to get these two away from him. We didn't save them to lose them again."

"Right, I'll go get them. They are napping behind that house. It was the best protected spot."

Danton followed Brill to retrieve the others. Laidan was heavy eyed, but smiled when she saw Danton. "You're back. We were worried."

Eneit blinked at him and nodded.

"We have to leave. We will try one of the smaller towns," Danton explained.

"What's wrong?" Laidan asked.

"Danger," Brill said quickly. "It's far more dangerous than we anticipated. A lot of the people are already dead. We can't help them."

Eneit's eyes widened. Laidan appeared to sense the other girl's distress and put an arm around her.

"Ready?" Danton asked. When he received nods of agreement, he added, "Keep your weapons handy. I don't expect trouble, but you never know. Stay alert."

Danton checked the street before they emerged and then Laidan and Eneit followed. Brill brought up the rear. The stepped quietly, but quickly. A shriek cut the air around them and Danton couldn't help but start.

"Keep walking," he said.

They turned the corner and the area seemed deserted, until they heard children crying. Brill pointed and they saw a school. Whimpers and weeping leaked out of the building. Danton bit his lip. He'd received a fright already. He'd seen the baron and had a nasty reaction, something that made him doubt himself and his ability to fight and lead.

"Shall I check it out?" Brill asked.

Danton gave him a quick nod, then moved Laidan and Eneit to shelter close by. No streetlamps were lit, and the strange crimson sunset cast an eerie glow. Danton hated how his heartbeat thudded, like he had no control over himself. Closing his eyes, he fought for calm, for that place where he normally went when he was fighting. He had to fight this fear now, because if he didn't conquer it the baron had won. The baron had cut bits off him and taken Danton's essential soul with it. Danton didn't really believe that his soul was lost but he feared it, like a persistent nightmare that came so often it impinged on reality. He wasn't going to let the baron win. At the same time, he knew he couldn't fight what was happening in the city, not with Laidan and Eneit to protect. They had learned to fight well, but if anything happened he would be responsible and the fate awaiting them was not a good one. Not even a quick death. No, not for them. They were worth more alive. He couldn't do that to Mandin's memory. Mandin had given everything to save her daughter.

Steps drew close. Danton pulled back and unsheathed his blade, and then relaxed when he saw it was Brill returning.

Brill crouched down and whispered. "There're about twenty children under guard."

"How many guards?" Danton asked.

"Six," Brill said. "I think we can take them."

Danton quailed. Laidan came forward, brandishing her stave. "We want to fight to save those children. It's what we came for."

Danton studied her, her pale skin ruddy in the light. "Me too," Eneit said.

Danton lifted an eyebrow to Brill. The boy cocked his head, thinking. "We have to try. To leave without trying…well, I don't think I could live with myself. No matter how many people we rescued from other towns."

"So what's the plan?" Danton asked Brill, who had seen the layout.

Brill squatted down and drew an imaginary map. "Two guards are stationed inside the main entrance. Two guard the rear entrance and on the inside two are free-ranging among the children, scaring them for fun. I think we may as well go for it. You take out the ones at the front and I'll make for the ones at the back. Then we meet in the middle."

Danton nodded. "Eneit, you're with me. Laidan, stick close to Brill."

Laidan's grin was feral. "It's about time."

Eneit was like a shadow as Danton approached the door. He hardly knew she was there. Brill and Laidan snuck along the outside to the rear door, ready to dart through once the first two guards were engaged and hopefully out of commission.

Danton waited, counting out the steps for Brill and Laidan to get in place. Then he nodded to Eneit and rose to kick in the door.

The door hit one guard in the face, but didn't take him down. Before Danton could get in, Eneit had hit the guard in the jaw with the end of the stave, knocking him backward. He landed with a thump and lay still. Danton hadn't even shifted his gaze when Eneit engaged the other guard. The room was a large hall, allowing him to see clear to the rear door.

At the other end of the building, Brill kicked in the door and ran inside with Laidan close behind. She twirled her stave, making it thrum in the air.

The guards positioned at the rear door gave guttural roars. One ran forward and the other tried to get out the door. Going for backup, most likely. Danton heard a crunch and saw Laidan break the other guard's nose. A guard charged from the middle of the room and Danton had no attention to spare for Brill and Laidan. Eneit tripped the guard and sent him sprawling. Then she went in and stabbed him between the shoulder blades with the tip of her stave. Seeing that Eneit had it under control, Danton went for the guard on his right. There was one guard left among the children and he posed a danger. That hopeless creature saw Danton was coming and picked up a child to shield him. The child screamed hysterically and Danton pulled up short. How as he going to take down the guard without harming the child or the guard harming the child?

The guard yelled suddenly, and Danton saw that children now clung to his legs and had their teeth in his flesh. The guard dropped the child and kicked and shoved to dislodge the small ones. Danton threw his blade and caught the man in the chest. He fell to his knees, making the children scramble out of the way. Instinctively, Danton ducked as a spear shot over his head. Another free-ranging guard was shoving children out of the way as he headed to engage Danton. This one must have been hidden from view when Brill had assessed the place. In his peripheral vision, Danton caught a glimpse of Eneit. She was tagging behind the guard. Stave ready. The guard caught the direction of Danton's gaze and turned. His head shot back as Eneit struck. Then he doubled over as she followed up with a blow to the gut. When he fell to the ground, the kids swarmed over him.

Danton checked on Brill and Laidan. The latter was twirling her stave, making her quarry back away. He saw she was enjoying herself, but she needed to move quickly before the guard counterattacked. The more she twirled the more time he had to assess her weaknesses. As if she heard Danton's thoughts, she halted the twirl, jerked back the stave and pistoned it into the guard's face.

The guards were down. They had a small window of time to get the children out. They had no idea whether there were other guards close, or if the children were expected to be moved at any moment.

"Come on, you lot. Come with us," Eneit shouted. The children turned to her. "We are taking you to a safe place, where there is good food and nice people."

The children were talking loudly. Eneit twirled her stave. "We have come to help you, but you have to help us too. We are going to leave by the front door. Don't run. Help those who can't walk, or who are sick or weak."

She pointed the stave. "That there is Laidan. He is Brill, and that guy there is Danton. It's their job to help people, understand? Not hurt them. We only hurt the bad people who were keeping you here and who are hurting people outside."

The children were quieter, so Danton gave Brill a signal and he ran to the front door. Laidan followed behind. They went out and then came back in. "All clear. We need to move."

Eneit turned to the children and gave a big sweep of her arm. "Come on and follow me."

She turned and the children started following. There was some pushing and shoving, but in among them Danton saw older kids helping smaller ones and others supporting injured children. Danton stayed near the back door so they wouldn't be taken by surprise by anyone entering that way.

"Faster!" he heard Eneit call. Danton sweated. He dared not leave the door until all the children were out, but he feared something was wrong. Frightened cries from some of the children were like a cold knife in his guts. Abandoning his post, he ran and chivvied the last children through the front door. Then he saw that Laidan, Brill and Eneit were fighting more guards. They looked to have the situation under control for the moment.

Danton ran to the front of the column of children. "Come on, keep going." And he led the children on, leaving the others to fight.

☙☙☙☙☙

More armed men came at them as they were leading the children away. Laidan had never been so scared and focused in her life. She whirled her stave and jabbed and thrust, keeping her attackers at bay. As they were all engaged in defending the children, no one was coming to help her any time soon. She was on her own.

A gap-toothed guard in ratty clothes blocked her stave thrust with his arm, then turned his hand and pulled the stave and Laidan went with it. He punched her in the face and Laidan reeled back, hot liquid in her mouth, dripping down her chin. In that moment, there was only her and this man. The guard dropped the stave to lunge at her. A mistake. She gripped the stave hard and flicked it up. It caught the man in the thigh close to the groin. She lost her grip and the stave fell to the ground. Her attacker stepped on it and kept coming for her. As he lunged, hands outstretched for her neck, she lifted her knee and thrust out with her foot. *Thump! Ooof!* The man fell to his knees, face infused with blood, then she surged forward and hit him across the cheek with her fist. It hurt and she shook out her hand, while also kicking the man off her stave as he lay across it.

The stave broke when she pulled at it, losing its top third and leaving a jagged edge. Laidan was frowning at it when someone else loomed. A hand grabbed her shoulder from behind and she turned, stave at the ready. The dirty, bearded face of another guard twisted in agony as he fell back, the remains of her stave sticking out of his gut.

For a moment, Laidan wanted to heave and then the noise of the fighting intruded. She was suddenly free of opponents, so she beckoned to a huddle of children, caught between Danton's line and the fighting. "Come on! Let's go!"

The lead children were wide-eyed. "Don't look at them. Look at me."

Laidan waved to them and when she saw they had overcome their inertia and were moving, she led the way. Vulnerable without her weapon, her knees shook. Eneit's grunts reached her where she fought alongside

Brill with a pile of men around them. They were winning, but Laidan didn't want to take any chances. The children needed to be saved.

A lone guard appeared before them. Laidan's mind went blank. She waved her arms and let out a guttural cry with her charge. The guard stepped back and as she kept on coming, mouth emitting the most frightening sound, and the guard turned and ran. Laidan followed and then faltered, all her might and fright leaving her as she bent over and breathed. Her heart rate was out of control and she had an urgent need to pee.

She had no idea how she had done that. Turning quickly, she kept the children going. Footsteps pounded the road behind her and Laidan struggled to find that ferocity again. When Danton came into view, she breathed out in relief and wiped at the tears that had suddenly appeared in her eyes. He had the rest of the children with him.

Not long after, Brill followed, with Eneit running along behind. She had blood running down the side of her face and she limped. Her stave was missing, too.

Laidan went to the head of the children and continued moving. "Well done. Good thinking, Laidan," Brill said. "Getting the rest of the children out of there made it easier. You okay?"

Laidan wiped at a tear and smiled broadly. "Oh yes!" Danton was grinning at her. The scar was scary, but she grinned back at him.

"Not far now," Danton said as he pointed to the building where they needed to turn to reach the sewers. "Brill?"

Brill nodded and darted ahead of them to make sure there were no more guards lying in wait. Brill sent back a whistle, an all clear. "Do you think we can get them to run?" Danton asked. "We can carry the ones that can't."

Laidan turned to the children. "Let's have a race. See if you can beat me."

Laidan made sure the children were watching and then she charged off. About half the children followed behind her. Laidan nearly faltered, but when she checked she saw that Danton had picked up little ones under each arm and he squatted so another could cling to his back. Eneit had a kid on her back. Brill darted past her as he went to get the remaining three. *Right then*, she thought. *Let's do this.*

Laidan kept up a steady pace. Two of the children started to flag, so she grabbed their hands. "We can win this."

Chapter Seventeen

REUNION

The lane that led to the sewer was close. Laidan dared to hope that they would make it without further incident.

The grating voice that roared through the air made her heart stop and she stumbled, falling to her knees. It wasn't in front of them. It was somewhere else. "Keep going," she said, waving the children on. That voice came again. It came from behind and that sound made her wet herself and roll into a ball, hand crammed into her mouth to hold back the screams. Danton drew close. "Laidan, get up, damn it!" he yelled.

She couldn't respond.

Danton kept coming, wriggling children uncomfortable being carried like sacks. "If you don't move he'll have you, Laidan. Do you want to be his again?"

Her eyes widened and it was as if her heart had stopped beating in her chest. A claw ripped into her mind, shredding flesh and blood. "Oh, source!" she wailed.

Brill stopped and knelt beside her. His fingers gripped her shoulders painfully. "Move, Laidan. It's a memory. Just a memory."

She gaped at him. "Just a memory?" Then she screamed.

Brill yelled at the children. "Run. Quickly. Follow the others."

He tried lifting Laidan and she cuffed him across the ears.

"Don't touch me!" she said in a voice she didn't recognize. Laidan struggled to keep her fear under control. The roar sounded again and she bolted aimlessly. Brill grabbed her hand. "That way," and swung her so she ran in an arc, ending up going in the right direction.

Laidan went at a dead run. She didn't know how she did it for she had never run so fast. She leaped over obstacles and caught up to the tail end of the children. Brill was panting hard behind her.

Danton opened the door to the Way Gate and Laidan splashed through the filthy sewage, heading for the dark opening. The Ways were a good place to hide.

Danton glanced up, saw her and nodded. Laidan kept going and felt more in control. Eneit carried the children who couldn't move fast enough over the threshold. Laidan gathered two by the hand and made them move faster. The dark doorway loomed over her. The roar sounded again and Laidan sobbed as she passed into the Way.

"Brill, to me," Danton called. "Trouble."

☙☙☙☙☙

Squab had heard something. A noise. Not armed men. She cocked her head. There was a girl's voice. No, two. Squab carefully peered out into the street. The girls were young and carrying staves and guarding a group of children. Squab nearly fainted when she saw who was with them. Brill? Who was the other? Her neck stretched as she caught sight of Danton as they turned the corner. *He lives!*

Squab came out in the open, too late to advertise her presence. Other sounds intruded. Armed men on their trail. Squab wanted to run to Danton and the others and warn them, but that was a stupid idea. It was better to wait and follow the troop of guards following them.

Squab tilted her head as the guards came past. They were making no attempt to hide their approach. Maybe they hadn't detected the others yet. At this rate though, both groups were going to stumble upon each other. Squab eased her pack off her shoulders and checked the weapons she had stashed on her person.

Stepping out into the street behind the group of men, she called out. She could have killed them with a knife in the back, only where was the fun in that? She was no assassin.

Five of the six men turned, and the sixth stumbled and landed on his rear in an attempt to save himself. She'd startled him. No sense in wasting time, so she took him out with a knife to the throat. She'd meant to hit him in the chest, but his ducking at the last minute put her off her aim.

Next, someone chucked a rock at her. "Come on! Really?" she jibed as the remaining five ranged out around her. What was she thinking? That dragon wine had made her cocky. Normally, she wouldn't take on five against one. Time to even the odds. She plunged both hands into her belt and flipped out two hurling blades. With a *thunk* they hit their marks.

"That's a little better," she growled out. "Three against one."

The leader spared a look for his fallen comrades and then came at a charge. The two others had to step over their downed mates. Squab lifted the sword with a sideways tilt to deflect the oncoming blow, rolling through with a kick to the man's balls. His sword fell and she kicked the hilt so it spun away. The one behind him did a little dance as he jumped over the whirling blade. Meanwhile, Squab followed through with her blade from when she had deflected to a sweeping arc that slashed the other guy on her left. He didn't see it coming and failed to block. He went down in a spray of blood and landed hard, his guts falling out to stain the ground.

That left the other who had recovered. The one with mashed balls was still writhing on the ground. She crunched his foot as she stepped to meet the blade dancer. He was unshaven, with heavy eyes that glinted with hate. His jaw clenched as he lifted his sword. Squab met his blade and pushed him back. He was strong. She was stronger. The dragon wine sang in her blood. She moved as if she had never been injured before in her life.

Restraint and caution were dead buddies. Squab pushed and then followed up with a thrust and jab. She caught her opponent on the shoulder and he yelped.

Then he shook himself out and hunkered like he was going to charge. Squab dipped and flipped up a hurling blade. It got him in the neck. She grinned as arterial blood spurted. She had hit her mark, right where she was aiming. A groan from the ground alerted her to the remaining live one. She turned, took a step and forcefully kicked him in the head. His limbs spread out, lifeless. Her job here was done.

Letting out a sigh, she surveyed the damage. Then two things happened. She realized that this carnage would advertise her presence and the sound of fighting reached her. *Danton!*

Stopping to retrieve the hurling blades, she wiped them on the downed men's clothes. Squab picked up her pack and ran.

A few turns and she came up behind the fighting. She hid behind a wall and could see Danton and Brill were guarding a sewer entrance. Squab surveyed the scene and found what they were protecting. The two girls she had seen before were helping children flee through a door. It was one of those things Brill had told her about. A tunnel in the earth that led somewhere safe. That is how he had described it when they attacked Eternity. It must be true, because here was Danton and Brill alive after that city had collapsed under the cliff.

No time for niceties. Squab threw two hurling blades and then ducked out of view.

Peeking around the corner she realized that the troops were too engaged to notice the two fallen ones. She needed something more.

In her pocket was the little bomb. This called for good timing. She had to warn Danton and Brill but she had to do it so she didn't alert the attackers too quickly. First, she had to let her friends know she was here. She rolled away and gained her feet. She threw two more blades into the pack of attackers. Squab looked up and could see that the children were nearly through.

A shrill whistle left her mouth. "Danton," she yelled. "Incoming!" She waited a moment, caught a glimpse of her friends. Danton looked up, grabbed Brill and ran. She lobbed the bomb into the attackers, some of whom had turned. The bomb went up in a tall arc just as she intended. She threw herself to the ground and covered her head. There were yells, but it was too late. Gravity was working as normal. The bomb went off and dirt and bone and blood fell from the sky.

Dusting herself off, Squab then ran and eased herself into the sewer and into the chaos that awaited her. The stench of ruptured guts was overpowering. She covered her nose and ran to where Danton and Brill were entering the doorway.

A pale hand waved at her. "Come on," Danton shouted. His voice was muffled in her ears after the explosion.

Behind her, she heard more attackers coming at a run. She ran faster than she ever had in her life, leaping mounds of bloody flesh and trying not to skid.

Reaching out, she touched Danton's hand. He in turn gripped her and tugged. Squab fell through the door and it snapped shut behind her.

"By the dragon's holy ass, Squab. It's good to see you."

Danton hugged her and she squeezed back.

"We'd better move," Brill said. "Thanks for the help, Squab."

It was dark inside the cave or tunnel. She moved closer in while Brill fretted that their attackers would follow and would have explosives. Little voices shivered in the dark. Danton introduced her to the young girls with the staves. Squab could tell even in the gloom that one of them was the loveliest creature she had ever seen. Laidan was the name. The young one was Eneit.

"Squab is one of the best and meanest fighters I know. We couldn't have made it without her," Danton said.

Squab grinned and luckily the dark hid her ugliness, because they thanked her and slapped her shoulders. Squab had found a purpose again.

ꙮꙮꙮ

After being introduced to the rebel woman, Laidan and Eneit moved ahead to keep the children in order.

"Danton! You are safe. I didn't think. I didn't hope..." Squab was saying in a scratchy voice. The door had shut, and the little light of the beacon shone in the gloom.

While Danton, Squab and Brill greeted one another, they all moved toward the beacon light, but something dark rose up in Laidan's mind. A dark red bruise of pain. Falling to her knees, she let the children pass ahead.

"Laidan?" Brill asked as he squatted next to her. "What's wrong?"

She couldn't move. The dark stain spreading in her brain consumed her. "Come on!" Brill said and then, with a grunt of annoyance, he pulled her up. Laidan followed, tugged along by Brill, but her mind was occupied sorting through images and feelings that she could not comprehend.

"What's wrong with her?" Squab asked. "Can I help?"

A confusion of bodies separated them. Laidan couldn't speak, didn't want to, not to a stranger.

That voice. That roar. It had triggered something. The memories came crashing in, crushing Laidan's mind. A wail escaped her lips.

Brill pestered her, asking if she was all right, but she couldn't answer.

Danton's voice sounded above her head. "What's wrong? What happened?"

Brill made an exasperated sound. "I don't know. She's not injured as far as I can see."

"We need to get moving in case we were seen. Squab's here to help. We need to put out the beacon lights as we pass them. You understand?" Danton's voice was light, as if finding his friend had lifted his spirits.

"Yes, so we can't be followed easily," Brill said, "if they blow the Way Gate."

Laidan heard the rustle of Danton's clothes as he crouched down beside her. She knew it was him, because he spoke softly to her. "Laidan, if you are remembering what happened to you before, that's all right, understand. I know what those painful memories can do. But right now, I need you to get up and to move. You don't need to think or talk or do anything but walk. We will guide you."

Laidan whimpered.

"Can't you see she's sad?" Eneit said and she came up to Laidan and rubbed her back. "You take the children. We will follow and put out the lamps."

Danton stood. "Are you sure?"

"Yes, I'm sure. I can do it."

"Right then. Brill, take the lead with a couple of the less able children. Squab, if you don't mind herding the older ones, I'll bring up the rear with the others."

Squab grunted. "Herding children instead of rebels. No problem."

Danton chuckled at her levity. The sound was good to Laidan's traumatized ears.

The sounds of footsteps faded as they moved away.

It was quiet, except for Eneit's breathing. The girl hugged her. "Don't lose yourself in the past, Laidan. You are special and I love you."

Laidan wept at the words. They meant so much to her. Her? A whole raft of memories assaulted her. The roar. The pain. The attack. It was him. Oh, what had he done? Eaten some of her flesh and tried to pry her mind open like some kind of ripe fruit. Why had she been there? She had been running, running away from Salinda and Garan. Garan, who she had hurt more than one could bear. She knew he loved her, but she had been cruel and mean. She'd loved Brill, too. How could that be? She felt nothing for Brill now. Nothing like the kind of love she'd thought she had. *Oh my!* She had slept with Brill. Her first time had been with Brill.

In an instant, there were two Laidans, separately watching each other. Two of her lives spread out behind and ahead of her, two paths. The two Laidans fought each other, each trying to climb on top, to be the person Laidan was meant to be.

The new Laidan observed her old self with calculation. She assessed her personality as it had been. The new her was crying, wailing, trying to ground herself, and was losing.

How insipid and stupid she had been. Laidan cried harder, her face wet with tears. *But I'm not like that anymore. I am strong and I can fight. I am a better me.*

The two Laidans stayed separate and Laidan pressed her hands against her head, trying to contain them. *No. No!*

Instinctively, she knew she was at a crisis point and that she had to fight to survive. The memories were terrible. Each scene kept coming back to that attack. It had been no one's fault but her own. She had run into danger, because she had been a child, but she was that child no longer. She was strong.

The two Laidans continued to battle, but the new Laidan, the strong Laidan…she was winning. She didn't like her old self. She wanted it gone, wanted it cut out of her, but that wasn't going to happen because that was her, too. She had to accept what she didn't like, had to embrace it.

Slowly, the raging battle in her mind calmed. The old self accepted the new and the new self embraced the old. The terrifying separation of mind she had experienced gradually diminished. Laidan knew there was an old her and a new her, but it wasn't an impediment to living her best now.

Sitting up straight, she squared her shoulders and looked about her. *Dragon tits! What am I doing here wallowing? Putting myself and others in danger?*

Wiping her face on the knee of her pants, she stood up. The memories were still cascading in her mind. Nils. Salinda. Thurdon...her chest grew tight just thinking of him. He had died. She could do nothing about it. Then Lenk and the bandits and Gercomo...the dragon beast.

But she could function. She was no longer paralyzed.

Lifting her hands, she watched them shaking. Eneit put her arms around her waist and clung to her. "Remember who you are," Eneit said, crying. "Don't let it take you."

"It's okay," Laidan said quietly. She lifted a hand to pat the other girl on the shoulder.

Eneit looked up at her. "Really? I thought you had lost yourself to the dark thoughts. They call me sometimes." She shook her head. "I don't go with them. I can't."

Laidan lifted her lips in a half smile. Eneit understood because Eneit had been there, had seen things no little girl should, knew her mother had died for her. "Yes. All under control now."

Eneit dared a tentative smile. "That's good."

"The children?" Laidan said, wiping her nose with the back of her hand and snorting back snot in a most unladylike fashion. She used her sleeve to dry the remnants of her tears.

Eneit stood back, her earnest eyes assessing Laidan. "You're all right?"

Laidan considered herself, brow furrowed. She was the new Laidan who remembered the old Laidan. She pictured Salinda and the horrible things Laidan had said and done to that woman in the past. Then she thought about Salinda now and how gentle she always was. Laidan wished she could be more like that. Smart. Brave. Compassionate and strong.

"The children are safe. They have gone with Brill and Danton and some funny-looking woman called Squab. She was a rebel, apparently."

Laidan grinned. "Well, we'd better move before they get too far ahead of us." Laidan glanced over her shoulder at the Way Gate and narrowed her gaze. "Just in case they come after us."

Eneit agreed. "I don't think they will come in here, but we are to put out the beacons. Then we need to catch up with the others. The children will be afraid."

"They can't stay in N'Barek by themselves. They are too young. We will need to get some abodes ready for them in Barrahiem."

"Yes," Eneit said and smiled. "I'm glad you are okay. You fought so bravely."

"So did you. I saw."

Hand in hand, they walked toward the first beacon and then checked the path ahead before extinguishing it. They were heading home. Home to Barrahiem with a purpose. They had saved some children and that felt good.

Donna Maree Hanson

Chapter Eighteen

THE TRUTH
IN RHYME

Nils brought Karol with him to his office. As he was still reading Trell's book and Salinda had impressed upon him the importance of finding certain information, it was the best course of action. He could instruct Karol on reading the archival language.

Karol stood there looking around, astounded, while Nils rearranged furniture. He put some heavy tomes on a chair to boost the child to desk height.

"What is this place?" Karol had asked as they descended below the city to where the archives were held and where Nils had his office.

"This is Barrahiem, the major city of the Hiem, your ancestors."

"I never thought it would be like this. My grandfather never told me what his city looked like."

Nils drew in an excited breath. "So your grandfather was from Barrahiem?

Karol frowned and studied the walls of the narrow corridor. "No, I don't think it was called that."

"Was it an underground city like this one?" Nils prompted further.

"Yes," Karol said and then continued to walk, "it was. We were never to talk of it with outsiders."

"Do you know why your grandfather left the city?" Nils asked, trying to mask his curiosity and failing. "Did he tell you?"

"No, he didn't. Not me, anyhow."

"Did anyone know why?" Nils asked, taking a gamble that Karol was taking his questions too literally.

"Father said it was because he fell in love with a human."

"Oh?"

Karol looked up at him gravely. "Grandmother was human and they made their own settlement. We had our own clan."

"I see. That would explain a few things."

"Later on, other Hiem came to live with grandfather and our clan grew."

"It did?"

"Yes," Karol replied.

"And did *they* talk about their city?"

"No, no one talked about why they left or where it was." Karol stared into space, thinking about the past. "This is not...I mean...I think they were from the same place...but I don't know why I think that."

Nils picked up a simple text and laid it in front of the boy. "Can you read this? Do you recognize the text?"

Karol frowned and ran his finger over the script. "I was a bad student. I have seen text like this, though," he said, facing Nils with a solemn expression. "I wish I had paid better attention."

"This is the script our people used to record the happenings of the world. Would you like to learn it now? Then you can read anything in our archives."

Karol's face lit up. "Truly, you are not angry with me? I hear anger in your thoughts."

Nils pulled back slightly. "No, of course I am not angry. You will learn it. I taught Salinda, you know, and she picked it up even though she isn't Hiem...well, only part.

"If you sense anger in me, it is only general. Not directed at you." Nils sighed and sat back, becoming conscious of his overall demeanor. "I am angry at my people. Angry that they are gone and I am left alone. Or, I was alone. Now there are more of us."

"You mean Salinda is part-Hiem like me?" Karol asked.

Nils pursed his lips, not quite sure how to proceed. "You look a lot like me and I am a full Hiem. Do you understand?"

Karol looked down. "I think so. So Salinda is only a little part. And the girl, Laidan, she is more of a Hiem?"

Nils's frowned at himself. "Yes. That is right."

Karol reached up and pressed a hand on Nils's forearm. "I like you."

In return, Nils laid a hand on the boy's head. "Likewise. So let us begin." And he pulled up a chair and wrote out the script and explained how it coded the words people said.

After an hour, Karol was tired and put his head on the desk. Nils stood, stretching his spine so he could return to his own work. Trell, his grandsire, awaited him.

Nils found it hard to keep emotions tamped down. Having the boy close helped him control them. He thought he knew and understood his grandsire, but this diary could have been written by a stranger. How could Trell so abandon his own kind, his own way of looking at this world?

Nils found he did not like the woman that Trell was so taken with and skipped over the parts that talked of their intimate moments. This growing disgust allowed him to read faster, just as Salinda had wanted, and then he found a section on the machine. There was a drawing of a squarish structure with a domed roof. Four had been built, each in a position to reach Ruel moon from different points on Margra's surface. Nils noted down the location of each of them so he could look at their positions on the map. He considered the destruction of the surface of Margra and realized he would have to draw a new map. Two of the machines were had been destroyed, he was certain, because they were right in the middle of the rift on the Strega continent where part of Ruel hit. One had been built on the Stoli continent but had been swamped in the great inundation. The other was on Arvoli.

Many of the scientific explanations of the machines were beyond him and he realized then that not all the technology had been invented by the team. At this, Nils rocked back in his chair, hands dropping to his lap. Trell had accessed Moon Binder technology. He had raided the warehouse at Stregahiem, where the best collection of the alien technology had been stored.

Nils found that there were tears falling down his cheeks. He glanced at the boy, who had woken again, and was diligently practicing the script, and quickly brushed his tears away lest Karol see his distress.

Trell had committed a major crime, far greater than the one Nils had. Hiem did not do what Trell did: they did not betray their very existence to Sundwellers. They did not use Moon Binder technology that was barely understood.

Wiping his eyes, he read further. Trell had identified the technology by his study of Ruel moon. The bindings—the red bands of power that held the fractured moon together—had been put there by the Moon Binders. Legend pointed to this and Trell, through his observations, had identified the bands of power and, later, he had located the device that had made the bands among the Moon Binder artifacts. Here, again, the words were too difficult for Nils, but what he understood was this: part of that alien technology had been placed in the machines and it was this hybrid technology that changed the substance, the mass, of the split parts of Ruel moon and made them have a lesser impact. It was this machine that had saved Margra from total destruction.

He read on, eager for the end of this chapter, combining what Trell and his companions intended with what had occurred. What they created destroyed parts of the moon and changed larger chunks of the moon. Not all of it fell. What had been blasted away had formed a debris field: Shatterwing.

That was why everyone was in danger now. The rest of it was coming down, drawn to the surface by gravity and the disruptive orbits of other solar system objects. Nils thought back to what the observatory had described happening in the Wing. Some fragment had been blown out on an oblique orbit and was moving back into the Wing, sweeping all before it and destabilizing the whole thing. Trell had worked to save some of the planet, and he had achieved that for a period of time, but the delay was almost over. The end was getting closer.

He shook his head. He must not give in to despair. Salinda would not have it. She thought there was a chance that this machine, or machines, could be used again.

He read on, hoping beyond hope that there was more description of where they were. And how the machine was operated.

❧❧❧❧❧

Later, Karol and Nils drank tea in the quiet of Nils's abode. After good progress with the book it was time for rest.

"Do you know any rhymes?" Karol asked.

"Rhymes? What do you mean?" Nils responded and took a sip of tea. He had to admit to having a headache, probably from clenching his jaw while he read Trell's diary. He had pushed himself, and Karol had sat quietly, leaving him to focus. He was grateful for the child's patience and self-control, so he forbore asking the boy to be quiet and let him rest now.

"Stories that have words that rhyme. You know, so you don't forget something. My grandfather taught me one."

Nils drank his tea and studied the boy. He thought hard, trying to ignore the ache behind his eyes. "Perhaps, when I was young like you, but I fear I do not recall them. Did you want to sing one?"

Karol nodded. "Yes. You will like it. We are only to sing it among the clan and as you are full-blooded Hiem then you are clan."

Nils's ears pricked up. "Only among the clan?"

"Yes." The boy straightened his shoulders and leaned his head slightly to one side and sang:

Through the Valley of the Eye
Until you see the sky
To find the path forbidden
To the ancient city hidden
Too many turns do you take
Until you bathe in the lake…

"By the source, can it be!" Nils exclaimed, nearly dropping his cup.

Karol narrowed his eyes. "What? Do you not like it?"

"Yes, of course I like it. Do you know this Valley of the Eye?" Nils asked.

"It is only a rhyme."

"No, it is a map. A map to where you came from." Nils blinked away tears. To think this was the clue he had been hoping for. He had been asking Karol all kinds of questions to find the city his clan came from. All

179

the time it was there in the child's rhyme. He racked his brain wondering what other Hiem settlements there were. He had lived in the largest city, but that did not mean that other Hiem settlements did not call themselves cities. If there had been a doubt about the child's heritage, this little verse proved it beyond doubt. "The Valley of the Eye," he repeated quietly. There was something familiar in that. Something recently familiar, for he doubted the geography was the same as before Ruel moon fell, which meant it was a modern map. Were there any of his kind still alive?

Hope fluttered in his chest and then stilled. They did not use the Ways. Nils would have detected it. Then he reasoned that just because they did not use the Ways, did not mean they did not exist. They could be living there in the Valley of the Eye. He would have to think on it. Nils had been totally caught up in his musings, for when the boy touched him gently on the shoulder, he started.

"Are you angry with me?" Karol asked.

Nils's mouth dropped open. "Angry? No. No! You have given me hope where there was none. I think we should look for this hidden city."

"Really. You mean the rhyme is true?" Karol had a puzzled frown.

"I think it is, or was. There is no guarantee, but I think we might find your kin if we follow the directions in the rhyme."

Karol let out a *whoop* of joy. "Really, truly? Do we leave now?"

Nils smiled at the lad's joy. "Not yet. When I figure out where I have seen this valley."

"Tomorrow, then, in the morning?" Karol asked excitedly.

Nils grinned at the boy. "How I wish it was so."

The boy had that otherworldly look and Nils's skin chilled. "You will remember," he said. "I see the image of it there in your mind."

❧❧❧❧❧

Nils's sleep was disturbed. Trell's words stormed about in his mind and he dreamed of the Valley of the Eye, running toward it, but finding on turning a corner that it was gone.

Karol woke him early, asking again if they could go and Nils shook his head at the wonder of it. He was willing to. He had almost finished reading Trell's book and the others were gone. Why not venture out and retrace his steps? He had to have seen or heard of the Valley of the Eye on one of his earlier forays before he even met Salinda. It was not near the valley where the observatory sat. Nils was almost certain of this as he had not traversed there.

"I've packed us some food," Karol said, eyes bright.

"Very well. We will head north and see what we can see. But no promises, Karol, because I do not know if we can find the valley, which is the key to your rhyming map."

Karol cast his eyes down and his head lowered fractionally, his disappointment dampened but not quashed. Nils understood that in the boy. He was young and resilient, but he had also lost everything. His mother, father and kin. Nils had been much older when he had lost everything and he had found it hard enough to cope. He only worried he had given false hope and that he could not bear. He did not want to wound the boy.

Nils took extra time to fashion some shrouds for them. Danton talked about how someone had been able to see him in his shroud, but Nils had to hope that such an ability was not widely available. Regardless, it would be better to be cautious.

Karol examined his shroud in wonder. Holding out an arm, he grinned and then looked down the length of himself. "This is a Hiem invention?"

Nils nodded as he slipped on his own shroud. He demonstrated where the pockets were and how to power it on. Karol eyes grew even wider. "I don't remember anyone talking about these, but they would have helped us hide. Maybe we wouldn't have been found so easily. We took precautions, you know, and we were well hidden but they found us anyway."

Nils crouched down in order to be closer to the boy. He studied the boy's face and used a thumb to shift a lock of hair from his eyes. "We do not know if shrouds would have saved them. We have to deal with what we do know. You are here with me and we are Hiem."

Karol sniffed once and wiped the tip of his nose with the back of his hand. "But…" he began.

Nils felt around his pocket for a cloth for him to use. "Your ancestors survived a lot of terrible things to live until now, until you. We will go see if there are more of us. It may be futile. They may have gone now, because these were your grandsire's people and we do not know what happened after he left. But we will do our best...understand?"

Karol sniffed again and took the cloth that Nils handed to him and blew his nose. "I understand...I shouldn't get my hopes up."

Nils's gut twisted. The excited gleam in the boy's eyes was subdued and he hated how he had done that, brought the lad down. Was it better to do that, or let him crash emotionally later if they were unsuccessful? Nils wished that he could ask Salinda for advice for he knew that his own perspective was shaped by his experiences and his reactions to them. Nils was naturally negative in outlook and that realization shamed him.

"Shall we go?" Nils said and pushed to his feet.

Karol grabbed hold of his hand and Nils, at first repulsed, decided that it was best to let the child cling to him. He had done enough damage already.

For some reason, there was clarity in his mind that morning, despite the troubled sleep. He had decided on a place, near where he had first heard the dragon's wing beat. There had been a city there once, and close by would have been a Hiem settlement.

They entered the Ways together and as the boy walked Nils grew conscious of something. The in-between glowed. At first it was so slight and subtle that Nils thought he was imagining it, but then as his eyes adjusted to the gloom he was sure. He turned to the boy, but he was oblivious. Nils shook his head and kept walking, listening to Karol chatter about his childhood and his favorite games. Sometimes he let slip details about happenings from his time in the camp. The boy had been so hungry all the time and he knew his mother gave up her portion to him and he would sneak it back. He lost weight. He stopped growing. He thought he was going to die, or that he would get thin enough to slip through the break in the fence and escape.

"Karol," Nils interrupted.

"Yes," Karol responded.

The light that glowed as the boy passed intrigued him. "What do you recall about your time in the in-between?"

Karol frowned and looked about him. "The in-between?"

Nils gestured to the substance that surrounded them. "Yes, the in-between where I found you."

"Not much," Karol said, giving the walls a steely look. He reached out a hand and where his fingers touched, light erupted. He did not pull his hand back, but stared at the light play as he moved his fingers. His eyes took on a faraway look.

Nils grew concerned. "Karol..."

The boy did not respond. Nils put his hand on the boy's shoulder and Karol stepped back. He looked up at Nils in surprise. "What's wrong?"

Nils shook his head. "Nothing. Let us keep moving." Nils was thrown. It was bad enough that they had one mysterious boy in their midst what with Garan and his power, and now Karol. But they were not the same. Karol's power was slight, more intrinsic to the Hiem. Was the in-between sentient? Nils had never thought to ask that before.

Such a question absorbed Nils's mind until they reached the Way Gate they were to exit from. He thought about how the Ways were in his youth. The Ways were to the Hiem as the veins were to the body taking blood and nourishment to all the parts. Living, breathing Hiem constantly traversed the Ways. It was part of them just as they were part of it.

In these latter days, there had been only Nils and the humans using the Ways. At first, the Ways seemed dead, then, over time, they had started to awaken. Nils had grown more attuned, could sense when someone was within the Ways and where. Nils had used the in-between and it had drained him. Was that it? Was that the signifier? He had detected Karol while in the healing tray. Karol had called to him. Or...the Ways had. That was remarkable, to say the least.

When he had used the in-between it had taken his life energy, almost killing him. For Karol, it had done the opposite. It had captured and maintained the child's life. Or had it? Nils shook his head, giving the in-between a baleful glare. Had the Ways changed the boy?

If Nils had not killed Nakel himself, he would not have known that Karol had been in the in-between for only a short time. He might have supposed that Karol had been there since Moonfall.

As he walked, Nils studied the in-between, hoping to see…what? More Hiem kept whole there? *No.* He shook his head. *No. You are starting to invest more in this than what is plain. You are starting to dream the impossible dream.*

૭૭૭૭

The Valley of the Eye was where Nils suspected it was. He and Karol scampered across the desolate plain with their shrouds engaged. Karol was not as hampered as Nils was. Nils gripped the boy's hand so tightly his fingers started to tingle as blood flow decreased. His jaw hurt, too. His innate fear of the outside, fear of the humans, or what remained of the humans in these parts, made him afraid, made him meek. He did not like that sensation, but realized he could do nothing at the present time to stop it.

Karol's gait was awkward due to the shroud, but his pace was quick. No jutting boulder or eroded ditch thwarted him. Nils sighed, envying the boy his youth and energy.

Now that he knew what to look for, Nils located the gate fairly easily.

"Can I open it?" Karol asked excitedly, hand already reaching for the symbols.

"Yes," Nils said, standing back to let the boy perform the task.

Once again, something odd happened to the boy. His body went still, his breathing became slow and deep, and Nils saw by his face that the boy was in some kind of trance. The small white hand reached out and touched the symbols on the groove in correct order. The boy's mouth was still, though. He did not chant as Nils would do. Nils cocked his head as the door opened. "How did…"

Karol shook himself and stood up, face somber. "You first, Nils of Barr."

Nils shivered in spite of himself. The maturity in the boy's voice and words belied his age. "Very well," Nils replied, equally somber, gathering up his shroud and moving forward.

Obvious signs of damage filled the Travel Way. After a short walk to the usual staircases, they found only one stair. The others were shattered into fragments. Nils peered into the gloom and where the stairs had been nothing showed but emptiness. A chill ran up his spine.

"Shall we go that way?" Karol asked.

Nils demurred. There was only one way to go. He peered at the damage and how evidence of other Ways had been erased. This was not damage caused by a failure of the Way's structure or through upheaval within Margra. It was deliberate.

☙☙☙☙☙

Garan studied the charts Epen had made. They were detailed and gave coordinates so that objects could be shot down even when not seen. There was a large cluster, just within range of the observatory. Choices needed to be made. Could Garan trek across the plains to another mountain peak to fire at them with greater accuracy? Epen would need to accompany him.

"We do not have sufficient time," Epen said. "It's coming soon. Skyfire. The precursor to moonfall."

Garan tried not to give in to despair. "What about we start hitting them from this angle? We might deflect them."

Epen bit his lip. "I could do the calculations. They are already affected by the planet's gravity."

"Let me try it now. It couldn't hurt."

The meteor he had diminished had not disintegrated. A hard core remained that would smack against the planet's crust with devastating effect. Smaller than before, but not destroyed. Garan had had a good evening, though, because he had shot down so many bits of Shatterwing that he thought it was a record.

Epen had developed a special scope that could aim their crystal beams with a higher degree of accuracy. With Garan's enhanced power, he could shoot farther than the others and this scope was built to withstand a greater explosive force.

Epen carefully set the gears on the scope, adjusting the crystal for height and distance. The chute was then loaded with a precisely cut crystal. "Why is the crystal faceted like that?" Garan asked.

Epen looked up from his map. "We found that it better focused the power. You will see."

Garan slipped into the old habits and hummed until the crystal glowed. He thought perhaps the hum helped his power to harmonize with the crystal.

Epen double-checked the settings and stepped back. "You can release now," he said before scrambling to his own scope.

Garan loved how the power growing inside him felt. Like his skin and his teeth and his hair were alive. The crystal glowed brightly and Garan shut his eyes, still able to see the crystal as well as taste the power with his eyes closed. "Now!" Epen shouted.

Garan's eyes snapped open and he focused on the sky. He could not see the meteor that he was aiming at. He looked to Epen. How could he see?

There was a flash in the distant sky and then Garan understood.

"How will you know if I hit it?" Garan asked.

Epen looked up from his scope. "I won't know until the sky clears enough for a direct observation."

Garan sagged. "Oh. Shall we keep trying?"

Epen smiled sadly. "Garan, even you, with your amazing talent and power, cannot clear Shatterwing from the sky." He came over and squeezed Garan's shoulder. "You have been of great assistance. You have helped me test my theory. Rest now. I hear you have a lot to do in the morning."

Garan glanced up. "What?"

"Salinda sent word a few hours ago. The messenger we sent to Vanden is returning with the townsfolk who are willing to flee into the lost city. You are to be dispatched to the doomsday cave and do the same. While we worked, scaffolding was erected in the cave that leads to the Way Gate so that people can pass without danger or too much effort."

"But I…"

Epen shook his head. "You have to work with Salinda. You can't stay here. This is not where moonfall will land. Understand? You must travel to where it will. I hope Salinda will find the machine she is looking for."

Garan lowered his head. "Me too. Are you going to stay?"

"Yes. There are those of us who will stay until there is nothing left for us to do. Until we can no longer do what we can."

His eyes wet with emotion, Garan turned away and headed off to find Salinda. He had some things to do before he slept. Somehow, he understood he would never see the observatory again. He didn't know if it was because he was going to die, or because the building and all it stood for was going to be destroyed. The cadre told him that the observatory had been destroyed before and risen again. If Garan did what he planned to do, if they succeeded, there would always be a Trithorn Peak observatory on this spot. Despite what the cadre said, Garan felt the weight of grief on him. Life had been so much easier before. Although he also understood that the events unfolding would have unfolded anyway. Nothing he did could change that. All he could affect was the outcome.

ᗧ ᗧ ᗧ ᗧ ᗧ

Salinda looked in on Garan before going to sleep herself. He looked so peaceful, so innocent and young. He had taken word to the doomsday cave and now they were getting ready to move to the Hiem city, just like the Vanden people. She shook her head, wishing that the world was a better place so that Garan's gift could be used to make people's lives better, instead of using it to save the planet.

She withdrew and headed down the hallway. The cadre was warm tonight, filled with sorrow and emotion. That just made Salinda angry. There were so many questions she wanted answered. What was it that Garan had detected in the bowels of Barrahiem? Was it important? In her gut she thought so. It was not that machine they had found because he said it was not. Yet, that was also important. If only they had more time, but everything seemed to be crumbling like some overbaked cake that could not defy gravity any longer. It was crumbling in her hands. The world was going to end while she was still trying to find answers.

"You can only do the best you can," she said to herself and then realized it was the cadre speaking to her in a prosaic manner.

It is all right for you. You are already dead. Why can't you be helpful for a change?

The anger was sudden and hot. "What use were you? What use are you? I wish...I wish..." But she couldn't bring herself to regret being gifted with the cadre. If she hadn't possessed the cadre when the Inspector had captured her, torturing and drugging her into slave-like devotion, she wouldn't have survived. She would have let herself die. She would not have fought for life for the cadre. She did understand that the cadre was why she was here, right now, that all her paths had led to this. Self-recrimination wasn't helping things. She was doing the best she could and more. The baby kicked and then kicked again. She felt the pressure on her bladder.

The annoyance brewed hotter. She couldn't decide whether it was better to give birth now or later. If there was going to be a later. It was so frustrating because she had no control over her body just when she needed to be at her best. "Damn."

In her room sat the glide. She was going to be using that tomorrow. Had to. She sat on the bed and looked at her swollen ankles. She had been on her feet all day, going over plans, organizing supplies. The observatory had quite a lot of food in storage. Now they were emptying it out. Transporting it through the Ways was logistically difficult. Stacking it in the cave would suffice for now.

Out her window, she gazed at the red sky. She thought it was less red and more naturally clear now. Belle moon's light penetrated feebly but it was getting through at last. It was a dark, angry purple.

Part 2

The truths we hold dear, die in the wine we drink...

Donna Maree Hanson

Chapter Nineteen

A TRACE OF DUST
AND A FLICKER OF HOPE

It was difficult to keep Karol from skipping ahead. He could not blame the child but Nils's inherent wariness made him cautious.

"Stick close, Karol," Nils repeated, again unheeded.

The Way showed little evidence of recent use. Dust sat in layers on the path and the in-between seemed resistant, harder than what Nils was used to. Nils reached out a hand and frowned at what met his fingers. It was firm, but not rock hard. Nils could not push into this in-between. More and more he suspected that this particular Way had been separated from the network of Ways deliberately.

Fear and hope warred in his chest. Sweat beaded on his forehead. He was not given to excitement easily, but his heart rate picked up its beat.

Again, they came to a staircase that had been partially destroyed. One pathway led out of the Ways. Nils found himself holding his breath.

Darkness loomed. Karol took Nils's hand. "Is this it?" he asked.

"Yes," Nils replied, "shall we step through?"

Karol bounded ahead to the symbols on the door. He repeated his performance to Nils's wonder. How did he know how to open the gate?

The door slid open. Bright sunlight caused Nils to falter and he raised his arms to shade his eyes. Karol blinked. "It's not an underground city," the boy commented.

Nils increased the shroud's light filter and when that kicked in, he lowered his arms and narrowed his eyes.

"No!" he blurted as he took in the baked shell of the small town. It had been a Hiem settlement once, but it was exposed to the elements now. Houses collapsed in like crushed eggshells. Stepping down the stair before him, Nils saw the high sides of the bowl in which the city had sat. Long ago, the city's roof had been eroded away.

They walked farther in. The outer edges appeared long deserted. Streets empty of life, but full of rock and stunted growth that had taken root in the cracks of houses and walkways.

Karol pulled on his hand. "Can I go look?"

Nils gripped the boy's hand. "No, let's do this together. There could be danger."

Moving deeper into the oval-shaped city, jagged shapes of upper balconies loomed overhead, effectively hiding the bulk of the city from view. The rustle of wind as it sang through the deserted streets put Nils on edge. It was not something he associated with Hiem dwellings. Nils had the urge to turn back. Danger itched at the back of his neck. Just as the city was exposed so was he exposed, like nerve endings twitching after being severed.

Nils had thought seeing Barrahiem as a ghost city for the first time had hardened him. Even Gateshead had not affected him as much as this.

The sound of a rock hitting rock echoed around them. Nils stilled and clutched at Karol's shoulder. The boy turned his head, mouth opening to voice the question poised on his lips. Nils shook his head and lifted a finger to his lips, signaling for quiet.

More rubble tumbled somewhere below them. They were not alone. There was a light wind, not something that should cause rocks to fall. Slowly, Nils crept forward and leaned around a decaying balcony support and froze.

A dragon was there, tail twitching, claws worrying at a tumble of rocks that looked once to have been a set of abodes. Karol pressed against his leg as he, too, leaned out. He let out a slow gasp. Nils prayed to the source that the dragon had not heard. He pulled back and drew Karol back by the shoulder. He rested his back against the crumbling building and thought furiously. Why was the dragon there?

Food was the answer. What kind of food would be in a deserted Hiem city? *Hiem!*

His palms were wet with stress. He dared not raise the boy's hopes, but somehow they needed to distract the dragon or wait until it was gone. Either was so nerve-racking that Nils wanted to bolt back to the Way and flee.

But the possibility of other Hiem living in these ruins made him stand his ground. This is what he had dreamed of since he first awoke and the solid evidence of Hiem blood in others was a clue that his people had not all died. Nakel and his son Karol were proof that the Hiem also kept up some kind of coherent cultural and biological identity. This ruined city was the first chance he'd had of finding some of his kin with ties to their home.

Hot breath brushed against his face. Both he and Karol had their shrouds engaged so they should be invisible to the dragon. Unless the dragon's vision worked differently? The dragon inhaled and Nils's knees jerked when he realized that the dragon could smell them. What was worse was that this was a different dragon, a second beast. Karol squeezed his hand and Nils felt gratitude that Karol kept quiet. The boy tugged and urged Nils to step sideways. Not being able to think due to fear, Nils followed the boy's prompting.

Around a stone pedestal they edged and the boy pulled harder on his arm. There was a crevice, small, but they could scramble inside. Nils chanced a look over his shoulder and saw a large clawed foot thump on the ground right near where they had been standing.

Karol scrambled in ahead of him and Nils prayed to the source that the dragon would not notice them until Nils was inside. Sharp rocks tore at his shroud as he crawled along the ground behind Karol. The small tunnel opened out into a large space where there was a staircase leading down. Karol threw off his shroud.

"Quick, down the steps before the dragon blows fire!" Nils urged.

Karol was off and Nils, with one look at the dark cleft they had crawled through, followed. Just as he reached the top stair a great bellow reached him and a fireball pierced the darkness. Nils stumbled and fell down the stairs. Darkness...

Nils came to with hands slapping at the flames from the remains of his shroud and Karol calling his name. "Nils! Nils! Wake up!" the terror-edged voice urged. For a fleeting moment, Nils understood the boy's fear. If anything happened to Nils, the boy could be stranded.

Taking a breath, Nils closed his eyes to focus on his body. He hurt but until he moved a leg or an arm or tried to sit up he would not know how bad it was.

"Help me to sit up," he said to Karol.

Nils moved an arm. It twinged, but it obeyed his command. The other arm was better. His knee hurt when he flexed his leg, but it worked. Same with the other. Karol helped him into a sitting position. Nils breathed and his body told him nothing was broken. "I am all right." A big sigh eased through Nils's lips.

Karol launched himself at Nils and threw his arms around his neck. It was then Nils realized the boy was crying. Moved by the child's concern, no matter how self-oriented it was, he lifted a hand and patted the boy on the back. "It will be all right."

Karol squeezed him hard and then let go, sitting back on his haunches and wiping tears from his face with his right hand. "I'm okay now. Sorry."

"Help me to my feet, will you?" Karol nodded, and sprang to his feet with Nils's hand in his. He pulled and Nils clambered awkwardly upright. He wavered for a moment and then the world stopped spinning. The passage they were in went along farther with the ceiling riddled with fractures. Above, they could hear the rage of screaming dragons and the sound of rocks being dislodged as claws gouged them away. For the moment they were safe. "Let us see if we can find your kin."

Karol took Nils's hand in a firm grip and led him on. Nils limped, his knee aching. However, this was a minor injury and Nils counted himself lucky. It could have been so much worse.

Signs of habitation drew his attention, and Karol's, too. The boy stared up at Nils and then back down at what was before them. The passageway was clean. Perhaps it was regularly swept, kept free of dust and debris. He contrasted it to the streets of Barrahiem when he'd first awoken, where the dust from the remains of his departed kin had rolled and churned along the passageways, stirred up by Nils's steps.

Nils wanted to call out. Only his innate caution kept him quiet. He drew Karol in behind him as they trod the path. The space wasn't large. Nils scanned the ceiling and guessed the area had been used for storage, taken over for living space when the city became exposed.

The path curved, and when they rounded the bend they saw the first body. Nils stood stock-still and Karol peeked out from behind him and let out a squeak. It was an older Hiem, shriveled and emaciated in death. The body lay sprawled to the side with only a twisted foot on the path.

Nils's hopes sank. Taking Karol by the hand, he skirted the body and they kept going. Two more bodies littered the path and Nils near wept. They were Hiem and they were dead and he was too late. Hope leaked out of his heart and regret pressed inexorably against his mind. Why had he not explored all known Hiem settlements? Why had he given himself up to despair when he could have done something sooner?

A faint sound reached him and his head jerked up and then over to the right. Something moved there. "Wait. We mean you no harm," he called.

He turned to Karol. "Who or what was it? Did you see?"

Karol shook his head. "No. I don't like it here."

The stone roof above dipped lower the farther they went in. Some of the fractures looked recent, with a fine dust raining down. There were no signs of vegetation. No obvious place where food was stored or grown. If the dragons had been attacking for a while, these people could be hungry, starving. He thought those bodies had been of old people. Would they have sacrificed themselves for the young?

"We will sit here," Nils said, choosing the remains of a stair to sit on. "Do you still have the food I gave you?"

Karol sat opposite him on the ground after sweeping some stones out of the way. "Yes," he answered. "Why?"

"Do as I do," Nils instructed. He reached into his deep pockets and brought out a number of loaves of Garan's flat bread. The bread stored well and was good for travel. It had been the last of the supply Garan had baked before leaving for Trithorn Peak. Nils then drew out some lairn apples fresh from the orchard. Karol added some dried fungi and a flask of water.

Then some dried berries, of which he had a lot. Nils guessed they were the lad's favorite food.

Nils shifted and glanced around him. "There is food here. Come, eat. We will not harm you."

Silence filled the space around them. They waited patiently. Karol fidgeted. "Nils, I want to look around."

Nils blinked. "Look around…but…"

"I can get into small spaces…I can find them."

"You need to be careful."

"I will be."

Nils considered for a moment. His ploy had not worked. Perhaps the boy would have more luck. "Very well, but watch out for yourself."

Karol jumped to his feet, took a quick look around him and then scampered over the rubble in the direction from which they had first detected movement. Nils hoped that this effort would not be in vain.

After a few long moments, a squeal cut through the quiet and Nils jumped to his feet. A head popped up and then disappeared. Then something ran over a path through what he thought might be houses. It happened so fast he was not quite sure what he saw. Another scream, and the sounds of rocks falling and feet scrambling reached him.

Karol's head popped up. "Did you see them? There are about ten of them hiding here." Then the boy disappeared again.

Nils, on his feet, began to call out. "I am Hiem. I am kin. Do not be afraid. We have food. We have come to help."

A shout had Nils spinning on his heel. A blurred shape plowed into him and he fell back. Wrestling with his assailant, he tried to reason. "Stop. Please."

Still the hands reached for him. Pale, thin hands. "I am from Barrahiem. I am your kin. Kin!"

The hands stilled and retreated. Nils sat up and stared at the female squatting opposite him. She was mostly naked, with rags draped across her middle. She was young by the look of her. For a moment, Nils thought she could not speak. That she was the Hiem version of the Lesserens.

"Kin," she said. "Kin are dead."

Nils shook his head, pushed back the torn remains of his shroud so that she could see him clearly. "I am Nils of Barr, from the city of Barrahiem. We have come to find you."

"You are an old one. The old ones are dead."

Nils caught a glimmer of movement out of the corner of his eye. Others were drawing near, all in the same state as the female.

Nils picked up the bread and broke it into sections, handing the first to the female, and then Karol appeared at his side to distribute the rest. "What has happened here?"

He looked meaningfully at the surroundings.

"The beasts came and they kept on coming. We could not get out. Food ran out. Our parents chose to starve so that we might live." She looked at the bread in her hand, studied it.

Nils mimicked putting his hand to his mouth and biting. "It is good," he said. "We can take you where there is more."

"How?" she said and took a bite. She chewed quickly and swallowed it in a big lump. "The dragons block the way."

"We will help you. We will find a way."

She shook her head. "No. It cannot be done. Many tried and then died."

"I found my way in here," Nils said with a shrug. "What may I call you?"

She hit her chest. "Avenal."

Nils nodded. "Pleased to meet you, Avenal. I have come to take you home." Tears filled Nils's eyes as he took in the ten youthful Hiem who surrounded him. His people lived. Alas, not many, but they were Hiem. Same silver eyes, same white hair and skin. If only he could promise them that the world was not going to end.

"This is Karol. I believe he is your kin, too. Closer in blood than I am. It is his words that led us here to find you."

Avenal turned to Karol, tilted her head and grinned. She inclined her head. "Thank you, kinsman Karol. We are in your debt. While I thank you for the food, you have yet to convince me that we should risk our lives with the dragons."

"There should be another way out," Nils said. "We just have to find it."

Because Hiem cities and towns had similar layouts, Nils was able to establish that there was another Way Gate. It was difficult, however, with the city in such disarray and buildings being destroyed. After discovering where the Hall of Elders had been, he oriented himself by confirming the position of the gate he and Karol had used.

"The Way Gate should be there." He indicated the direction, which was currently occupied by a large tumble of rocks and boulders and completely impassable.

Avenal turned to him, a quizzical expression in her silver eyes. Karol grinned. "We go down?" he guessed.

Nils stood and brushed off his robe. "We do. I assume you know the way down?" he asked Avenal.

She stood when he did and motioned for the others to join them. She did a quick round of introductions. Not all had Hiem-sounding names. "Jokun, Helum, Miraka, Olenka, Dinn, Polu, Wenka, Tomu and Elenki," Avenal said.

The motley bunch of youths had seen hard times. Dirty hair filled with earth and dust. Some, like Jokun and Miraka, had short hair that stood up in filthy spikes. Olenka and Wenka, sisters apparently, each had a single plait down their backs. The rest had their hair loose. Their clothing was but mere rags, holey bits of material tied or strapped on. Stick thin, sunken cheeks and stooped shoulders. Nils would have given them up for lost souls if not for the brightness in their silver eyes.

"Polu, you lead the way. You were down below most recently," Avenal said. Polu scrambled forward. He looked to have a bad leg, some unhealed injury. Nils's heart twisted. If only he had searched more thoroughly, he could have saved these children sooner. He could have soothed his hurt at the loss of his kind. But there was no use in lamenting what he had not done before. It was now, this moment, that he needed to exert himself for these children of the Hiem.

Nils gathered up the edge of his robe to assist his passage through the small tunnel that Polu led them to. It looked like the tunnel had been excavated from a previous collapse. Just as he entered, a rockfall filled the space where they had been talking. Nils's head jerked around when the deafening screech of a dragon filled the air. "Hurry," Nils urged as he pushed the others ahead of him. Rocks beat at the earth where they had just stood as if the dragon sensed its prey was escaping.

The rockfall was undermining the stability of the tunnel they were in. Nils detected vibrations against his fingers as shock waves shifted the rocks overhead. It was dark and Nils had trouble seeing where they were going, bent over and crawling in the space behind Karol. To his relief, as the tunnel angled down, he noted they were moving into a Hiem passageway, free of the stacked debris of the wrecked city. Here they could stand up straight, but as the muffled cry of an enraged dragon reached them, they ran. Just in time, too, for Nils was the last one out of the tunnel, which collapsed just as he stepped through. The structure falling in was due to the weight of the pursuing dragon.

They continued in haste until the passageway met a stair. They followed it upward and Nils found his body tensing, hoping beyond hope that the Way Gate was intact. So much of the city was in ruins. He recalled with clarity that one of the stairs to a Way Gate had been blocked in Barrahiem when he first tried to venture out, and he had had to use the north-west stair instead.

As they climbed the stair out of the layer of rubble, they were once again exposed. It was the triumphant roars from both dragons that told them they had been spotted.

"Run!" Nils urged. He had no desire to be dragon fodder. Then, as though they'd discovered hidden energy reserves, the children ran and Nils pelted up the stairs after them. If the gate was not functional, they were doomed.

Karol pushed his way through the children who were blocking access to the Way Gate. "Hurry!" Nils called, unable to hide his panic. He could not bring himself to look behind, to see the jaws opening. Already the breeze from the wings of the dragons disturbed his hair, making it float around his face.

Nils had no more time to think about that. Karol opened the gate. The children rushed through and Nils bolted after them. Then he stopped and looked down. A claw had caught his leg. Heart thumping, Nils turned and recoiled as a hot breath washed over him. A scream sounded. It was not his own, but others' voices joining together and their hands waving. Distracted for a brief moment, the dragon released its grip, enough for Nils to free himself from that single claw and run. The children backed inside, Avenal hauling him through by his hand. The claw came again, but this time Nils was through. The door shut, the fetid stench of dragon breath the only remnant of that threat.

Nils lay on the ground, panting. He had never been so scared in his life. Previously, he had been fascinated by dragons; now, he had had his fill. That was too close. The children gathered around him, silver gazes expectant.

"Now," Nils said, as he sat up and arranged his robe with more dignity, "we shall go to Barrahiem."

Chapter Twenty
MIGRATION

Surprisingly, Salinda was refreshed after a rather restless night. Perhaps it was the thought of returning to Barrahiem; perhaps it was the thought that Nils had answers for her. She didn't really know why, although being horizontal had taken the pressure off her feet and the swelling was less. Whatever it was, she was fit enough to face the day. The work to facilitate the migration of those coming to Barrahiem was complete. What was once a fairly treacherous path was now a wooden walkway, complete with stairs. Seated on her glide at the entrance to the cave, she waved to Titina and Wylie who had come to say farewell.

"Why won't you come with us?" Salinda asked, one last time.

"We have nothing to offer the next world, but we can work here to lessen the destruction of the smaller firestorm. Skyfire could do damage and, if by chance you do stop moonfall, our early success would mean less healing to do afterward."

Behind them, Garan ushered people through the caves. Each had bundles of possessions and backpacks full of food. It would be enough until they could arrange transport for the rest of the supplies. Vanden folk were in among them and Salinda silently rejoiced that they had managed to convince the majority of them to come. Some were understandably reluctant, having seen and gone through too much to consider life underground as any sort of life at all. Salinda respected their choice and was glad that those who would remain did not attempt to stop those who chose to leave. *To live*, Salinda thought. They had chosen to live.

As the day progressed, weariness knocked at the door of her mind. A voice whispered that everything she did was for naught. That was not the cadre, that was her own self. The part of her that had lost hope. Every breath sometimes seemed to be a struggle. Yet looking at the people of Vanden and the observatory folk marching into the cave, chatting and smiling, gave her the power to smash that negative voice.

Salinda lowered her glide a tad so that she could kiss Titina and Wylie goodbye. "I will always think of you," Salinda said, suddenly finding her eyes moist and her chest tight.

Titina wiped a tear that decided to slide down her cheek at that auspicious moment. She looked at her moist finger in wonderment. "I didn't think I had any sorrow left." She lifted her lips in a lopsided smile. "Take care of them for me."

Salinda tried to smile, but she feared it was more of a tight-lipped grimace that did nothing to reassure these elders that she was going to achieve anything. Having said their farewells, they turned away and started back up the path to the observatory. Salinda engaged her glide and followed the people into the cave mouth.

As she neared the Way Gate she heard Garan's reassuring tones guiding people inside, where they waited in a line to be led to Barrahiem. That was Salinda's job and she was late, as soon became apparent when she tried to enter the Way. People had to move out of her way and she apologized to those she bumped into with the glide.

After an uncomfortable time working her way to the head of the line, she hovered there. "Follow me to your new home."

And then she saw that they lifted their bundles and adjusted their packs and she turned and headed through the Ways. These people were destined for N'Barek and if that didn't work out then she'd convince Nils to let them inhabit Barrahiem. Although with skyfire imminent and moonfall soon after, it might be a moot point discussing anything. The Hiem city would offer some protection, but with the planet devastated by moonfall, how long would any of them last?

ᗢᗢᗢᗢ

Garan waited for the stragglers. He kept looking to see if more people were coming but when, after a few hours there were no more, he stepped into the Way Gate and shut it behind him. He had passed his time transferring the crates of food and supplies from the cave into the Way Gate. Perhaps it was just a nagging fear that someone would steal them. He laughed at himself when he thought of that. It seemed tidier somehow to have it all within the Ways rather than in a cave. When he came back for the supplies with a larger slide, he would check the cave once more to see if there were any stragglers or elders who had changed their mind.

On his way, he found a few people who had lost the tail end of the line of people following Salinda. They were distressed, crying and wailing, but when they saw him they stopped and ran up to him. These were Vanden folk.

"'Tis all right now. 'Tis only a tunnel. Keep walking. I am here with you." They settled after that, but the ones in front looked over their shoulders at him, eyes showing white in the gloom of the Ways. Garan did not try to explain the nature of the Ways. He figured calling them tunnels for now was the best course of action. Besides, it was Nils's place to explain the Ways. Garan still could not grapple with the concepts. To him they defied gravity at times and at others they didn't. In any case, he was able to navigate them well enough.

The leaders had candles that were getting low so Garan turned on his Hiem light. The people accepted the illumination without getting too interested in the source. One of the males in the group he recognized from the observatory. A workman, he recalled. Not everyone at the observatory had, or needed, talent with crystals or higher learning. There were lots of unskilled tasks that required attention. Garan nodded to the man. This was one of those who had volunteered to go with the Vanden women and rebuild the town. There was a woman with him. They held hands and that made Garan smile. They had found some love and affection despite the despair around them. It warmed Garan's heart to know that.

"Take the left-hand stair," he called out to the leaders. They obeyed the instruction and led everyone onward. The walls of the in-between were lighter than before. Garan slowed his step to examine the wall closer to him. It was glowing faintly. He put his forefinger against the wall and pressed. Little flickers of light spread out from his fingertip. The substance of the Way was soft, almost like thick mud. He pulled his finger out and examined the tip. Nothing. Just a finger. The wall of the Way stayed lighter.

Garan frowned and then hurried to keep up with the last of his stragglers. *The Ways are alive,* he thought, and the cadre warmed. Having so many living beings pass through had awakened something. *Is that bad?* he queried the cadre.

No, it returned. *Normal for the Ways.*

One of the cadre's holders had been a Hiem. Of that he was sure. How else would they know about the Ways?

"Who is that answering my questions?" Garan queried.

We are answering your questions.

Garan gritted his teeth. He could discern no change in flavor in that response. It was the cadre speaking as it always did in the same voice. He couldn't shake the thought, though, that it was a particular member of the cadre who answered.

When they came to the exit, Garan shuffled through the people to get to the front of the line. "Excuse me, please," he said and then grunted when someone turned suddenly and elbowed him in the gut. "That's right. Let me through to open the gate." As the people stepped back and rested against the in-between, Garan saw the wall lighten further. The sight made him shudder. He couldn't help thinking that the in-between was feeding off these people. The door opened and he stood back to let people pass one at a time. "Just wait in that space over there and I will take you down."

He had opened to the path to N'Barek. He wished these people were to settle in Barrahiem, but for now he had to be content with them being safe with a possible future ahead of them in N'Barek. Nils's reluctance to have them in Barrahiem had to be respected. They were all there on his sufferance. The Hiem could have said no, but Garan suspected that if pushed, Nils would not refuse. The Hiem did have a caring heart, after all.

Down in the city, Salinda sat on her slide, but looking so tired Garan thought she would fall off. "That way," she said, throwing out an arm. "Take any house that isn't occupied. You will need to clean it and set up your possessions. No fighting, please. There are plenty of houses and they are all much the same," Salinda said to those filing past her. Some stopped to ask questions. "Yes, you can take a place near your friends." "By the lake is fine." "Yes, up high is fine."

Garan hurried over once the last of his group was through and the Way was shut. "Let me continue with this. You need to rest."

Salinda sighed and visibly slumped. "You are such a good man, Garan. I confess I am very tired. Shall I see you back in Barrahiem?"

"Yes, I will come as soon as I can. Everything looks like it is going along well. Any sign of Danton and the other people?"

Salinda pursed her lips and shook her head. "No. I do hope nothing went wrong."

Garan threw up a false smile. "I am sure it all went very well. See you soon." Garan waved and turned to direct someone to an empty house. Then he answered a query from a young family, asking to have two houses together. He directed them to a section not yet occupied and told them to lay claim to what suited them. Even with this many people, there was space in N'Barek.

It filled Garan's heart with gladness that they had potentially saved hundreds of people. His mind could not encompass the many thousands who would perish. With these hundreds of people, there was hope for the future and he had a hand in that.

By the time the last of the refugees were sorted and all of the extant queries were answered, Garan could hardly keep his eyes open. A fatigue so strong threatened to overwhelm him. By rights, he should have found an abode and taken a nap, but he wanted to get back to Barrahiem. He wanted to see what had happened to Danton, Brill, Eneit and Laidan. To Laidan especially. Were they safe? Had they achieved their goal? He would not find out if he did not return to the city.

Then there was Salinda, anxious to know what Nils had found in his grandfather's book. Garan's stomach lurched when he thought of what would happen if Nils had nothing, or if Trell had left no clue. Garan had no idea what they would do or where they would start. It was too hard to even contemplate.

So with shoulders slumped and dragging feet, Garan let himself back into the Way for the short trip to Barrahiem. Half asleep, he took step after step, sometimes tripping over his feet because in his fatigued state he was not paying enough attention. The Way remained lighter, he noticed, looking up and wrinkling his nose in puzzlement. As he neared Barrahiem, that presence he often felt sharpened. He rocked to a halt, bathed in a pale blue glow, and examined his surroundings. He turned full circle until he came to a point where the feeling was strongest. Through the wall of the in-between lay that presence. He was certain of it.

Garan lifted a hand and laid it on the in-between. If only he could walk through like Nils had done. But that was dangerous. Garan went to draw his hand back and noticed that it had sunk into the wall. Tentatively, he put his weight behind it and his arm slid in to the shoulder. Garan was going to pull back but his cadre, normally placid, urged him on with excited whispers. *Yes, yes, yes!* So, on the cusp of pulling back, Garan changed direction and lunged into the in-between. It sucked him in, drawing him down. Garan could not breathe, could not feel air. His arms moved, his feet, too, and he struggled. Then his cadre calmed him down. *Think. Focus on where you want to go.*

Garan didn't know where, just that presence. In the panic of his mind and with lungs keen for breath, he reached out to find that presence, that mind that seemed to call him from afar...and found it. Garan detected movement. He was sliding through walls. The in-between was a lattice of connections built into the very fabric of Margra. For a fleeting moment, he was the Ways, and then he was spat out into a corridor. Garan gaped at his surroundings. He was not in the Ways. He was in the corridors below Barrahiem. At least, he hoped it was Barrahiem.

Ahead was an archway and Garan climbed to his feet, sucked in a breath and staggered forward. In the next room was inky blackness. He fumbled for his light and switched it on. A large statue stood there. It wasn't an image he was familiar with. Lizard-like, with clawed hands and feet, a long pointed head and three eyes. Was it a statue of a god of some kind?

Garan faltered as he looked around at the patterned wall. That presence had to be here, but there was nothing else in the room except the statue. The wall pattern was a geometric design in black and white. Not something he had seen before. Dizziness hit him. Suddenly he was weak and tired. He reached out to the statue for support and a tingling ran up his arm. With a cry, he pulled back. He was too late, though, for before his eyes the statue cracked open.

A cloud of blue haze seeped out into the room. Garan backed up against the wall, heart thumping, fatigue banished. Eyes wide, he watched the haze roil and roll into a shape. Then the presence noticed him. "You," it said into his mind. "What took you so long?"

Garan was not sure it actually spoke, but that was what his mind made of the communication. The presence seemed to be still for a long moment. Garan barely breathed because he thought that whatever it was, its attention was elsewhere.

"Fools," the presence said to Garan. "The moon is split."

Garan had an urge to answer it. Frightened out of his mind and yet he wanted to answer. "Yes, thousands of years ago. Who are you?"

"I am a daemon of the most high. You are scum."

Garan nodded. "Yes." His heart thumped like crazy. He had no idea what a daemon was. He looked at the broken statue and back to the roiling, blue mass.

"Are you a Moon Binder?" he ventured.

A noise like a hiss filled the air. "Moon Binder? We are the rulers of this system, this sector of space."

Garan furrowed his brow and took a huge breath. "Did your people bind the moon?"

"Yes." There was might behind that brooding spirit.

"Your bindings failed."

Again Garan got the sense that the creature was focused elsewhere.

"The vermin are everywhere," it commented.

Garan did not know who the vermin were. It could mean humans. "What are vermin?"

A spear of something lanced into Garan's brain. A vision peeled away the outer layers of his mind. The cadre recoiled at the onslaught of power, hiding itself deep. A dragon's wing unfurled and a vast maw issued flame. "This is the vermin."

"Dragons," Garan was able to say after the image dissipated and the presence vacated his mind. Garan shook himself, surprised to find himself still whole. The dragon had seemed so real he thought he had been fried by the flame.

"Fools," the presence said, and then it roiled fiercely and changed shape. Garan just stood there in shock when it arrowed up, and then dove straight at Garan.

Cold pierced Garan's gut and then shrouded his mind. The world went black.

Chapter Twenty-one
BARRAHIEM LIVES

Danton frowned at the empty city of Barrahiem. No Nils to greet them, or to negotiate with. The trip to Sartell had been dangerous, perhaps ill-conceived, but finding Squab had been a bonus. She stood there frowning, with her scar twisting her features into a sneer.

Laidan had convinced him that bringing the children here was better than taking them to N'Barek to fend for themselves. Something was different with Laidan, but Danton was too distracted to think much about it. The encounter with Gercomo had triggered something in her. Danton had not seen her horrific injuries, but knew them in detail because Garan, Nils and Salinda had separately told him of them at different times during his convalescence.

Brill had also weighed in on Laidan's inability to remember him and what they had been to each other. Danton decided that Brill took it well and in no way betrayed to Laidan or anyone else that they had previously been intimate. That situation could change and, if it did, Danton wasn't looking forward to it.

"I guess we just find some abodes and put them there," he suggested to the others.

Laidan nodded and then strode off confidently up the stairs toward the Barr family node. "Where are you taking them?" he called after her.

"Next to us and one level down. There are three abodes and that should be enough."

"Come on," Eneit said to the children they had rescued. "We have some work to do to get a place ready for you to sleep."

Eneit looked up and glared at Brill. "Some food would be good," she said.

Brill's eyes widened and then, taking in the line of children, said, "Yes, I am on it."

Danton continued to frown at nothing in particular. He had expected Nils to be there so he could negotiate, but Nils wasn't there. Danton decided that Nils would just have to live with the situation.

"Is everything all right?" Squab asked. Her frown was less severe now that the children had been taken to their abode. "Anything I can do?"

Danton nodded. "All good. Go find yourself a place to live. Brill and I share that abode over there. There won't be much in the way of comforts, but we can manufacture something for you later."

Squab grunted and strode away. He grinned when he saw that she had taken an abode in the same node as them.

Danton continued to scowl over the view of the city. Salinda wasn't there either, and that made him cranky. She was too far along in her pregnancy to be doing any work, and that she wasn't back where he could keep an eye on her annoyed him. And just where had Nils got to? There had been no discussion of him abandoning his post before they left to carry out their various tasks. He should have been working on that damned book.

Danton took the long trek to Nils's study. He wasn't there, and neither was Karol. They were both gone. Worry gnawed at his belly as he came back to the Barr family, but his mind could not even imagine what the problem might be. Damn them all for not leaving a note.

"You coming?" Brill asked when he came back from below.

"Where?" Danton replied, a tad grumpily. He was still feeling ill-used by everyone.

"Gardens. We need to get more food for the children."

"Oh, yes." Danton got grounded really quickly. "Food. I'm coming."

Together they took the path to Barrahiem's overgrown gardens. Brill suggested Danton raid the food stores to supplement the meal. They had the children to feed and to settle into their abodes and maybe some explaining to do when Nils came back from wherever he was. Danton had enough to do, and worrying about what the others were doing was a little stupid, he realized now. They were back safe. They had saved some children. Gercomo was with the baron. That was a tasty piece of news that Salinda really needed to know and he really wished he didn't have to tell her. More trouble was brewing. He felt it in his bones.

ᏨᏨᏨᏨ

Laidan and Eneit worked methodically to clean out the unoccupied abodes. Eneit swept and Laidan coughed. "What…" She hacked up some dust. "Er, what are we going to use for bedding?"

Cloth was rare everywhere and that included Barrahiem. Nils fashioned cloth. He had made her robe and she racked her brains to remember how he had done that. He had shown her and Garan, but Laidan hadn't had to make cloth. Did she have time? She would have to cut the palm fronds and then feed them into the machine. But she didn't know what settings Nils used. She scratched her head.

"What?' Eneit said, pausing from her vigorous sweeping.

"It will take time for bedding. Do you think they will mind sleeping on the floor?" Laidan asked.

The abodes were empty of furniture. Nils had slowly furnished the other abodes. *I wonder where Nils went?* she pondered to herself as she wiped the round windowsill. It contained neither glass nor shutters, being an opening to merely let in light; there was no wind or rain in Barrahiem.

Basically, they could only supply empty houses. For the moment, at least.

"I'm sure it will be fine," Eneit said as she surveyed the cleanliness her broom had created. "As long as we feed them, I think it will do for now." Her eyes met Laidan's and a haunted expression came into them. "At least they are safe. That's the most important thing."

The children were sitting in the courtyard. Eneit went off to sweep the next abode clean and Laidan went to sit with the children.

"Where is this place?" one asked her as soon as she joined them, sitting cross-legged on the ground.

Laidan saw their large, troubled eyes, their expressions of wariness and fear. To the last one, they had that hungry look of dread. "We are in a safe place, deep underground. You are with good people who will care for you." She looked around. "Food will be here soon. Danton and Brill have gone to get it."

"But why?" asked a precocious girl. "Why here?"

"Because of moonfall. Large sections of the old moon are going to fall and this is the safest place."

"It's because of the meteor," one of them commented and nodded to his neighbors. His shock of red hair and lightly tanned skin made him stand out.

"Yes," Laidan replied, "that was just the beginning. There is going to be more, and then some really big pieces of Shatterwing are going to come down. When that happens, and maybe even before then, it will be very hard to survive on the surface. So here in this place is best."

"How do you know?" her first inquisitor asked.

Laidan cocked her head and tossed her hair over one shoulder. "Well, I use my head. This city survived Moonfall thousands of years ago. And look, it's perfectly fine. So while I can't say for sure that we will be good this time, I think this gives us the best chance based on past experience. There is food here, too."

"What about dragon wine?"

"Yeah. Dragon. Wine. Dragon. Wine." The children picked up the words to make a chant.

Laidan frowned, perplexed for a moment. "We don't have much dragon wine, but that's okay because we don't need it."

"But what will we drink?"

"Water…and, um, tea."

The children looked at each other, eyebrows knotted in skepticism. The sound of crunching gravel alerted her to someone approaching. Standing up, she caught sight of Brill. "Here you are. Food is coming. I'm going to help Eneit clean your new homes. I'm afraid there's no furniture at the moment, but we will fix that soon…I hope."

Laidan flashed Brill a smile, waggled her eyebrows, and darted away, ostensibly to help Eneit. "Give me a turn with the broom, will you?" Laidan said to her friend.

Eneit paused, looked at her and lifted an eyebrow. "What's wrong?"

Laidan adjusted her posture and lifted her chin. "Nothing. Now give me the broom."

Eneit handed it to her and then went to the door and peeked out. Then, after listening to Brill who was handing out food, she sauntered out to help him.

Laidan took out her frustration on the dust, sweeping it into a pile, and then out the door. There was another abode to sweep so she headed over there. Eneit waved to her as she went to get the flat piece of metal they used to gather up the piles of dust and dispose of it.

The last abode needed sweeping along the ceilings and walls, as well as the floors, as dust hung everywhere and dead shuwai plants clustered in the corners. They should have been more prepared for visitors. New arrivals were meant to go to N'Barek and fend for themselves, but that was when families and adults were included. Not lonely, frightened children.

A memory of sleeping rough surfaced in her mind. Remembered the mound of blanket across from her being Thurdon. Laidan hadn't minded sleeping that way. She might have complained in later years, but when she was young she'd thought nothing of it. The dust from her broom coalesced into a roiling cloud. Laidan slowed her strokes, batted her hand in front of her face and stepped away from it.

"You are doing it wrong," Eneit said from the doorway.

Laidan flicked her a cross look. "I can see that."

"Sweep slower, longer strokes. It will take a few turns before the dust is less. You won't get rid of it all. My ma always said that cleaning was an investment."

"An investment?"

"Yeah, you invest your time, but you never get a reward. The dirt always comes back, along with the mess, and the next meal needs to be done."

Laidan was tempted to comment on Mandin's maxim, but didn't. She was Eneit's mother and possibly trashing a dear memory was beyond what Laidan knew was right.

Danton arrived with more supplies. He dropped them off and ran back up the stairs to fetch some more. As Laidan had asked for the broom, she couldn't run off now and do something she preferred, like raiding the stores. Then an idea came into her brain. "Eneit."

"Yes, what?" She had stepped outside but came back in.

"Do you think the rugs on the floors of our abodes could be brought down here? Better than bare stone."

Eneit nodded. "I think it's a good plan. I'll talk to Brill."

With renewed energy, Laidan set to her task to reduce the amount of dust in the abode. Given the time it had taken to get the children here, she guessed it was way past their bedtime. Laidan didn't think she could sleep herself until she knew they were comfortably bedded down for the night.

☞☞☞☞☞

Eneit crept up to Brill and Danton's abode and hissed through the window. Brill's head popped up and startled Eneit.

"What?" Brill asked, blinking a few times. "What are you doing, creeping about?"

"I wanted to talk to someone."

Brill grinned. "I'm someone. What's up?"

Eneit looked over her shoulder. "It's Laidan."

"What?" Brill's eyes widened. "Is she all right?"

Eneit nodded and then shook her head. "She remembers."

Brill cocked his head. "Remembers?"

"Yes, everything apparently. You need to talk to her. Garan and Salinda aren't here. Neither is Nils. That leaves you or Danton. But..." she bit her bottom lip, "you are probably better."

Brill looked sideways. "I will be there soon. I just have to talk to Danton and he is busy talking to Squab."

"All right. Don't be long."

Eneit retreated to the abode she shared with Laidan. It wasn't that she was reluctant to go back alone. It was just that everything had changed. She'd thought she known Laidan. The older girl had been recovering from brain injury, and Salinda had said that it took time and that Laidan hadn't always been like that. Now, Laidan was a hyped-up mess of pacing and muttering and crying and Eneit didn't know what to do. Salinda wasn't here to give advice. Garan wasn't either and he'd always been good at getting Laidan to behave in the early days. It had been ages since Eneit hadn't been able to cope with Laidan. They had shared kiddie games and told silly stories to each other. They had had food fights and giggle sessions. They had cuddled and tickled each other until they'd fallen asleep, exhausted. This new Laidan was not that Laidan.

Laidan surged to the opening just as Eneit arrived. "Where have you been?" Laidan asked and then looked about as if she suspected someone would jump her.

"A walk. You all right?"

Laidan turned bloodshot eyes toward her. "No! Yes! I don't know."

"Can I come in?" Eneit pointed to the doorway

"Oh, sorry." She stepped back, her hair a tangle as if she'd been pulling at it. The careful plait that Eneit had made had been wrenched apart while Laidan battled with her inner demons.

"Are you hungry?" Eneit asked, feeling her own stomach pump and pound.

"No! I can't eat." Laidan paced the floor, tugging at her hair.

"I'm hungry." Eneit turned her back on Laidan and went into the alcove where their food was kept. She pulled out some flat bread and some fungi stew and put them on a plate. What she really wanted to do was go into their room and hide under the blankets, but she knew she couldn't do that. Laidan needed her, even though Eneit didn't know what to do or how to help. Brill should be along soon. Eneit swallowed two mouthfuls of food in quick succession. What if Brill made things worse? Maybe Eneit should have waited. Then she shook her head. Eneit couldn't wait. Laidan needed someone now.

"Hello?" Brill called from outside.

Laidan's head jerked around and she narrowed her gaze at Eneit accusingly. "You!"

Eneit called out. "Come in, please."

She didn't know if that "You" was for her or for Brill. Either way it was laced with betrayal.

Brill slipped through the narrow doorway. "Hey, there. I thought I'd drop in and see how you were doing. Danton's catching up with Squab."

Eneit nodded. That was a good opening, casual and true. Eneit wasn't sure how she felt about Squab. The woman was big and ugly, but she had helped them, and Eneit had to trust that. And she was friends with Danton and he was a good person. Like Brill was.

Brill reached over and mussed Eneit's hair. She slapped his hand away. He had to stop doing that. She wasn't a kid any longer. Hadn't been since she was kidnapped. Yet, she couldn't help liking Brill's smile and twinkling eyes. He had charm. Yeah, that was it: charm.

Brill stood and put his hands on hips. "What the hell's happening?" he asked a pacing Laidan.

"Nothing," Laidan said, with a sob in her voice. "Everything!"

"Talk to me," Brill said. "I'll just sit over here." He angled past Laidan, who had stopped pacing to glare at him, and took a seat on the couch. Eneit decided that she wasn't that brave so she lowered herself to the ground and sat cross-legged on the threshold to the alcove. She took another bit of bread and then a mouthful of the spicy stew. Here she could witness what was going on, but stay out of the way.

Laidan, caught off guard, stepped one way and then another as if trying to stop pacing.

Brill put out a hand and gestured to the other sofa. "Why don't you sit down and tell me what's up?"

Laidan hovered indecisively, and then made up her mind. She stepped over to the sofa and sat on the edge of it. She was dressed in her Hiem gown and nervously plucked at it and made no eye contact. The corner of the room seemed to hold great fascination. Eneit frowned, wondering what it was.

Brill let out a breath. "So, Laidan, do you want to talk about it?"

"No," Laidan said sullenly. Then after a moment added, "I need to, though."

Brill nodded, his lips thinning into a very bad attempt at a smile. The straight line of his lips seemed glum to Eneit.

"I'm listening."

Laidan sat still for a few minutes, just breathing. Her shoulders rose and fell and her hair swayed. Eneit took another bite of bread and chomped.

"I remember..." Laidan began and her eyebrows drew together. "I remember us."

Brill sighed and smoothed his trousers along his knees with both hands. "Good." He nodded. "That's good."

Laidan targeted him with her stare. "Good? You left me. Abandoned me. After we..."

Laidan turned her head away from Brill and cast a glance at Eneit. Eneit wasn't moving and missing this. So Brill and Laidan were mated. That explained a lot...kind of...

"I had a duty to perform..." Brill began, gesturing in the air with both hands. Eneit didn't think that would cut it with Laidan.

"You could have spoken to me. You left me. I was..." Laidan's eyes crinkled up as she tried to think. "I remember how I was. I hate myself. I—"

"You shouldn't hate yourself."

Laidan shot to her feet and started pacing back and forth. "You don't know what I did. What I thought. I hate the old me. I hate the new me because the new me is empty and there is this bridge inside me that stretches out over an empty space between these two mes. I am conscious that something in me died. I hurt Garan." Her face turned to Brill again, her faced creased with lines of stress and pain. "I hurt Garan. I willfully hurt him. Why did I do that?"

Brill shrugged and wrinkled his own brow. "You liked me better, I suppose," Brill ventured. Eneit cringed and watched Laidan.

Her mouth dropped open. "I liked you better? That's it. Why didn't I think of that?"

Eneit watched Brill. Did he detect the sarcasm in Laidan's tone?

Laidan turned away, still crunching her robe in nervous fingers. "You were charming. You charmed me. I was..." Her brow crinkled again. "I was traumatized."

The heel of her hand went to her forehead and she rubbed as if she was trying to erase a memory. "I don't want to remember. Stop!" Her voice rose in pitch at the last. Brill flinched.

Brill sat forward on the edge of the seat. "Look, Laidan. You have been through a lot. But nothing is set in stone. You can be who you were meant to be. Try to forget."

Laidan's jaw clenched and her pale skin blushed dark red. Brill, awake to the fact that he had spoken ill, leaned back.

"Forget. Forget? FORGET!" Laidan smashed her fist against her chest. "I remember Gercomo. The beast and what he did. It keeps replaying in my mind, over and over. He ate pieces of me. He split me down the middle. He put his foul claws into my brain and you say I should forget it?"

Laidan launched herself forward and the slap was over before Brill could react. Eneit shoved to her feet, ready to intervene, but Brill was stunned, holding his cheek and blinking away tears. "I'm sorry. I'm so sorry, Laidan. If I could undo it, I would. I didn't mean to make light of your suffering. I didn't know you remembered the attack."

Laidan put her hands over her face and sobbed. Eneit ran to her and clung to her waist with both arms. She caught Brill's eye and jerked her head toward the door. Laidan could recover now she'd got that out. Eneit could deal with this.

Brill nodded at her unspoken command and slipped around them to the door. "I'll let Danton and the others know."

Eneit nodded and clung to Laidan as she sobbed and sobbed. Soon she would calm down. Gently, Eneit led Laidan to bed and the girl followed without words, too numb to speak, Eneit thought.

Tomorrow was a new day. Laidan could start over then. She would get better. Eneit felt this to be so. Her own demon memories raged inside her. She knew Laidan could carry on, just as Eneit had.

ᏬᏬᏬᏬᏬ

After talking with Laidan, Brill had trouble sleeping. His mind was full of Laidan and Sartell and what had happened there. Where had the people gone? He shuddered, thinking of them being rounded up for food, or being killed on a whim. And poor Laidan. She remembered it. Remembered them. Brill knew now that Laidan didn't and couldn't love him like she used to. At least, that is what his heart told him.

Nils's absence worried him too. The Hiem had not mentioned he would be going somewhere. Brill's general state of anxiety made him fret about the city being empty at a time like this, when so much needed to be done.

Brill must have fallen asleep because he was woken up by a loud voice. He blinked and shook off the shroud of sleep. That was Danton's voice. He listened again and that was Nils's voice. Something was up. Brill threw off his bed cover and lowered his legs over the side to draw on his pants. There was always light so Brill tugged aside the cloth he'd put over his window and peered outside. The conversation was continuing and it sounded like it was coming from Nils's abode. Brill pushed his feet into his boots and grabbed his shirt on his way out of the door Something was up.

He came at a run, stopping on the threshold of the courtyard. Karol was there with a bunch of skinny Hiem kids. Brill couldn't help gawking. They were so thin and rangy and pale, but each had the distinctive long fingers, bony brows, white hair and silver eyes, the latter looking at him like tiny mirrors. "Oh, hello," Brill said lamely, his attention divided by the Hiem children and the conversation going on inside Nils's abode.

"I thought you were going to take them to N'Barek," Nils was saying.

"I know, we were, but we could only save children. We couldn't put them in N'Barek by themselves."

"But I was going to put the Hiem children in that node," Nils complained, his voice taking on a high-pitched whine that Brill hadn't heard before.

"Well, it's kinda full right now. Laidan and Eneit cleaned the three abodes so the children could sleep there."

Nils grumbled something unintelligible. Brill flashed a grin at Karol and indicated Nils's abode. "I think I'll just step in there."

Danton's face was flushed and his hands were on his hips, one leg bent in a posture that was meant to be relaxed, but was disguising annoyance. Nils stood rigid, which for him indicated outrage and annoyance.

"What's the problem?" Brill asked, giving Nils a salute, a quick flick of the hand from the eyebrow.

Nils's silver eyes flashed when they centered on Brill. "I have Hiem children that need to be housed and fed."

"And washed, by the looks of them," Brill added.

"I was not expecting other humans to be occupying Barrahiem." Nils's robes quivered with his suppressed outrage.

"Yes, I know. But as Danton said, we can't leave those kids to fend for themselves. Can't we put them together? At the moment the children are sleeping on rugs as we have no bedding or furniture for them." Brill turned and looked through the door. "And I think your lot need to be fed first. We have some food already up here that they can eat."

Nils blinked. "That sounds...reasonable."

Brill grinned again and caught Danton's eye. The rebel was frowning and then nodding slowly. He pushed his fingers through his dark hair. "Yes. Food first. Once we settle this lot down, Nils, I think you have an interesting story to tell."

Nils, his mood quite recovered, lifted his lips. The closest to a smile Brill had seen on the Hiem. "Yes, a wondrous tale." Nils steepled his hands together and bowed to Danton and Brill. "I fear I had a negative reaction to your guests, a rather uncalled-for negative reaction. I can claim surprise and excitement as an excuse. My mind was preoccupied. I had not expected to be in this position. I had not thought that I would be successful...I mean, we would be successful. I owe it to Karol and his history for the discovery of my kin."

Danton flashed him a wide grin. "No need to explain, Nils. I suspect our visitors were a shock to you, as well as bringing this lot of yours in. Wait till Salinda sees them. I am sure it will warm her heart."

Nils cocked his head and studied Danton. Brill wondered if he was trying to gauge the rebel's sincerity. Often Danton joked, but Brill knew Danton spoke from deep feeling. They had attempted to rescue people from the surface of Margra. Even with their small numbers, it was something. It was a chance. It was hope. If they survived what they couldn't stop then there was a chance that both peoples would live on. That there would be a future beyond the now. There was some instinctive need for them to have that hope, even if the future was bleak on a broken world. Life was hope. Life was future.

Brill and Danton started to clean the next set of abodes in the node adjacent to the one where they had put the Sartell refugee children. They slept on blissfully unaware while Danton and Brill swept. Nils was with his Hiem children, talking to them and feeding them. They had discussed what to feed them because they were malnourished and had been for some time. In the end, Nils had decided on a broth and a small portion of Garan's flat bread. If they were able to manage that, then they would expand their diet the next day. After food, he took them down to the lake to wash while Danton and Brill worked.

Nils said he would have to locate some furniture and make some cloth. It was going to take a while given they now had nearly thirty children to cater for. The Hiem children had nothing but rags. At least the Sartell children had clothes.

Brill cast a look at N'Barek. When would Salinda arrive with her refugees? Nils would have a meltdown if she brought more refugees to Barrahiem, he suspected.

The abodes had water so Brill went to fetch small bowls for the children to use as drinking vessels. Also, he raided Nils's store of Pardu tea and a pot. The abodes had a functioning little stove—a small burner. Tea would be good for them. Then he went to his abode and stripped Danton's and his bed so that he could use the blankets on the floor, something to put between the Hiem children and the stone of the floor.

The children came into the abode. They all wanted to stay together in the one place, understandably. An ache in Brill's shoulder was one he wished he'd thought about before he swept three abodes clean. Danton clenched his jaw and Brill suspected he thought the same. The children's dirty rags had been replaced by cloth that Nils had ripped up for them, which they had bound around their waists. Fatigue was starting to weigh Brill down. When the last child drifted off to sleep and Nils ushered them outside, Brill could barely keep his eyes open.

"Thank you for your assistance. Karol will sleep with them and tend to them in the morning. I suggest you take your rest," Nils said.

Brill yawned and shook his head. Danton grabbed his elbow and led him back to their abode. "Get some sleep. I think we have a big day tomorrow."

👁👁👁👁👁

In the morning, Brill woke and sat up, almost at the same time. "We didn't ask him if he found the machine," he blurted out. Danton groaned and turned over in his bed. When Brill moved, his muscles were stiff and sore. He groaned and shuffled to the bathroom. As he shuffled back, he remembered they had a lot of work to do getting the accommodations into shape. The thought sent him back to bed where he flopped face down on his mattress. Sometime later, Laidan banged on the door.

"Hello, we need help. It's time to feed the children," she called. She banged louder. "All the children. Hello. Brill! Danton!"

"Coming," Danton said, in a low, tired voice. "Give us a few minutes."

"That's not fair. Come on, we agreed." Laidan walked away, grumbling to Eneit about Brill and Danton already slacking off.

Obviously, Laidan didn't know that they had been up half the night preparing the lodging for the newcomers.

A pillow landed on Brill's head. "Come on, kid. Time to face the masses." Danton went into the bathroom and water gurgled as he proceeded to wash. Brill struggled out of bed and fuddle-walked into the cooking nook to put on some tea. He crumbled some flat bread and munched on it while he made up the pot. A steaming bowl was ready for Danton when he emerged washed and dressed, then Brill took his turn. The tea had woken him up somewhat and, after splashing cold water on his face, he felt alive enough to interact with other people. It annoyed him that Laidan thought they were shirking, but he knew there was work to be done, so they would just get on with it. His father had told him that not all worthy tasks were noteworthy. Winning a battle was noteworthy, but feeding refugees was worthy. He nodded to himself, understanding at last, when they caught up to Laidan and Eneit in the children's abode.

Brill nudged Laidan away from the large pot she was serving porridge from. "Let me do it."

"Sure," she said, and sniffed as she walked away. Eneit looked up from handing out the bowls.

Danton carried over another pot and placed it next to Brill. "They cooked the meal and carried it here."

Brill nodded and spooned a portion into the bowl held up by the child in front of him. This one looked to be around seven years old. He had large dark eyes, dark hair grown long, and rosy cheeks on dusky skin. Brill grinned at the boy, who said nothing, taking the food and walking away. The next child took his place.

Nils brought his Hiem children down for breakfast. That caused a stir, although Laidan and Eneit did not seem surprised. Brill guessed that they had been briefed by Nils earlier.

"Good day to you. My kin are able to eat a half portion of the porridge. Is there sufficient?" he asked.

Danton looked at the pot and the remaining children to be served. "I reckon so."

Nils leaned down and instructed the Hiem children to form a line. The Sartell children openly stared. It was their first time seeing Nils and the Hiem children. Whispering began. Brill's brow furrowed. He didn't like this turn of events. Danton nodded at him, as if inviting him to speak.

Brill cleared his throat. "Hello everyone. I would like to you to meet Nils of Barr. This is his home. This whole city is his. And he has kindly agreed to let us stay with him. Say hello to Nils."

A few of the children said a tentative hello. Brill let that lie for the moment. "With him are some children of the Hiem. The Hiem are a race that used to live with humans before Ruel fell. They lived in underground cities like this one and they helped humans and both peoples lived together in harmony. After Moonfall, humans forgot about the Hiem people, but they still lived. Not many of them, because they died like the humans did. So I want you to be respectful and friendly to all of them, as well as to each other. Understand?"

There were a few nods. A couple of the children stared at him, brows wrinkled as if they were trying to understand. "Any questions?"

A hand came up slowly. "Yes."

"Why do they look funny?" the girl asked. She was about eleven or twelve, Brill thought.

Brill swallowed. "Well…um…they look like they are. Just as we look like we are. We look funny to them. Right? They are Hiem. They came to Margra with our ancestors. They are a different people. A very clever people. And we should remember to be respectful to them because we are in their home now. They are helping us survive."

"Shatterwing is falling down," a teenage girl said.

"We are going to die," one child cried, and then started bawling.

"I hope we are not going to die," Brill said. "Let's think about how we can live together when the danger is over. All right?"

A few of the children nodded and others kept eating their food, eyes drifting over to the Hiem children, who sat huddled together eating their porridge slowly. Silver eyes were wary. Brill didn't blame them.

He had yet to hear their story from Nils and Karol. But by the look of them, they were close to death and owed Nils their lives. Yet they lived and they were looking better today and that warmed Brill's heart. He smiled at them and nodded. One of the older Hiem acknowledged him with a nod of his head.

Danton startled him when he slapped him on the shoulder. "Come on. Let's eat. I'm famished and we have some manufacturing to do. Nils is going to show us how to make cloth."

Brill rubbed his shoulder. "Sounds wonderful." He went off to grab some porridge for himself, as Laidan and Eneit had brought down a fresh pot.

"I'd better fetch Squab," Danton said. "She's probably feeling shy."

Brill's head jerked back. "Shy. Squab? Don't make me laugh."

Danton chuckled as he climbed the stairs.

⏳⏳⏳⏳⏳

"There are lights in N'Barek," Danton said to Brill the next night. Danton had just come inside. He'd been sitting by the lakeshore looking across the water waiting for a sign. When the lights came to life, a weight lifted from his heart. Salinda was safe. She had brought refugees to N'Barek. Eventually, they would have to start sending food across to them, but that was in some future where they survived moonfall. Right now, Danton didn't have to think about that. He was so weary from the exertions of supplying their small band of refugees that the thought of more labor brought tears to his eyes.

Squab had proven to be useful. She was good at organizing people and soon had the children going to the gardens to harvest and bring up supplies, and she'd set up a storage shed in one of the spare abodes where the Hiem children lived. She had also doled out some clothes to the Hiem kids as Danton and Brill brought them up from where Nils manufactured them. Soon all the children were wearing Hiem tunics.

Danton let out a sigh as his mind returned to Salinda. He hoped she would return by the morning. He worried for her. She was so late in her term that she should be resting, not running around saving people. Not that it was his business, but that didn't change his heart or his worry over her.

He had tried to pry information from Nils about the text, but Nils said it was better left until Salinda returned. Then they would all hear it. Then they could plan. Nils wouldn't let him talk about Salinda, about what was best for her and the baby. It was as if the concept of a birth and newborn were distant. Salinda should stay behind, give birth in safety and let them deal with moonfall. That damned cadre put the kibosh on that. She had the cadre...she had to go because it was somehow essential in saving the planet.

Bloody Mez. Why did he do that to her? Put that thing in her, which had given her nothing but grief. Danton didn't know for a fact that the cadre had endangered her. He just resented the thing that placed Salinda in danger, even though, if he believed Salinda's version of events, it was the cadre that had saved her from a witch's pyre. It was the cadre that had recognized Nils for what he was.

The cadre was so alien, Danton thought. Garan had been weird enough before he got one. Sometimes Garan just amazed him. Danton could not shoot down meteors or cause flame to appear in his hands. He looked at his scarred fingers, the traces of nicks and scrapes on his palms. He was just a man with ordinary skills. All he had was his heart. His source. His will to survive. His desire to help others. Compared to Garan and Salinda, Danton sometimes felt useless. He refused to accept that he was, though. Even without mystical power, he knew he could help. He would guard their backs, share his knowledge with them, feed them, care for them. He belonged and he wouldn't let his lack of a supernatural power stop him from trying to make life better for everyone.

Danton shook himself again. Why was he letting that wodge of insecurity surface now? He'd not felt it before. Fear. He was afraid. He was afraid it was all for naught and he didn't like that one bit. Even Nils, well-known for his chronic despair, had hope now. Finding some remnants of his people had energized him, filled him with hope.

Danton did not want to fail.

ꙶꙶꙶꙶꙶ

Weariness crept up Salinda's body, despite being transported by the glide. Salinda took her time in the Ways, hoping to let Garan catch up with her. Surely there weren't that many people to organize after he had come through with the last of them? But when he didn't arrive after too long a time, she grew concerned. *What is he doing?* she asked the cadre, since they could detect one another.

It was as if the cadre was distracted; it didn't answer. Rolling her eyes and giving a big sigh, she pressed on. With no Garan to pull the tether, she was basically moving at a crawling pace. It was hard to stay awake.

After a while she noticed there was something strange going on with the Ways. The walls were lighter; the general air of gloom had lifted. Something to mention to Nils when she saw him. Thinking of Nils made her think of the book. She had so much tied up in that book saying something useful and that Nils would find it. Because if there was nothing, then they could do nothing, and that was not acceptable.

Even in Barrahiem, they wouldn't survive long after the initial impact. Life was dependent on air and water and many things. They were insulated to some extent, but if the planet finally died, then so would they. It was just a matter of when.

Sitting up straight, she rubbed at her distended abdomen. The child moved and it was uncomfortable. Fighting despair, Salinda thought about the cadres. They couldn't be worthless, and they were for saving the planet. She grunted, annoyed at the train of her thoughts. All this mulling over stuff she wasn't sure about was aggravating, causing her unnecessary angst.

She had travelled farther along the Way when something happened with the cadre. A sudden tug that nearly made her fall out of the glide. Gripping the sides with her hands, she shook her head, trying to make sense of it. Her heart leaped and thudded in an uncomfortable beat. *Garan!* Her cadre had detected the other one. Something bad had happened.

Salinda stopped the glide and swung about, hesitant. She should get help, but the tug of the cadres meant it wasn't easy to do that. No, she had to go after Garan right now, but he wasn't where she thought he should be. Confused that her cadre couldn't easily locate him, she studied the walls of the Way, the in-between. Could she? Dare she?

After forbidding Nils to use the in-between, she couldn't contemplate it herself, could she? Once again she shook her head, fighting for decision, direction. Calming her mind, she reached out to the cadre: *Do you know where the other cadre is?*

It glowed and its surface roiled as if it was having some kind of internal struggle. *Yes,* it said at last.

"Can you show me?"

Yes.

Salinda sagged. Thank the source for that. Then she commenced the search. Salinda headed toward Barrahiem, which went against her instincts, for surely Garan was in N'Barek, but she followed the warm sensations the cadre provided. When she reached Barrahiem, the cadre directed her down. She was tempted to stop and try to contact Nils and the others, but there was an urgency to the cadre, a burning desire to get to Garan.

Down she went, sitting on the glide. As much as she had hated the contraption at first, with this foray into the bowels of Barrahiem, and all the stairs and corridors, she was grateful not to be doing it on foot in her condition.

The narrow corridors that morphed into rock seemed familiar. They had come this way when Nils had guided them, in search of the presence that Garan had told them about. Could he be there with that presence? How? He would have had to pass by her in the Way. It made no sense.

Salinda came to a wall. She could go no farther. The cadre urged her on. She climbed off the glide and walked up to the wall, placing her ear against it to see if she could hear anything. "Garan," she called. "Garan!"

Nothing. She banged on the wall with her fist and then placed her ear against it again and listened. There was a muffled sound. He was in there. Somehow, Garan was in that room. *"Garan!"* she screamed.

Standing back, she surveyed the wall, looking for some sign of a door, anything. The cadre grew frantic—she needed to get through right now. She leaned in close, pushing both hands against the fabric of the wall, trying to sense, to hear. "Garan?"

Salinda backed up as far as she could, moving the glide behind her. She was going to need it again. Her unborn child decided to do a cartwheel and she groaned in frustration. The movements of the child were distracting and she couldn't touch the power of the cadre.

Breathing through the discomfort, she readied her mind. The child grew quiet in her body and the cadre was there, excited, ready. She reached out for the power. Flame enveloped her fist. She let it build and grow in intensity and then threw it hard at the center of the wall. The force of the explosion sent her flying back and she landed on her rear and then rolled to her side. Dust and rock billowed out and she covered her head with her hands, coughing all the while until it settled. She was not badly hurt, although her rear hurt and her lower back twinged.

Gingerly, she climbed on all fours and then, using the wall for support, she pushed upright. Cradling her abdomen, as it was suddenly heavy and dull, she stared through the hole in the wall. There was a room behind it. Stepping carefully around the rock and debris, she made her way into the room. "Garan," she called ahead, "are you in here?"

All her senses were on alert. A sweat broke out on her forehead, her upper lip and the back of her neck. A feeling of faintness washed over her and she steeled herself to keep going. There, standing in the room, totally unaware of her, was Garan. His muscles were rigid, his jaw clenched, but his eyes were blue fire. "Garan?"

Like his body was resisting every movement, Garan looked directly at her. Salinda screamed.

Chapter Twenty-two
SECRETS UNDONE

Nils had been enjoying a nice conversation with Danton and Brill after putting all his charges to bed. Poor overworked Eneit and Laidan had retired for the night, barely able to lift their feet. Nils experienced a warm feeling toward the world and he had overcome his surprise at finding additional humans in Barrahiem. Once he understood the reasons, he was at peace with the situation. Of course they could not let the children fend for themselves in N'Barek.

"We will need to set up some kind of roster for food and supplies for these children. Squab is working on it," Danton said.

Nils sat bolt upright.

"Nils, are you feeling all right?" Brill asked.

Nils could not speak. Pain twisted his innards. Salinda was in trouble. He had noted when she entered the Ways, but had since been conversing and concentrating on what was going on around him, not focusing on her progress. Now, she was below. Deep below the city and in trouble.

Danton stood up and leaned down. "Nils? Don't do this, buddy, because I'm getting scared. Is it Salinda?"

Nils nodded and took a few deep breaths to get hold of himself. Her distress echoed across their bond. "We must go!" he said urgently.

Danton recoiled and Brill moved from one foot to another, an anxious tread with no direction.

Danton's face hovered before Nils. "Tell us where and what if you can. Is she giving birth?"

Nils unclenched his jaw and shook his head. "Danger," he said, "she is in danger. Below." He tried to explain in a painfully thin voice. He swallowed. "She went below where I forbade her to go."

Danton's brows furrowed. "Below? By the great dragon's holy ass, what is she doing there?" He pointed to the lesser city where the beacons still flickered. "She was meant to be there and coming back here with Garan."

Garan's name jolted Nils. He knew where they were, just as if they were standing before him. "Garan is down there too," Nils said.

Danton's face creased in confusion. "Garan is down below as well? Isn't that a bit strange?"

Nils stood up, wavered a little and was steadied by Danton. "I must go now."

"All right. We are coming with you. Brill, can you wake Squab and let her know where we are going? Tell her she's in charge until we get back."

Brill nodded, but frowned. "I don't like this plan. All the key players placing themselves in danger. We don't know what the issue is, what the threat is or even if we can deal with it."

Nils explained that Garan had detected a presence or an awareness in the depths of Barrahiem and when they'd searched for it they found a wall, as if something had been sealed off. Brill's normally pale face became even grayer. "A presence? What does that mean? Are you talking a ghost, or a relic of times past?"

Nils shrugged. "How do I know? It is not my mind that detects it. Garan is special. None of us understands his power or from where it derives. I can feel Salinda's fear. I must go to her. Stay or come, but I know what I must do."

Danton stood by, listening and rubbing his chin. His beard was long gone and in its place was a heavy stubble, which abraded his fingertips. "Brill, you stay here. You are perfectly right to question, but I must go. I must help both of them, understand?"

Brill's eyes looked liquid, as if he was moved by great emotion. "Yes, I'll stay here. Please be careful. Don't take any risks. I can't do this without you, without Nils, or Salinda, or Garan." He wiped the end of his nose with his sleeve. "Understand?"

Danton squeezed Brill's shoulder. "Yes, I understand. You are stronger than you think. Bringing a full deck of cards to a game is something I appreciate. We will bring them back whole."

Brill nodded and turned away. Danton lifted an eyebrow. "I'm ready. Do we need anything? Weapons?" He patted his belt where a dagger perched. If he had other weapons, Nils did not know of them. There was no time to make shrouds even if one was going to help them. "Let us go."

Nils gathered up the end of his robe and made for the stairs, of which there were many, and they did not have much time. Danton's boots tapped out a tattoo behind Nils. The feeling of getting closer to Salinda grew stronger the deeper they went. Nils paused at an intersection, trying to align his memory of the corridors with where he sensed Salinda's presence. He rushed off and hunched over to enter the room through a large dark space. The ground was littered with pale rocks and gravel, the remains of the wall.

"Salinda? Are you there?"

There was no response. He took another step and then Danton placed his hands on Nils's shoulder and moved him to one side.

"Salinda!" Danton called, his body coiled, ready to strike. Dagger clenched tight in his hand, shoulder muscles clenching, knees slightly bent, Danton was full of barely repressed forward motion.

"In here," Salinda said in a shaky voice. "We're in here."

ↄ৩ↄ৩ↄ৩

Garan knew what was going on around him. Unfortunately, he did not have control of his body. His hands clasped Salinda's face and lifted her so that only her toes met the ground.

"Who are you?" his voice said. Garan tried to fight this possession, but his attempts proved to be ineffectual. It was like he was a puppet. He was appalled as he had no wish to harm Salinda. Her eyes glowed and the daemon inside him twittered with menacing glee.

"What are you? I feel your power. Tell me!" Garan's voice had taken on a hard, raspy edge. Perhaps his resistance was working. Garan sought other means. He tried not breathing, but the presence just reverse punched him in the guts and forced him to breathe.

Nils stepped into the room and the presence looked up. "You. I know your kind." With that comment, Garan was assailed by images and emotions that near overwhelmed his mind. It was like a storm.

Nils paused, his gaze going to Salinda who was still held tight in Garan's grip. Garan wanted to let her go, but he had no will of his own.

"Release the woman," Nils said.

Garan cocked his head, studied Nils. It was the beast. The thing inside of him. Curious and curiouser. "You want this vessel holding power within?"

"Yes," Nils said.

Danton loomed behind the Hiem. Garan was shamed. His body was being used to hurt Salinda and both Nils and Danton loved her. Garan mounted another struggle against the creature. A futile struggle.

Yet, his fingers slowly released Salinda. Her nose bled and his fingernails had dug into the soft skin of her face, leaving trickles of blood trailing down to her chin. Salinda stepped back and collapsed into Nils. "What is it?" Salinda asked Nils in a voice that sounded like a sob. "It's not Garan."

Praise the source! They know I did not do this. Now, if they could only help me.

Nils's attention was focused on the statue. He let Danton embrace Salinda and stood up, skirting Garan as he toed the fragments of the statue where the creature had been imprisoned. Nils scooped up a portion and turned it over in his hands, inspecting it closely, even sniffing it.

"What is it?" Danton asked, as he paused in his wiping of blood from Salinda's face. He was using a cloth he had tugged from his trouser pocket.

"Hmm. I think it is a Ufak Monta."

The creature hissed with Garan's mouth.

"A what?" Danton asked as he lay Salinda's head against his chest.

Salinda wept. It was probably shock. When she looked up, she had a forlorn expression. Nils had not seen her so lost before. The creature must have really frightened her.

"A Ufak Monta is a Moon Binder artifact that was deemed harmful. I have not seen one before, but the warnings I read about them are apparently justified."

"Great. I'm glad your research is justified. How do we get rid of it?" Danton said, his anger unable to be disguised.

Salinda's head shot up. "Moon Binder? But...but they are gone. No one...you said no one really knew much about them, just their artifacts." Salinda wiped at the blood still running from her nose. Her gaze never left Nils, who was studying the fragment of the statue.

"We had these. I read about this one in particular. It was said to resemble the Moon Binders. We could not be certain. They could have made this image in the shape of some deity or legendary creature, rather than a replica of themselves. We had no way of knowing if this reptilian representation was a Moon Binder."

"Fools," the creature said with Garan's voice. "You have let the vermin take over the surface. We imprisoned them for a purpose."

Salinda groped her way to her feet, Danton's hand supporting her from behind. "You mean the dragons? You imprisoned them in Ruel moon?"

Garan swung toward her, but Nils stepped in front of her. "Careful," Nils said, "this is my mate you threaten."

The creature inside Garan assessed Nils more closely. "Ah...you are not as they. Why did you free them? This vessel says the power that bound them within the moon waned."

"It did. And the moon broke apart and some parts of it fell to Margra's surface. I surmise that is how the dragons appeared on the surface after Moonfall. They ate the dead and they multiplied."

A growl emitted from Garan's throat. A sound he did not think he could recreate. "You must put a stop to it."

"Tell us how," Salinda interjected. "The rest of Ruel moon is set to fall. Tell us how to stop that."

The creature laughed. "If I was a living being I could help you with that. I am not." The creature paused in its speech and Garan detected something—the creature grew distracted as if its attention was elsewhere.

"Danger is near," it said. "You must go to the machine that the others built. It waits for you."

"Where? Tell us where!" Salinda begged.

The creature regarded her, studied her. "You have part of the solution in you, as does this vessel. Divided, it won't work."

"What do you mean?" she asked.

"No more. Set me free."

Danton stood behind Salinda. "How do we do that?" he asked.

"Destroy this vessel."

Garan froze. *No. No.*

"No," Salinda said. "We cannot. We will not."

"You will do as I command." Garan's voice was deep and ominous.

Salinda drew power into her, her eyes filling with a glow. She was ready to fight this being. "We will not."

"I can strike you down where you stand."

"Try it!" Salinda said through gritted teeth.

Protests arose from Nils and Danton, but she ignored them.

The blast of power from the Moon Binder rocked her back a step, but did not harm her. She had used Garan's trick of weaving power. Nils and Danton, though, were forced back with arms raised to protect themselves from flying debris.

Salinda didn't attack. "We need him whole. Return him to us."

"You have a power I can detect. It resides in this one."

"Yes, he is important to us. Release him. Leave him."

The beast growled again. "Fools. I cannot free myself."

"But you drew Garan here. Why?" Salinda asked.

"Because he has a quality that I understand. I can mesh with him easily."

Garan tried to push the creature out, but he could not find the edges of him, could not find a way to edge him out, no grip, no wedge. It was immense.

"Then help us. Let Garan control his body, but stay with us and we will do our best to help you. Help us, please."

The beast's mind grew quiet. Garan trembled. He wanted the beast out. He did not want to carry it around with him. The cadre had fled, now but a tiny flame inside his mind, and Garan's mind felt as small as a nut.

"You wish to bargain with me. I can do nothing to assist you. I am not corporeal."

"But you know dragons and Moon Binder technology. You could help us. Advise us."

"Why would I do that?" Garan detected the creature's derision. It thought of them as nothing.

"Because if we all die, you will die. There will be no vessels. There will only be dragons—the vermin you despise."

The beast was quiet. Garan stood immobile, waiting like the others for a response. Nils's silver eyes glowed as he stood beside Salinda.

"I agree. I will ride this vessel and help you save Margra. I warn you, do not enrage me. I cannot contain myself when I am impassioned. I will overwhelm this weakling mind and snuff him out. Not because I want to, but because I am too powerful."

Salinda sighed loudly. "Good. Give Garan back to us."

Garan drowned. He could not breathe, could not see, and then the ground hit. Control returned slowly. He lifted a hand, an arm, turned his head. Danton knelt beside him, fingers clawing through Garan's curls. "Garan?" he asked hesitantly.

Wearily, Garan nodded. "Yes. 'Tis me."

"Is it still there inside you?" Danton asked, and even though he tried to mask it, his revulsion was evident in his features.

"Yes," Garan replied. Inside him were two small flames. A blue one, which was the Ufak Monta, and a white one, which was the cadre. Garan could not touch either of them.

"Can you stand?" Danton asked.

Garan did not answer; he just rolled over and climbed to his feet. He was perfectly fine and normal. The beast was quiescent. It said nothing, tried nothing and gave off nothing. No emotion or anger or wisdom.

"Fine, let's get out of here," Danton said, grabbing Garan by the arm and tugging him forward. Nils had Salinda and was assisting her over the debris. Her glide was in the other room. Nils found it and helped her onto it. A good thing, too, for she looked as if she could barely walk. They headed back to the Barr node.

Garan's heart was heavy. Even though they gave nothing away, he was aware of the two consciousnesses inside him. The beast had severed Garan's connection to the cadre and he did not know what he could say to Salinda, or whether it was safe to say anything with the beast listening.

Garan had the overwhelming urge to weep. Something significant had happened and it was yet to be determined if it was good or ill.

Nils was chatting excitedly to Salinda about his theories of where the dragons had come from. "I knew they could not have evolved in such a short time. There is much to understand about the Moon Binders and their relationship with the dragons. If only the beast were not so lethal to life. Kill Garan, indeed. That is out of the question. But think, Salinda, think of the possibilities, the knowledge. The archives would be enhanced so much if only I could get the beast to talk to me, to show me..."

Salinda made an annoyed sound. "Really, Nils. It almost killed me and took possession of Garan. It is dangerous and we have a dragon by the tail in this beast. This Moon Binder spirit. It could end badly and I fear it will end badly."

Nils stood up straighter and moved his shoulders around as if he was reestablishing a burden upon them. "Yes, well, moonfall will make it end badly. We cannot get worse than that."

"True," Salinda agreed. "I'm so tired. We should meet in the morning. I'm afraid I need to rest. It's been a big day." She put out a hand and snagged Danton's sleeve. "Can you see to Garan? Keep him safe?"

Danton grinned. "My pleasure."

Garan warmed inside, knowing that these people cared for him.

Chapter Twenty-three
TRELL'S CLUE

It took a while for Salinda to get to sleep. As well as the emotional and mental drama, her body was physically hurt in various places from her encounter with the possessed Garan. The lad was strong at the best of times. Enhanced by the Moon Binder, though, he had a huge potential for destruction. She was still surprised the beast hadn't used Garan to squash her for standing up to it. Her back hurt a lot more than she thought it ought to, and even though she had been on the glide most of the time, her feet ached with a *throb, throb, throbbing*. And being so pregnant, finding a comfortable spot in the bed proved to be near impossible.

In the end, she sprawled out with various pillows supporting arms and legs and let fatigue take her. Her eyes closed and she slipped from worried reality into worried dreams. She dreamed she was awake stressing about the day's events. She was conscious that she was doing that, but it was in a pattern she could not break. Sometime in the night, the cadre welled up full of light and made her sleep. Salinda was conscious of Nils being in bed with her, but when she woke the bed was empty, and when she looked at how she was placed on the bed, she wondered how Nils had even found space to rest.

When she went to move, she cried out. Her back muscles had seized up and made their position clear. No getting out of bed. It was difficult to see her feet, but they felt swollen and ugly. "Nils?" she called out.

Nils came into the room, dressed and looking refreshed. "Yes," he said, inclining his head in that way he had. His long straight hair looked neatly combed, but she knew it always looked that way and, other than brushing it away from his face when he washed it, his hair didn't really need much attention. Salinda reached up and touched her own hair. She had failed to braid it and now it was a crazy mass of tangles. She shook her head. "I need help to get up."

Nils frowned. "Are you injured?"

"No, just sore."

Nils nodded and then cocked his head again. "Danton provided this advice. He said to tell you to stay put. Then he instructed me to bring you tea and breakfast. There is no rush this morning."

Danton might not think there was a rush, but moonfall had other plans. How could she rest when there was so much to do? But as she tried to move once more, she realized that she had to stay put if she was to have any chance of going anywhere again.

"How thoughtful of him. How is Garan?" she asked as she rearranged the pillows behind her and punched them into shape. It looked like she had no other choice, but to take Danton's unasked for advice.

Nils didn't reply so she tried another question. "Can we discuss Trell's book?"

Nils shook his head. "I am to make tea. To save explaining more than once, I will wait until the meeting."

"Can't you give me a hint?" Salinda asked him, exasperated.

"A hint? What do you mean?" he asked just as he ducked out of the room. Salinda threw a pillow to vent her frustration. She fumed at the ceiling while rotating her feet at the ankles to exercise them. If she didn't try to move her body, her back also didn't hurt, so minor exertion like foot exercise was a good idea.

"Did Trell provide any useful information?" Salinda demanded when Nils returned. He poured a cup for her from the pot.

"Trell's information is priceless to the Hiem archives."

Salinda growled quietly. "I meant to our quest."

Nils's silver eyes met hers. "You should rest. You do not look well. If we had more time I would suggest a time of light healing in the tray."

"Nils!" she yelled.

Nils got up from the edge of the bed where he had been sitting. "You do not think the healing tray would help at this time?"

"Nils," she said, her rage contained, but only just.

He grinned. "Trell had a lot to say that will be useful to us."

Salinda sagged with relief. "Thank you. I will wait to hear it." She picked up her tea and sipped it. She recommenced circling her feet to ease the ache in her ankles.

Salinda didn't get out of bed until noon. Nils brought her hot packs to ease the strain in her muscles. They were quite effective. Salinda was pretty sure she was not in labor, but that scenario did worry her for a time when the ache persisted. Rubbing her belly, she said to her unborn child, "Just a little longer, please."

Nils brought her a meal and talked to her about Danton and Brill and their manufacturing process. He discussed Squab and her efficient organization. If they continued on in the afternoon, they would have sufficient clothing prepared for the children to have a second set of clothes each. More work would be required to provide bedding. After locating some furniture in the storage shed, Garan had helped to bring it up on the large glides, which he had got working.

"He's useful, isn't he," she commented.

"Yes. Garan has asked permission to go back to the cave to bring the supplies to N'Barek. He said most were inside the Ways and only a few larger items remained in the cave."

"Oh. Do you think that is wise? What about..." she tapped her head, "the Ufak Montu thing?"

"It is called Ufak Monta and Garan tells me it is quiescent."

"Can we spare someone to go with him?" Salinda wanted to go, but realized she was in no fit state and needed to keep her thoughts on the meeting ahead. Much had to be decided. Not only their plan of action, but how to manage things here. They had many people to care for now and that was a problem, one she hadn't worked out how to deal with.

"Perhaps we should put together a list of items to be discussed at this meeting, otherwise it will take forever. Unless you want to have separate meetings about separate issues?" Nils spread his hands indicating the city and she understood what he meant.

"A list, I think. Can you ask Danton to think on the issue of the refugees."

"He is thinking on it. Manufacturing cloth is quite conducive to thinking once you have learned how to do it, and your rebel friends found it easy to master the process."

Salinda lay back against the pillow and sighed. "Thank you for everything, Nils."

"You are welcome. We have come far, you and I, since we first met. I feel like I am a different person."

"Indeed, so do I. I mean, I too feel like a different person and, yes, you have bent and swayed with events. I think you are still essentially you, but now you seem lighthearted and that is strange. Why is that?"

Salinda knew something good had happened, but they had had to deal with Garan and she hadn't been able to talk to Nils until now. She had been so tired last night.

Nils smiled at her, eyes sparkling and reflecting silver. She caught her breath. It was not something she could say she had seen often in Nils. Her heart surged with joy and love. She reached out and clasped his hand. "Nils, tell me."

"I am pleased to have found a small Hiem town, with Hiem still living in it." His voice was a soft whisper.

"Yes, that is wonderful." He had told her last night, when he had a chance, but not the details.

"Yes. They were near the end of existence. The city had been exposed and decayed and dragons were attacking them. Karol had a rhyme, you see. A family song that spoke of their origins. While you were away, Karol and I ventured out to find the place that was in the song. It was a puzzle, but we found it and we saved ten Hiem youths. Their parents were all dead. I was too late to help them.

"I think if I had not given myself to despair, I might have found them earlier…"

Salinda squeezed his hand. "You have found a lot of evidence that the Hiem survived. In my blood, in Laidan's. Then you found Karol. It is wonderful, Nils, that you found more. Without Karol, though, you may not have found this settlement."

"I could have been more methodical. I could have checked every known settlement, but instead I let myself become morose."

"Oh, Nils. You had a very hard time. You woke and found your kin, your people, gone. Your response was natural. Please don't blame yourself. You are doing what you can now."

"I suppose you are right. I can do my best for them now."

Salinda's smile died. "Stopping final moonfall will help them. It will give them a chance at life."

Nils lifted her hand, studied it. "You have great focus, Salinda. You are right, of course." He lowered her hand, running his long white forefinger along the outside of it, brushing against her knuckles. "You should rest now. Then we will have our meeting."

Nils smiled at her again and Salinda couldn't help responding to it. She didn't know this Nils. He was so much lighter and happier. It was a profound change. Salinda was keen to meet these Hiem youths who had so transformed her mate.

☐☐☐☐

"Are you sure you want Garan involved in this meeting?" Danton asked. "With his...um," he motioned toward his head, "possession?"

Danton's words only mirrored what was in Salinda's heart. How far could she trust this Ufak Monta and its seeming retreat within Garan? Garan was acting himself...but the cadre? That was hiding, too, and Salinda didn't like that.

Garan definitely had to be involved in the final play against final moonfall, which meant that excluding him from the discussions would not achieve much. If Nils had any way of evicting Garan's alien hitchhiker, that would be good. But Nils was reluctant to try. He was too fascinated by the phenomenon to actually see the danger. Salinda was left having to accept the Moon Binder spirit's presence, for good or ill.

"We need him," was all she said to Danton as she took her seat. Eneit pushed a cushion behind Salinda's back, for which she was grateful.

Danton's brows drew together and his already downturned mouth thinned into a line. Salinda looked away and saw that Nils had joined them. Laidan looked strange, as if she was seeing everyone anew. Salinda didn't have time to ask what was wrong. Maybe after the meeting.

Brill sat on the ground, and when he noticed Laidan his eyes widened. Laidan smiled at him and then looked away to watch Garan. The Skywatcher loomed into view, not quite sure of his welcome, Salinda expected. She patted the seat beside her. "Come sit here, Garan."

Nils drew out a long piece of paper and Salinda glared at him. "What is that?"

"The agenda," he replied. "The faster we get through this, the better."

Salinda chuckled, then choked. "Agenda! You're serious. What is item one?"

"The refugee situation," Nils said and ticked off the first item.

"What about it?" Salinda asked.

Danton picked up on her comment. "I have rethought my position and I think, logistically, all the refugees should be located here, where there is ample food and water. The abodes are also in better condition than N'Barek's."

"Relocate them?" Salinda said, not quite parsing the comment. "Why? I mean the real reason."

Nils shifted on his feet. He was standing there, robes draping his body, with the list in his hand. He glanced up at her. "We are going on a quest. Someone has to mind the children."

"So that's it." Salinda mulled it over and then noticed Danton and Brill nodding.

"Squab can take charge," Danton said. "But it makes sense if we aren't going to be here to set up the transport of food. We don't know how long the observatory's supplies will last."

Garan raised his hands. "I still have to go fetch them from the cave. I'm ready though."

Danton cursed under his breath and she understood his frustration. They had deposited the observatory and Vanden refugees in N'Barek at Nils's instruction. Now that he had a city with children in it, he needed help. Then it finally struck her: they were going on a quest. Nils knew the location of the machine. Her heart lifted and she smiled. "Oh, Nils."

He gave her a sideways look. "We are not at the agenda item yet. Who is going to stay behind to watch over things? That's item two."

"Not me," Brill said.

Danton had thunderclouds on his forehead. "Me neither."

Salinda put forth her opinion. "We need Garan and me and Nils. So that leaves Laidan, Eneit and Karol. Oh, and this Squab. I haven't met her yet."

"She's down in the gardens with the children, showing them how to harvest food," Danton explained with arms folded.

Then Eneit, Laidan and Karol started complaining at the same time, sounding like cats fighting.

"Enough," Danton yelled. "You will stay behind as ordered. There are important things to do here."

"But…" Eneit said. "I want to fight."

Danton shook his head. "You have fought. Now you fight here, keeping people alive. Your mother would have wanted it this way."

Eneit shut her mouth and scowled. Laidan's gaze drifted from Brill to Garan, and she bit her lip as she concentrated. Salinda had the distinct impression that Laidan recalled everything from her past. She said nothing, though. Karol, too, remained quiet. Salinda thought that they would probably lobby after the meeting.

Nils looked around. "I take it that we are in favor? Relocation of the refugees and leaving the children behind with Squab, Laidan, Eneit and Karol to look after things?"

Salinda surveyed the group. Danton gave her a tiny salute and Brill a nod. "Yes."

"Item two. Trell's book."

Salinda's heart leaped. All her bets were going to pay off. Nils would save them. He would give them the information they needed to avert final moonfall.

Danton, Brill, Garan and Laidan leaned forward as one. Salinda found she wasn't breathing. Nils regarded them. Salinda let out a long breath. "Yes."

Nils relaxed as he started to talk. "Trell's book details the last days before Moonfall, when he and six other scientists worked on a plan to avert such an event. He talks of four machines, but only two were built in time. One of which they used. Both of the machines and the buildings they were placed in were located at similar angles, so that they could aim at a fragment of Ruel moon."

Danton shook his head. "How is such a thing possible? I have to admit that I can't get my head around it."

"Indeed," Nils replied. "It took me three run-throughs of the book to make sense of it, because it was dotted with personal accounts of Trell's love life and some ruminations on his kin."

"So, Nils, does it say where these machines are and how we can use them?" Salinda asked.

"Yes, and not precisely." Nils looked around the group. "Where did Garan go?"

Salinda glanced around. Garan had slipped away. "How odd."

Danton put out his hand and waved it. "Keep going. If Garan doesn't want to listen, we can't wait."

"Oh, yes. The means by which this machine worked are unclear to me."

Salinda chewed her bottom lip and eased her right side with a light stretch as the baby was pressing down uncomfortably. "Tell us what you do know."

Nils turned his head and met her gaze. The silver in them flared. "I know where they were. I have to use the archives and access some post-Shatterwing maps to determine where the remaining one is and how we might get there."

"Do you think you can do that?" she asked.

"Yes, I think so. I may need a day or two to draft the map."

General conversation broke out then about whether the machine still existed, whether it worked and what they could do otherwise.

"We have no choice. The machine is all we have to work with. The Moon Binder didn't have much advice, did it?" Salinda questioned, gazing around the meeting.

Danton frowned, shook his head and shifted his feet uneasily. "That's true."

"We do this, or we do nothing." Salinda jabbed the air to make her point.

Salinda sat back as Garan returned and placed a large square box in the center of the group. She shared a look with the others, then she examined the box, its familiar lines jogging her memory.

"'Tis an energy source...for the machine."

"Garan, how did you..." Nils began and then paused and shifted in his seat, and stared at the device.

"I can tell," replied Garan. "I have a feeling we will need it."

Salinda swallowed the saliva that had pooled in her mouth. For the first time, she felt uneasy about Garan and the Moon Binder spirit inside him. Nils knew a little about the Moon Binders, and Garan being infected by something that Nils classified as dangerous was distinctly disturbing.

It occurred to her that Garan had been found in a sealed room. She had had to smash her way in. Way in... "Garan," she said quickly, "how did you get into the room with the Ufak thingy?" Damn pregnancy was making her pea-brained. Nils corrected her and she flashed him an embarrassed grin.

Garan scratched behind his ear. "I was..." he began and then finger-ruffled his curls and let out a gasp of exasperation. "I was walking back through the Ways and I sensed the presence." He frowned and jerked his head back as he recalled the moment. "And it called to me..."

"But how did you get into that room?" Salinda persisted.

"I went into the in-between...or the in-between took me. I noticed it was getting lighter in color and I remember reaching out to touch it."

Salinda sent an accusing stare in Nils's direction. His eyes went wide. "You went into the in-between?" Nils said, appalled.

"Yes, and then it put me in that room."

"Nils," Salinda said in a curt voice, "what haven't you told us about the Ways? They wouldn't happen to be a Moon Binder artifact, would they?"

Nils's expression grew puzzled. "I...I am not sure. The cities were built originally by the Moon Binders so perhaps the Ways were too. I never thought about it before. They have been giving me an uneasy feeling of late."

"Great...I wonder what other surprises the Moon Binders have in store." She lifted an accusatory eyebrow at Garan.

He shrugged and said nothing, just stepped out of the center, leaving the dark box there.

245

"We depend on the Ways to get in and out of the Hiem cities. Previously, they have been benevolent. There is no reason to think that they are suddenly hazardous." This came from Brill who sat on the ground cross-legged. "If we believe they are, then we have to abandon the cities and live on the surface."

"We can't do that," Danton said impatiently.

"I know, "Brill responded, "so there's no point in getting paranoid about the Ways or the in-between. We just deal with it and be careful. Garan has a Moon Binder spirit inside him. That is not necessarily a bad thing."

Garan chortled derisively. "'Tis all right for you to say."

Salinda rolled her eyes. "So we will know where this machine is soon, right, Nils? And we have a power source to bring along and we have the cadres. I saw a vision of those who formed the cadre. They went into a machine. Somehow the machine made the kernel of the cadre. Whether that was deliberate or not, I don't know. The cadres contain lifetimes of power and knowledge and we will bring this to bear on the problem." She turned to Nils. "I think, yes, the machine somehow formed the cadres."

Nils's eyes widened, but he said nothing because Danton interrupted. "Nils, can you tell us whereabouts you think this machine might be? It will help us plan."

Nils drew a ball out of the pocket of his robe and tossed it in the air. A map was displayed. Dazzled by the lights, Salinda couldn't make head nor tail of it. She cast Nils a sideways glance and he explained. "The map is pre-Shatterwing." He stepped into the display. "This is what is now known as the rift where the largest piece of the moon struck. It was the Strega continent. Not much of it is left now, as I understand it." He waved his hand to the side. "This is the Arvoli continent, which we know is partially under water."

"And where are we?" Danton asked, his eyes bright as he studied the map. Salinda was envious that they did not seem to be dazzled by the Hiem technology like she had been. Salinda hazarded a glance at the girls and both Laidan and Eneit were open-mouthed in awe. Brill's brow was creased as he studied the map and Garan just had a stupid smile on his face, but he loved technology, so perhaps it was just his pleasure showing through.

Nils waved a hand. "This is the Stoli continent where we are now. This is what it used to look like in outline. Much was lost of the coastal and low-lying areas."

Danton harrumphed. "Tell me, Nils, do the Ways travel to these other places?"

Nils cleared his throat. "Of course they did. There was a lot of damage, but I think we may find a passage to Arvoli, where the machine is, through the Ways."

"The machine is in Arvoli?" Salinda asked.

"Yes." Nils inclined his head in acknowledgment. He gripped his hands together. "Trell's book talks of four machines." He pointed to the map. "One remains and it is here on this side of the Arvoli continent. Apparently multiple machines gave them the best chance of blasting the moon and also a chance at a second shot."

"A second shot?" Danton asked. "What do you mean?"

Nils waved his hand and the map disappeared. Salinda blinked at the sudden dimness. "Trell and his fellow scientists thought they needed two shots at the moon. They only managed one before the end."

Salinda frowned. "So the other machine is damaged?"

Nils's head jerked up. "I did not say that. What I fear is that the damage around the machine they used was too great for them to make their way to one of the others."

Salinda nodded, thinking the planet would have been a mess. It was still messy now. "Yes, the damage to the surface…"

"No, not the surface. To the team. The machine was deadly. There was only one survivor."

"Who was that?" Salinda asked, though she knew straight away. It had to be Trell because he wrote the book.

"It was my grandsire. He notes something strange happened to him and he was unable to travel to the other machine in time. He said the Strega machine was unusable afterward."

Danton shifted his feet. He was leaning against the outer wall of the abode in a relaxed kind of way. "This machine thing was going to blow up the moon and it didn't work?"

Nils let out a sigh. "It is more complicated than that. I must confess it is a bit difficult to comprehend or explain. There was too much of the moon falling to Margra to blow up, but they developed a beam that reduced the mass at the same time as blowing some of it away. They succeeded in that. The second machine was meant to finish off the remaining debris. It was this latter task they did not accomplish."

Danton nodded slowly. "So, this second machine we can use to finish off the remaining debris."

"If it is still there," Brill said.

"And functioning," Salinda added.

"That's a lot of ifs," Danton replied.

"There is only one way to figure it out," Garan said and patted the top of the power box he'd brought along. "We go there and try."

"Garan's right. We have no choice. So now we plan." Danton's gaze ranged out over the group. "I have to talk to her about it, but does anyone object if I put Squab in charge of everything here?"

Eneit's hand shot up. "If Squab can manage everything, then maybe we can come too. I want to fight."

"Now, Eneit..." Salinda began.

Eneit shot to her feet, fists tightly balled at her side. "Don't tell me I can't because I'm a kid. I'm not that much younger than Brill or Karol or Laidan for that matter. I want to fight for my future and I will feel deprived if I sit here feeling as if I'm doing nothing."

"I agree," Laidan said. "What was the point of teaching us to fight if you are going to leave us behind like we are still crawling babies? Either you respect us as individuals, or you don't."

Salinda waved her hand, trying to quiet them. "Is it wrong to try to protect you? You are the future. Without the young to live on after us, there is no point in trying to save the world."

"It is wrong to take the decision from us. We've been part of this," Laidan said, "from the beginning. Admittedly, I wasn't too willing at first. I understand why you might not want me around. But I'm not like that anymore. I care. I belong and so does Eneit. We haven't discussed this with Karol and he's got a right to make up his own mind as well."

Karol piped up. "Yes, I must be there to help, too."

"You have other children here, plus the refugees," Eneit argued. "There is hope for the future in them. I don't know about you but I want to take a risk. I want to fight."

A tightly held breath hissed out of Salinda. She didn't know what was going on in their minds, but she remembered her fight. She'd been younger than Laidan when she joined the rebels in Sartel. Closing her eyes, she remembered how that felt and concluded she had no right to deny these youngsters a choice. Her head hung down. "Wing dust! All right, then. You choose, but I want you to think about it and let me know tomorrow. Just you three. We can't accommodate anyone else that has a mind to help out."

Laidan held her gaze and nodded. Eneit patted Laidan on the back and Karol grinned.

Salinda rubbed at a sore spot on her belly. The baby was moving again. Who was she to talk? She was taking this unborn child into danger. Would that she'd given birth a month ago. When was it ever safe to do so? Not then. Not now. "How long will it take us to get there?"

Nils tossed the map ball from one hand to another. "It will depend on the Ways. As we have seen, some are damaged and discontinuous. So we might have to trek above ground where there are breaks in the Ways."

"We don't have time for that," Danton commented and Salinda nodded in agreement. The end was days away, not months or weeks.

"I can guide you," Garan said. His eyes were strange and staring and Salinda shivered.

"Is that you, Garan, or the Ufak...thing?" Salinda asked.

Garan's head turned and she looked deep into his eyes. It was the Ufak Monta talking if the blue glow was anything to go by. So much for giving Garan back control. "You need me."

Salinda rubbed her upper arms. "If you can find us passage through the Ways, then we do."

Garan's voice spoke, but it was the Ufak Monta speaking. "I can. Do not underestimate Garan. He has an affinity with the Ways too. Together we will be invaluable."

Salinda nodded, still not feeling more at ease with the Ufak Monta's assurance. "As long as we can get through safely."

Garan cocked his head. "The Travel Ways are not tunnels. They are not material as this..." He stamped his foot. "They exist in a space betwixt, not quite in this world and not quite out of it. The same for this city. It is here and it is not here. Not all cities are built like this. This was ours, but the other cities that I can see in Garan's mind were Hiem built. They were modeled on this one—they are not the same as this."

Salinda's skin crawled and she straightened and stretched her spine. She wasn't quite sure what the Moon Binder spirit meant, but Nils nodded as if he did.

"Right." Salinda smiled, but it was fake and she knew it was and, from their expressions, so did everyone else. "We need to get organized. We need food, supplies, weapons—in case we meet unfriendlies—and some means to transport everything."

Nils glanced at his list. "Those items are next on the agenda."

"Danton, you and Brill can see to the logistics. Laidan, Garan, Eneit and Karol will help."

Danton nodded, almost giving her a salute.

She was met with nods and the group started to break up. "We check in again tonight before bed. We leave as soon as Nils has finalized his map so get those supplies ready."

"Come on everyone. Let's get cracking." Laidan led the young ones to get orders from Danton.

Garan's violet-colored eyes scanned the group and he shook his head as if just waking up. "We can use the glide. I have to take it to bring back the remainder of the supplies. I will do that now. Then we can start loading it up for our trip."

"Take care, Garan," Salinda said. "Don't dawdle."

Garan had turned away and his head shot round, sending his curls roiling. "I do not dawdle."

Salinda grinned and received an answering smile from Garan. The Ufak Monta had retreated for the moment. The blue had faded from his eyes.

Chapter Twenty-four

SKYFIRE

The glide moved easily under Garan's hand. The pleasure he felt in having fixed the alien device was muted. It was hard to think and feel properly with two alien entities in his head. The cadre was generally the less invasive of the two. It didn't take over his body and shunt him into the background. Twice, now, the Ufak Monta had done that. The last time hadn't been as bad as the first. It had just moved forward, blanketed Garan's will and took him to fetch the power box that Garan had detected when he had been on a quest with Nils and Salinda. A quest to find the Ufak Monta, although Garan had not known that at the time. He had been answering a mysterious call, or presence, the sense that someone was looking at him.

Now that Garan understood what it was, he was no less comforted. Why did it target him? How did it summon him through the Ways? The Ways were even more alien than he had been led to believe. They were connected to Barrahiem, Barrahiem was connected to the Moon Binders, the Moon Binders were connected to the dragons. He shook his head lest he start putting the pieces to rhyme and begin humming a tune.

The Ufak Monta was a grim feeling in his mind, a repressed sense of violence. Garan was small in its eyes. *Did you really look like your statue?* he asked.

In answer, a vision of a ferocious beast roared in his mind and Garan recoiled. He shook himself and panted in fear, resting his hand on the in-between to keep his balance. The substance of the Ways grew sticky and he plucked his hand away with a cry. He had been sinking into it and after his previous visit to the in-between, he did not trust it.

The interesting thing he noticed about the vision was the creature's similarity to a dragon. Smaller, smarter perhaps, but there was some kinship there, as if evolved from the same species. *Are you related to the dragons?*

Garan crashed to the floor, writhing in pain, gasping for breath. *Noooo!* came the reply, but the pain, the raw anger, told Garan something else. The Moon Binders were related and that concept was abhorrent to the Ufak Monta. This knowledge certainly put a different shade on things. A history of the world that Garan would never know, not in detail at least, but it affected them now and bound them together: dragon, Moon Binders, Hiem and human. What a melting pot Margra was. Garan climbed to his feet and wiped the spittle from his mouth. He grabbed the tether for the glide and gingerly recommenced walking in the direction of the observatory cave.

Wanting to get there without another attack, Garan sent no more questions to his alien stowaway.

The glide was big enough to take a sizable load. Some supplies he had left outside the Way Gate, so he prioritized them for collection. As expected, they were where he had left them. There were no stragglers left over from the refugee line that had fled into the Ways with Salinda. No one else sought shelter in Barrahiem and he felt some sadness.

The thought that he would not see the observatory again oppressed him. He piled box and barrel onto the glide until it was full and then started back to Barrahiem. Something made him stop. He looked back at the interior aspect of the Way Gate, its distinctive markings visible now that the Ways were giving off low-level blue light.

One more visit would not hurt, he thought. The supplies were not urgent. The observatory had been his home for so long, the place where he had grown up and learned and achieved. With a wide smile, he recalled how good it felt to have gained the rank of Skywatcher, and how much he had treasured being of use to Margra, saving people he would never know or see. He let out a big sigh of sorrow, but not regret. He was on a larger path now. They were going to save Margra, he was sure.

But the elders had remained at Trithorn Peak. They stayed behind to save what they could. And if he ventured a little from the mouth of the cave, he would see the turrets and the sky and feel the wind on his face. Something he missed the most. Maybe he would catch a glimpse of Belle moon in all its glory.

Do it! The Ufak's impatient voice sounded in his mind.

Garan knew the creature was playing with him, but nevertheless he took long strides to key open the door. The planking and ladders that had been set up for the refugees were still there and in no time at all Garan was at the mouth of the cave. He stilled and blinked. The light was strange, flashing orange and red and sometimes white. He stepped farther out and the silence of the cave was obliterated by the sound of meteors screaming through the sky and explosions all around. He blinked. Streaks of light bled from the sky. Most of the meteors appeared to be hitting out on the plains.

A beam of light shot out from the observatory and killed a meteor high in the sky. Garan bit his lip and peered out farther. So many meteors that Garan's mouth dropped open. It was like rain. Small meteors interspersed with large. Another beam of light shot from the observatory. The elders were fighting.

Heaviness filled his chest. How could they beat this? How could anyone? Their own quest to find the machine seemed futile in the face of this apocalypse falling from the sky. Yet, this was only the precursor. The skyfire preceding final moonfall. The larger pieces of the fragments of Ruel moon swept all before it. It was hard to see how Margra could survive this. Finally, he really understood why Barrahiem was important. It sheltered them from skyfire.

A large meteor bore down on his position. Two beams of light hit it and there was an explosion, but when the flame cleared a large rock was still coming. Garan shouted, "Kill it!"

Another beam shot out and hit the rock with a glancing blow. Garan was thrown backward. Rock and dirt rained down on his body. He turned and ran in a crouch, cradling his head from the debris, seeking the shelter of the cave mouth.

Turning, he saw the turrets crumble and collapse. He watched a large section of the huge building sink in on itself. Then Garan realized it was falling on him. With superhuman speed, he scrambled into the cave, then sprang to his feet and ran to the Way Gate.

Tears tracked down his cheeks as he entered the Way. Even then the earth shook beneath his feet. He picked up the tether of the glide and ran and ran and ran. Crying and moaning. He had seen the observatory fall. His home and his hope. Gone. Just obliterated.

The elders had died fighting the sky until the sky killed them.

Weeping, Garan moved mechanically as he transported the supplies. How was he going to tell them that the observatory was gone, destroyed in skyfire?

EPILOGUE

The bed's frame rocked violently. Gercomo surged awake in the darkened basement room and glanced around. The baron stood there, foot poised to kick the low, wooden bed again. "We're leaving. Get up."

They had taken shelter in the series of rooms beneath the baron's house. A basement that was separated from the house above by a thick layer of earth. The baron's mansion was a ruin. The air was tinged with smoke and ash, the result of the skyfire that had rained down for a day and a night. The baron had a cloth wrapped around his face.

Gercomo squinted into the gloom. By the stench, the baron had some of his men in the room with him. Gercomo wasn't sure if he wanted to retch or eat them. "Wheresss arth we goinsth?"

"On a quest and I have need of your skills." The baron kicked the bed again, making it rock. "We leave in five minutes. Be out front, or be left behind."

Gercomo grinned. Of course, he was going to be ready He had nothing to pack and there was nothing left to eat in Sartell anyway. His only chance of survival was with the baron.

Out front, a fully loaded wagon stood in front of fifty fighting men arranged in rows. The street had been cleared and only the black, charred remains of houses stood witness to their departure. Piles of ash lined the edge of the street. Wind stirred up tendrils of smoke and drew designs in the air. A familiar sight: fire and smoke and ash. It brought back memories of the vineyard and of Salinda.

When Gercomo climbed onto the wagon, the baron lifted his hand and everyone started forward. The burden beasts groaned at the load as they pulled.

After a few turns, Gercomo realized they were heading to the wharf, or what remained of the wharf, after the bombardment. "Wheres arth we goinsth?" Gercomo said, gesturing to the water.

"The quickest way I know how," the baron said.

Gercomo still didn't know where, but he had found out the why.

At the wharf, their supplies were unloaded. Barrels were rolled across planks onto the deck, then another bunch of seamen lowered them by ropes to the hold below. Gercomo growled. They contained salted meat. Salted human meat. He knew because he'd harvested it and watched them being prepared. A few barrels had dragon wine, the last they had been able to salvage from the rebels at Eternity. Gercomo didn't need wine anymore. That taste he had taken that near ripped his guts out, had taught him that much.

He was a dragon now. It was in him. He just needed food. Gercomo eyed the fighting men who stomped along the ramp to get onboard. These were the pick of the baron's men. Good fighters. He saw a cage, full of people, young and fleshy, and nodded as they were placed on the deck. It didn't hurt to keep the livestock around. If the salted meat ran out, then they had fresh.

The sky was a roiling mass of dark gray, black and red. A storm was brewing. Was it wise to cast out to sea in that? Two mainsails went up and quickly caught the rising breeze. Gercomo leaped on board and staggered as the vessel moved under him. Where was the baron going? Gercomo peered over the side. He didn't like the sea. It was wine-dark and menacing.

Stepping back from the rail, he surveyed the ship. If worse comes to worst, he could transform back into a dragon and fly away.

The Dragon Wine series concludes in

Moonfall, Dragon Wine: Part Six

Preview of *Moonfall*

Dragon Wine: Part Six

Chapter One

The Quest Begins

Salinda surveyed the group heading into the Ways for the trip to the Arvoli continent, noting it was larger than she had anticipated. She had wanted to leave the younger ones behind, but there was no point in trying to keep them safe. If they didn't succeed, there was no safe.

With some difficulty, Salinda shuffled beside Nils, holding the underside of her distended abdomen to relieve the pressure. The glide was there for her to use, but for the moment she needed the exercise, needed to work off some excess energy and ease the strain in her lower back. Otherwise, she would sit on that glide and fret and nag and nobody would benefit from that.

Her mind was busy with "what ifs?"—What if they didn't find the machine? What if they didn't know how to use it? What if they were too late?

She sought comfort in the cadre. It glowed in her mind and she sensed that it had a keen edge as if its purpose was on the verge of being fulfilled. That did comfort her. At least, the cadre was not telling her she was going the wrong way.

She glanced sideways at Garan. His cadre was quiet, had been since the Ufak Monta had taken possession of him. Even though the Moon Binder spirit had stepped back to allow Garan control over his body, he was subdued and that worried her. Was it the Moon Binder spirit that brooded, and planned, or was the change in behavior just a side effect on Garan? If so, there was nothing she could do about it. They needed Garan and it appeared they needed the Ufak Monta. Yet, they also needed the cadre.

"Garan, can I lean on your arm?" she asked. She patted Nils on his forearm to signal the change in walking partner, thus giving Nils freedom to chat to Karol, who had come alongside.

There were a few more stairs to go before reaching the Way Gate. "Of course," Garan said and transferred the tether attached to the long glide that held most of their supplies to his other hand. He eased his elbow out so she could place her hand there.

"How are you feeling?" she asked him, surreptitiously studying his face.

"Well. Perfectly well," he responded, keeping his eyes ahead. He slowed his pace and put his arm around her to ease her up the next riser. "You should use the glide," he said with a grunt, as if she weighed as much as a boulder.

Giving him narrow-eyed glare, she responded, "I will when I get to the top." She let out a sigh and studied him. "Garan, tell me how you really feel…you know…inside."

His violet-colored eyes met hers and he looked away, his cheeks turning pink. "Scared," he said under his breath. Then he faced her, lifting his eyebrows. "Affronted. Curious." Finally, he shrugged. "And more besides."

Salinda nodded as she heard the words. If it had been her, she'd feel that way. Maybe enraged and angry, too. Garan, though, was a gentle soul, so it didn't surprise her that those terms were not used to describe his inner state. "Curious? Why?"

Garan chuckled, a low sound in his throat. Salinda narrowed her gaze, not quite sure how to take his reaction. "I have an alien being inside of me." He grimaced, and then shrugged helplessly. "What can I say?"

Salinda grinned. "You do, but you had a cadre inside you, too. Didn't that prepare you? You know, for another presence inside your mind?"

Garan's eyes widened and he looked ahead to assist her up the next riser. Nils was several steps ahead of them, leading the way, with Karol chatting away excitedly. Garan turned and tugged on the glide tether. "'Tis not the same. The cadre is mostly inert. Its sense of personality is muted. There is power there, but it generally waits for you to touch it and wield it. The Moon Binder spirit has a strong will and sense of identity. It takes over without asking. It dominates. It is so big it makes me cringe. I am lost when it comes forward."

Salinda brushed her fingers across his chin. "That is why, Garan, you have to fight it. You have to find a way to touch and hold your own strength of purpose and identity when the Moon Binder tries to take over."

"That is easy for you to say."

"You sensed this being, this spirit, when none of us could. It called to you and summoned you through the Ways and the in-between. No one else can do this except you."

Garan wiped his mouth, rubbed his chin and shook his head. "I know. That is why I am scared. I am not sure I am strong enough. I do not want to fail."

Salinda straightened her posture, her features schooled into a mask of purpose. "You cannot fail. You must not fail!"

Salinda didn't make it to the top of the stairs before needing assistance. "I think I'll use my glide now."

Garan inclined his head. "I will fetch it." Garan untied it from the back of the supply glide and brought it to her, doing the necessary work to help her get seated.

Once she was on the glide, Salinda could not talk so intimately with Garan. By the look on his face, he was relieved. *Poor Garan*, she thought. *So much power in him and he is so young.* Life was unfair sometimes.

The cadre warmed within her. *What about the cadre?* it suggested into her mind. Salinda frowned. *What about it?* she retorted.

She knew the answer. The Moon Binder's presence in Garan's mind interfered with the cadre and, possibly, Garan's inherent power. She would have to test that theory during the journey. They had to know where they stood before reaching the machine, possibly well before, so that they could plan.

Salinda usually found long journeys in the Ways tedious, so having a deep problem to think about would help pass the time. No time to be bored. She hoped no one tried to talk to her because she wasn't up for being sociable right now. There were complications. Again.

Nils reached out and touched her hand as she was passing through the Way Gate. "Are you well?" he asked her.

"Yes, quite well." Her response was automatic. Truth be told, her feet hurt and her ankles were swollen. She could hardly walk, let alone run. The baby was putting a lot of pressure on her bladder and her nether regions. Yes, she was very well indeed.

☐☐☐☐

Nils consulted his mental map when he reached the third junction. The Ways looked to be intact and the in-between glowed healthily. That gave him confidence to continue on. This was a section of the Ways that he had not travelled, not since awakening from his prison of sleep. Even then, he had only come this way once before. This was the section of the Way that led to the continent of Strega and Arvoli. The great city of Stregahiem had been destroyed when Ruel split. Arvoli was severely damaged, with many of its people fleeing to the Stoli continent.

"Is everything all right?" Danton asked him from behind his shoulder.

Nils turned. "Yes. I am assessing the health of the Way before we proceed."

Danton flashed a grin. "It looks fine to me."

Nils smiled thinly. "To an untrained human eye, perhaps. You have not been here before to blow it up." There was a thinness ahead, like the substance of the Ways was nearly dead. It appeared whole at this stage, though, so they might be able to get through.

Danton grunted. "Still sore about that, eh? Well, it kept the nasty folks out of your precious Ways and city. And didn't you do your share of blowing up? I thought Brill said…"

Nils straightened his shoulders. "That demolition cleared a dangerous section of the Ways that were discontinuous and—"

"In danger of being compromised by nasty humans."

Nils inclined his head. "I concede your point. I withdraw my adverse comment."

Danton slapped Nils on the back and it was all Nils could do to stop falling over. "No need. I understand. These Ways mean a lot to you." He cocked his head to study the walls of the Way. "I have to say they have been helpful. Saved our skins a number of times."

"Yes, they have. It is just that having humans use the Ways freely makes me uncomfortable. I worry that my elders would not like it, even though they do not exist anymore. Old habits are hard to break."

"Is there a problem?" Salinda yelled from the back of the line.

Danton waved a hand and called back. "All good. We're moving."

Nils stepped ahead of Danton, his shoulder aching from the impact of the man's heavy hand. Danton may have lost weight, but he had certainly lost none of his strength. Surely the dragon wine they had plied the rebel with had not had this effect. He pondered Salinda's enthusiastic avowal of the wine's properties. Nils half-turned to regard the rebel then heard Salinda repeat her question. "No, no problem," he replied, knowing that Salinda would hear him as sound carried farther in the Ways.

He took a step into the next section and nothing bad happened. The world did not stop turning or fall down on his head. He kept walking, a smile lifting his lips at his fanciful thoughts. Examining the in-between around him, he detected the weaknesses there. For now, the Ways were fine, but as he peered ahead, he was not so certain. His affinity with the Ways was not so acute here, but there was something ahead, something to worry about.

"Can I walk next to you?" Karol asked.

Startled, Nils jumped, and looked down at the Hiem child. He was too small to be called a youth. Karol had barely left his side as they left Barrahiem and was only forced to move away when Nils opened the Way Gate and ushered the group through. "Of course. Perhaps you can tell me what you know about the Ways and I can embellish your understanding. It will pass the time."

Karol peered up at him. "They are alive."

Nils's skin prickled, the boy's comment unnerving him. The Ways were alive, or had been, but not living and breathing like Hiem or Humans. "Alive? In what sense?"

Karol kept walking but peered at the in-between, his hand reaching out to caress it lightly. His white fingers glowed faintly when they skimmed the surface of the wall and pale blue light spread out from where his fingers touched. "It lives and breathes, and perhaps thinks and feels."

Jolted, Nils nearly cried out a "no'" in denial. Quickly, he calmed himself. This was but a child, an untaught child. Theoretically, the Ways had a symbiotic relationship with the Hiem. Energy gleaned from those passing through kept it energized. Yet, in these latter days he had begun to think that that "life" had been lost. However, the increase in the light emanating from the in-between had indicated otherwise. Ever since he had found Karol, to be exact. The way Karol spoke of the Ways indicated that his views came from experience and observation rather than learned knowledge. Perhaps Nils should not judge too soon. The child may know more than he himself. Nils licked his bottom lip before speaking again. "Do you know what it thinks?"

Karol blinked and gazed at the in-between. He shook his head. "It is trying to say something, but I can't grasp it. Maybe the longer I am here I will figure it out."

Nils shuddered, a sensation of death creeping over him. He decided to stop asking the boy questions and gave the in-between a hesitant and slightly resentful look. It had never spoken to him.

They walked along in companionable silence until the next junction. Here the Ways were less well preserved. There was moisture in the air. They were passing under the New Straits that separated Stoli from Arvoli. It had once been the shallow Arvlen Sea, but the inundation caused by Moonfall changed it. There used to be an isthmus that connected the continents, but that had collapsed in the aftermath of Moonfall, or so the archives said. His work to prepare a map for this quest had shown him the true extent of damage to the world.

Nils raised a hand, signaling those behind to halt. He grabbed Karol's shoulder to make him stop, too, because he had kept walking as if in a dream. The boy started. Karol gasped and turned around to face Nils, arms rising to clasp his upper arms as if warding off a chill. His face was a picture of misery. Tears gleamed on his upper cheeks.

"It hurts!" he said.

Nils stared and then shut his mouth. The child could be unnerving at times. He was referring to the Ways. Nils glanced about him nervously. *Can they feel pain?*

Gathering his courage, Nils turned to Danton, and Brill, Laidan and Eneit, who stood waiting close behind. "I need to inspect the Way. I suspect its condition is not good."

"Do you need help?" Brill asked.

Nils was about to reply in the negative when Garan came forward, passing the tether of the supply glide to Brill. "I will help you."

Nils let out a slow breath. He did not know who was speaking. The Ufak Monta or Garan. Garan had had an affinity with the Ways, even before his possession. Yet something in the tone suggested the Ufak Monta was in control. Nils damped down his nervousness. "Thank you."

Garan stood shoulder to shoulder with Nils. "Water is leaking through the roof."

Nils could not see water coming through, but he could sense the dampness and faint sounds that indicated trickles of water. "I suspected as much. But we must pass this way, as we have no means of floating on the sea."

Garan's gaze glowed and Nils backed up a step. This was an effect of the cadre and not something he had seen in the Ufak Monta. The lad was truly unnerving.

The light faded from Garan's eyes. "'Tis sturdy enough for our passage. The return I cannot vouch for." The voice was dead flat, devoid of emotion. It must be the Ufak Monta talking. "We should move now before more seismic disturbances alter the structure of the Ways." Then, casually, he put his hand on the in-between. A bluish glow spread out from his hand. The walls of the Way, which had been duller than the previous section, brightened. Nils kept his wonder in check. He had no time to throw questions at Garan, whoever he may be, whatever he may be.

Garan turned and took the tether back from Brill with a nod of thanks and resumed his place next to Salinda in the line. With one last look at the in-between, which had now faded back to dull gray, Nils raised his hand and signaled to keep walking. Karol clasped his hand and smiled up at him.

"Did you see that?" Karol asked in a rapt voice. "How did that human do that?"

Nils turned and brushed away the wet strand of long hair that was clinging to the boy's face. "A very special one. Let us move along quickly. The Way is stable now but it may not remain so."

Nils had a fleeting desire to hold Salinda. Suddenly, he was overwhelmingly grateful that she had come into his life and enriched it with these humans. If not for rescuing her for his own selfish reasons, he wouldn't be here now in this company. He wouldn't have kin around him. He wouldn't have a reason for living. Or a reason for dying.

A note from the author

It is with great pleasure that I present this book to you. It's been a long time coming and I hope you enjoy it. The final installment, *Moonfall*, will follow in August, 2018.

I want to thank a few people. My partner, Matthew Farrer, for moral support and cups of tea, thank you for getting the whole "I must write until I die" thing. Thank you to Liz from Canada for being a faithful beta reader and providing insightful comments. A big thank you to the amazing Stephanie Smith for editing this book and for stepping in when Brianna could no longer edit the series. Thank you to Jason Nahrung for proofreading with such a hawkeye view of things. I want to acknowledge the support of the Canberra Speculative Fiction Guild—an amazing group of writers who believe in paying it forward. I don't think I'd be here if I hadn't joined them back in 2001. For general industry tips, I give thanks to Patty Jansen and her dragon team of indie publishers. Also, a big thank you to Frauke of Croco Designs for the covers. I also want to thank Russell Kirkpatrick for the map.

I hope to one day come back to Margra and write more in this world. There is so much to be explored, from prequels about the life of Margra before Ruel split, to some future times just waiting to be envisaged.

But now I must continue working on *Moonfall*.

With love and thanks
Donna
July, 2018

Donna Maree Hanson